HERLOT OF ALONIA

HERLOT OF ALONIA

MARIA ROSESTONE

Proofreading and Formatting
by Allusion Graphics, LLC/Book Publishing
www.allusiongraphics.com
Cover design by Staci Hart

SYNOPSIS

Herlot of Alonia, the medieval fantasy debut from Maria Rosestone, is the first book in a trilogy of ancient magic, golden hearts, unicorns, and the desperate quest for survival from the epidemic bestowed on the land of Eraska by the wrath of a murderous King.

Delivered into the hidden land of Eraska under the lullaby of a willow tree, Herlot of Alonia has displayed unnatural abilities from a young age. Her village fears the strange happenings surrounding her and deems her a bad omen. Pushed into isolation, she befriends a unicorn and engulfs herself in a magical world; however, the magic soon comes to an end when she is forced to realize that her imagination may actually be the source of her suffering.

Just as Herlot reaches adulthood and has found her place in her village, her land is invaded by King Felix, a man willing to perform unspeakable acts in his search for a source of power to conquer the Empire of Ipta. Herlot's land is now under attack by strangers attempting to poison her family and friends. In the midst of chaos and torture, Herlot's magical friend returns and saves her from the King's wrath. But now it is Herlot's responsibility to not only save a magical world, but her people, as well. Is the magic real and can she use it to complete her mission? Can she not only trust herself, but a Prince and two Iptan warriors who pledge that they will lead her and her friends into safety? Or will she have to become the leader of a quest she never asked for, let alone develop the magical abilities she will need to succeed?

"Before you turn the page and enter this tale,

which lies invitingly before you, close your eyes,

expand your own glorious breath within,

and let go of any belief in limitation.

Give yourself the gift of remembering

that all Magic begins in imagination

blended with curiosity, and all Real is

made true through a chosen Yes

and release of limiting belief. Enter."

~ *The Marys*

PROLOGUE

E VERY NIGHT, BENYAMIN OF the village Bundene would climb on top of his thatched roof and watch the night sky, which spread uninterrupted until colliding with the flat land of Eraska. Benyamin lived beyond the forest, rolling hills, cliffs, and waterfall of his kingdom, where the land of Eraska plateaued before a mountain range obscured it from the rest of the continent. There, lying back with his elbows crossed underneath his head, with an owl who occasionally landed on the roof and kept him company, he entertained himself using his unique gift. Night after night, he watched the infinite number of stories the stars had observed. Sometimes he'd pick one and see the images unfold in front of his mind's eye, other times he'd look at several, seeing several different stories or the same one just from different perspectives. He loved that stars, like humans, had their own preferences for stories.

Benyamin had learned many things from his years of watching the stories of the stars, but most of all, he had learned that nature could perform magic—as surely as the wind buffeted his face or the night sky curved overhead. He had learned long ago to keep this knowledge to himself, for there was no way he could present anyone with the necessary evidence. His family would only insist that he take his healthy spirit tincture if he ever were to utter a word about magic. Establishing traditions to nature's magic was a futile attempt. It was nature's nature to scatter standards apart and create a path for magic to flow through and create its vision. When it interplayed with humans, magic was either enormously present in that it appeared normal and went unnoticed, or remained hidden when on the brink of being discovered. But if anything, magic was real, so very, very real. At least that was what Benyamin chose to believe.

CHAPTER 1
Alonia

"ILVY, WILL YOU STILL be one of us after the baby is born, or are you going to go back to being an adult and never chase butterflies again?"

Ilvy nudged her wooden sled forward with the tip of her boot to the crest of the hill. She reached over her belly and pretended to adjust the sled while she thought about how to answer Elvin's question. With full cheeks and curious, seagrass green eyes, Elvin always found a way to poke at the most uncomfortable of subjects, but she couldn't help smiling when she thought of the first time she had chased a butterfly during her pregnancy. That was also the first time her baby had taken control of her body, though Elvin didn't know that. No one knew of her baby's abilities.

Last summer, while turning the hay with her rake, a warm force had spread from her belly into her head. At first she thought it was because she had stopped taking her tincture for nerve illness. Oliver, the healer, had told her not to take it if she was with child. But then the force lifted her chin up and focused her eyes on a purple-winged butterfly. Yes, her nerves often got the better of her, but never before had something taken control of her body while she was in one of her states. She felt the butterfly's sporadic dance in her belly and under

3

her skin, making her body tingle all over before she chased after it without thinking. Once the butterfly flew away, the sensation ceased, but for the rest of the day it had been impossible to walk a straight line. Her best friend, Merle, had asked Ilvy if she had accidentally drunk the strong ale that morning.

Today, Ilvy's afternoon plans had been to stay home while her husband Ernest took their son Ambro out on the boat to fish. She needed to weave a new basket since the one forgotten outside had been stripped for nest pieces by the early morning birds. However, the water carriers had returned with news that had stirred the baby—the snow was still intact in parts of the woods. Warmth spread from her belly to her legs and there was nothing she could do to stop her body from finding a sled and inviting Elvin, Maurice, and Kristen.

"Yes, Elvin," she finally said. "I will still chase butterflies." She honestly hoped she would.

She looked down at the three, her solaces, scratching their temples under their wool hats. Unlike her friends, Agatha and Bee, who had assembled a village meeting after having caught Ilvy climbing an elderberry tree and forced Ilvy to endure a speech on the dangers of acting like a jester in her state, the children adored each and every one of her childish endeavors. However, she couldn't tell anyone the whole truth: that her baby had made her do these childish things. Pregnancy delirium they would have called it. A bad omen.

"Now, on to the matter at hand," Ilvy said. "Who sleds first?"

"Let's pull sticks!" twelve-year-old Kristen said, gathering several muddy twigs. "We will have to watch the tracks. And avoid the areas with grass showing through. We'll save a lot of time cleaning the mud off the sled and avoid getting stuck. But no matter what, watch out for the birches."

"Watch out for the birches," Ilvy repeated in chorus with Elvin and Maurice.

Kristen wrapped her hand around the bundle. One by one, they each pulled a stick.

Ilvy gasped in delight. First! It was her lucky day.

Elvin took his hat off and gave his sweaty matted hair a shake. "And if someone comes along? Agatha told us not to allow Ilvy to act like a jester," he asked. "Does sledding count?"

"According to *The Tales of Geraldus and his Travelling Jesters*, pregnant jesters don't perform stunts, but they can dance as long as it is ten backflips away from the nearest steep drop," Kristen said. "Or was it nine?"

"That's just a story—" Ilvy started.

"Definitely ten!" Maurice exclaimed. "Mother read that story last night before bed."

"Ten backflips, it is," Kristen said. "So now we must decide whether or not sledding is considered a stunt. I say it's not. And if someone were to come along, as long as Ilvy is not on the sled, we can just say she was watching us."

Ilvy grimaced in shame. It was not right to make the children tell fibs for her.

"If someone comes along, each and every one of you will tell the truth," Ilvy said, "and, Elvin, pull your hat back down or you will get sick."

"I told you Ilvy was still an adult," Maurice murmured into Elvin's ear, just loud enough for Ilvy to hear.

"She's not. If only I could get her to sneeze on someone, I'd finally have proof."

Ilvy rolled her eyes and took a seat on the sled. Elvin was referring to a tale she had come up with herself—the one about the fairy who sprinkled a woman with fairy dust to turn her into a child again. And not just any child—a child with a magical sneeze. In the tale, each time the woman sneezed, fairy dust would splash onto other adults and they would become children again.

Ilvy wedged the heels of her leather boots over the wooden runners. As the sled balanced over the steep, narrow drop, she eyed the smattering of birch trees below. No matter—she could avoid them with focused maneuvering.

"Big push or little push?" Elvin asked.

"Big," Ilvy said.

Ilvy's hood flew back and her wheat-yellow hair rippled behind her. She prepared to lean away from the first birch. The sunlight flickered against her cheeks as the sled flew by tree trunks while sparrows raced alongside the branches. Snow splashed into her golden eyelashes again and again, but not once did she blink.

The hill merged into flat ground, but the sled did not lose momentum. The frozen stream ahead hurtled toward her. The sled was going too fast. She squeezed her eyes shut, bracing for the impact with the cold water and stones, then opened them to realize she was not shivering wet when it came to a halt. Right at the edge. Lucky. She clapped her hands while the children raced down the hill after her.

"Ilvy! You almost went into the water!" Elvin cried.

"Ah, a little water never hurt anyone anyway," Ilvy said.

A sharp pain in her belly forced her to crouch forward.

"Ilvy!" cried the children.

Her jaw shook in an attempt to breathe through the shock of the pain. Another sharp cramp pierced through her nerves, an awful ripping sensation that spread all the way into her forehead, paralyzing her balance. She swayed forward.

Kristen dropped to her knees just in time to steady her. "The baby is coming," she stated calmly, though her brown eyes were wide with fear.

Ilvy pressed her palm over the midsection of her wool dress. "Yes." A strong, invisible pull lured Ilvy's attention across the stream to a willow tree. Heat pulsed from her belly. Ilvy broke out in a sweat. *Is that where you want to go, little baby?* Ilvy thought. As if in response, the sensation began to burn like fire. *Yes,* her baby seemed to say. "Kristen, help me cross the stream so I can sit under the willow."

Kristen turned Ilvy's shoulders so that they were eye to eye, meeting Ilvy's gaze with an expression of a much older woman—a woman who understood the importance of Alonia's birthing tradition. The dangers awaiting Ilvy. Every child was born in the village center, as a true Alonian part of a larger village family. "You will not be like Thilda, not in my hands. I know the village is a long walk away, but I will pull you on the sled the entire way."

Ilvy shuddered at the thought of Thilda, a woman who had wandered too far away on the beach when she went into labor and didn't make it back to the village. Thilda's baby had not survived and Thilda, overtaken by grief, wandered into the woods and was never seen again. What if Thilda's baby had also had special abilities? What if the baby had *made* Thilda walk so far away on the beach?

Ilvy bit her lip. She did not want to be like Thilda. She looked down at her belly. *There will be plenty of time to go by the tree when you arrive.* "Kristen, take me home."

Kristen nodded but before she stood, she touched Ilvy's forehead, a sharp crease forming between her eyebrows. "You have a fever."

"I am well. Do not worry." Ilvy smiled, which only made Kristen's face grow more concerned. But what could Ilvy do? She wished she could explain that it was the baby's ability to send waves of warmth through her body, not the feared labor fever. However, Kristen's worry was a fair exchange if it meant that no one would speculate that her baby may be a bad omen.

By the time they reached the wheat field waiting to be ploughed, Ilvy was ready to rip her hair out between the contractions and fighting the baby's urge to run back to the forest. Beyond the field stood about fifty circular stone huts with thatched roofs. Through her blurred vision, Ilvy could make out several figures carrying wood. Her baby thrashed against her insides at her sight of them. Warmth poured from the left side to the right side of her body and threatened to knock her off the sled. She gripped the edges and the warmth rushed to her lips instead. Ilvy ground her teeth to stop herself from shouting to turn the sled around as Kristen pedaled her feet against the mud. A contraction weakened her control and the baby won. In one powerful swoop, the baby knocked her off the sled and forced her to claw her way toward the forest.

"Help!" the children called.

Ilvy threw images of Thilda's story at the baby, hoping the baby would understand the urgency of getting to the village. *If you win and take us away from the village, we both die.*

The exclamations of the villagers arriving at the sled were unbearable to Ilvy's ears. Someone grabbed her underneath her armpits and lifted her to her feet. Questions filled the air around her, making her ears ring.

"Why didn't you tell someone you were going into the forest?"

"Kristen! How could you have allowed Ilvy to go sledding?"

"Stop scolding her and fetch Agatha! Can't you see she has a fever?"

Ilvy felt trapped in a swarm of bees. She swatted at the direction from which the voices were coming in an attempt to keep them away. The baby kicked frantically, attempting the same. "Quiet!" she shouted, her voice cracking.

Everyone stopped and stared. Ilvy had never shouted at anyone before, let alone in such a petrifying voice, but she didn't care.

"Quiet," a voice echoed—deep, warm, and steady. It was the only voice that could calm the kicking in her belly, the unbearable heat rushing to her limbs. A voice she had fallen in love with over and over again.

In a flash, Ernest's strong arms lifted her from the sled. The smell of the sea on his hide coat rippled memories of comfort through her. Her urge to return to the forest dissipated while her pains mellowed. Ernest carried her through the paths that wove between the stone-hut homes, where countless footsteps of Alonians were imprinted into the dirt. The baby moved in her, bringing her attention to footprints for some reason.

Once they reached the center of the village, Ernest paused around the hearth. Ilvy heard several villagers barging into homes, asking for Agatha's whereabouts, for she was the one always in charge of deliveries. Ilvy noticed a pair of footprints in the dirt that matched Agatha's—they were of boots comparable to the size the men wore and were spread rather wide apart.

Before she could suggest to the others to track Agatha using the footprints, Ernest ducked and carried her through the entrance of Agatha's home and lowered her onto the straw mattress as if she were a fragile seashell.

Ilvy sighed with relief. She had made it and the baby was not fighting her anymore. *See? This is the perfect place for you to come into the world.*

Ernest took hold of her hand. "Don't worry, they'll find Agatha soon enough."

"You mean Agatha will find us soon enough. She has the instinct of an owl hunting a mouse when it comes to knowing when a woman is in labor." Agatha had never missed a delivery, and even if she were on the other side of the forest, she would find a way to Ilvy right now. In spite of the pain coursing through her, Ilvy giggled, picturing Agatha swinging from branch to branch toward the village.

Ernest brushed a strand of hair from her face. "What are you laughing about?"

"I think I'll wait to tell you until later. It just might have to be my next story," she said.

"Then I look forward to hearing it." The skin at the corner of his eyes creased. Ilvy, like all Alonian women, was an expert at detecting her husband's smile by his eyes rather than his mouth, which was hidden behind a beard and mustache. Alonian men avoided the tedious task of trimming and shaving unless they did it using a sharp piece of flint to occupy their time while searching for eels hiding amidst the sea grass.

But there was something else besides a smile that she noticed in Ernest's eyes as he wiped the sweat off her forehead. Tension was hidden in them, and there was no doubt he feared that she had labor fever, like Kristen had thought.

He was the only one she had wanted to tell about their baby's abilities; however, every time she started to, the baby's warmth raced to her lips and prevented her from shaping the words. She had a feeling the baby wanted to keep its abilities secret. Her mind was on the brink of sinking into a quicksand of unanswered questions—but she gathered herself. Right now, Ernest needed to have his mind put at ease the same way he had put the baby at ease about coming to the village.

She pressed her palm against Ernest's cheek. "Have you thought of a name for if it's a girl?"

He nodded and a glimmer returned to his eyes. "Herlot," he said.

Agatha squeezed through the small opening of the stone hut, carrying a bucket of hot water. Her rust-colored hair was pinned up with twigs and she was breathing heavily. "See? I told you. Instinct," Ilvy whispered to Ernest.

Without a word, Agatha marched to Ilvy's side and checked her forehead. Then she began to search through a chest on the dirt floor, pulling out every oil jar she could find. Agatha hummed a merry melody, but through gritted teeth. *The fever is not what you think, Agatha,* Ilvy wished she could explain.

When Agatha ran out of oil jars to pull out, she cleared her throat and sent Ernest on his way.

Normally, Ilvy was fond of Alonian childbirth traditions. If she was not one of the helping hands inside the birthing home, she was outside leading the children in rehearsing poems that would be recited to the mother and newborn child, or placing hot stones from the fire into a bucket to keep the water warm. But right now, she despised it. The pains returned, twice as malicious as before, as if a boar was trying to tear its way out of her, and she cursed tradition for forcing her to give birth inside a smoke trap that made it impossible to breathe.

Ilvy managed to catch a reflection of herself in Agatha's eyes as she lashed at the hands attempting to help her. She did not recognize the bewildered woman in the reflection and the white skin of her anguished face.

● ● ●

"No worries, my friend. Any moment now, you and Ilvy will bring a fresh, new story into our world," sang Rudi of Alonia. He handed Ernest a cup carved from oak and filled to the brim with ale, then sat next to him on a stone warmed by the fire.

Moments ago, Rudi had retreated home with the rest of the Alonian villagers who had waited with Ernest at the hearth to welcome the baby. The others had left Ernest because it was rude to keep up celebratory pretenses while Ilvy was struggling so—Alonians knew the difference between the sounds of birth pain and of dying in childbirth. Ilvy's were the latter.

However, Rudi could never leave his friend in such a time. He had left with every intent to return with ale and a friend's support for the father who could be left without a wife and child tonight. The moonlight streamed in through the hearth, pouring its light onto Ernest as if announcing to the entire night sky that there sat a soon-to-be lonely widower. No. Rudi would not allow the moon to make a spectacle of Ernest tonight.

Another shriek erupted from Agatha's home. Ernest winced as if the fire had spat sparks at his face. He closed his eyes until Ilvy's cries ceased.

"A fresh story," Ernest thought out loud. "A new story... is there really such a thing?"

Rudi stuttered. He had meant to ease Ernest's mind about the childbirth, not trigger a complicated discussion. But, at the moment, it seemed to have done the trick and given him something to ponder.

Ernest took a sip of the ale and then stared into the fire. "It seems to me that our lives are nothing like the stories we tell. No clear beginning. My story started with my father, grandfather, great-grandfather, and beyond because, without them, I would not be here. How far back does it go, do you suppose? Ah! And no finite endings either, now that I think about it. We leave behind legacies of which we will never know. Just imagine, Rudi, all the toy figures you carve! After you pass, think of how many children of Eraskan land will still play with them. Is this not strange to you?"

A gust of wind blew the fire's smoke at Rudi. "Yes," he managed between coughs. He loved the idea. It felt as if he had travelled to all the places his toys had and that a part of him would continue travelling even after his time came.

"I have a wish for my newborn," Ernest said, looking at the stars. "My child, may your life be a new, fresh story. May you face life's challenges with an open heart, and may you dance in your legacies before it is your time."

That was lovely, Rudi wanted to say, but he stopped to think of a more masculine expression. Enchanting? No, that was for fairy tales. Delightful? No, that was Merle's favorite word when she drank milk, and Ernest's wish was much more... *lovely.* Well, then. He would just have to say lovely because there was no other word for it.

"That was—"

"That was lovely, Ernest," a woman's voice interrupted. Bee hunched through the opening of her home, careful not to step on her hair that dipped into the dirt. She straightened and lifted a wool blanket off a rope line.

Rudi scowled. "Now, Bee, last I heard, you were in charge of getting the young ones to practice their welcome poems for the baby, but instead, you're eavesdropping on our chat and snatching my words. I have heard nothing but silence from the wee poets since the moment that there log began to burn, and if those children sound like a jumbled thatch endeavor, I'll be the one to tell Ilvy exactly why that is so," he said, then crossed his arms and slouched.

Bee folded the blanket over her arm and reached for another on the line. "The children," she articulated, "are resting so that when the time comes, they do not sound like a grumpy man who has run out of things to complain about." She tossed the blanket, and it landed on top of Rudi's head. "I suggest you join them."

"That might not be a bad idea," Ernest agreed.

Rudi refused to unwind his frown as he watched Bee pat Ernest's shoulder and offer him the other blanket. "Forgive my interruption, but your wish really is lovely and I think it would do everyone good to hear it. Rumor has it that Sira and Viktor wished little Manni a chest of gold. A chest of gold! In Eraska! Imagine that. The skies only know where their heads were when they thought of that."

"If it's true, let's hope it is only the skies that heard and not Cloudian. It'd break the old king's heart. I hope our people know better than to spread such a lie," Ernest commented.

Rudi agreed. He'd be the first to disclose Sira and Viktor's betrayal to King Cloudian if it were true. It was the only law in Alonia and the other five villages of Eraska: neither the citizens nor their kings would seek gold. It had been like that for generations. It was why he had the luxury of living a peaceful life of woodwork and carving without having to worry about greedy, gold-seeking thieves—or kings—invading his home.

However, no one knew the *real* reason why no one was allowed to seek gold in Eraska. Only King Cloudian and one chosen person from each of Eraska's six villages knew. And Rudi was Alonia's chosen one.

Not even Rudi's wife Merle knew about his secret duty. He was King Cloudian's eye in Alonia, under oath to help the King in a mission outlined in a letter that had been handed down to each King of Eraska. The letter had been written by a Wiseman named Brom who wrote of an awful tragedy that he had caused, a tragedy that he had too little time to fix. He begged the Kings to ban gold from Eraska and believed that if this law were abided, a solution to the misfortune he had caused would arise. Brom wrote that nature would send a sign upon the arrival of that solution.

Rudi hummed with the thought of this responsibility, somehow heavy and light at once. What Brom's tragedy had been was unclear, but Brom warned in the letter not to seek it.

King Cloudian was desperate for the solution. Rudi was, too. How many ages had gone by in this strange hold of knowing and not knowing? Of waiting? Yes, Eraska was at peace, unlike the other kingdoms of the world, but how much of the world were they being deprived of because of their isolation? And how much longer could Cloudian keep Eraskans isolated from the other gold-bearing kingdoms of the world? More and more often sailors docked and visited Alonia while world wanderers visited the other villages. They carried gold, and many Eraskans caught a glimpse of the precious metal. What would happen if Eraskans found out that the glory of owning the precious metal had been taken from them all because of a silly letter? How long could freedom from invasion and a promise of peace be a good enough reason to withhold the desire to touch it, to own it? Rudi even wished he could touch it, even if just for a moment to see what it felt like.

Rudi had to admit that Brom's letter sounded like an Alonian story. He could even imagine Ernest spinning it. But what if there really had been a tragedy and a solution that would arise all thanks to centuries of Eraskans keeping their land free of gold? What if they were part of something bigger, something even bigger than the adventures people outside of their kingdom were having?

Rudi would never forget the first time he had touched the letter. Up in King Cloudian's tower on a windy night, his father and the King had told him the story and informed him of his task. He didn't believe it until the letter rested in his hands. The writing was on a grey material that had the texture of a leaf. And it felt warm, alive. There had to be *something* different and special about Brom and the world he lived in. No piece of parchment in their times could compare to the mysterious material of the letter.

Rudi drew circles in the dirt with a stick as he listened to Bee talk to Ernest about a new story she had read. Neither one of them knew that the only reason their ancestors had learned to read and write was because of Brom's letter. Alonia was the only village close to the sea, which stimulated many curiosities about the outside world. Rudi felt bad for the fellow who had been the King when Alonians by the dozens arrived at the fortress to see a docked ship and to speak with the sailors. He could almost see them eagerly asking to go on the ship. The exact opposite of isolation indeed, Alonians sailing off into the horizon to explore the world of gold. The only solution was to quench their thirst about the outside world, and what better way than to give them stories and the means to read and write them? And here they were today, eagerly awaiting King Cloudian's stewards to come by several times a year with all sorts of goods the King traded for—boots, coats, tools, glass jars—and for Alonians, books, parchment, and ink.

The sound of a clay pot shattering sounded from Agatha's home, followed by a thud. Rudi spilled his cup of ale as he rushed after Ernest toward Agatha's.

"Ilvy! Stop!" Agatha cried.

Ilvy of Alonia stumbled out of the dwelling, looked both ways, and then took off in the direction of the forest at a pace more inclined toward challenging a deer than a human.

Rudi blinked, stunned. That was not Alonian tradition. That was not like anything Rudi had ever seen. He was right behind Ernest as they charged after her. Once they reached the brink of the forest, Ilvy was nowhere in sight. Rudi stopped in his tracks, distracted from a flash above. He gazed up at the night sky and watched in awe as all the stars pulsed in unison. He came to the realization that he was witnessing something very out of the ordinary. For the first time in his life, he stepped into his role of being King Cloudian's eye in Alonia as he entered the forest in search of Ilvy.

● ● ●

Crisp air poured into Ilvy's lungs. Now that there was no smoke, she could finally breathe. The full moon beamed. Soaking in the natural light of the white birch bark, she knew that she had never made a better decision in her life than to grant her baby's wish to leave the birthing hut. No, she was not Thilda. She would not be cursed for delivering her child outside the village.

The pains were still there, but they grew gentler now. She wasn't sure where she was going, but the baby seemed sure, having taken full control of her legs.

All the wildlife background on her favorite path for picking berries seemed to emit a pulse that she felt in the air around her—even the pebbles on the path. Ilvy knew the names of many plants and trees that grew in the forest, but now it was almost as if each plant, blade of grass, and tree had a unique name of its own, each singing a unique tone. She attempted articulating one of them. *What a lovely sound*, she thought. *I didn't know my voice could do that.* Joy whirled in her belly, a sign that the baby liked the sounds. Ilvy continued to sing the mysterious tunes.

Soon she found herself in an area where a family of willow trees stood by the stream. The warmth in her legs receded slightly and slowed her pace. Still singing, her attention was drawn to the sway of one of the willow tree's leaves. Her receding pains transformed into waves, mimicking their rhythm. A tide-like pull invited her to approach the willow, and she laid down under its canopy. She sighed and closed her eyes, the ground more comfortable than even the freshest of mattresses.

The leaves brushed soothing patterns and shapes across her belly. These, she realized, were the assisting hands her baby had called for. When Ilvy opened her eyes, she gasped: a scene of magic greeted her that even the most imaginative storytellers would not have been able to come up with—several leaves supported her baby's head and the rest wrapped around the torso until her little girl swayed above her, cradled, her sweet cry joining the melody of the forest.

"Holy Basil..." she whispered in wonder. Her eyelids grew heavy and her vision blurred. It looked like a family of fireflies was dancing around her baby, the newborn wrapped in a gentle glow. Slowly, the willow tree leaves lowered Herlot into the crease of Ilvy's arm. That was the last image she saw before another willow leaf appeared before her and caressed her eyes, and she heeded sleep's hypnotizing call.

Ilvy's awakening was the most beautiful of her life. Not a single ache infiltrated her body. She felt strong, not weak like she had felt after giving birth to Ambro. The sun warmed her face through the willow leaves, and everything was a perfect pitch of quiet. The morning birds singing, the water rolling over the rocks in the stream, and most beautiful of all, her daughter's cooing—and Ernest's humming.

Ilvy looked to her right to see her husband sitting alongside her, his back resting against the trunk of the willow tree with their daughter in his arms. Several images of the willow tree leaves reaching for her and the delivery flashed across her mind, but reason flushed them away. It must have been a dream. She must have run off in a labor-fever delirium and collapsed by the willows when she finally reached exhaustion. It was a miracle that she had even been able to deliver her baby and she wished she could remember it.

She watched Ernest and her daughter as her breaths grew deeper, enjoying the sight of them. What would he say of her running off? How did he find her? But the questions didn't last long. Ernest soon noticed she was awake. They could always tell when the other was awake just by sensing the change in their breathing pattern.

"Good morning." Ernest leaned forward to give Ilvy a better glimpse of their daughter.

Love burst into her cheeks for every part of her precious daughter's face, especially her small nose, so intent on breathing, and the delicate hairs matted to her forehead. "Good morning, Herlot," she said. Her smile faded when she glanced up at Ernest's exhausted face. How long had he been looking for her? "Ernest—"

"Don't apologize. You are safe. Herlot is safe. I would like to know why you ran, though."

Ilvy swallowed. A lot of people would be asking that question.

"It was so hot in there, and I had a fever. There was so much smoke and I couldn't breathe. All I remember is wanting fresh air. Oh, Ernest. What will the others think? How can we convince them that I am not like Thilda?" Or was she?

"We don't need to convince them of anything. Herlot is alive. Thilda's story was a tragedy, but it does not mean that a mother and her child will suffer an ill fate if the child is not born in the village."

If only everyone thought like Ernest. She needed him to reassure her. "I don't know if I can go back there yet."

"You're right. They may be suspicious at first. And I'll gladly stay in the woods with you for ages, but what about our home and friends? Look at our daughter, Ilvy. All they need is time to see that everything is fine and they will love her like every child. They are our family, too, and I know that we both want Herlot to grow up with them."

Ilvy's eyes found her daughter. "What do you say? Is it time for you to meet your village family?"

They entered Alonia from the south, where their home stood. It was farthest away from the center hearth and closest to the forest trees. Ilvy set her jaw tight as Alonians, busy with chores, came into view—but it did not stop her lips from trembling. What would they say? Brooms brushed against the dirty entryways, eggs were inspected, and hands were nudged aside by calves well aware of their right to drink first. Those who did regard her entrance only threw a few scowls the baby's way. Sira lifted her daughter, Manni, away from the carrots in the vegetable garden as if she were protecting her from some danger.

She was about to break into tears when she noticed Elvin helping his mother carry fish into the smokehouse, waving at her. He dropped the fish, slipped from his mother's attempting grip, and skipped over to Ilvy, folding his hands in front of him.

"Welcome to our home for you,
From all of us not just a few,
Even though you are still new—"

He seemed to have forgotten the next phrase and fell deep into thought as Ilvy's heart delighted at more welcomers—her best friend Merle holding Ilvy's three-year-old son by hand. Just when Merle opened her mouth, most likely to help Elvin with the poem, he shushed her. It looked like Elvin had decided to make up his own phrase.

"And one day we'll have to share my favorite stew,
As long as the sky is blue,
My home is open to you!"

He stood up on his toes and kissed Herlot on the cheek.

"Oh, Ilvy, she is an orchid. May I hold her?" Merle asked.

Ilvy nodded and rubbed a happy tear away. Along with the others, Ilvy sat on her heels as they got a closer look at Herlot. Ilvy delighted in Ambro's first moment with his new sister, as he brushed Herlot's cheeks with the side of his finger. Then he did the same against her hands, which were curled into fists. All of a sudden, Herlot was scooped away by Ernest.

A cold voice penetrated the air. "She wasn't born in the village. It's a bad omen."

Ilvy turned around and almost stumbled back when she was met by Sira's scowl. Behind her stood the entire village, each wearing the same scowl. Fear plucked at her heart. How had they gathered so quickly?

"Out of my way, superstitious fools!" Rudi's voice rang. Ilvy caught a glimpse of him as he shoved his way through the crowd that had assembled, hopping on one leg between two women who were stubborn in letting him through.

"Holy Basil, do I have news," he announced. He leaned over and kissed Herlot on the forehead. "Welcome, princess. You really are a fresh and new story." He winked at Ilvy before he faced the others. Whatever the wink was about, she was certain he felt confident about it. She hoped with all of her heart that it was something to save her daughter from being deemed a bad omen.

"Alonians! I have news that will make even your shadows turn to light and help you forget your silly fears. Eraskan bells would not ring if Herlot were a bad omen. Come! Follow me! To the sea cliffs!"

Everyone broke out in curious murmurs. Bells? What in the world was Rudi speaking about?

"Eraskan bells?" Bee's husband said.

"But there are no bells at the fortress! King Cloudian said so himself!" Sira said.

"No, no, no. He said there were bells but they were *broken*," Bee said.

Impossible, Ilvy thought as she followed the crowd down the path to the sea with Ernest and Ambro at her side. Even from the sea cliffs, the fortress would be too far away from them to hear the bells if in fact they had been fixed.

Then she heard them, even over the sound of the vigorous waves splashing up water at the protruding cliff as they crashed into the jagged rocks below. Ringing and vibrating metals alternated in rhythm in two distinct pitches. Beautiful, much more so than the clanking of iron pots that she had imagined.

One by one, she watched everyone line up to greet Herlot in Ernest's arms.

All of a sudden, Rudi's arm was around her shoulder. He gazed at the crowd as if watching a sunset.

"I hope you are feeling very proud of yourself," Ilvy said.

"Ah, yes, yes."

"As you ought to be. But, Rudi, how is it possible? How can we hear them from this far away?" She gazed at the fortress that was but a dot on the horizon where the sea met the shore. The bells were too far, yet the ringing was deafening and seemed to be right there next to them on the cliffs.

"Let's just be grateful that everyone is too caught up by the beauty of the sound. There couldn't be a clearer sign that Herlot is not a bad omen. Hey, Agatha," Rudi waved over Agatha who still stood on the path with both hands on her hips. Slowly, swaying her hips side to side, she walked right by Ernest and Herlot and squared her shoulders off at Ilvy.

"I stubbed two toes trying to go after you," she said.

Rudi covered his mouth and whispered under his breath. *Are you sure it wasn't your toes that stubbed the chests?*

"I'm so sorry, Agatha. Really—" Ilvy started.

"And you know what the worst part was?" Agatha's whole face trembled, and her eyes squinted shut. "I was so worried about you and the little one! I used up three candles waiting for you to come back. I even promised that as long as you came back, I wouldn't ever deliver a baby again."

Before Agatha could get any more riled up, Ilvy threw her arms around her. Never, ever, would she want someone else delivering babies. "I am so, so sorry for causing all this trouble, and every mother and child are lucky to have you. I just needed some fresh air. That was all."

Agatha wiped her nose on her apron. "Just fresh air? Well, this is good to know." And at last she looked at Herlot. "Can I hold her?"

"Of course," Ernest said and placed Herlot on Agatha's chest. Agatha rocked side to side to the rhythm of the bells until Rudi asked for his turn.

Ilvy couldn't believe how wonderful the morning had turned out. She had the best home in the world. Each one of them was lucky to have been welcomed into the world with so much love. The only thing more pleasing was seeing her own child be on the receiving end.

"Hungry," Ambro tugged on Ilvy's dress.

As if awoken and reminded, Ilvy's stomach grumbled.

"I agree," Ernest said. "What do you say, friends? Shall we celebrate this wonderful morning with hard-boiled eggs?"

A high-pitched, continuous cry emanated from Herlot and Ilvy's arms extended for her. "Sounds like we aren't the only ones who are hungry," Rudi said.

Then, right as Ilvy and Rudi's arms touched, Herlot between them, Ivy's hair flew into her face from a wind so strong it threatened to unravel Herlot from her blanket. It slid over the top of Herlot and then turned to glide underneath, carrying the ringing tone of the bells in a circle around her. Based on Rudi's dropped jaw, Ilvy knew he was just as shocked as she was. They stared at one another, each holding onto Herlot, afraid to move for fear of the wind sweeping her away. And then, just as suddenly as it had started, it stopped. The air was void of any bell ringing, only the waves and seagulls could be heard like on any normal day at the sea cliffs.

Ilvy held Herlot close to her chest, readjusting the blanket. Rudi seemed unshaken. Had she imagined that he had witnessed it, too? He simply stared off into the distance, toward the fortress.

"Rudi?"

He just kept staring. She nudged him with her shoulder.

He turned to look at her, brows furrowed together. "You go on ahead, Ilvy. I'll catch up," he said and smiled sadly before turning back to look at the fortress.

Ilvy rushed toward the path, her only wish to get Herlot away from the cliff. While everyone celebrated her daughter over breakfast, she couldn't stop thinking about the wind and the bells and how the wind had targeted her daughter. She was stirred out of her thoughts by a tap on her shoulder. She turned to look down at Elvin who had a half-peeled egg in his hand.

"I just saw the first butterfly outside. Come, I'll show you and you can chase it."

Ilvy frowned. "Elvin, why in the world would you think I'd want to chase a butterfly?"

"You said you would still chase them after the baby was born."

"I said no such thing." Ilvy took the egg from Elvin and peeled off the rest of the shell. Sometimes children had the silliest of ideas. Ilvy hadn't chased a butterfly since she was a little girl.

● ● ●

King Cloudian raced barefoot and robeless up the cracked stone steps of the fortress, his morning routine utterly forgotten. His stewards were right on his heels as Cloudian pushed the ceiling door up, pulled himself onto the plank, and gazed up at the bells swinging—no bell ringer or ropes in sight. It was as if the wind itself was pushing them like a child on a tree swing. *A sign from nature.* His knees buckled in relief and hit the old, wooden floor. He didn't even notice the screw that dug into his worn skin as he dropped his face into his hands, relief pouring out of his pores like a maple tree's sap on a warm day in spring.

Cloudian grasped for the large amulet that hung around his neck and took out the small scroll that was hidden inside. Like every king before him, he had sworn a secret oath only shared between one Eraskan king to another. He had promised to sacrifice any desires for gold in duty to this message he often questioned was real. He skimmed the words that he had recited on so many occasions when he was certain his life as a king was of no worth. No gold, no cities, no army. He had nothing compared to the rulers of other kingdoms in the world.

But he did have this letter. If the contents were true, maybe he had something that was just as valuable, if not more.

Dear future King of Eraska,

I have done something terrible and our world suffers endless wars over gold because of it. For years I have studied my mistakes and my enemy—our enemy—and believe that I have found a solution. I cannot tell you more than this, for if I share my knowledge of who our enemy is, your life will be endangered and you are not strong enough to face him. Trust me when I tell you that it is complicated beyond sense and requires a long time for crucial events to unfold. By this time, not even a trace of my existence will be remembered by anyone in your world. My solution requires crucial events to unfold, and it is imperative that you not allow a single Eraskan to possess gold. Our enemy has already won, but if you follow my instructions, we just may have a chance of not letting him win forever. Keep your people isolated. Support their joy and peace in any way you can. This, I believe, will foster a place, if given enough time, for my solution. The wind will give you a sign when you are on the correct path.

With shame and hope in my heart,

Brom

Goosebumps spread across King Cloudian's body as he felt the power and changing direction of the wind above, as if ignited by an important message that the clapper was beating against the bells' hollow insides. If this was not the sign every king had waited for, nothing would be.

CHAPTER 2
Footprints

I LVY HELD HER EAR to the door of Alonia's barn.

"Mother, what are we doing?" her eight-year-old son, Ambro, asked.

"Having a competition. Who can stay the most quiet?"

Ambro pointed his thumb at his chest. He took after Ernest with his smooth, light brown curls, narrow eyebrows, and strong jaw, but she had no idea from whom he had gotten his competitiveness.

A moth flew off the door as she opened it a sliver, silently asking it not to creak, to peek inside. Just as she had expected. Sira. Bee. Melody. All perched on haystacks like owls, and the sweet little mouse in the middle, their prey—Herlot, throwing oats to the chickens.

Herlot had long, golden waves of hair that tangled easily, fog-gray eyes, and long eyelashes. She had pink cheeks, with a mole on her left one and dimples just below when she smiled. She was tall for her five years, nearly as tall as Ambro, but clearly not tall enough to stand up for herself.

"Is anyone out in the woods right now?" Sira asked.

"I think I overheard Simon say he needed to gather more wood," Bee said.

"Perfect. Herlot, do you think you could help us find Simon?"

Those slug trotters. They were tricking her again to search for someone to prove their ghost story right. Ilvy shoved the door open, allowing it to creak in all its glory.

"Oh! Ilvy! How is your afternoon?" Melody asked.

Herlot's mother smiled. "Soon to be lovely. Herlot, come here, please. Ambro, take your sister home to play blocks."

She pressed her palm against Herlot's cheek as Ambro guided her out of the barn. The chickens scattered out of Ilvy's path as she stomped toward the "hide and seek" gathering.

Once she was close enough to have invaded their clan space, she put her hands on her hips. "I'm only going to ask this once. Stop making my daughter into a spectacle."

"We just wanted to play—" Melody started.

"I have heard the rumors the bunch of you have been spreading around the village like a winter cold. Calling a little girl haunted? A ghost that helps Herlot find people when she takes off her shoes? Shame on all of you. She just likes to be barefoot and search for the people who are special to her. Unfortunately, she is too young to understand that you should not be one of them."

Bee and Melody's shoulders slumped. Sira, however, leaned back onto her haystack. The only other being more relaxed in the room was Milly the Cow, who chewed on hay with her eyes half closed.

"I'd only feel shame if it were a rumor, but it's not," Sira said. "I suspected it even before she played hide and seek. You were all there at the beach when she learned to walk. You all saw. She didn't walk to Ilvy or Ernest. She reached out her arms toward someone none of us could see." Sira crossed her ankles. "A ghost. Herlot walked into the hands of a ghost. That's the truth."

Bee and Melody sat up straighter and leaned toward Sira. "Tell us, Sira, why do you think she has to take off her shoes?" Melody asked.

Ilvy's jaw dropped and she felt the roots of her hairs stand up in frustration.

"The ghost must have been a noble who had his shoes shined every day. He simply can't stand the sight of our worn shoes and tells Herlot that he won't help her unless she takes them off!"

Ilvy kicked the bucket in front of her. Milk splashed all over Bee and Melody's skirts.

"Ilvy, have you completely tangled your wool? Oh, how I hate scrubbing milk stains," Melody said.

Ilvy almost laughed at how little she cared. "One more rumor and I will make sure King Cloudian hears about the gold coin wedged somewhere between the stones of Sira and Viktor's home."

It was Sira's turn to have her jaw drop. Ilvy had walked out on a tree branch with the accusation. Sira's daughter Manni liked to boast. Based on Sira's expression, the boasting was based on truth.

"Have a lovely evening." Ilvy turned on the worn heels of her boots and marched out.

The cold wind kissed Ilvy as she walked the path home, as if it were congratulating her for taking a stand. Yes, even she agreed that it had looked like Herlot was walking to something that was not there when she learned to walk, but that didn't mean there actually was something there. However, the real problem had begun recently, and it was all Ilvy's foolish fault. She had started a game of hide and seek in hopes of getting Herlot to play with the other children while she and the other women planted cucumber seeds in the garden. Herlot took off her shoes, and one by one, found each child without checking a single empty spot. Since then, everyone wanted to play the game with her. That was fine. However, when her best friend Merle told her that Sira had spread a rumor about Herlot being haunted by a ghost that helped her find people, she knew she had to do something.

"Would you look at that! Just in time," Ernest's voice shook Ilvy from her thoughts and she noticed the clusters of snowflakes falling around her. Just around the corner of Bee's home, Ernest and Rudi appeared carrying a door made of pieces of wood tied together. Rudi really had finished just in time.

"Rudi, I cannot thank you enough for your hard work. Especially after just having returned from your trip," Ilvy said as she caught up to the men. "Please join us with Merle for supper tonight."

"Supper with our friends on the day of first snow. I can't imagine a better way to celebrate," Rudi said.

"Wonderful." Ilvy admired the door—each piece was carved into a perfect circular shape so that, when stacked together, no space showed through. Rudi was a master of woodwork. Once a year, King

Cloudian's stewards took him on a trip to the villages so that he could help build and repair anything from wood-carrying carts to Cloudian's wagons themselves. However, his favorite way to apply his skill was for the children. There was not one child in Eraska who did not play with a toy carved by Rudi or his forefathers.

Once inside, Ilvy lit the fire under her hanging pot while the men worked on detaching the former door. She opened her chest and took a quick sip of her healthy spirit tincture before returning to her pot. She watched Herlot and Ambro while she waited for the water to boil. They were a sight to see in their play headpieces made of colorful bird feathers that shook each time they leaned over.

"What was the word again?" Herlot asked.

"Jungle." Ambro nudged the letter E toward her. "Mother, will you help us find a new word?"

"Certainly." Ilvy crawled over and flipped through the pages—what was left of them—of a damaged book.

"Herlot, did you know that only Alonian children learn to read and write? Nobody else in Eraska knows how, right, Mother? That sailor who came by last week couldn't believe that we could."

"Yes, Ambro," Ilvy said.

"Don't you think that's great, Herlot?"

Without a word, Herlot continued to sort through the blocks, as if she were in her own world. A part of Ilvy wished she could actually put Herlot into a different world, just for a little bit, until she knew Sira wouldn't bother her again. What if Sira was right? The thought was an awful lump in her throat that she couldn't swallow away. She scanned the page trying not to think about the wind that had wrapped around Herlot when she was born. "Lizard," she said, and rushed back to her pot as she waved her hand in front of her body, trying to cool herself down. Her heart was beating so fast and she was so hot even though it was cold outside. *What if the wind had been a ghost?* She didn't realize she had gripped the iron edges until she heard her skin singe. She suppressed a yelp and plunged her already blistering palms into the water bucket.

"Mother?" A block rolled off Ambro's lap as he stared at her with a worried expression.

"I'm fine, dear. Go on, keep playing," she said as she poured her prepped vegetables into the bubbling water. Then, she snuck another quick sip of her tincture.

"Not a single drift will bring in snow this winter," Ernest said as Rudi tapped the new door a few times.

"Children, won't you thank Rudi?" Ilvy said.

"Great door. Thank you, Rudi," Ambro muttered.

"Herlot," Ilvy said, with a small warning in her tone.

"What? Oh. Great door. Thank you, Rudi." Her grey eyes beamed as she smiled at Rudi.

"You're welcome," Rudi said, smiling back.

A series of knocks sounded and Rudi scattered to the side right in time as it flew open. Not bothering to say hello, Agatha swung the door back and forth, then blew between two pieces while pressing her hand against the other side.

"We need one just like this," Agatha mumbled. Then she leaned toward Ilvy. "Just walked by Sira and Viktor's, all sorts of a ruckus going on in there. Sure sounded like someone hiding a piece of gold to me." She winked.

"Rudi!" Agatha shouted as if Rudi were not standing right next to her. "Could you walk me home? I'd like to discuss a new door for Simon and me if you have the time."

As Ilvy watched Agatha pull Rudi along like a little child, she felt safe knowing Agatha was on Herlot's side and hadn't believed the rumor about Herlot. And, if there was a ghost, Ilvy knew that Agatha would find a way to scare it away.

It wasn't long before Ilvy greeted Rudi, Merle, and Lupert for supper as they shook snow off their coats and boots. "And you will all stay the night. I will not let you walk back home in this storm."

"Thank you, Ilvy." Merle rolled up her leggings that she always knit too long for her short legs. "Oh, I can't believe we have to wait at least four moons to see the heather and grass again."

"Oh, speak for yourself." Rudi bounced Lupert on his hip. "I, myself, am looking forward to long evenings inside and a break from all those hearth gatherings."

Ilvy didn't know if it was the storm outside combined with the fire inside, or her guests' happy remarks about her stew, but she slipped into a state of ease and enjoyed the fish, beets, and potatoes. "Healthy appetite," she said as Lupert crawled into Rudi's lap and opened his mouth to be fed.

"Twee," Lupert said. Ilvy pinched her lips together as did Herlot and Ernest. Ambro bit down on his spoon and Merle covered her mouth with a handkerchief. "No, Lupert. Pa-Pa," Rudi said.

"Twee."

How was it possible that Rudi had still not caught on to the reference? There was no nice way to put it. His dry hair stuck out in all directions, creating a half halo around his head that resembled the leaves and branches of a tree. Ilvy had laughed an entire looming session when Merle had told her about how Lupert had swished his first attempt of a word around in his mouth while looking at Rudi. Instead of the hoped-for "papa," Lupert had said, "Tree."

"Sto-wee," Lupert said with food still in his mouth.

"Yes! Father, tell us about the sea monster," Ambro said.

Merle groaned. "I've heard Finnigan feed jelly biscuits to the sea monster one too many times. Ilvy, let's clean up and have our chat."

Once they were settled sipping ale and dunking bowls into the bucket, Ilvy knew Merle was going to ask about Sira and the gold. "Did you do it?" Merle asked as she dried a spoon with a cloth.

Ilvy took a long swig of ale. "Yes. But now I'm afraid she's going to do something worse to get back at me...maybe even use Herlot to do it."

"She won't. Especially if Manni was telling the truth about the gold."

Ilvy wrung the water from her cloth. "I can just see her telling the kids something awful about Herlot. She rarely plays so little with them as it is."

"Now Herlot you don't worry about, my dear. She's...different. In a special way."

"She seems so lonely to me."

"Eh, lonely from what? Remember the fight the children had over the seashell Elvin found? Inga bawled because Manni pulled her hair and Maurice's knee bled a flood when he fell on and broke the shell. And then there was Herlot, yes, alone, creating the loveliest shape out of some stones in the sand. It's like she's in a world where our fusses don't exist." Merle sighed. "Would be nice."

Tearing fabric brought Ilvy's attention to Herlot who was mid-sitting back on her heels. Ilvy was about to ask if she had accidentally ripped her dress when Herlot switched to having her ankles crossed in front of her. Then she leaned to her right. Then her left. What was making her fidget so?

Ivy's eyes followed Herlot with suspicion as she inched toward Ernest and whispered in his ear.

Ernest chuckled. "Our Herlot wishes to hear a story of a real magical creature."

Ilvy sat up. "Oh my. Herlot, real magical creatures don't exist." The last thing she needed was Herlot searching for a magical creature with Sira on the watch. "Ernest, tell us the one about the elk."

Herlot clasped her hands in front of her and gazed up at Ernest with big, hopeful eyes. *Oh no. I know that look.* Ilvy cleared her throat to get his attention. Futile attempt it was.

"I just might have something for you." Ernest pushed himself up and began to search through one of the chests. *Please don't let it be anything that can blow smoke out of its nostrils*, Ilvy thought. When he returned, he carried a roll of parchment, the edges ruffled with wear. Ilvy flung her rag into the pot. *Of course he would pick that one. Of course!* Ilvy watched on in defeat as Ernest lifted Herlot and Ambro onto his knees and unrolled the parchment.

"This here is a legend. I cannot promise you that it is true, but legends are often based in true history," Ernest started. "A long time ago, before Alonia and before the other villages of Eraska—Lorfin, Temes, Ruelder, Noray, and Bundene—people lived with magnificent pearl-white horses that had a glowing alicorn on the center of their foreheads"—he stroked the space above Herlot's nose—"and wings that carried them high into the sky. They called them unicorns. Every morning, the people climbed onto their unicorns, and together, they flew up high, higher than the clouds, and greeted the sun together. And, every morning, the sun shined its rays in response to the iridescence that glistened above our world."

Herlot's eyes glistened like Ilvy had never seen before.

"But, one day, all of this changed when a boy decided not to greet the sun.

"What was his name?" Ambro asked.

"It doesn't say..."

"He needs a name! It's not a story if he doesn't have a name," Ambro said.

"It's a legend though," Ernest said.

"I want to hear the story," Herlot said.

"I still think he needs a name," Ambro said.

"Very well. Give me a moment..." Ernest said.

"Hurry, Father, I want to hear more about the white horses!" Herlot tugged on his sleeve.

"Rudi, help Ernest," Merle said.

"Brom. How about Brom?" Rudi said.

Ernest smiled. "Very well. "Brom and his unicorn set out for an adventure before the first daylight could be seen. His people did not see him for many days. When he did return, he was without his unicorn, and the others soon began to change. They stopped greeting the sun and forgot about their unicorns. Instead, they spent their days searching for gold."

Ambro rested his elbow on his knee. "How foolish. Who would rather play with a piece of gold than a unicorn?"

Rudi chuckled.

"Father, keep telling the story," Herlot said.

Ernest flipped a page over. "The unicorns felt deep sorrow, and one day, their wings dissipated, for they had no need for them anymore. Flying was not the same without their companions. Eventually the humans remembered the unicorns again, but for awful reasons. They began to hunt them for their golden alicorns. Many unicorns died during this time, but magic was on their side. To save themselves, the remaining unicorns hid inside a tree, where they remain today, waiting for a better time when the world is safe for them again."

"It is an awfully sad story, Father," Herlot said.

"It is. Real stories are often sad, but they are never without hope. Remember, they are waiting to come back again. Now, as for the tree, it is said by some that it grows in our forest here near Alonia."

Ilvy frowned as she thought she saw Herlot's lips tremble. Was she about to cry? Herlot never cried unless she injured herself.

"Let's go find the tree! I want to see a unicorn! Let's go right now!" exclaimed Ambro.

"Have you lost your little head of curls? In a snowstorm?" Rudi said.

In the firelight, Ilvy noticed Herlot's eyes begin to water.

"This is not the time to go searching for magical creatures. It's time to do the most boring thing in the world for a little boy and girl. Sleep," said Merle.

Herlot's face scrunched together.

"Aw, really? Hey, Rudi, why don't we have a look at the door?" Ambro said.

And then she did. Cry. Like Ilvy had never heard a child cry before. *Someone comfort her!* she wanted to shout, as her spirit collapsed in shame because she knew she wouldn't be able to. The sorrow in her daughter's cry was something she had never experienced. Based on everyone else's stiff postures, she sank even more knowing they felt the same.

Herlot threw herself into Ernest's chest and gripped onto his tunic. He wrapped his arms around her, and for what seemed like moon cycles, rocked her back and forth. As much as she wanted to cover her ears, Ilvy listened to every heart-ripping cry, it was the least she could do. As Herlot's cry dissipated to a whimper and finally, thankfully, a stuff-nosed snore, Ilvy wished she had a sword from one of the stories to fight whatever had caused Herlot so much pain. She didn't budge a finger as Ernest lowered Herlot onto her mattress and Ambro covered her with a blanket, afraid that she'd awaken and it would all start over again.

She didn't blame Rudi and Merle for not saying anything as she helped spread out a fresh barrel of hay for them to sleep on. But she was glad they were there. If the sorrow followed Herlot into her dreams, at least she was not alone here.

They wished one another a goodnight before settling into an awkward silence, only the raging wind outside and the fire crackles were telling a story now.

"Why was Herlot crying like that?" Ambro's voice rang across the room.

"I don't know, Ambro," Ilvy said, her voice hoarse. How could she be a good mother if she couldn't guess at what had made her daughter cry with such sorrow?

"Could it have been the story?" Merle asked.

"Possibility," Ernest said. A long silence followed. "Possibility and the things that destroy it."

● ● ●

Ernest's boat danced on the waves. His surroundings were blurred unless he focused right at them—an obvious clue that he was dreaming. A white figure materialized on the beach. Its mane whirled in the wind and wings tucked in at its side.

A unicorn!

"Wait!" he called between puffs of air as he paddled toward the shore. The clouds emitting from his mouth blurred his vision. When they drifted away, the unicorn was still standing there. The moment he reached the shore, the unicorn took off into the forest.

Ernest chased after it for what felt like years and years of dreams. Just as he was beginning to worry the dream would never reach its climax, the tips of the trees bent in toward one another. Their browns and greens turned grey until eventually they transformed into a cave tunnel. Far ahead, a glow emanated from the unicorn's alicorn. It had stopped.

"Please, wait!" he called. "I won't hurt you, I just want to tell my children about you!"

Ernest treaded closer. When he was a rock's throw away, his dream heart dropped when he realized it was just a painting on the cave wall. However, the alicorn was still glowing.

He spun toward a creaking in the wall to his right. The crevices were taking the shape of a face, and it seemed to be protruding out of the wall. He leaned forward for a closer look and came face to face with a pair of hollow eyes. A hand extended from the wall and gripped him around the neck. He fought to free himself but his dream hand slipped through the stone arm. The mouth of the face opened wide, a crack spread from its cheeks.

"Seek the rest before it's too late. Do you understand?" It repeated that question until the motions of its mouth caused its entire face to shatter and all that was left was the arm.

Ernest awoke gripping his neck. He could feel indentations in his skin.

"I must have done it to myself. It was only a dream," he mumbled, his heart pounding.

Careful not to step on anyone, he made his way to splash water on the back of his neck. He closed his eyes as the droplets cooled the nerve burn from the nightmare. Before lying back down, he watched Ambro and Herlot's innocent faces and chests rising and falling to Lupert's cooing in the background. He kissed them on their foreheads. "I hope your dreams are magical and kind."

Seek the rest before it's too late. Do you understand?

Ernest swallowed, still unable to shake the feeling of someone clutching his throat. As beautiful as the unicorn had been, Ernest would never utter a word of the nightmare to Herlot and Ambro, for fear it might follow them into their own dream world.

● ● ●

Herlot pulled her knees to her chest to escape Ambro's tickling fingers, his favorite method to wake her. Except this morning, she was already awake, but had no desire to open her tear-dried eyes. All that awaited her was the hollowness that had appeared after her father finished the unicorn story. At first she had felt wonderful, as if part of her had left and reappeared on the sea horizon, riding a unicorn with majestic wings. Then she realized that most of her was stuck on the beach facing a tide that would never allow her to reach the Herlot who flew riding a unicorn above the horizon.

"Wake up, Herlot, we are going to go find the unicorn tree," Ambro whispered.

She opened an eye. It could be a world without unicorns. It could be a world with hidden unicorns. And maybe, just maybe, it could be a world with hidden unicorns who might come out and say hello. She opened her other eye. "How do you know where they are?" she asked.

"There was a drawing of a tree on father's parchment with the legend of the unicorns. Rudi showed me a place with really old trees once, I think that's where it is."

That was enough to make her slide out and begin to twist a scarf around her neck while Ambro wrapped fur strips around her boots. Winter clothes always made her feel like a Herlot animal that fit right into the forest. She placed her headpiece snugly over her forehead. Ambro followed suit. "What does that say?" she pointed at the letter blocks that Ambro must have arranged.

"Snowballs. Woods. Now we have to be quiet. If Mother wakes up and asks us where we are going, she'll know if I'm lying. The trees are farther than I'm allowed to go without an adult."

Once outside, Herlot could not tear her eyes away from the infinite pieces of sky that had covered the world in a blanket of fluff. "Good morning, snow," she said. She stomped her foot forward, mesmerized by the crunch. Like biting into a crisp apple. Her mouth watered to taste the fresh snow.

When she looked up, Ambro was more than halfway to the tree line. Had it been a snowball fight, she would have felt no need to rush, but by no means would she miss out on a unicorn hello. She pumped her knees to her chest as she struggled through the high snow. Ambro still showed no sign of slowing down when she made it to the small hill that led up to the forest path. She had to run faster. Her foot slipped from underneath her and her mouth opened to squeal right as her face made contact with the snow. She lifted her head, blinked the snow out of her eyes, and licked her lips. "Ambro, wait!"

Thankfully, Ambro appeared on top of the hill and slid down to give her a hand to the top. Herlot allowed herself a glance at the bare branches covered in snow before putting all of her focus on not slipping and keeping pace with Ambro.

"I was thinking, since the unicorns are afraid of humans, maybe if we wrap our scarves around our faces and get on our hands and knees, they'll come out thinking we're a magic animal, too."

Herlot froze. "I'm going home," she said.

"What? Why? We are more than halfway there. Mother and Father will be mad at me for letting you walk home alone."

"I don't want to trick the unicorns."

Ambro sighed. "It's not like it will harm them. They'll come out, see we're good, and that will be the end of it."

It took everything for Herlot to rip her hand out of Ambro's grasp because there was nothing more that she wanted than to meet a unicorn. "Don't you remember the story? They don't trust humans enough already. If you and Elvin trick them, they might really never come out again."

"Elvin? How did Elvin come into the story?"

Herlot shrugged. "He's your favorite person to go on adventures with."

"Fine. We won't trick them," Ambro said. "We'll even take our headpieces off."

Herlot scanned his expression. "Promise?"

Ambro nodded and took their headpieces and hung them on a branch. "By the way, I wouldn't have taken Elvin. You were the only one I wanted to go on this adventure with."

Herlot squeezed her palm into a fist imagining she had clasped the words, and then held it to her chest, telling her heart to remember each one.

"I think this is it," Ambro said after a while.

Herlot would have known even if Ambro hadn't said anything. Not only were the trees wider and taller, there was something about the air that said this was a special place, a little like the graveyard, a place where it was important to not disturb the peace.

Ambro knocked on a trunk. "Unicorns! Are you in there?" Nothing. He moved on to another tree.

Herlot rolled her eyes. If she were a unicorn, it would take a lot more than a knock to make her come out. Like Ambro had said, they had to show the unicorns that they were good and just wanted to play. Perhaps a song, or a game would do. She checked her dress pocket to see if maybe she had left her wooden lamb toy there. No luck.

A glimmer caught her eye. It came from a chestnut tree Ambro had overlooked. The trunk was so wide that it could have easily fit two

Milly the Cows. From far away it looked like any other tree, but once she got closer, the bark seemed to have all the colors of the rainbow entwined in its deep shades of brown.

"Ambro, it's this one. Just look at how beautiful it is."

"I already tried that one," Ambro replied, his voice carrying a hint of frustration.

Herlot wasn't sure what to do. She did not want to be rude and knock, so she grabbed her dress and curtsied. "Hello, hello, I am Herlot," she sang.

Ambro trudged over to her side. His eyes danced from her to the tree. "Why are you singing to it?"

"It's what princesses do in stories." Herlot was about to explain about the colors when a root pressed into the bottom of her boot causing her foot to slide over to the right. Strange. It had not been there before. Could roots move that fast? She'd have to ask Rudi.

Her sight, hearing, smell, and taste slowed like hardening mud except all she could focus on was the skin at the bottom of her foot and a growing warmth in her chest. An image of a footprint in the ground danced across her mind. She kicked off her boot and wedged her foot through the snow.

"Herlot! What are you doing? You'll freeze your toes!"

But Herlot was not bothered by the cold because a warmth was pulsing from the ground. As if guided by an unknown force, her toes oriented themselves over the shape of the warmth—a footprint.

The warmth in her chest pulsed like a star and what felt like a thread of warmth travelled from her chest to the footprint in the snow. She gasped as another flavor of warmth belonging to the footprint flowed into her and toward her heart. Yes, another flavor was how she could describe it. Warm but a different warmth from hers. It was like she had paths within her body just for these warmths. It was wonderful.

Until her world began to spin. The trees and sky became whirling streaks of grey and brown. Somewhere amongst them was Ambro's voice, muffled to a point where she could not tell where one word ended and another began. Time itself seemed to spin backwards, too. The rhythm of the day, the beat of the night, once flowing toward the sea was now running from it.

The spinning stopped and she felt suspended in air. Light as chickling fuzz in the breeze. Nothing to see, hear, or smell. All that existed was the warm pulse in her chest. This. Had happened before. She knew it. For the briefest moment, like a surprise sun ray on a clouded day, an image of willow tree leaves and a woman on the beach came to light in her mind. The leaves, rocking and singing to her. The woman, her open arms inviting her to walk into them for a hug.

May I share a memory with you? A voice, not her own, asked within her mind.

"Who...who are you?" she asked, but for some reason could barely hear her own words, as if someone far away had spoken them.

My name is Brom. You stepped on my footprint that I made long ago. You must have a golden heart. Please, may I share my memory with you?

All the adults always said to not speak to the wanderers and sailors alone. Herlot wasn't sure if she had to wait for an adult in order to speak to a footprint man. But she was curious about what a footprint man wanted to show her...

"Alright. As long as it does not hurt," she said.

Wonderful. All of a sudden, Herlot's heart felt like a cauldron. She felt her flavor and Brom's flavor of warmth stirring together. Then, just as quickly as her senses had disappeared, they slung out to her head, arms, and legs. No more chickling fuzz. Heavy, alive.

Her eyes blinked open. The trees were thinner, shorter. So many green leaves filled the canopy, vibrant in the heat and sunlight. She felt farther from the ground and realized her body was different. She was taller, with several added layers of muscular strength.

Her head was incredibly busy. From what she could tell, she still only had one, but if her thoughts and emotions were a row of wheat, another row had been planted right next to them, and just as difficult as it was to distinguish one stalk from another, she wasn't sure which thoughts were her own. The confusion and wonder about what was happening most likely belonged to her, then there was the shame, anger, fear, and most of all—urgency that belonged to someone else.

The sound of a stick breaking sent her lunging behind a bush. It was as if her legs had moved on their own, or were controlled by something or someone else. She wanted to look at her legs and touch them, to make sure they were hers, but her eyes stayed focused on the chestnut tree she could barely see through the leaves. Then a figure appeared next to the tree. She could only make out the figure's bare feet and bottom of her dress. *Blue* dress. How could the color of the sky appear in a fabric? It was beautiful.

Emrys, I told you to be more careful. What if you had seen me? You would have lost your golden heart, too! she wanted to say, and then her lips began to mouth the words but it wasn't her voice she heard; it was one much lower in tone than hers, Brom's voice. Now she understood. This was Brom's memory. She was Brom! Her mouth wanted to drop in shock, but stayed firm.

Before Herlot could learn who Emrys was, why Brom was upset with her, and how Emrys had made blue dye for the dress, the spinning started again. Time rushed forward toward the present, colors changed from summer greens and blues to winter browns and greys. Just as shapes of her forest surroundings were beginning to settle back into place, something that looked like a swarm of black maggots that had taken the form of a crooked hand materialized through the whirl. The awful thing inched closer and closer, the maggot fingers reached for her heart. She couldn't find her voice to scream or her hands to slap it away—anything to prevent it from touching her. So close now she could reach out and touch them if she wanted to. She would never want to touch something so awful. *No! No! No!* Something pulled at the warmth in her chest and it began to leak out of her. Just a finger's length from her chest now.

Her bottom hit the snow and her legs went flying into the air. "I said stop it!" Ambro shouted.

Herlot sat up and shook her head. Why was she behind the bush? She had just been at the tree. Why was Ambro angry? Had he pushed her? "Did you push me?" she asked, head spinning.

"I had to! I know you do strange things like finding people but this, whatever this was, don't ever do it again." He took off a glove and chucked it at the ground.

What strange things? "Ambro, I just wanted to tell you about the colorful trunk," she said.

"You were *not* talking about a trunk. And you sure weren't hearing me. You were talking to someone who wasn't even there. An Emrys."

Herlot rubbed her forehead. The name sounded very familiar. For some reason she couldn't stop thinking about a blue dress. Emrys. Emrys. She was thinking so hard she could feel the blood pulsing in her forehead. "Ouch!" she exclaimed at the sharp pain behind her eyes. "Oh, Ambro, I don't know what you are speaking of. Are you playing a trick on me?"

"No!" Ambro's shoulders rose up and down he was breathing so hard.

"Well, why don't we go ask Mother about Emrys. Maybe she will know. Or Agatha. She knows everyone."

"That is the last thing we will do!"

Herlot turned her cheek as if slapped by a gust of wind. Ambro had never been this angry before.

"The others think you're strange, that you talk to ghosts, and sometimes, I think you do, too." Ambro's skin flushed pink, his eyes wide. "And we will not utter a word of this to anyone, *especially* Mother. She's worried enough as it is."

Herlot felt as if she had swallowed a collection of rocks that threatened to rip the inside of her belly apart. Tears stung the corners of her eyes. "I don't want to worry Mother," she managed.

She watched Ambro walk over to the chestnut tree and pick up her boot. He returned with a pained expression on his face. "I'm sorry," he said as he slid the boot onto her foot. "How *do* you find everyone when you play hide and seek?"

"Are you going to yell at me if I tell you?" Herlot asked.

"No. I do want to fix this, though. If you tell me, maybe I can help. So...do you see a ghost?"

"No!" Herlot exclaimed.

"Phew. Alright. Then it can't be that bad. So why *do* you take off your shoes?"

"Why footprints, of course. It's easier to imagine where the footprints are when I have my shoes off."

Ambro's eyes crossed. "Imagine? What do you mean imagine? Why are you imagining footprints?"

39

Herlot hugged herself. "Uhh—"

"So you take your shoes off. You imagine the footprint of the person you're looking for. And then you see their footprints and follow them?"

"No." She hugged herself tighter. Didn't everyone do this? Maybe she really was doing something very strange. She didn't want to be strange. She wanted to be like her village family.

"Well, then, how, Herlot, how?"

"I don't know!" she shouted. His questions felt like hot sticks poking the truth out of her. "Look. I take off the shoes. And there's footprints. *I* don't see them. *My feet* see them. And then I follow them."

They both stared at one another. Now that Herlot had said it out loud, she realized how strange it really was.

"Your feet are like animal noses," Ambro said.

Herlot let her body fall into the snow. She swallowed the awful truth as she gazed up at the grey sky. "My feet are like animal noses," she repeated. "My feet are story monsters. I'm a story monster."

"No, no. You're not a monster. But it is strange. And I don't think it's good. Feet are supposed to have a smell, not be able to smell. But, Herlot, what did just happen now? How did your feet make you... disappear? That never happens when you play hide and seek, right? I really was scared that you were gone."

Herlot sat up again. "You were scared? Well, I am more scared. How would you like to disappear and not know you disappeared?" Her eyes were beginning to swell with the tears she was fighting to hold back.

Ambro rested his hands on her shoulders. "We just can't let you disappear again and then we won't have anything to worry about and neither will Mother. Look, I think I know what the problem is. The strange things happen whenever you take off your shoes. Maybe if you only take them off before bed or bathing, it won't happen anymore."

What an awful solution, she thought. She'd never feel the sand or grass or snow, as cold as it was. But Mother was much more important than sand or grass or snow. And so was her village family. And by all means, she did not want to disappear. Herlot nodded. "I won't take them off anymore."

Ambro's face lightened. "Good. Now let's go home. Elvin and the crew probably already started the snowball fight." Herlot forced a smile and took one last glance at the chestnut tree. Way at the very top hung a leaf the color of the freshest green as if it had neither tasted the fall nor beginning of winter.

On the walk home, Ambro rambled on and on about snowball sizes and shapes. "The whole trick is to pack it tight so that it does not fall apart when you throw it, but you can't waste too much time on the packing part. Pack, throw, move, that's my art!" At least he was not angry anymore. She, on the other hand, wished she had a wand that could make the day go away. She had hoped to find a unicorn. Instead, she had learned that she was strange.

The smell of fireplaces poked at her nose. She looked up just in time to see a sphere of snow whizz at her shoulder. It splattered into her coat and several kids jumped out from behind the trees, congratulating Manni on her aim.

"Get Ambro!" Maurice called.

Ambro took off in a zig-zag as four more snowballs flew by aiming at his back.

Herlot dropped to her knees and squished a chunk of wet snow together. Maybe the snowball fight could be her wand, something to help her forget the awful day. She focused on packing the perfect ball. She squished from the other direction but realized she must have pressed too hard because her ball had flattened into a potato cake. She tried again but then stopped. What if Ambro's plan failed? What if she still did something strange even with her shoes on? Maybe it was a better idea to play alone until she was certain no more of the strange things happened.

Elvin and Manni ran by her, each holding a snowball. Ambro stuck his head out from behind a tree and stuck out his tongue. In unison, Elvin and Manni chucked their balls at him. He ducked just in time, laughed, then sprinted farther away. The rest of the children chased after him, disappearing into the woods until Herlot was all alone with their footprints in the snow. *I'll find a nice game to play at home*, she thought.

Once home, she added a piece of wood to the fire and took off her winter clothes, but not the boots. She sat down with her two wooden toy figures that she kept under her pillow, a butterfly and a bear. She tied a string that hung from the thatched roof around the butterfly and pushed it so it flung back and forth. Then she took the bear and weaved it between the butterfly's movements until the bear did not move out of the way in time and the two collided. The bear was injured and needed help. With a piece of straw, she made a bandage around his leg.

She stopped her play when the door opened and her father walked in. He set his net in the corner and stretched his neck from side to side. She wanted to run to him so that he would pick her up, the way they always greeted each other, but she couldn't find the cheerful song in her body that usually guided her movements. "Oh, Herlot, I didn't know you were home," he said when he turned around.

His face turned to one that reminded her of Ambro after he had pushed her. Oh no. Was she hurting Father, too? She waited quietly while he sat down next to her. He picked up the bear and rolled it around in his palm. She hoped he would tell her why she had upset him, too.

"Where are you hiding your smile?" he asked. That was strange. His voice was not angry. It was kind. Gentle. Maybe he wasn't mad at her.

"Is it here?" he poked her knee. She shook her head.

He poked her belly, right where the stones sat. "What about here?"

"I think you found it," she said.

"How come you hid it there?" He made the bear climb onto the butterfly and then he floated them in the air while she thought about how to answer him. She hadn't found a unicorn. Her feet were strange. She couldn't take off her shoes anymore. But if there were unicorns, they were still hidden and safe, even though she might never get to ride one. If Ambro's plan worked, no one would know her feet were strange. Neither problem had a happy ending for her, but it did have a solution. But what really hurt her stomach was that she had *disappeared*.

"I—I went somewhere," she blurted.

Her father stopped. "Does it have to do with playing hide and seek?"

She shook her head. "Yes. No. Maybe."

She remembered the colorful bark and then falling into the snow behind the bush. Something had happened. She had done something. It was as if someone had covered her ears while a story was being told. She couldn't hear it, but the story was there. For the briefest moment the shortest memory she could imagine surfaced, fast, slippery, and out of her reach. No. Not even reachable. Like trying to catch a wave. But it had been there. It was that something. It had a feel to it, but she couldn't find a word that even hinted at coming close to it. The frustration of it was causing her breath to come faster.

"Easy, daughter, easy. You don't have to explain."

"I can't find the word, Father. There's so many but none of them are the one!"

She let her Father pull her to his side and then she rested her head against his chest.

"You don't have to find it now. You can always tell me when you do. I'm not going anywhere."

"I will, Father, I promise."

Over the years, Herlot's urges to take off her shoes disappeared, and no more strange moments happened. Sometimes, if she saw a new book, she would search for words that would help her keep her promise to her father, and explain the strange things that happened to her. But she never found any words that came close to her experience, at least to the best of her memory of it.

There would come a day where she would know the words, but by then, it'd be too late to keep the promise.

CHAPTER 3
The Oak Tree

T HREE-AND-A-HALF YEARS had gone by since Herlot and Ambro listened to the legend about the unicorns. It was deep into summer in Eraska, and even the leaves on the trees seemed to sweat in the heat.

Herlot adored the summer heat because it forced all of Alonia out of its morning routines. Instead of gathering eggs and feeding the chickens while they pecked at her ankles, she, along with everyone else, went to the beach to eat breakfast while enjoying the sea breeze.

She had just finished drinking her broth and was preparing to bite into her favorite bread made from freshly ground wheat with honey, but first she had to savor the sight of the honey sinking into the spaces in the bread. She waited for the current wave of wind to end so her hair would stop swishing in front of her face. She didn't want to waste any of the honey by getting it stuck into her hair.

The breeze stopped, and already she felt sweat forming at the bottom of her neck, but she trusted that the next breeze would come right as the heat became overbearing and she took a small bite of the bread. "Delicious," she thought to herself. "Next time I will bring some of the chickens with me. They could use a break from their routine, too."

She was shaken out of her meditation by choking coughs coming from Ambro next to her. She handed Ambro his cup of milk and watched him take a large swig. Covered in crumbs and honey stains, he was already stuffing an entire egg into his mouth.

"If you don't start taking smaller bites, we'll start feeding you in portions like a little child," Rudi said, joining in.

Herlot noticed Ambro sneak a glance at thirteen-year-old Elvin, his idol and best friend, who was teasing a seagull by pulling a piece of bread away out of its reach right as it pecked. Ambro ripped off a small piece of bread and watched Rudi the whole time as he chewed. "Now, count to at least twenty before you swallow," Rudi said.

Giggles broke out from Manni and the other girls at the shore. "Elvin, watch out!" Ambro called. The seagull had finally had enough. Some of its friends showed up and picked at Elvin's breakfast until he was forced to drop it. Another dozen arrived, and all of them seemed to know Herlot and those around her had more to spare.

"Looks like we have to cut our time on the beach short this morning. These seagulls look hungry," Herlot's father said. "Ambro, don't forget to stop at home to get your pack for trunk sitting."

Trunk sitting. Herlot's eyes widened. Once in a while, Rudi took the children into the forest and helped them climb inside a few wide-girth oaks, which had been hollowed out from the top, where they would spend the day watching for animals. For years she had only listened to Ambro's stories of sighting deer—and once, even a bear—and she couldn't wait to be old enough to go.

"Herlot, would you like to come?" Rudi asked.

She gripped the edge of Rudi's tunic. "Yes!" she squealed, jumping up and down.

"She's still too yo—" her mother started.

"Eight years old. Manni was seven her first time," Rudi said.

But Herlot had prepared for this occasion. Her mother never allowed her into the woods alone, but she did always push Herlot to play with the other children. "Mother, think about it. I won't be alone, Rudi will be with us on the walk, and then I'll be with the other children the rest of the day. Oh, and how I'd really like to see the animals. It's not the same as when we go for walks. They always run away if we get close." Herlot released her grip on Rudi's tunic because her mother's expression remained firm. Disappointment welled in her chest.

"Think about your times in the trunk. Oh, Ernest," he started. Her father's voice raised a few pitches to mimic that of her mother's, as did his gestures. "It was the most magical time. The family of deer frolicked in the area for an entire afternoon while their fawn learned to walk."

Her mother's eyes softened. A smile played at the corner of her lips. She turned to Rudi. "Promise me that you will sit her in a trunk with Ambro. And, Ambro, promise me that you will take care of your sister," she said.

"What do you mean by take care of her? She'll be in a trunk. Nothing ever happens in there—unless a lightning bolt strikes us. And, in that case, I'd need taking care of, too. What could possibly happen?"

"Bug bites," Herlot's mother answered matter-of-factly, "and hornets. Check the tree for any nests before you go in. And wanderers. Don't talk to them. B-butterflies. Don't chase them."

"Butterflies?" Herlot's father asked. "What could a butterfly possibly do?"

"I don't know!" Herlot jumped at her mother's outburst. "Apologies, I didn't mean to shout. Just be careful and think about things that might be dangerous even though they seem harmless."

Herlot wondered if the other children's parents were so flustered every time they went into the woods. However, she did not mind as long as she could finally go.

"Yes, Mother. I'll be her hornet-fighting knight. And, if they come close, I'll warn them away with my sword and protect us with my shield," Ambro said, acting the scene out in front of Herlot.

Herlot didn't waste a breath falling into character. She gasped and squeezed her knees together before calling out the direction of attack to Ambro. "Right in front of you! Bzzz! Up above you! Bzz!"

Elvin, with two seagulls on his tail, lunged into their scene. "There're too many! We must run!" he called. Then he swept Herlot up and threw her over his shoulder as he ran into the woods. Her imaginary sword appeared in her hand and she swung it at their pursuers. Once in the woods, Elvin set Herlot down. "Are you coming with us today?"

"Yes!" Herlot's excitement faltered as she noticed Manni over Elvin's shoulder. Manni's eyelids were lowered in a glare that seemed to aim her presence right at Herlot like a very focused ray of sunlight. It was outright fascinating. Herlot widened her eyes and noticed how her own presence touched a little bit on every element around her, a tap on the trees, a sprinkle on the other kids, and a pet on the rocky path. Then she dimmed her eyelids on Manni, smiling at the sensation of having floated right in front of Manni without taking a single step. Manni had long, raven-black hair as smooth as a spider's webbing and her eyes were teal like the sunset sea. Herlot finally understood why all the girls loved playing with her, especially if she had more interesting games like this focusing sun ray one. Herlot switched back to wide sun ray focus, then back to the glare. Back and forth she went, seeing how fast she could switch between the two.

Elvin snickered. "Herlot, why are you making such weird faces?"

"It's a sun ray game." She was about to ask Manni to explain, but Sira came up the path and rushed Manni home to prepare her tree sitting pack. Herlot did her best to show Elvin and Ambro as they walked the path, and then laughed along with Ambro when Elvin went cross-eyed.

Before long, Herlot stood still in front of her mother as she slung her very own pack over her shoulder. "She wears it with honor," Elvin said.

"That she does," Ambro said.

Herlot swiveled side to side, allowing the pack to float above her dress. Not a single berry or nut. She couldn't be more prepared for the adventure lying ahead. Her mother shook the collar of her dress and then wiped a bead of sweat from her brow. She took a breath and then focused on Herlot. "Don't eat everything at once," her mother said, tapping her on the nose, and then she turned around and walked toward her chest.

Herlot waved to Rudi who was followed like the head of a pack of ducklings by the other children dressed in shades of tan tunics and dresses. "And our last stop, Herlot and Ambro's home. Ah, there you are, Elvin, I almost thought you had decided you had better things to do." Herlot gazed in awe at Rudi's head. It was so hot out that even his hair had been matted down by the humidity.

"Come on, let's go to the back of the group. There we can do fun stuff while Rudi rambles on about everything and nothing," Elvin whispered and pulled Herlot along. Each kid that she passed could be one of her partners in the trunk. Finding out who it would be was almost as exciting as thinking about the animals that she would see. Once their pack got moving, Herlot coughed from all the dust their shuffling and scuffing kicked up. Just as they reached the top of the hill, she turned and waved to her mother and father. Then she took her first step into the forest as a girl who was old enough to go tree sitting.

● ● ●

Herlot couldn't believe she was going to spend an entire day in her favorite place. There was always something new and different in the woods, a new nest or cluster of herbs, something blooming, something falling, something singing, freezing, melting, the possibilities were endless. Today it was a bug festival. A butterfly sat on her satchel, a beetle fell off a branch leaf and landed on Maurice's shoulder, and several flies took turns poking at Ambro.

"And here we have a gallnut," Rudi called from the front as he approached the trunk of an oak. Herlot stood on her tiptoes to see. "Who can tell me what we use it for?"

Next to Herlot, Elvin cupped his mouth. "Ink!" he called.

"Thank you, Elvin. Next time let the younger ones answer!" Rudi called back. Elvin, Maurice, and Ambro snickered. Herlot wondered what that was about. Rudi rarely got irritated.

Their duckling walk continued on and Manni pushed her way between Herlot and Elvin and hooked her arm in Elvin's. "Elvin, come up with something fun for us to do."

"Why don't we walk off the path and see if we can keep up?" Ambro said.

"Yes!" One of Manni's best friends, Coral, wove her way between the trunks, sending several squirrels scattering up the trunk of a beech tree. As several of the others followed, Herlot didn't know if she was up to the difficult task of not getting stuck or tangled in bushes or branches. She decided to stay on the path and try to listen to Rudi, which turned out to be not that much easier. She could barely hear him over Elvin telling the others about how he had hidden in the fields and listened to a story Bee had told the other women. "I tell you, they would never tell a story like this at the hearth. There were fairies and knights, but there was...romance. *A lot* of it."

"What do you mean by romance?" Maurice asked.

"Do you even know what the story was about?" Coral asked.

Elvin rested his arm on a branch. "Uhh, something about waiting to say 'I love you' so the lover is not scared away."

"Well, that's silly. It's such a nice thing to say, I can't imagine anyone ever being afraid of it," Herlot said.

For a moment all that could be heard was Rudi ranting about the wings of a bird ahead. "You think that ghost tells her he loves her?" Herlot heard Coral mumble to Manni.

Herlot wiggled her shoulders. It was what Ambro and her parents told her to do if she ever heard it mentioned—the best way to respond to a rumor is to shake it off and ignore it, it will only make it worse if you try to fight it—but she really wanted to say the truth: that she didn't talk to a ghost.

"I agree," Elvin said. He turned around and smiled at Herlot. "It is a nice thing to say." Herlot beamed. It was easy and fun to be around Elvin. She understood why everyone liked him so much.

"I don't say it! Only girls say that," Maurice said. Ambro cheered in agreement.

Elvin began walking backwards, facing them. "Well, shame on you. It's actually the most grown-up thing you can say. It shows that your feelings are strong. My father says that strong feelings grow strong muscles. So when I meet a girl I love, I will tell her right away so she knows I have the muscles to build a home and work in the field."

Ambro and Maurice erupted with comments about the things they loved such as tug of war, ships, and their mothers. Herlot was about to say how much she loved her bear toy when a prickling irritated the back of her neck. She turned around to be met by Coral's bulging eyes and curled upper lip.

"Are you feeling ill?" she asked. "I'll tell Rudi we need to wait if you have to go into the bushes."

Next to Coral, Herlot noticed Manni's fists tighten at her sides before she stomped over a cluster of heather. "Manni? You, too?" Herlot asked.

"Ey! Herlot! Why don't you walk with me for a moment?" Rudi called.

Herlot rushed ahead to fall into step with Rudi. "All is well?" he asked.

"I think so. It's just that some of the girls look rather ill..."

"Not to worry, my dear, I am sure they are fine. Come, let me show you something."

Rudi squatted down next to a group of white mushrooms growing near a fallen trunk. "Do you know what these are?"

"Why, they're straw mushrooms, of course. They're delicious, Mother picks them," Herlot said.

"Are you certain? Look closer."

Leaning closer, Herlot did, in fact, notice several differences. The tops reached out to the sides more and there were traces of a faded mint color in some spots. "It's called a fool's mushroom," Rudi said. "Very dangerous. A few bites, and even if we called for Oliver of Lorfin, you wouldn't make it."

"Why does such a mushroom exist?"

"Good question. I suppose it exists to maybe give a bug a nice place to stay dry during the rain or hide from the sun. They like to grow by trees, perhaps they make good company."

Herlot pressed her cheek against the ground and looked under the mushrooms. Not a single bug was there. They didn't seem scary at all, and she found it pretty how the green mixed in with the white. They seemed so soft to the touch, so *harmless*. It was disorienting to her. Until now, it had always been easy to know what to be afraid of—the fierceness of the waves during a storm, the dizzying height of the cliffs, the piercing, sharp teeth of a rat—they all made her feel afraid just by the sight of them. How could she know what to trust or what to be afraid of when pretty things could be harmful, too?

"Suppose someone picked it on accident?" she asked.

"Won't happen. As you grow older, you will learn to recognize them just as your parents and I learned. For now, only pick the ones your mother tells you to."

"What if someone wants to hurt me with it?" She surprised herself by how easily and quickly the question had escaped her lips. It seemed like she hadn't even had time to think it before she asked it. However, it had come with an unexpected sense of relief, as if it had been something she had waited to ask a long time, like when waiting to ask Mother for a cup of milk while she was having a conversation.

Rudi frowned. "I promise you, Herlot. No one in Eraska would ever hurt you, especially in Alonia. We are all a family, and family only wishes to do good for one another. Sometimes at your age, other children can be difficult because of teasing. But it's something we all grow out of."

Something about Rudi's answer didn't put her at ease. "What about outside of Eraska?"

"Well, there *are* places where people would use a fool's mushroom to cause harm. King Cloudian told me all sorts of stories that he has heard from sailors. Outside of Eraska, people hurt each other a lot, mostly over gold. We are lucky to not have any gold, Herlot. If you did and you lived outside of Eraska, someone just might sneak the fool's mushroom into your food, wait while you struggle, and then take your gold."

"What if they come here?" Herlot asked.

"Now there we have nothing to fear. No gold, a small land with too little flat space for large fields of crops, no King would waste his time." Rudi's voice lowered several pitches. "But just in case, if there is ever something that frightens you, you can always tell me, alright, Herlot?"

"Yes, Rudi."

"Even if it's a bug."

Herlot giggled. "I'm not afraid of bugs!"

Rudi wrapped his arm around her shoulder. "I know, I know."

Herlot yawned. It was only the beginning of the day, but she felt unusually tired, as if she had just drunk her after-supper warm milk.

She knew based on the stories she heard that there was a different world outside of Eraska. She also knew that gold was not allowed in Eraska and that in the outside world there was much. Yet she had always imagined the outside world as pretty as Eraska, not a place where people made each other eat poisonous mushrooms. It felt as if a dark cloud covered the light in her imaginary pictures, and she didn't like it. She wanted to search for something to make it light again.

A sweet smell interrupted her thoughts and she lifted her head to search for where it was coming from. Up ahead was a honeysuckle shrub. Several rays of light penetrated through the canopy, illuminating the yellow flowers. As they walked closer, she spotted a colorful butterfly on one of the petals and joy stirred within her belly as the butterfly waved its wings.

How silly of me to be sad over a little mushroom. I had breakfast at the shore, Elvin rescued me from the hornets, and I'm about to go trunk sitting for the first time! And no matter what, I have Rudi at my side.

She immersed herself in Rudi's lessons about the forest, so much so that she wasn't aware of any other voice but his, at least until he turned around and scowled at all the children listening to Elvin. "What does he have that I don't?" Rudi asked.

"Romance," Herlot said.

"Romance? What in the world does Elvin know about? Holy Basil, I was hoping we'd stumble upon one of these! From a fallen tree but still fresh enough to eat, let me show you, Herlot."

Using his knife, Rudi cut at the outside bark of a fallen tree limb, stripping a piece of the cream-colored inside for Herlot to try. "Mmm, if you imagine eating it with honey it's delicious," she said.

Rudi smiled widely, exposing his teeth, then frowned as the other children laughed at something Elvin had said. He shook his head. "Thank you for listening, little Herlot."

Herlot swallowed her last bite of bark. "My pleasure," she said.

Soon they arrived at the first hollowed oak. "Time to farewell my competition," Rudi said, winking at her. She patiently watched Rudi lift two children into the tree. "Elvin! You, too!" he called.

The others sounded their complaints as Elvin hauled himself in without Rudi's help.

As they made their way to the other trees, Herlot was no longer the only one listening to Rudi. "Romance. Ha!" Rudi said, when even Ambro followed a trail of droppings he had pointed out.

At the fifth and final tree, only Ambro, Herlot, and Manni were left. Rudi held Herlot by her armpits, asking her to say when she was ready to drop. It wasn't a long way down, but she felt a rush in her belly before her feet hit the bed of leaves on the bottom.

"I will see you three around sundown," Rudi called into the peephole. "Don't eat all of your food at once!"

Herlot called goodbye to him before he disappeared into the forest.

"Now what do we do?" she asked.

"We watch nothing happen." Ambro yawned and sat next to Manni with his back against the trunk.

Herlot watched eagerly out the hole. Some leaves scattered, and a rabbit raced by. She had expected more to happen, but nevertheless found it exciting to be hidden, even if it was just from a rabbit. Soon, the sun was straight above them.

"High sun. Time to go," Manni said.

Herlot frowned. Rudi wasn't supposed to return until sunset.

"Not today," Ambro glanced at Herlot. "I can't leave—"

Manni flicked her long hair over her shoulder. "Come on, Ambro, help me."

Without another word, Ambro interlaced his fingers on top of his thigh. Manni put one foot on his hands. "On three. One. Two. Three," Manni said. Ambro didn't budge, staring at Manni with a hypnotized grin. Herlot had never seen her brother make such an expression before. He looked as if he were about to fall asleep. Manni knocked on the top of his head three times and he shook his head before springing his leg. Manni grabbed the top of the trunk and lifted one leg over it. Just as Herlot was beginning to worry that she'd fallen and hurt herself, she reappeared on the other side of the trunk. "Goodbye, unless you changed your mind," Manni said.

"Where are you going?" Herlot asked.

"To meet Elvin," Ambro said. "We're going to have some adventures outside of the trunk where it's not boring. Herlot, look, hold your hands like this," Ambro said. Herlot laced her fingers together and placed them just as Ambro had before. "Now really bend your knees and then stand up quick."

Herlot almost toppled under his weight, but she gritted her teeth and hoisted him up, not wanting to disappoint him on her first day of tree sitting, or tree escaping, for that matter. Ambro vanished over the top. Now Manni would sit on his shoulders so Herlot could grab onto her hand. How else would she get out? Herlot waited but no hand appeared. She looked out the hole to see what was taking so long. They were already a ways down the path. Her belly tightened.

"Wait!" she shouted. She gripped at the bark surrounding the hole in the tree. "I want to come, too! Don't leave me here alone!"

"We'll be back later!" Ambro called, but he didn't turn around or even slow. He just trotted after Manni as if she had a rope tied around him. But Manni did. She smirked and waved her fingers at Herlot.

She tried not to cry, remembering how safe she was in the trunk and nibbled on seeds while imagining what the other children were doing. Then she felt like crying again—not because she was afraid, but because she was alone and Ambro had forgotten about her so easily. How could Ambro do this to her? He had even made a promise to their mother! Yet he had acted as if she were invisible, as if the promise had meant nothing. Did he even remember making it? A spider dangled down next to her, and she comforted herself in that she was not entirely alone.

She watched the sun lower toward the canopy horizon, only her frequent yawns breaking the silence, when a screech made the hairs on her arms stand up. She clasped her hand over her mouth as a giant elk stepped into view. A wide, strong neck supported antlers that branched out above him. Then another elk appeared, facing the first; however, this one only had one antler. Something about the encounter made her certain that they were not friends.

The first one screeched again as it extended its neck and then crouched. The other was quick to respond and in a flash, they attacked one another with their antlers. It sounded like two pieces of wood clanked together and she was surprised that their antlers had not split in half.

The first one was stronger and taller, but the one with only one antler wasn't afraid, and Herlot rooted for him. A cloud of dust formed around them as they pushed against one another, the one-antlered one taking the advantage and sliding the other backward until they receded from Herlot's view.

More than anything she wanted to see if the one-antlered elk would win. She tried to press her face closer to see, the bark scratching her forehead, but the peephole was too small. She fanned her hand over her chest that had suddenly become very warm. She readjusted her collar to allow the air to flow. Flashes of willow tree leaves crossed her mind, followed by a woman extending her arms to her on the beach. Then a view from behind a bush—someone's feet, beautiful blue fabric.

Suddenly, the bark seemed to soften. Her skin seemed to callous all over, and her toes lengthened and sensed a worm near the roots of the tree.

Next thing she knew, she was outside the tree. Free. She backed away from it, frowning. She had expected the trunk to be damaged from her barging through, but it wasn't. *I must have been so focused on seeing the elk that I don't remember climbing out*, she thought. *But how did I climb out?* She flexed her arm and poked at it. She didn't know she was so strong. But why in the world could she not remember climbing? It must have been the heat. Yes. She remembered feeling warm. Her mother always complained about not being able to think straight when it was too hot outside.

Another screech caught her attention and shook her from her disorientation. She still had the chance to see if her elk had won. She raced deeper into the woods, where the sound had come from. A strong wind blew her hair in her face, and she puffed to move it out of the way. She had to keep her hands free to move the shrubs and branches aside. She had to find the elks and at least make sure that the one with only one antler was not injured.

It wasn't until a raindrop fell on her nose that she paused to take in her surroundings.

"Where..." she muttered. She spun around, having lost all sense of direction and finding herself in a part of the woods she had never been to before. A shadow spread across the forest floor. She looked up.

The day's clear sky had transformed into a colony of gray clouds. She tried to backtrack by using her footprints as a guide as the raindrops quickened until there was no end to them, as if the sea was pouring from the sky. They felt like icicles biting into her skin and made it difficult to keep her eyes open. She couldn't stop bumping into trunks and shrubs. It was impossible to see any of her footprints. Her arm stung, and when she looked down raindrops smeared with the color red trickled down it from a deep scratch she must have gotten from fighting her way through a shrub.

Darker clouds pushed the gray ones aside, and as the thunder clashed around her, she felt caught between blankets being shaken out. A lightning bolt struck a tree in front of her, leaving a ringing in her ears. She looked up in horror as the giant tree creaked and plummeted toward her. She threw her body forward. She covered her head and pressed her face into the mud, silently shouting to the tree to miss her. The crash rumbled through the ground beneath her body. She looked behind her and cried at how close she had been to being crushed.

Legs shaking from fear and cold, she tried to raise her body onto her hands and knees, but they gave out underneath her. "Mother! Father!" Her helpless cry wouldn't be heard even if by some magic they had searched for her in this part of the forest. If they even knew she was gone. Her mind raced. Rudi probably had not even returned to the tree yet. She stretched past the bone-shattering fear that pulsed through her body to remember anything Rudi may have once said about being caught in a storm.

Another lightning bolt cracked, and this time the fear was too much, shooting through her body with such strength she was certain the pain would shatter her bones and her world went black.

● ● ●

A loving warmth stirred Herlot awake. *I am home and safe. They must have found me*, she thought. *Home is the most wonderful place to be.* She couldn't hear a fire, so she must have been covered by a blanket; however, this had to be a new blanket, woven of some new material, because it was so light that she couldn't feel it, yet it still had the ability to penetrate her clothes and skin with a warmth that melted everything in her into comfort. But why couldn't she hear the fire? There was always a fire in the evening.

Then she felt the rocks and the roots of a tree under her back and her eyes flew open.

No story or legend could have prepared her for what she saw.

The creature standing before her was beautiful, whiter than the freshest snow she had ever played in. His coat was a pearl white, so vivid it made her squint. His eyes were the color of dark-blue sea water interwoven with every color of the rainbow. He had a royal golden alicorn that arose proudly from his forehead and casted a warm glow around them.

Herlot knew exactly what he was, this creature she had met in so many daydreams and imaginings of her mind. The creature that part of her had ridden off with into the sea horizon.

"Unicorn," she whispered, laying her hand on his muzzle, "you are so very lovely."

She had reached Herlot on the horizon. She was whole again, any way her story would unfold from now would be perfect because she would be traveling with her dream come true. This felt right. This was the way things were supposed to be. This was... home. She was home.

The unicorn nuzzled against her palm, exhaling. Refreshing air trickled down her arm and toward her ear.

"My name is Devotio, and I would like to take you back home to Alonia, Herlot."

"Oh!" She was startled by the words, only because she did not know where they came from. The voice, though, was something special. It was kind with a hint of playfulness that made her feel safe, like falling asleep to her mother's lullabies. She sat up to see who else was with them but there was no one in sight. That meant that the voice had come from—

No. It couldn't be. She turned back to the unicorn. His mouth hadn't moved. Or had it? "You can speak? You. You are Devotio?" she asked, turning the name in her mouth.

The unicorn lowered his muzzle to his chest and then back up again.

"But how? How is that possible?"

Once again, he exhaled and the same breeze surrounded her ear. "With my breath. I can send it to whomever I wish to hear what I wish to say."

Herlot giggled at her reaction of surprise to the explanation. He was a unicorn, of course there was a wonderful way in which he would communicate. "Of course!" she cried out, pressing her fists toward the night sky.

"One breath, if breathed the right way, can share much more than just words if you know how to listen," he said.

She frowned and stared at her nose, trying to understand what that meant as Devotio took a step forward and drifted his alicorn over her dress. The parts still drenched in cold rainwater dried instantaneously under the warm glow.

"Your mother put much care into this dress when she made it for you," he said.

"Yes. She made it on a loom with wool from Ruelder. How do you know that she made it?"

"I can sense her care in the fabric. She must be looking for you and very worried. Let me take you back to your village."

Herlot rose to her feet, her muscles flexible from the warmth. She touched her toes and then stretched her arms high up above her head. Devotio bowed in front of her. "Climb on."

She leaned over his back and jumped up, grasping his side with her hands and kicking her feet as she began to slide backwards. She managed to haul herself up, so her belly lay over his back. Then, undulating like a worm, she turned to face forward.

"Hold on," he said, and whipped his mane back and forth.

She took hold of the mane and let out a gasp at the feel of it. It was fine and silky, yet strong. She let go and all the strands fell perfectly next to one another.

Devotio kicked up on his hind legs and everything blurred, and the next thing she knew they were headed right at a family of shrubs. She winced at the memory of being scratched.

"Watch out!" she shouted.

But Devotio ran through with ease, smoother than her father's boat gliding through the sea water. Devotio wove through the trees and bushes, nothing like Ambro, Elvin, and the other children who had fought their way through the forest while walking off the path. It reminded her of pictures in old storybooks of princesses dancing in royal ballrooms. They had long dresses that they held out to the side when they twirled. She had pretended to be one of these princesses many times, and now her fantasy seemed to have come alive. Of course, she was not wearing a royal dress and there were no other people around, but it was like all the trees and plants of the forest were her and Devotio's dance partners. Oh, how wonderful this was. It was better than she could have imagined. If only she could tell her younger self, the Herlot who had been so disappointed to not meet a unicorn when she and Ambro went looking for them in the forest, that this would happen. What more wonderful things would happen from now on? She spread her arms wide, as if she could hug the entire forest.

The air around became heavier for a few breaths, right around her torso where hugs were felt. Had the forest hugged her back? She breathed in the scent of wood and raindrops. There was a new scent in the delicious forest aroma. It smelled like home. Home. There it was again. Being with Devotio and seeing the woods illuminated by his glow gave her the same feeling she had when returning home after a long day in the fields—stepping through the door she would sigh and feel warmth, familiarity, and trust as she took in her surroundings lit by the sunrays filtering through the thatched roof. But now she felt the same in the forest, and it made her confused about where home really was. Surely one could only have such feelings in one place. Everyone had only one home. Now she had it in Alonia, in the forest, and most of all, in Devotio.

The light shining from Devotio's alicorn allowed her to catch glimpses of the forest's creatures who had come out of their hiding spots. She cried, "Hello!" to a family of deer as if she were one of them and blew a kiss to a squirrel that had popped its head out of a tree. The forest was itself one large village, each tree home to a family of forest creatures.

Devotio jumped a fallen trunk, and she realized it was the same place where Rudi had shown her the fool's mushrooms. "Wait, please," she said.

Devotio came to a halt just as an owl hooted from its hiding place somewhere in the branches.

"There is something I would like to check," she said as he bowed and she slipped down.

"Thank you." She curtsied, because that's what princesses did after a dance.

The mushrooms were easy to find thanks to Devotio's alicorn's glow. She crawled to them, just as several raindrops fell from the leaves above, one landing on top of a mushroom and gliding down its side. She peered below.

"Oh!" Surprisingly, she saw what she had hoped for—two slugs curled into one another, sleeping under the roof of the mushroom. "Forgive me for waking you, little slugs."

She stood and brushed some of the dirt off her dress, and then a tear off her cheek. She kept her focus on Devotio's hooves because she was afraid that she wouldn't be able to stop the tears if she looked at more of him.

"Why are you sad?" Devotio asked.

She forced herself to look up, her vision blurred from the tears, at the magical creature from her father's legend.

"I'm not sad—I'm happy. At least, I think I am. It's so nice when a magic you hoped for becomes true."

And it was true, she thought as she climbed back on, it was too wonderful to be a dream. Even the nicest dreams had a daze about them. This, on the other hand, was crisp. Not just Devotio, but the forest and herself, too. Everything felt more real than her normal days when she was awake. But it was different from normal. Could it be some sort of other dream? A too awake that would eventually slip away? No, that couldn't be. She couldn't allow it, not now that she really knew what it felt like to fly above the horizon. As soon as they were home, she would introduce Devotio to her family and the rest of the villagers. Nobody could dream the same dream, and that meant no one could experience the same too awake. They would see, touch, and hear him just as she could, and she would know it was all real.

Devotio trotted at a slower pace. "I also know what it's like to hope for magic," he said.

This took Herlot by surprise. What magic could he possibly hope for? He *was* magical.

She began to recognize more and more of the trees. Off in the distance, villagers roamed the forest with torches while calling her name. "I can't go any farther. This is where I must leave you," Devotio said.

"But you have to meet my parents. I have a brother, too. And Rudi, you definitely have to meet him," she said as she slid down. "And the other children, Devotio! They will want to be friends with you, and now maybe even with me, too! You know, Devotio, they think I'm haunted and don't really want to play with me because of that. I'm not haunted, though, don't worry, but do you know how wonderful it will be if I can be the one who introduces you to them? Surely a girl who made a unicorn friend can't be haunted." She twirled when her feet met the ground. "They are going to love you so much and tell you stories, lots of stories." She circled his body, petting him, until she came face to face with him.

"Herlot, you have to promise that you will never tell another soul about me," he said.

Herlot's bare feet sank in the mud. She opened her mouth to speak, but then pressed her lips together. How could she make such a promise? She had just met the most wonderful being in the world and she couldn't even introduce him to her family? How could she hide Herlot flying on a unicorn on the horizon? And how could she know that this was real if someone else couldn't experience it, too?

Then, her heart sank into her belly as she remembered the legend. Devotio didn't have wings. In the legend the unicorns had lost their wings out of sadness. They didn't want to fly and greet the sun anymore without their human companions. She stared down at the ground as if she could see the sea water that Herlot and Devotio on the horizon would sink into. They couldn't fly in this world. This world had hurt them. "My father once told me a legend about people who hurt unicorns for their golden alicorns. Is this why you hide from us? Is the legend true?"

"Yes."

She threw her arms around his neck. "I'm so sorry."

At that moment, Herlot decided that she would never tell a soul. She would never risk anyone finding out about him and doing to him what the humans in the legend had done. Just the thought of someone hurting Devotio for his alicorn was far worse than keeping him a secret. "I promise."

She stepped away, letting her tears flow freely. She was proud of them, they were tears of a magical dream come true that she loved, that she would protect. Then she remembered his comment about magic. "What is the magic that you hope for, Devotio?"

Devotio looked off into the distance where the torchlights danced. He was quiet for so long she thought he wouldn't answer.

She stood next to him, matching his gaze into the distance. Perhaps there was something else he saw of interest among the villagers.

Once again, the cool air tickled her ears as he spoke. Finally, he said, "Friendship."

"You don't have friends?" she asked.

"I do. And family. But I have dreamed of a human companion for...forever."

"Oh! Well, I could be your companion. Unless of course," she paused, embarrassment slipping into her chest, "you'd rather wait and find someone else. Someone with more color in their eyes, perhaps." It was definitely not a human like her. Her tangled hair was a tragedy compared to his mane, and her grey eyes dull compared to his colorful blue ones. He could cast light in the night and warmth where it was cold. What was it that she could do? By the day's events, the only talent she had was getting lost and causing a lot of worry and trouble.

Devotio turned, coming face to face with her. He looked into her eyes and not once did she feel the usual need to blink or look away when holding eye contact with someone for a longer period of time.

"There are many wonderful things about you, Herlot, but most of all it is your spirit that shines through your grey eyes and gives me a glimpse of how colorfully you perceive your world. If I had the chance to find friendship with one of your kind, I believe we would be a perfect match."

"If?"

Devotio lowered his head, as if in defeat, his alicorn aiming straight at her heart. She couldn't help taking a step back, realizing how sharp it was, like some of her father's fish knives. After all, he always warned to be careful around them. But then she took a step forward again, sensing Devotio's sorrow. His shoulder bones jutted out as if tired from bearing a heavy weight. No. He wouldn't hurt her. If anything, someone could hurt him in his vulnerable pose.

"I broke promises tonight," he said. "Promises meant to protect my family. Some may say I even betrayed them. I should not have shown myself to you."

Herlot covered her heart with her hand. He had taken a risk to save her from the cold. He had helped her even though she could hurt him. From now until forever, Devotio and his family would live knowing that Herlot could decide to tell the world that unicorns were hiding in Alonia's forest. She hoped she was worth the trouble. "Devotio, I can't thank you enough for helping me. I will never hurt you or tell anyone. I hope you and your family can believe me when I say that."

The corner of Devotio's mouth seemed to curl in a smile. "I know. I will go home and tell my family about the girl I met with long, tangled, golden hair and a warm touch that made me question their endless warnings about humans. This I will do, but even if they understood, we only risk coming to your world once every twelve moons. I should have been back already."

"Why once every twelve moons?" Herlot asked.

"Our home is...complicated. If we stay there too long, we won't be able to come out. That is all I can tell you."

Herlot straightened. "Then our friendship will be one of once every twelve moons. Please. Please, let me see you again. I don't care how long I have to wait." She squeezed her hands into fists and prayed he would say yes.

Devotio grew taller and his rainbow-tinted eyes seemed to shimmer. He no longer looked as if he were carrying a heavy weight. "It shall be so. Our friendship will be one of once every twelve moons," he said.

Herlot let out a sigh of joy and breathed in the cooling night air. It was almost as if the air entering her chest was buzzing with the wonder that had happened between her and Devotio. As if it knew that for the first time in a very long time, human and unicorn were friends once again.

The villagers and their torch lights were drawing nearer. Herlot knew it was time to go before they could get any closer and discover Devotio. "If only we had a little more time tonight," Herlot said. "Will you go home now, too?"

"I should. My family will be upset, but this one time I may wait to return tomorrow night."

"Does that mean we don't have to wait twelve moons just this one time?" Herlot almost squealed.

"Come into the forest tomorrow night," Devotio said. "If I'm not there, I will find you in twelve moons. Now go, my friend, your family is looking for you."

Herlot wrapped her arms again around Devotio's neck. "Until tomorrow, my friend," she said, then headed toward the torchlights. She stopped to jump in the air and clap her hands before waving goodbye, but there was no trace left of Devotio where he had stood.

She neared the area where candlelights flickered among the trees like fireflies and shouts calling her name echoed into the night. Simon, Agatha's husband, must have been so intent on finding her he almost didn't see her when she stepped right in front of him.

"I'm here!" she announced.

Simon cupped his hands around his mouth, his chest inflating as he took a deep breath. "I found her!" he blared.

Another villager bellowed, "We found her!"

Another joined the chorus, and then another, until echoes from as far away as the village made their way back to Herlot, and not one word could be deciphered from the other. The invisible pauses between words had vanished, just like the distinct lines between imaginary stories and real life. She loved these echoes.

The whole time Simon carried her she wanted to explain to him that she could walk. Her body had never felt better. When she was finally put back on her feet at the village, a group of women huddled toward her with blankets.

"Only a miracle will save this child from catching a cold! Out in the rain for who knows how long!" Agatha cried.

Herlot held up her hands in protest. She had never felt warmer. Not the kind from being out in the heat or from a fever that was overwhelming. It was just right.

Agatha's mouth fell open when she skimmed Herlot's dress with her hand. "It's perfectly dry," Agatha stated.

"Unbelievable," said Bee, and followed suit to examine the dress. "She is right," she said to the other women.

Herlot loved her fellow villagers, but couldn't wrap her mind around how often they mustered in on things like a pack of wolves. Like now, all the women couldn't take Agatha's word that the dress was dry. Each woman had to touch it.

Agatha squeezed Herlot's wrist. "She's not even cold! How is that possible?"

"Unicorn glow," Herlot wanted to say, but she pressed her lips together. She would not break her promise.

"Herlot!" her father's voice sounded from the forest. He was running faster than she had ever seen him run, dropping his torch into the nearest pit before he slid in front of her and scooped her into his arms. Next thing she knew, he was lifting her up toward the sky as he shouted, "Thank you, stars, for bringing my daughter home!"

"Stars? No father, it was a unicorn who helped me," she wished she could say.

Looking down at the villagers from above, she watched her father's shout breaking through the worried and frightened atmosphere emanating from the looks of the rest of the village. As she watched her people's faces raise into smiles, she delighted in the knowledge that her father's joy could be contagious.

But it wasn't the villagers that needed his contagious joy. As they went inside, she understood why Devotio had been in a hurry to bring her home.

Her mother was pacing back and forth, Merle trailing behind her with a cup of tea that filled the room with the scent of sleep herbs. "Struck by lightning. Attacked by wolves. And, oh no. No. What if the forest took her? It's where she wanted to be. She didn't want our hands, she wanted the willow leaves," her mother said. Merle shielded the front of the teacup and stepped back, as if afraid of Herlot's mother.

Herlot's stomach knotted. Her mother's words made no sense. "Ilvy," her father said. "Look."

Herlot's mother whipped around and her pupils seemed to do a dance before they focused on Herlot. Did she not recognize her? Part of her seemed to be gone, a light missing from her eyes. *It really is me, Mother. Don't worry anymore, please*, Herlot thought as she and her mother made eye contact. Something about her mother's eyes made her certain that spoken words would not reach her in the way she wished. So Herlot took a breath and blew her thoughts her way, hoping they would reach her like Devotio's words could.

Herlot's mother threw her arms in the air. "Oh, my darling, oh, thank the skies!"

Herlot scrunched the back of her mother's dress as she embraced her. She never wanted to lose her. And she never wanted her to disappear from her body again like she just had. She shivered at the thought.

"Oh, my child, we must get you under a blanket right away. You need rest, rest, and a sprinkle of rest. It will be a miracle if you don't awaken with a cold. Ambro, you, too."

"I'm not tired," Ambro said from a spot near the fire. Herlot had not noticed him before.

"I don't want another word out of you. You broke your promise to stay with your sister. You're lucky she didn't break her neck trying to climb out of that tree. Now, to bed," Herlot's mother said.

Ambro hid his face behind his shoulder as he walked by Herlot and climbed into bed. Merle and Herlot's parents finished saying goodbye as Herlot settled into her spot. Ambro didn't budge from his position facing the wall. Herlot closed her eyes and pretended to sleep. Just as her father began to snore, her mother climbed out of her mattress and went over to her chest. The hint of a bitter smell filled the room as her mother took a sip of something. Her mother returned, and soon Herlot could hear her mother's light snore, as well.

She gazed up at the thatching illuminated by the fire's glow and remembered her night with Devotio. She promised that she would do so every night so she would never forget a single moment. She was just beginning to drift when Ambro stirred next to her.

"Herlot? Are you awake?" he whispered.

"Yes."

"I'm glad you're safe."

"Me, too."

"I'm sorry I left you."

"It's alright," she said. Herlot almost giggled. In a way, Ambro and Manni leaving her was the best thing that ever happened to her. She would not have met Devotio otherwise. A lump formed in her throat at the realization. If she wanted to be Herlot on the horizon, were those the seeds she would have to trade? Could people who met magic ever be the same and fit in with the other children? With their village family?

"Really? You're not mad? At all? Wait, you sound almost *happy* about it. Did something happen? Tell me."

Oh, how Herlot wished she could kick the blanket off, ignite the fire, and reenact what had happened. But she couldn't. She had made a promise, and unlike Ambro, she would not break it. But she didn't know how to answer Ambro. She didn't want to lie. "I'm happy that Mother is not worried anymore," she said. That was true. But not all of it.

"Oh." Ambro plucked out a piece of straw that was sticking out of his pillow.

"So, how did you climb out?"

Thank goodness he asked a question she could answer honestly. "I don't know. I just did somehow. I don't remember."

"You came back barefoot. We found your shoes in the trunk," Ambro said.

Herlot had completely forgotten about her shoes. She couldn't remember taking them off, though.

"I suppose I did take them off," she said.

"Herlot, you can't do that. You remember the strange things that happen when you do. Don't do it again. Maybe you wouldn't have climbed out if you had left them on."

"I won't," she said. At least he wasn't asking about what happened after she climbed out. She couldn't help feeling sad that real magic had happened so close to everyone in the village, and no one would ever know. She remembered how years ago Ambro had said that she was the only one he wanted to search for unicorns with. Devotio was the most wonderful thing Herlot could ever tell her brother about. She would never see his reaction, the wonder of taking a bite of magic and how wonderful it made the world after it was swallowed. In her heart she knew she would never be the same again after having tasted something so delicious. Before Devotio said their meeting had to be a secret, she thought this would bring her closer to her village family. If anything, she was more different than she ever was. Even though she was in her home in Alonia, she had never felt farther away.

"Remember when we were kids, well, when I was a kid—you're still a kid—the same day you stopped taking off your shoes? For a moment I thought you were happy because you might have met a unicorn." Ambro giggled.

"What a silly thought, that could never happen," Herlot said. Her first lie to Ambro. He was less than an arm length's away, but as soon as she spoke the words, a distance grew between their hearts.

CHAPTER 4
Pinecones

HERLOT CRAWLED AFTER LUPERT until he disappeared under Merle's dress. She sat back on her heels and waited patiently as the morning sunrays warmed her dress and her mother and Merle tried to understand why there were no eggs left in the chicken shack. A wooden lamb toy peeked out from below the hem of Merle's skirt and Herlot reached for it. Lupert shrieked with joy. So did Herlot. But for other reasons. She was about to burst from the excitement that had been building in her all morning. Tonight she would see Devotio again. It would be the best wait of her life. She sat back again and waited for the lamb to make another appearance.

"She's fine, Ilvy. Stop staring at her," Merle said. "Go on, give your body a shake and welcome a new day. Our woods have yet to swallow a child, and lightning strikes gentler on younger spirits."

Herlot's shoulders sank in shame. Merle was talking about her. If only she could tell her mother what had really happened that day in the woods, instead of worrying that Herlot could have died out there, her mother would be celebrating the truth that unicorns really existed.

Herlot gritted her teeth together to keep the truth from slipping out. She had to keep her promise, no matter what. If Devotio thought that he could not trust her, he would never come near her again, of that she was certain.

Her mother's chuckle stirred her out of her thoughts. "Well, then, I pray lightning never finds us a target. We are not the young spirits we once were!" Herlot smiled. There. Her mother had managed to laugh without having to hear about Devotio. For now she could go back to counting down the moments until she would see him again.

"So, what do you say?" Merle asked, extending a bucket. "Shall we go see what the storm washed ashore? That is, unless the egg thief already beat us down there."

Herlot's mother took the bucket. "It's Simon. I just know it. Poor man is starving." She lowered her voice and nudged Merle. "Agatha has been trying new recipes."

Herlot held Lupert's hand and followed behind her mother and Merle. They found Ambro doing the only chore he ever woke up early for: tug-of-war rope maintenance. He had it stretched out along the path and jumped to his feet as they approached. A breeze shook the fabric of his tunic but he stood strong against it, not budging a muscle.

"Walk around. You are entering Captain Ambro's territory and I must prepare my rope for my sailors. There have been sightings of a sea monster."

Nodding, Merle thanked him for his hard work. Then, Herlot saw tragedy strike—at the beginning of the rope was a bird pecking at the rope fibers, clearly curious of the material. "Ambro!" she cried and pointed.

Ambro's face scrunched in horror, and he threw seeds to distract it. Herlot thanked herself for doing her duty and helped Lupert skip over the rope while Ambro was not watching.

Just as they reached the spot where the small chunk of wooded path down to the seashore started, Merle stopped and stared at a willow tree. "Why so quiet, Merle?" her mother asked.

Lupert tugged on Herlot's finger and waddled toward the edge of the path where a butterfly had landed on a flower. She squatted next to him and studied his purple colors.

Merle cleared her throat. "What if the forest took her? It's where she wanted to be. She didn't want our hands, she wanted the willow leaves."

Those were the words her mother had spoken last night during that awful moment when she seemed to have disappeared. "Does that mean anything to you?" Merle asked. Herlot stole a glance at her mother and then pretended she was not listening. She asked Lupert if he liked the butterfly.

"I'm sorry, Merle. It doesn't. Should it?"

Merle shrugged her shoulders. "Ah, no. Just a silly something I heard somewhere."

Why didn't her mother remember? It was not normal to say things one day and not remember them the next. This was something Oliver was usually called for, like when Bee's mother wasn't able to recognize Bee. Herlot realized how careful she would have to be to sneak out and meet Devotio again. By no means could she let her mother worry again. She would have to be very attentive for an opportunity. During story time by the fire would probably be her only chance, and she would have to make sure to sit far back so no one would notice her sneak away.

Merle sniffled a few times. "Say, where is the smoke coming from?"

"There," Ilvy pointed at the dense smoke fog emerging from above a shrub. "Say, Herlot. Go check and see if it is Simon. I would bet two rosemary sprigs he's cooking the eggs."

A loud creaking and crunching erupted behind them. Herlot turned around just in time to see Sira and Viktor's roof cave in and collapse. Next, a strong-pitched whistle sounded as her father ran out of the wood shack—straight toward the caved-in home.

"Father!" Herlot shouted, running toward the heap of home with the others. Ambro ran from the other side, his eyes wide in horror, as if his very own bones had been snapped in half. He reached the home at the same time as Herlot—just as their father plunged through the doorway, which was now guarding only a maze of broken timbers amidst clouds of dust.

"Manni! Manni!" Ambro cried, trying desperately to move the debris out of his way. But before Ambro could disappear inside, Rudi appeared and pulled him back roughly by the shoulders. Ambro kicked at the air, struggling to free himself from Rudi's hold. He finally surrendered, panting against Rudi's chest.

Red-faced, Rudi surveyed the onlookers who circled the area. "Everyone alright?"

"Of course, they are," Ambro said, voice ragged. "The people you should be asking are inside."

Including their father. Herlot squeezed her fists together wishing that any moment her father would come out again and that nothing collapsed more before he did.

A series of huffs and grunts emitted from the home and her father emerged, tugging on a half-asleep, dust and hay-covered Viktor.

Ambro rushed to Viktor's side. "Where is Manni?"

"Sira and Manni are at the shore," Viktor said between coughs. "They woke me to tell me before I went back to sleep."

Ambro covered his heart with his palms and fell to his knees. "How sweet the feeling of relief."

Herlot frowned. Ambro never read or liked the poetry books or recitations, let alone spoke them.

Viktor sat in his tunic and no slacks, scratching the back of his head. "Now that is one snake bite of a way to wake up. Thought Sira found out what I was dreaming about."

Ambro laughed along with the other men at Viktor's remark. Herlot had no idea what was so funny. Why would Sira be upset about a dream?

"Alonians!" her father called. "Viktor's belongings need to be moved in case another storm sets in. Gather any pieces that can be reused and we will need a group to begin thatching a new roof. Herlot, Ambro, you help, too."

By noon, Herlot decided she could push and carry chests every day. She also wouldn't mind threshing wheat for a week straight. Back and forth she would go to the stream, bringing fresh water to each family in the village and cleaning every fire pit, even the ones that didn't need it. If she ran out of things to do, she would come up with new chores, ones that no one had ever heard of, and she would do those, too. She could do anything as long as she had seeing Devotio to look forward to. She had her plan all set. At the hearth, she would sit in back and wait until it was her father's turn to tell a story. She would wait for one of the exciting parts to slip away. No one would notice, especially if all their attention was deep into one of father's stories. Of that she was certain.

"Come on, Ambro. Heave-ho!" she cried. But Ambro, it seemed, had had enough. He slouched his body over the chest and yawned. She gave another shove, causing the chest to glide forward and Ambro to slip off.

She turned around, leaning her back against the chest and crossing her legs, clicking her tongue and watching the cloud formations in the sky, all while wondering about Devotio. If the legend was true, he had been up there, right next to the clouds, and through them. She wondered what they felt like and could not wait to ask him. But then she faltered at the idea, because according to the legend, unicorns had lost their wings, and as magical as Devotio was, he did not have wings. If she were a unicorn, she wouldn't want to be reminded of the wings she had lost.

"My father says I'm supposed to help you."

Herlot startled from her daydream, not having heard Manni approach.

"My father likes to fish. Would you like to try one?" Ambro stuttered.

Herlot giggled. Every Alonian was well aware that Herlot's father liked to fish, and Manni had definitely tried them plenty of times. What a silly thing to ask someone. Manni flicked a dirt pebble off her sleeve. "No, thank you. I have plenty of fish," she said.

"Oh." Ambro looked defeated. Since when was he so intent on sharing their father's fish?

"Tonight we'll eat some of the fish together," Herlot said. "Now let's worry about moving this chest. Manni, can you clear the rock out of our path, please?"

Herlot got into position as Manni strolled toward the rock. Finally, after what seemed like two bedtime stories, Manni reached the rock and nudged it right into the center of Herlot's path.

"The other way," Herlot said. She pointed in the direction the rock should have been moved, but Manni didn't budge. Herlot was beginning to wonder if perhaps something had happened to the two of them after they had left her in the tree because they were both acting strange.

"Everyone, drop your oars and open your doors! Cloudian's stewards are arriving!" Agatha belted. "Out of my way!"

Herlot and Ambro staggered back as Agatha lifted the front of her dress, wiggled her elbows to gain momentum, stepped up on the chest and came down hard on both feet. As she swished toward the meadow, Herlot made out several wagons pulled by oxen beyond the wheat field.

"Come on!" Ambro grabbed Herlot's hand and together they merged into the crowd. For this, even the roof disaster could wait.

She found herself next to her parents, with only the sweat-stained tunic backs of several men to look at. She tugged on her father's sleeve and pointed at the sky, her signal that she had used for as long as she could remember to be lifted up on his shoulders. In a flash, she was taller than any Alonian with a perfect view of the wagons entering the meadow. Herlot watched the wheels roll over bumps in the grass. Not a single potato tumbled off. She bet they felt just as she had riding Devotio.

Several village men turned to cheer on Rudi. "Never seen finer wagons! Looky there at the one filled to the top with potatoes! Not even a queen could have herself a better ride!"

"Look! Children!" Herlot announced. At the back of one of the wagons were two children sitting next to a bald man—Oliver, the healer. And that was exactly to whom her family headed first.

"Oliver! It has been ages!" Herlot's father took a sack off of Oliver's arms when they reached the wagon. "And Holy Basil, you brought the twins!"

"Yes, Ernest, far too long." Oliver jumped down from the wagon. He was a tall, thin man with large joints and a bumpy nose. The top of his head shone, and his hair arced around it, starting at his ears. Herlot was surprised that he was strong enough to carry both children when he picked them up and set them down on the grass. Her heart fluttered with excitement as she realized the children looked the same age as she. They could be friends.

The boy, Mahtreeh, had many of his father's features. He was bony and fragile looking. His lips were full of lines that looked as if they had been painted on. He had dull, limp hair that seemed destined to fall out. But most of all, Herlot liked his eyes. They were kind. Friendly. With a hint of sadness. Like Devotio's, she thought.

His sister, Enri, had full cheeks and sleek, strawberry-blond hair. Half of it was tied back with a sunflower, its petals projecting past her head. She had eyes like Mahtreeh.

"Look at these two precious faces," Herlot's mother said, looking down at the children. "You must be Mahtreeh, and you, Enri, my, how much you resemble Sylvia. It must be very exciting for both of you to join your father on his trip."

"Thank you. It's because my mother lives on in me."

Herlot's mother clasped her hand against her chest. "Oh no, Oliver, what happened?"

Oliver reach for a strand of Enri's hair and tucked it back into the sunflower stem. "We were expecting. I—" Oliver took a breath. "I was at Temes when it started and by the time I came back, it was too late to help her."

Herlot's mother clutched Oliver's arm. "We grieve with you, our friend. Please, allow us to share our home with you and your children for your stay."

"Thank you, my friends," Oliver said.

Oh no, Herlot thought and bowed her head. Enri and Mahtreeh didn't have a mother anymore. Or a brother or sister. That was why they had that sad look in their eyes. From her view she was able to see Enri take Mahtreeh's hand. There was a strength there. She didn't have words to comfort these two children she had just met, but she felt a need to add to their strength. She reached her hand out and set it on top of theirs. She felt the tension in their hands relax, and when she looked up, she was met by a gentle smile on Enri's face.

Next to her, her father shielded his arm behind Oliver and invited them all to start making their way to their home. Just as Enri and Mahtreeh's hands separated beneath her own, Herlot's palm brushed against Enri's. Sometimes Herlot was drawn to a shell on the beach as if she knew it had ocean waves to listen to if she held it up to her ear. Enri's palm felt like one of those seashells now. It was as if it really had something to say but in a way that could only be communicated by touch. More than anything, Herlot wanted to press her palm against Enri's, to feel every crease and indentation, but she refrained and followed behind, her palm highly aware of Enri's the entire walk. She didn't know how she knew, but it was as if Enri's palm wanted to tell a story, one that was too heavy to be carried alone.

Enri turned around and Herlot's heart fluttered thinking that Enri had noticed, too. But then she realized that Enri's attention was on one of the stewards unlatching the oxen from the cart. Was she imagining things? It couldn't be. She could almost see the string of heat connecting her and Enri's hands.

"Oliver! Is this one yours?" one of the stewards asked, holding up a sack.

Enri's face lit up. "No, that one is mine. My dolly is in there!"

"I'll bring it over for you, little Enri!" the steward replied.

Just as quickly as it had appeared, the heat string vanished, but there was still sweat residue on Herlot's palm. She gasped when Enri rubbed her hand against the side of her dress at the exact same moment that Herlot did to wipe the sweat off. It couldn't just be her imagination. Once she was more acquainted with Enri, she would ask her about it.

Back at the village, there was already a line forming outside of their door made up of people eager to see Oliver. Herlot's father spoke. "Oliver has had a long journey. Unless it is urgent, let us wait until tomorrow."

"Please, tell them to stay. I would love to get to work right away," Oliver said. "It will remind me of the first time I met Sylvia when I was here. She had a sprained ankle..." Oliver went quiet and looked around the village. "I feel her here, in her first home. There's nothing I'd like more than to help right now. After all, it's how I met her."

Herlot remembered now hearing several stories about Sylvia. She had married Oliver and moved to Lorfin, one of the only people who moved to a different village.

"Very well, Oliver. Ilvy and I will be helping carry the supplies if you need anything. Children, have a seat and wait while Oliver gets to work," Herlot's father said.

Enri and Mahtreeh followed a steward with a sack inside Herlot's home.

"Maybe we could take Enri and Mahtreeh outside to play?" Ambro asked.

Now there was a good idea. The last thing Herlot wanted to do was be cooped up in the house when they could play a game outside with the children. She also didn't want to ask Enri inside about the palm where Ambro could overhear. He would most likely yell at her again about shoes and doing strange things. Then there was the issue of waiting patiently. How could she wait patiently and quietly when she had a unicorn to meet in the evening?

Herlot's mother bent forward and spoke quietly. "Enri and Mahtreeh have been through a difficult time. It is probably best that they stay close to their father until they are more settled in. Since they are your guests, waiting with them is the kindest thing to do. Help them feel welcome."

Herlot glanced inside at the brother and sister who had taken a seat on one of the mattresses. They both had their legs stretched out in front of them and palms folded in their laps. They seemed so stiff that Herlot imagined they'd break if forced to move too fast. Herlot couldn't help thinking about how sad their mother Sylvia would be if she saw them now. She'd want them to be happy in the place that was once her home. If not happy, at least more comfortable.

"Come on, in we go," Herlot's mother said as Oliver appeared at her side.

Herlot stepped inside, but out the corner of her eye noticed Oliver hand her mother a glass bottle. Her mother walked past her and put the bottle inside her chest.

"Don't you want to sit with your new friends?" Herlot's mother said as she straightened and brushed the dirt off her skirt.

Herlot sat between Enri and Ambro as her mother made her leave. Ambro soon started twiddling his thumbs. He seemed just as at a loss for words as she. Was it appropriate to ask them if they wanted to see the wooden toys, or was that something you didn't ask children who had just lost their mother? Maybe they didn't have play on their minds at all. If only they would say something first, she'd be able to decide whether to say something cheerful or not. She nudged Ambro only to receive a nudge back. This was anything but welcoming.

Oliver greeted his first patient, Agatha. Oliver had visited Alonia many times, but Herlot had never been inside to see what it was that he actually did. As the scene unfolded in front of her, she realized the work of a healer was even more difficult than anyone made it out to be. Agatha took her sandal off and held her foot right up to Oliver's face.

"Eee," Ambro said. He plugged his nose. Herlot suppressed her giggle, and the air rising up caused her cheeks to inflate. Then Mahtreeh and Enri giggled next to her—and just like that the stiff awkwardness lifted.

Oliver gave them all a warning glance. They did their best to stifle their laughter while plugging their noses and looking back and forth at one another. However, it was too much for Herlot, when Oliver touched Agatha's foot for inspection, and a loud snort escaped her.

"I hear you, child! Just wait until you get your first callus and have to walk to the stream every day!" Agatha threatened.

"Dearest Agatha, will you be fine waiting a moment?" Oliver asked. His tone of voice made it sound as if the callus were a matter of life or death. Herlot found herself leaning forward, curious to find out what exactly it was. As she did so, she bumped into Enri who was attempting the same.

Agatha sighed. "I suppose so."

They were left alone with Agatha and the mysterious callus on her foot.

"What is a callus?" Ambro demanded. He crawled to have a look, but Agatha set her foot down. "Oh, come on! I don't mean any harm. I just want to see it."

"I've seen one," Mahtreeh teased.

"You will see no such thing! What has your mother been putting in your porridge?" Agatha cried, trying to tuck her foot under her bottom. Failing to do so, she pressed the foot hard against the ground while Ambro tried to lift it. Herlot watched intently, hoping her brother would succeed.

"I...want...to...see...it," Ambro grunted. He tickled her foot and gained leeway. "Come on! Help me tickle her!"

He didn't need to ask twice. She, Mahtreeh, and Enri jumped to their feet and tickled her armpits and neck. "Ernest! Oliver! Someone! Help!" she clucked.

The door flew open and as Herlot's father peeled her and Ambro off poor Agatha, Oliver rushed in and clenching a sandstone between his teeth, his arms worked to restrain Enri and Mahtreeh.

"Apologize to Agatha, every single one of you," Oliver said. His tone was firm but Herlot could tell he was working hard not to smile.

After they each apologized, Agatha opened her arms wide. "Oh, come here. It's not your fault. Your parents ought to know better than to coop you up during a day like this," she said, directing her frown at the men.

Before Herlot knew it, she was scooped toward Agatha's chest, Enri and Mahtreeh's cheeks smushed against both sides of her face. "Agatha! I can't breathe," Ambro said.

"Now outside with all of you. Ambro, Herlot, show your guests what it is to have a good time in Alonia," Agatha said.

Once they were outside, Ambro faltered in closing the door and stuck his head back in. "Is having a callus like growing a turtle shell?"

"Why, yes, it is." Agatha's voice rang from the home with pride. "It protects what is beautiful and delicate on the inside."

At that, Herlot's father stepped outside again and guided Ambro away from the door. "No more questions," he said as he closed it.

Herlot gazed up, the bickering around her fading into silence as she looked at the full cloud floating into the sun's way, casting Alonia in a brief shadow. The rays shone through once again and she checked the sun's position. *Just a little bit longer and soon it will be dark. Then I can go see Devotio*, she thought.

"Elvin! Maurice! Over here!" Ambro waved to his friends standing in the line. "What do you say, Mahtreeh and Enri? Are you up for a game of tug of war? I've a rope that can withstand dragon fire!"

Mahtreeh gaped. "*Real* dragon fire?"

"Uh-huh," Ambro said.

Elvin arrived and rubbed his hands together. "Not just once. But twice. Never thought we'd pull Maurice back into the ship, but no matter how much fire that dragon blew, it was no match for the rope."

"Holy Basil! Can I see it?" Mahtreeh asked. His cheeks were flushed from excitement.

"Aye, Aye. You can even be the captain of your side when we play," Maurice said.

"I thought a captain had to be strong. Even the ones with only one leg are strong," Manni said, arriving at the scene.

Herlot watched Mahtreeh's cheeks flush red and his body sink as if he were going down with his ship. Never before had Herlot felt so much irritation because of another person, so much so that her arms shook. "And all sailors, captain or not, love the sea. Which means you shouldn't be on anyone's side because you don't have a heart."

"Herlot!" Ambro snapped.

Her brother looked like he might punish her with a chore. Manni just stood there with her mouth wide open. Even though all the other children adored her, Herlot did not care what they thought. Not anymore. There were a lot of things she found confusing, but one thing was clear—Manni needed a lesson on how to treat guests. And, looking at her, she couldn't help but understand why Devotio's family wanted to stay hidden. If someone like Manni could say something so mean to someone of her own kind, how would she treat a magical creature like Devotio? If Manni's family really was hiding a gold coin, what would they do if they saw Devotio's alicorn?

Ambro kept staring her down, but she had no intention of apologizing to Manni. "Enri, Mahtreeh, let's go warm our bodies for the game," Herlot said.

Mahtreeh stayed quiet as they spun in circles and touched their toes, but Enri stopped a moment to whisper in Herlot's ear. "Thank you for standing up for my brother. And I think that with our sailor hearts we will win the game, don't you?"

"I do. You want to know a secret? I actually like the part about falling in the mud," Herlot said.

"You like falling in the mud?" Mahtreeh asked.

"Uh-huh. It's like a bath, but better."

"I say we pull until we are a snail's glide away from winning, and then we let them pull us in the mud," Enri said.

"It will be a little like winning but without having to miss out on the best part," Herlot said.

Enri's plan worked perfectly. Herlot, Mahtreeh, Enri, and Elvin pulled against Ambro, Maurice, Manni, and Coral. "Now," Captain

Mahtreeh said just as Ambro's foot was at the edge of the mud pit. Herlot relaxed her grip on the rope and squealed in delight as she flew toward the wet soil. Once immersed to her satisfaction, she joined in on rolling around with Mahtreeh and Enri. Elvin grabbed at his hair as he kneed in the mud. "What happened? We were this close to winning!"

"We didn't want to miss out on the award," Enri said mid roll.

"Huh? Oh... Oh!" Herlot didn't need more evidence to know Elvin had understood as he made a show of falling into the mud backwards.

• • •

Herlot had never seen a parent so happy about muddy clothing as Oliver. He sang a tune about sunflowers from Lorfin as they scrubbed the mud off their skin, and Oliver and Herlot's mother soaked the dresses and tunics in a giant barrel. Every time Oliver glanced over at Enri and Mahtreeh laughing and repeatedly telling the story of the tug-of-war game, his voice raised another pitch and the song increased in pace. Herlot's guests felt at home and her mind was filled with beautiful images of Lorfin's sunflower fields as she awaited her evening with Devotio.

Herlot ran her tongue over her teeth, disturbed by the dirt stuck between the spaces. Enri had just finished slipping her dress over her head and was busy rubbing her finger against her teeth. Now could be the perfect opportunity to ask Enri about her palm. "Let's see if there's any water buckets left outside so we can swish the grit out," Herlot said.

Outside, Herlot and Enri swished and spat for ages. "Enri, have you ever noticed your palm talking?" Herlot asked when her teeth felt smooth again.

Enri giggled. "What a funny question. But no, I guess I have not. I didn't know palms could talk."

"I didn't either! But when we first met today, yours had a story to tell."

Enri stared down and poked at the center of her right palm with her left pointer finger as if she wanted to wake it up. She giggled again.

"Hmm, I don't think it's working," Enri said.

"May I?" Herlot asked.

Enri nodded and extended her hand. Herlot closed her eyes and waited for the sensation to start. Her tongue made its way out between her lips as she focused. Now that her hand was touching Enri's, understanding the story was easier. She just had to listen with her own hand.

"It's very warm. Can you feel that?" Enri asked.

"Yes." But there was more than just warmth, each crease and indentation in Enri's palm was like a letter in a book. A heavy mood settled over Herlot, as if she had put on a coat with way too many layers of fur. Pressure built behind her eyes. Sadness. "Oh, it's a very sad story, I'm afraid. Do we still want to hear it?"

Enri's face darkened for a brief moment, but the look passed. "I guess. Maybe it is just starting out sad. Something funny might happen. Do you...see anything?"

"Not yet. But I can feel it. I'll try harder." Herlot squeezed her eyes shut. At first all she saw was dark, but then her eyes began to sense something else behind her closed eyelids. It was much like trying to see in the dark. A fire appeared inside a home much like her own, and a woman curled up on her side next to it. And there was Oliver! "Your father is there," Herlot said.

"Oh! Father! What is he doing?"

"I think he's trying to help a woman. I think she's in a lot of pain. He's holding something to her lips," Herlot said.

Enri gasped and snatched her palm away. Herlot's eyes fluttered open to see Enri's gaze bore into her with anger—then terror. She raced back inside the home.

"Oh," Herlot grasped her chest which tightened with pain. She was certain she had just lost Enri as a friend. She had never had such a good time with other children before. This was her fault. She had to find a way to make it up.

That turned out to be a very difficult task. When all the children visited the stewards to show off their flower headbands and rock collections, Enri made sure to not be in talking distance of Herlot.

Devotio was still on the forefront of her mind, but she wished she understood why Enri had become upset so suddenly. Maybe Enri had thought Herlot was playing a game and then realized that Herlot really was seeing something, and that had scared her. Could there have been something about the story that she saw? Then the realization hit. How could she have been so awful and naïve? What if the woman she had seen was Sylvia? Herlot ran her fingers through her hair and they got stuck in a tangle. She pulled extra hard trying to push through, but it only made her scalp ache. She tugged again.

Why did she always have to be the one who made mistakes that others didn't? First it had been taking off her shoes, now it was hearing palm stories, and aside from that, everyone always seemed to have something to pick at about her. She was too quiet, she didn't participate enough, she didn't play enough, and when she did play, she didn't play the way they wanted her to. She hurt people. Mother, especially. What if she made a mistake that hurt Devotio just like she had just hurt Enri? She winced as her fingers charged through the tangle. She let the strands that had fallen out fall to the dirt. No matter what, she would try harder than anything she had ever tried at to make no mistake around Devotio. As for Enri, she hoped Enri might at least listen to her long enough for Herlot to say that she was sorry.

When the stars appeared, Oliver and the stewards' presence seemed to ignite the atmosphere of the village as the first fires were lit. No one could sit still to listen to stories, so they decided to sing and dance instead. Simon played a lively tune on his recorder while Merle and Herlot's mother hooked elbows and spun in circles. Agatha shook her chest and clapped the sides of her hips with the rhythm. Every time Herlot started to sneak away into the woods, someone pulled her into a dance.

Frustration ignited as someone else locked their elbow with her own just as she began to sneak toward the outskirts of the dance— until she realized that it was Mahtreeh. He smiled widely at her as they spun in a circle. They were still friends. Enri must have not told him about what had happened. Her frustration eased as they spun faster to keep pace with the fluttering recorder music. Then, when the song ended, they fell on their backs and watched the stars spin above them.

When the stars came to a still, Herlot adjusted to the change in mood of the music, for Simon had begun to play a slow melody.

She rocked from side to side to the song when all of a sudden, she heard a sound so beautiful that her body stilled, too. It was Mahtreeh. Whistling. Not the type of whistle her father used to gather the men, or the type the birds sang in the morning. Even Simon stopped because his recorder could do Mahtreeh no justice. Three different tones drifted from his lips as slow, low pitches braided with delicate, high ones. There was a kind of mysteriousness about his whistling. If there had been a tune that she could match to seeing Devotio when she opened her eyes after the storm, this would have been it. The music helped her remember every piece with clarity, like the slugs under the mushrooms and the exact shade of Devotio's pearl coat.

"Lovely," Rudi whispered, as entranced as everyone else by Mahtreeh's song.

As much as Herlot wanted to hear the end of the song, now was the perfect time to sneak away. She shuffled backwards a bit and checked to see if she had gained anyone's attention. Not even a turn of the head. She continued her shuffle until she reached the back of the crowd. Then, to the beautiful accompaniment of Mahtreeh's whistle, she finally was on her way to meet with beauty, magic, and adventure—Devotio.

● ● ●

Mahtreeh of Lorfin was constantly in a struggle with his ability to control the balance of warmth and cold in his body. It was as if everyone else had been born with a perfect mixture that could easily be brought back into harmony after being shaken from a cool rain or a soak in the blistering sun, and Mahtreeh had been born with something else entirely. Whatever that something was, he suspected it wanted him to struggle.

He had just endured a humiliating applause and was grateful to see everyone disperse to fill their cups before Rudi was to begin telling his story. It was a warm summer night and he had a close place by the fire, yet he felt cold as if it were winter. That is, winter for a normal person because that was the time of the year when Mahtreeh was always too hot and his morning ritual consisted of dunking his head in the snow.

He was certain his father had packed his wool summer sweater—yes, he was probably the only one in Eraska who had a summer sweater—but he hated to bother him for it while he was having a conversation with Ambro's parents. But he also didn't want to go fetch his sweater alone because the light from the fire didn't reach as far as Ambro's home, and he was afraid.

Enri tapped him on the shoulder. "You're shivering. Come, I thought I saw your sweater in one of the sacks."

"No, Enri, don't tell—"

"Ambro, will you show us to your home? I don't know if we can find it in the dark."

Great. The last thing he needed was for Ambro to witness his twin sister treating him as if he were *her* little brother. They followed Ambro into the dark, but just as they were nearing the home, a glimmer of candlelight flickered in the woods.

"What is that?" Mahtreeh wondered out loud.

"Shh. It's my sister," Ambro said. "Sneaking away into the woods. What could she be up to?"

"We should follow her," Enri whispered. Mahtreeh knew the curious look on his sister's face. She wouldn't stop poking, wondering, or whatever else it took until she was satisfied. Especially about Herlot. Enri had acted strange since the afternoon, keeping a fair distance from Herlot but constantly sneaking peeks at her and asking Mahtreeh if he noticed anything different about her.

Mahtreeh opened his mouth to protest, but Ambro finalized the decision before he could. "You don't have to say that twice. Let's go."

But what about my sweater? He wanted to remind Enri about it but didn't want Ambro to overhear. They formed a chain holding hands and before he knew it, he was in the forest. The very dark, dark forest. It made no difference if Mahtreeh closed his eyes—everything was black.

"We should have brought a candle," Enri said.

Mahtreeh nodded, and then realized it was so dark they couldn't see him. "You can say that again."

The trip only got worse. Mahtreeh squeaked whenever grass brushed against his ankle and spat and shook his head when he walked into a spiderweb.

A faint light to Mahtreeh's left pierced the dark abyss that had engulfed him the entire walk. At first, he didn't know if it was his imagination, but then he saw the outline of Herlot's face illuminated in the light. He wanted to speak, to tell the others he had found her. But as afraid as he was, and even though she carried the light savior with her that could protect him from any more spiderwebs, a larger part of him wished to just watch her. For the first time in his entire life he knew what serene joy looked like and he even got a taste of it. He wanted to watch and watch, and study and study, maybe even whistle a song about it, just for the chance to maybe one day feel that feeling, too.

"Stop," Ambro whispered. "I think I hear her."

"Devotio?" Silence. "Please come. I'm right here." More silence.

"Devotio?" Ambro wondered out loud. "Who is Devotio?"

"Look, Ambro. There's a light. I think that's her," Enri said.

A pair, or rather four pairs, of legs shuffled down Mahtreeh's neck. He scolded himself for allowing fear to take the better of him as he shook his hand free of his sister's grasp and marched toward the candlelight. He didn't care who or what Devotio was, just as long as he could stand by the light, away from things with many legs falling on him from places he couldn't see.

"Herlot!" he announced. "You shouldn't be out here. We are going to take that splendid candle of yours and head back to the village. All of us. Now."

He wasn't expecting the look of pure anguish on her face. He recognized it well: a type of fear that could make one's entire body hurt. He froze in his tracks with guilt from the realization that he had caused it. Herlot's serene joy shattered like a dropped clay pot right in front of him. Whatever it was that he had done by approaching Herlot, he seemed to have destroyed a dream that just a moment ago had seemed tangible for him—if one was lucky enough to find serene joy, it was the most fragile thing under the stars. How could he turn this around?

"You can't be here! Turn around, please, I beg you," Herlot cried. "He's going to think I broke my promise!"

"Herlot, what are you talking about?" Ambro said, snatching the candle from her. "Please don't tell me you have been taking your shoes off again. And who is this Devotio you were talking to?"

"Stop yelling at her. Can't you see she's in pain?" Mahtreeh said.

Herlot fell to her knees and dropped her head into her hands. "I broke my promise. I betrayed him. He will never come back again. I met a unicorn and I ruined it."

"I can't believe I'm hearing this. Herlot, after last night, especially after worrying Mother sick, how can you—"

A gust of wind blew through the branches and the candlelight extinguished. Just as Mahtreeh's panic rose to the surface, his sister grabbed a strong hold of his hand. "I'm right here. Don't worry—Holy Basil!" she gasped.

Another light surfaced in the distance, illuminating the trunks and the branches in a way no candle could ever cover. A white creature approached, its steps making no sound. Mahtreeh's heartbeat hammered in his throat, but not from fear. From exhilaration.

The creature towered over them, his golden horn casting them in a glow, causing any trace of cold to vanish from Mahtreeh's skin. He blinked non-stop in an attempt to capture the reality of the beautiful pearl white of its coat, the majesty of its golden horn, and the magic in its eyes.

"You came." Herlot slowly rose to her feet. She cleared her throat. "Devotio, I'm so sorry—I didn't mean for them to be here. They followed me. I didn't know—"

Herlot's speech faded and she tilted her head to the side, much like people would when Mahtreeh whistled quietly. It was as if she was listening to something, but he couldn't hear anything. Then she smiled. "This is my brother Ambro, and these are my friends Enri and Mahtreeh. And this, this is Devotio. He is a unicorn. I promised him to keep him a secret, but..." Herlot paused and glanced at Devotio, smiling wide. By some miracle, her serene joy had returned, and with her wide smile it seemed stronger. The impossible had happened. A shattered pot rearranged perfectly to what it had once been before, and this time durable enough to withstand another drop. "He wishes to meet you. I—I can share the magic."

Now Mahtreeh understood why Herlot had been so upset. He didn't know much about magical creatures, but he guessed that keeping them secret was a very serious matter. Mahtreeh felt the air swivel around his ears before a voice spoke.

"Hello, Ambro. Enri. Mahtreeh. It is nice to meet you."

Enri spun around in a circle. "Where did that come from?"

Herlot chuckled. "Devotio can speak, but not the way we do. He doesn't have to use his lips, just his breath, right, Devotio? Did I explain that well?"

Devotio nodded.

Mahtreeh felt giddy all over and gave up on trying to think before he spoke. He felt so safe, safe enough to be exhilarated like he had never been before in his nine years. "It's nice to meet you, too! You are, ah, splendid, beautiful, and I hope you don't get offended, but it's confusing meeting a unicorn, actually any creature that can speak. Anybody I have ever met before I have shaken hands with, and I feel like I'm not being polite without shaking hands. But you don't have hands so..."

The unicorn lowered his head in front of him, and Enri giggled. "Like this!" She extended her palm and pressed it to his forehead.

"Silly me," Mahtreeh said and followed suit. "Absolute magic," he said as he gazed up at the golden horn.

"It's called an alicorn," Herlot said. "Yesterday he dried my dress with it and he took me home when I got lost."

Devotio approached Ambro whose features were frozen. His mouth hung open, exposing his teeth and his eyebrows rose to his hairline.

"I can't believe you came," Herlot said.

"I wanted to meet you—Enri, Mahtreeh, and Ambro," Devotio said.

"Will your family be even more upset now? You've let four humans see you now," Herlot said.

"I will just have to tell them about Ambro's light-brown curls that stand up at attention like his spirit for adventure. And how his eyes are a display of blurred browns that remind me of spotting a racing deer out the corner of my eye. And I'll tell them about his freckles.

You see, some members of my family remember freckles, but not as precisely as I see them now. They aren't evenly sprinkled, there are less on his forehead and more on his cheeks and the bridge of his nose. When I tell them that, they may still be upset, but at least they will understand why I was tempted."

Mahtreeh would never see Ambro the same again. Or freckles. Or any person, for that matter. At once, people were much more interesting than he had ever thought, and he was looking forward to getting a closer look at them.

"Can we ride him?" Ambro squealed. Even though Devotio was right in front of him, he had asked the question to Herlot.

"I think so. Ask him," Herlot suggested.

"Can we ride you?" he asked.

Devotio bowed.

"Hooray!" Herlot exclaimed. "Wait until you see how fast Devotio can run."

Mahtreeh hesitated while his friends climbed on. "How fast?" he asked, nervously.

"Not fast enough for you to fall off, I promise," Devotio said.

And so Mahtreeh found himself going for a walk in the forest, in the middle of the night, on a magical creature, with friends. As he doodled shapes with his finger against Devotio's coat, he thought about his day in its entirety. A light had grown since the moment he met Herlot and Ambro and laughed at Agatha in their home. It felt like a full moon appearing after having been frozen in its new moon phase since his mother's passing. His mother didn't feel gone anymore. It was as if she was right there with them, inside the magic of their night adventure unfolding.

"So the legend father told, it must be real," Ambro announced.

"What legend?" Enri asked.

"The legend of the unicorns," Ambro said.

"I'd like to hear it," Enri said.

Devotio remained silent for a long time, keeping a steady rhythm in his walk. If Mahtreeh didn't know any better, he would have said he was deep in thought. "Maybe it's not a good idea," Herlot said. "It's such a sad—"

"You can tell them," Devotio said.

"Well, if you say so," Herlot said. Mahtreeh sank into the sound of Herlot's voice, quiet and warm, and her words, spoken softly and slow, as she told the legend of the unicorns. He learned about a people who lived long ago during a time when everyone had a unicorn companion. His heart fluttered when Herlot told the part about the unicorns carrying the humans up to the sky so they could greet the sun together. He sniffled when the humans forgot about the unicorns and the unicorns lost their wings out of sadness. And at the end, he was struck by grief when the humans began to hunt the unicorns for their golden alicorns, and how the unicorns hid in a tree to stay safe, never to show themselves to a human again.

Silence swept over them. Mahtreeh did not know what to say. He wished those humans so long ago had never done what they did. Their world could be so different now. All of Eraska could have unicorns walking the forest. He and Enri could have unicorn companions. He'd have the chance of greeting the sun with a magical creature every morning. What could have pushed those humans to cause so much harm to the most beautiful beings in the world?

Enri broke the silence. "Is it true, Devotio?"

"Yes."

Mahtreeh believed every single part of the legend except for the part where the humans abandoned their unicorns, let alone hunted them. Something awful must have happened to the boy in the story. Mahtreeh would have never been able to forgive himself if he were him. "What happened to the boy's unicorn?" Mahtreeh asked. "Were they able to find him and hide him, too?"

"She. Her name was Ola. Many believe her heart shattered when he left her. Some went searching for her but all they found were dozens of floating lights. She still lives on in this world. You call them fireflies," Devotio said.

Ambro began rocking from side to side. "Do you really hide in a tree? And how is that possible? Is it one tree or a lot of trees? And you all have to have a way of becoming really, really small in order to fit, right?" Ambro asked.

"And you used to have wings?" Enri asked.

But Devotio did not answer. Mahtreeh was relieved that nobody else asked more questions. Even though he was curious to know the answers to the questions about the trees and wings, he knew what it was like to stay silent when someone asked him a question he did not want to or know how to answer. And for him, this would happen only when the questions were about something that made him truly uncomfortable, like when adults would ask him if he needed someone to talk to about his mother. This question specifically caused him so much pain that he thought he might shatter like a clay pot if he would speak. These were only things he talked to Enri about, late at night when everyone was asleep, when he was wrapped in a blanket and did not have to worry about keeping his body upright when the grief hit. If Devotio's reason for staying quiet was similar to this, Mahtreeh's curiosity was not worth causing Devotio pain.

Devotio came to a halt at an opening to a meadow. "Don't worry, Mahtreeh."

That was exactly what Enri and his father always said to him before something frightening was about to happen, like a storm or a steep hill on a wagon ride. What did Devotio know that he didn't? Devotio raised his front legs and leapt in at full speed, so fast that Mahtreeh did not have a moment to worry about sliding off.

Before that moment, Mahtreeh believed wings were necessary to fly. Now he knew the truth: one didn't need to leave the ground in order to do it. He looked down at the ground and thought he saw a series of animal burrows raise up to support Devotio's hooves as they ran over a ridged part. He looked behind but they were too far ahead for him to be sure that what he had seen was real.

But did it matter? He looked ahead, and at the world speeding by them. This was what it must have been like to be wind. This was what the wind felt when it breezed through the meadow and knowing that stirred a wild freedom in his belly. He spread his arms wide, threw his head back, and howled at the full moon that had risen. His was not the only voice, though. Herlot, Ambro, and Enri were howling right along with him. They were flying together.

Once they reached the other side of the meadow, Devotio asked them to slide down.

"I have a gift for Enri and Mahtreeh. This way," Devotio said.

A gift? Mahtreeh wondered what kind of gift could be waiting for him in a part of the Eraskan forest he had never visited before. As they walked, he noticed Enri reach for Herlot's hand.

"I'm sorry for running off before," Enri said. "I...I was startled. I hope you understand."

"It's alright. I was startled, too. That's the first time that happened to me."

"What happened?" Ambro asked.

"I thought I heard Enri's palm wanting to tell a story."

Mahtreeh thought he noticed Devotio's step falter a bit, but then decided against it. He was too graceful to falter. Ambro, on the other hand, nearly knocked Herlot over he spun her so hard to face him. "Did you—" Ambro started before being interrupted by Herlot who pushed his hand off her.

"No, I did not take off my shoes." She sighed. Ambro had asked her the same thing just before Devotio showed up. Herlot looked at Enri and Mahtreeh. "When I was younger, the Alonians all thought I was haunted because I would take my shoes off and be really good at finding people when I did. Ambro had me stop."

"And for good reason. I just know you weren't wearing your shoes when you thought you were hearing a palm tell a story. Admit it—"

"It was just a game we were playing," Enri said, stepping between the two. "Right, Herlot? We pretended Herlot could see a story when she touched my hand. You Alonians are better story tellers than everyone says though. Holy Basil, was that a frightening story that Herlot came up with, it had us both scared. I avoided her because I was afraid that she would tell me another one and I wouldn't be able to sleep."

Ambro seemed to relax and Herlot just smiled and nodded. Mahtreeh was grateful that he hadn't heard it. His sister was always the strong one. If a story was able to frighten her, he would make sure there would be a mountain between him and the teller if it were ever to be told again.

They continued walking and Mahtreeh's thoughts drifted back to wondering what Devotio's gift would be, as if his presence alone was not a gift in itself. Devotio stopped in front of a pine tree, which was rare in Eraska. In that moment Mahtreeh knew with his entire heart what the gift was. He had visited this place many times listening to a poem his mother used to recite whenever a storm came. She had visited here many times. This was her pine tree, planted with her own two hands.

"*Off in the distance, the thunder rumbles,*" Devotio started.

Mahtreeh swallowed.

"*Under the drizzle, a pinecone sits humble,*" Enri recited.

She and Devotio continued together.

"*I feel a magnificent yearning,*
And my spirit is thirsting,
To greet this friend I do not meet much,
Who, in the rain, is soft to the touch.
Water streams between the pinecone's scales.
Drops sprinkle from my hair upon two snails.
The drops saturate the grass.
The soil serenades 'Alas!'
Now, the pinecone stands dry.
Water still slushes within my boots, I won't lie.
Soon, our journeys must part,
For we both await a new start."

They paused. Mahtreeh took a deep breath and finished the last line.

"*But, pinecone, even when your seeds transform into a beautiful pine tree,*
I will still, and always, recognize thee."

Devotio tugged at a pinecone with his teeth until it came free. He placed it in Enri's hand and returned with another for Mahtreeh. Mahtreeh eyed the pinecone in his palm for a long time, memorizing each ridge and sensing how light it felt in his hand. Finally, he pressed it against his chest.

His mother was certainly not gone, and he would never doubt that again.

After saying good-bye to Devotio, Mahtreeh thought about a lot of things on their walk back to the village. He gazed up at the stars and imagined they could see the magic that had happened in Alonia's forest that night. He promised himself that he would remember this night every time he looked up at the stars.

Mahtreeh's father visited King Cloudian and the fortress often in order to trade with sailors for supplies for his tinctures and salves. He often told him and Enri about the sailors and the lands they came from. They often spoke of luxurious golden items that had been gifted by the most powerful leaders of the world. Elephant statues made of pure gold as engagement presents, golden birdcages for a prince's birth. In the world outside of Eraska there were history books dedicated to the rulers possessing the largest amounts of gold, the first pages always dedicated to the most powerful, an Emperor of a place named Ipta. Not a single Eraskan would ever be written about in there. But, if gifts alone could have history books, Mahtreeh imagined that a pinecone gifted in the land of Eraska would be the emperor written about on the first pages.

CHAPTER 5
King Felix

A FLOCK OF SEAGULLS flew over the Eraskan fortress, their wings flapping with strength against the wind as they began their journey across the northern seas, to where no Eraskan had ever set foot: the capital city of the Kingdom of Isolda, ruled by King Felix, the city of Damalathum.

A meager Eraskan fishing boat would disappear next to the grandeur of Damalathum's sailing ships. One of their sails alone could clothe an entire village or a king's bride. There were armies with swords, spears, maces, and bows. War-bred horses. Gold mines. Some gold-filled, some gold-less. Palaces and dungeons. Cobblestone-paved streets lined with shops, taverns, and bakeries. Blacksmiths, carpenters, and stonemasons competing to be the first called on by their king.

Delicious aromas of lavender and gut-turning stenches of human waste.

Illnesses and epidemics. Schools, some specifically to keep illnesses at bay.

Flute festivals. Parrot parades. Marigold markets.

Families, friends, and lovers. Robbers, killers, and victims.

Bells.

The eight-o'clock bells in Damalathum sounded their last ring and the garrison guards began their routines to secure the city's walls for the night.

Ademar, Royal Chef Ademar to be exact, plugged his nose against the moat's stench as he raced across the drawbridge. His stiff, middle-aged body screamed at him to stop but he pushed on. He was on a royal mission to deliver a precious swan for the banquet of his most precious King Felix whether his knees liked it or not. King Felix's brother, King Robin of Berdania, was coming to visit, and Ademar could not stop imagining Felix's clap of approval at the splendid swan art assembled by his chef within such short notice.

These bridges always made him nervous. *My King, My King, my most precious lovely King,* he sang to himself as he held on to the neck of the swan, making sure it would not fall into the water. The swan. It was a putrid-tasting thing and only those with sharp, sculpted teeth could chew the meat, and even they would suffer from a sore jaw afterward. Nevertheless, it was the most important part of the banquet—a grandiose decoration to honor the guests. It had to have just the right color, just the right texture, just the right curvature to reflect King Felix's perfection for all the guests to see—especially King Robin.

That fool could learn a thing or two, Royal Chef Ademar thought. Here he was in a beautifully gilded apron—courtesy of King Felix— while King Robin's chefs were lucky to have a pair of shoes.

"Open up! Open up, I say!" he yelled as the portcullis crashed behind him.

His voice was scratchy from years of tasting foods that were too sour or spicy. He was well aware that his kitchen assistants joked that his voice reminded them of one of the yodeling sheep herders who lived outside the city walls. Let them joke was his philosophy. As long as they served him well, they served King Felix well, and if jokes helped them do good work in the kitchen, it was a minimal price to pay.

He kicked the door, shimmers of gold falling from his shoes.

A small window in the gate slid open. "No one allowed after the bells ring eight."

Ademar recognized the voice with a twinge of annoyance: Vincent, the newest and youngest of the garrison. "I am not no one. I am our

King's chef! Now, open the doors or your fate will be that of this swan."
Ademar lifted the limp bird up to the window.

"Hm. Tempting"—Vincent yawned—"but I do not believe it. You sound like a sheep herder."

"Oh, really? In that case, I don't presume a guard would be interested in a coin from a silly old sheep herder?" Ademar dug into his pouch and presented a gold coin. A strong hand with defined, muscular fingers snatched it. Metal clanked, and the gatehouse door opened wide.

"I would have let you in without the coin," Vincent said. "Do you need an escort to the palace?"

"Yes, by horse. I need to get back as soon as possible."

The space was small, and Ademar felt the eyes of the garrison guards who spied through the holes in the wall. Any moment, a hidden door in the ceiling could be opened to pour boiling water or oil on him. Or a set of spears would jab at him from the sides. Ademar jumped when Vincent pounded on the next gate.

The second door opened to reveal several guards frowning down at Ademar. "All that work into building a clock tower tall enough for people outside the walls to see. How does one find himself in a situation where the gate closes right in front of their nose!" one of them belted.

Ademar lifted his chin. "If it weren't for my menu, let alone milk from the best-bred cows in the kingdom, not a single one of you would be tall enough to look down upon me."

His comment may have had an effect on the men, but unfortunately, right as he finished speaking, his chef's hat fell off, throwing the other men into fits of laughter. Vincent bent over to retrieve the hat and set it back on Ademar's head. "I'll take you to the palace myself, Chef Ademar. I could use a change in routine. Anything is better than staring at a bowl of water all night."

In Damalathum, water bowls were placed in several areas of the city and checked throughout the night. If the water rippled, there was a chance an enemy was attempting to invade through a tunnel. Ademar sympathized with Vincent. Such a task would be like watching a pot of water that never boiled.

A group of guards marched by and into the dark alleys of the city's defensive walls. They carried bows, arrows, and unlit torches to be lit as signals of possible threats during the night. It took several hours for even the best-trained soldier to run the perimeter of Damalathum's defensive wall, and in the case of an attack, the torches were waved in specific patterns depending on the oncoming threat.

Shivers ran down Ademar's spine from the clanking of armor and sharpening of swords. Though the sounds were not much different from those of the knives, pots, and pans, the end result of his work was mouth-watering edible masterpieces. The end result of the soldiers' work were corpses.

Vincent headed toward the stables. "Do you want your own horse, or will you ride with me?"

"Wi-with me, uh, with you," Ademar stuttered. Horses had never been fond of him. He couldn't risk getting bucked and hurting his back, and the horse would be less likely to try if he was with Vincent.

While Ademar waited, three men and two women with golden skin that looked as if it had never missed a day of being burnished by the sun walked toward the defensive walls. They were Iptans, citizens of the richest and most powerful empire from as far back as history could recall—Ipta. They were draped in a smoky scent that brightened Ademar's senses. His attention fell to the instruments the Iptans carried on their backs—heavy, golden telescopes, and not just gilded. Everything but the lenses was pure gold.

Ademar pouted his lips, noticing how no guard questioned them in the gatehouse. Some even stepped to the side to make way for them. They opened the gates, dropped the bridge, and lifted the portcullis without a single scolding.

"Iptans," Ademar muttered. "I bet they don't get lectured about the clock tower." Then he stroked his cheek that had never experienced a single crowpox welt, unlike so many of Damalathum's citizens— at least before the Iptans had built a headquarters building inside Damalathum. As a gift to King Felix, they had given everyone a gold-tinted elixir to drink to protect them from the illness. It had worked. Perfectly.

Vincent returned on a silky, grey horse that was at least two heads taller than Ademar. "Easy boy," Ademar said as Vincent hauled him up. The horse flattened its ears.

"She's a girl," Vincent said.

Ademar patted the horse. "My apologies, milady."

As they trotted down Malt Alley, Vincent sighed as they passed a soldier seated in front of a barber's shop, half asleep, in front of a water bowl. "How is life as a garrison guard?" Ademar asked.

"Ah. Surprising."

"Surprising? So you have had interesting experiences. This is good."

Vincent chuckled. "What is surprising is that one trains to fight battles but ends up a scholar of paranoia. I once could disarm a soldier in my sleep. Now I find that my most-perfected skill is increasing my heartbeat each time I see fireflies beyond the eastern wall. I dreamt of being with the armies. Conquering and gaining is where all the glory is, not in protecting what's already here."

"Do not get discouraged, young Vincent. You are merely seventeen and have many years ahead of you for a chance to see battle and return in honor. And if not, there are many beautiful maidens seeking a garrison soldier whom they can see every day," Ademar winked.

They entered the city square where the palace stood. Fountains, sculptures, and guards decorated it all along its rectangular shape. Steps led up to its entrance, accented with bold, white columns. The night was still young enough for crowds to stand as close as allowed, trying to catch a glimpse of the King or his beautiful Queen. They held cups up and saluted, chanting, "Hail King Felix!" Pride rushed through Ademar's veins at the thought of his King.

"Move aside! Royal swan coming through," Vincent ordered.

Ademar, aware of the crowd's eyes on him, placed his hand as gently as he could into the soldier's hand that was extended to help him off the horse. They would all marvel at his royal gracefulness, he thought. The horse sidestepped and Ademar was forced to tighten his grip and before he knew it, he found himself embracing the guard chest to chest. As quickly as he could, he took his swan and saluted Vincent. Then, racing up the steps, he slipped on the polished marble floors and dropped the swan. Even his fingers had blushed. Wonderful. He was the color of his tomato soup. He could still hear the crowd laughing as he entered the grand palace hall and the guards shut the doors behind him.

When Ademar burst into his kitchen, panting, his staff of fifty froze and looked at him with expectation. He lifted the swan in the air in victory. Cheers and clanks erupted as his staff beat whatever they could find against the bronze pots hanging from the ceiling.

Later, Ademar, lured in by the harp music, peeked in at the banquet. He scanned the room to make sure that the servants had arranged the dishes exactly as he had trained them. But then he was distracted by something far more beautiful than his culinary masterpieces.

Seated at the high table of the banquet was the beloved Queen Magdalene of Damalathum. She was a melody prettier than any harp's. Her posture was perfectly straight but graceful, as if she were being held up by puppet strings. Her red, gold-embroidered, velvet dress had no folds or wrinkles. A petite face framed the gentlest of rosy smiles at her guests, and her long eyelashes fluttered along with the music. Not a single hair fell out of place from the intricate braids that held her hickory-colored hair in a fluid design.

His heart fluttered when she made eye contact with him and raised her goblet of wine.

● ● ●

Queen Magdalene smiled at Chef Ademar before she took a sip and set her goblet down. She couldn't imagine the amount of work he had put into tonight's occasion.

The melodic harp did little to diffuse the tense atmosphere at the head table in the banquet hall, much like the heavy tapestry failed at insulating the cold from the wall and prickling the back of her neck. She did her best to reflect the guests' merriness—she clapped at the end of the song and widened her eyes in delight as she tasted the rabbit soup.

But just as the tapestry covered a cold, empty, grey wall, she had to cover the conflict between her husband, King Felix, and his brother,

King Robin. Felix and Robin's dying father had deemed them too weak to rule the kingdom in its entirety, hence why neither one of the brothers would be crowned the sole king. Instead, the kingdom was split in half. Isolda for Felix, Berdania for Robin. Upon their father's death, the brothers became rivals in the world's race for gold riches and power, and tonight was an occasion for Robin to boast about his recently excavated gold mine riches and for Felix to show that he could retain his composure.

Luck of the purest kind had been on Robin's side but had spat in Felix's handsome, chiseled face. Robin's gold mine had yielded him a place in history for ages, crowning him the richest man in the entire world, after the Emperor of Ipta. Felix's mines, on the other hand, had yielded nothing.

"Ey! Get your buttery fingers off the pages," one of the knights said to another who had turned a page of the book one of the servants King Robin had brought with him from his kingdom was presenting for the crowd at one of the tables to view.

Along with the letter announcing his visit, Magdalene had managed to see something else Robin had sent to Felix. It was a page from the most recent history book. The writing mentioned Felix's mine yielding only dirty stones, while Robin was now the second richest man across all the known lands of their time. Knowing her husband, she was shocked that he had not declared war at once to take everything that was Robin's—including his place in the history books.

She would do everything in her might to prevent it for the sake of her people, for if it came to war, Felix would lose. She had to admit that the thought of making an escape and settling in a village far, far away had crossed her mind, but everytime it was followed by a wave of shame. It was her responsibility to do what she could from her position for the families within and outside the walls of the city. And if it were not for them, she would be forever bound to Felix for one reason—her son.

Around her, nobles and several knights conversed merrily. Sir Bigge presented Sir Feldour with a plate of broiled fish, inviting him to seconds. Sir Rainling tapped Matilde, the servant, on the shoulder and asked her to fill Sir Mitwin's cup with wine. Yet Felix and Robin had yet to exchange a word.

Magdalene knew for certain that Felix had had no less than ten servants tending to him in dressing for the feast; however, his brown, shoulder-length hair looked a tangled mess underneath his crown. Worst of all were his wrists. When he reached for the salt, they seemed to disappear under his satin robe sleeves. He'd lost weight, she observed, probably from nerves and envy.

Magdalene thought she heard a crack as Felix attempted to push his spoon past his gritted teeth. If only Robin or Felix would speak, she could say something to save Felix's pride. However, even though she was a queen, she was still a woman and was not allowed to speak first.

After everyone had cleared their plates, servants came to sweep the wooden tables of the first course and relight several candles. Robin slid his chair back and stood, twirling his mustache and jutting his belly out as he eyed the diners. Felix's knee tensed against Magdalene's.

"It is a great honor to be a guest in Damalathum," Robin said. "As my show of appreciation, I'd like to provide us all with entertainment while we wait to see if the second course is as splendid as the first."

Felix cleared his throat.

"And now, may I present to you Beadie, Bodie, Bonnie, and Beau," Robin announced.

A jester wearing a checkered costume skipped through the doorway. In a fluid motion, both of his legs kicked up into the air and Magdalene's hands instinctually began a rhythmic clap while he walked on his hands and the bells at the end of his hat jingled. Oh, how she wished to let her body move with such freedom. A second jester entered, jumped up and blew Magdalene a kiss while in midair. The hand walker toppled as if knocked over by the kiss. She turned her head, as if to catch the kiss on her cheek, and the diners cheered. She surprised herself by how natural her laughter sounded. Sometimes she couldn't tell the difference anymore between what was really real and what she had to force. *Thank you for the reminder, jesters,* she thought. But then the last two jesters entered. On top of their heads were not the bells that the crowd always loved. Instead, there were two, unevenly cut, overly decorated crowns. Crowns that twisted, smashed, and packed her laughter into a faraway place that she knew she wouldn't find for a while. Two crowns meant two kings. Felix. And Robin.

A taunt.

She watched helplessly as one of the jesters fell lower and lower into a split as the other pulled gold coins from his trousers. She didn't have to guess which one was Felix.

She could feel Robin's smugness cut the air as he took his seat and leaned toward Felix. Magdalene's tongue stayed helplessly wedged behind her teeth as the diners cheered the performing jesters. The consequences of where Felix would unleash his fury at this performance flitted through her mind, tremendous and terrifying. Didn't the nobles understand this? The least they could do was not display their enjoyment. How many times had they witnessed Felix's delirious decisions whenever he was humiliated, challenged, disobeyed, and worst of all, when he wasn't successful at anything, from a game of chess to the siege of a castle?

The nobles clearly could not have cared less. A candle fell over when one of the barons slammed his hand on the table amidst his laughter, and others scrambled to lift it before a fire could start. Then the marquess tumbled off the bench when he leaned back, clutching his belly in a futile attempt to hold his laughter in..

She dared to look at Felix as he unraveled from his slouched crumble and sat up straight. He watched the show but did not blink, and soon a steady, provoking smile formed on his lips. She recognized this smile. He was swimming in a sea of ideas for revenge.

Magdalene noticed one of the younger kitchen helpers standing in the doorway, watching the show. She was new, arrived at the palace about a week ago. Too new. Why wasn't anyone ordering her back into the kitchen? The Felix jester cried out in pain, having reached a full split on the floor while the Robin jester walked the room, balancing two towers of coins on his pointer fingers. The servant girl clapped along with the crowd.

Stop! Magdalene wanted to scream. She tried with all her might to make eye contact but the girl was focused on something else, too far to the right. *Felix.* As if the girl could feel his coldness, his threats, she hid back into the hallway. Magdalene was certain she wouldn't see the girl again.

Robin gulped his wine and then spoke as he wiped his mouth with the table apron. "What are you going to do, Felix? Seek revenge? Conquer Berdania? And tell me, what would you do if you succeeded at that? Hm? Then your next and only step forward would be to conquer Ipta!"

Conquer Ipta? Magdalene wanted to rip the cloth and send all the tableware crashing onto the floor to stop the absurd idea from reaching Felix's ears. Yet she was bound by invisible chains, and she had to listen to Robin continue his attack of savage taunts.

"It would destroy you. You'd be a leper attempting to seduce a queen. Let me give you a piece of advice—we are family, after all. Leave the matter at the satisfaction that, if you wanted to, you may actually succeed at conquering me. Find every way to prolong it and you will live happily and have the benefit of keeping your sanity."

Felix's knuckles turned white. Magdalene had to act. She couldn't use weapons or take part in discussions among Kings, but she could work quietly.

Magdalene waved to a servant. "Be so kind and open a window. It is awfully warm in here, and I feel faint," she said, even though all she felt was cold.

"Are you well, Queen Magdalene?" Robin asked.

"Yes. I just need a bit of fresh air and don't wish to leave my guests. It is so rare that we have the chance to enjoy a feast together, after all."

The servant bowed and then opened the window closest to her. At once the room echoed with calls of "Hail our King Felix!" from outside.

The diners stopped watching the jesters, raised their glasses, and joined the chant.

"Hail our King Felix!"

Magdalene's heart sighed in relief, but she did not let her composure show it. "I find it astounding that, all day and far into the night, they come to cheer. A king with such devotion from his people was destined to rule, wouldn't you agree?"

"Heh," Robin mumbled, baffled.

Magdalene never forgot one lesson from her mother: Kings start wars and Queens prevent them. She feared the best she could do was postpone this one.

Magdalene straightened the cloth on her lap while the second course arrived. She gave the servants several nods of approval as they packed the tables with bread and meats in all shapes and forms. The harp melody resumed, and Magdalene waved the servant with the wine pitcher over. "The new girl. She must leave first thing in the morning," she whispered as the servant leaned over.

Then she noticed that Robin had called one of his own servants and was whispering in her ear, as well. He was going to strike again. She watched him cut a piece of salmon and layer it with a slice of beef pie in hope of spotting a clue that would help her prepare a counterattack. *What are you up to, you weasel?* she thought.

He finished wiping his hands on the tablecloth right when his servant returned with two goblets engraved with Robin's coat of arms. The servant set one in front of Robin and filled it with wine. It was a direct insult for everyone in the room to see that the host's goblets were not good enough for Robin.

Meanwhile, Felix remained murderously silent. It was as if they were playing chess and Felix kept giving Robin another turn without making a move of his own. But behind his silence, Magdalene knew he was planning a larger move. A final move.

"I find wine tastes best when drunk from goblets of pure gold," Robin said. "Felix, do the Iptans who live in Damalathum drink from pure gold goblets, as well?"

Of course, he had to mention the Iptans—the saviors of Damalathum. Magdalene should have foreseen that.

Then Robin's servant set the other gold goblet in front of Magdalene's plate. She looked at the goblet with hunger, salivating more than for any exotic delicacy she had ever tasted. All thoughts of a counterattack vanished.

"The other, a gift for the queen," Robin said.

So much gold as a gift, just for her, to do with as she pleased. She thought about the dungeon guards she could bribe with it. She thought about seeing her son again. Could she resist?

The servant reached to take away her former one. She awoke from her stupor just in time to lay a hand on her original, only gilded in gold, goblet. "No, I prefer this one," she said. "Thank you, Robin, but I will drink from your goblet when we visit your kingdom. When I am home, I drink from my own."

She stared down at her lap, afraid that if she had another glance at the goblet she would change her mind. "Then it is my gift to you until such a time comes," Robin said.

Delight crashed through her sunken emotions, and light entered her being at the news. She would get to keep it. She would get to see her son. "Thank you. It will be a precious reminder of our merry visit," she said.

Thankfully, the rest of the merry visit remained uneventful and Magdalene collapsed against the wall when she finally returned to her quarters. After she took a few breaths, she ordered her body into its frozen state of composure. She still had a long night ahead of her, and she'd have to wait to release her terror and grief until she was fast asleep in her nightmares. She sat down in front of her oval mirror in her lace-trimmed nightgown as one of her ladies-in-waiting combed through her hair, which fell to her knees. On her nightstand were her two most prized possessions: a seashell and a wooden toy figure of a unicorn that had once been polished but now had burn marks, since her son, Prince Movo, had thrown it into the fireplace in anger. She had purchased the figure years ago, before her pregnancy, during times when she used to dress in a cloak and sneak out to the market. As soon as she'd seen it, she knew she'd wanted her future children to play with it, especially if she had a son. Even though his future had already been written to consist of endless military training, at least he'd have memories of playing with horses of a magical kind before he had to fight on the ones bred for war.

She held the seashell to her ear as she did every night. Magdalene's mother had comforted her before her wedding, explaining that Damalathum lay right on the sea and she'd be able to take long walks on the beach with her children. However, she had only had one child and one day on the beach where they had found the seashell that played the melody of the ocean.

In the reflection of her mirror, her other two ladies-in-waiting pulled her silk bedsheets back and fluffed the pillows. Cora, the youngest, whispered to Linette on the other side of the bed. "You have to believe me about the dream. Your grandmother appeared looking exactly as she had the last time I saw her. She wants you to stop wearing the necklace because it was never hers in the first place and she feels insulted. She said that you would feel closer to her using her spindle."

Magdalene watched a few feathers escape the pillows they were fluffing. She loved their ability to float, to be so light and free of burden.

"Well, that does sound like something she'd say. I would have thought the afterlife had, I don't know... What's the word? Softened her a little," Linette responded. "I won't wear it anymore. You'll let me know if she appears again, won't you?"

"Yes, but I don't like to dream about ghosts. I hope she doesn't come again."

"Ah, I know who you do like to dream of! Could it be the handsome Verius?"

Cora held her finger to her lips, stifling her giggles.

Normally, Magdalene would have asked about Verius to delight in a story of blossoming romance, but something else had struck her interest. "Cora, these dreams you have where spirits visit you, how do you find them?"

Warily, Cora crossed the chamber and added another log into the fireplace. "My Queen, the spirits find me. Sometimes if I really think about one before I fall asleep and ask them to come, they might, but beyond that I cannot influence the matter."

"Suppose you wanted to find someone else who was dreaming?" Magdalene asked.

Cora's shoulders slumped forward. "My apologies, my Queen, but that is not possible. At least, I do not know of anyone who has ever succeeded."

"But there is such a way?"

"Well...one would have to become a spirit."

"Absurd..." Linette mumbled as she poured tea into a cup.

Cora continued. "My mother once told me that only spirits can travel through many worlds—our world, the skies, the world of dreams. We can enter the dream world, but because we are asleep, we cannot maneuver through it."

"I see. Thank you, Cora."

Cora curtsied. "Of course, my Queen."

"Well, it has been a long evening. You both may retreat to your quarters."

"But, my Queen, you have not had your lavender tea," Linette said.

Magdalene covered her mouth and faked a yawn, thinking only of the golden goblet, sitting on the banquet hall table—the key to seeing her son. "Oh, I do not need it tonight. I will fall right asleep."

Both girls curtsied and left.

Magdalene slipped on a robe and waited until she was certain they were no longer in the hallway. Then she walked out barefoot and tip-toed down the rugged staircase.

Once in the banquet hall, she marched to the head table—only for her stomach to sink. The goblet was gone. Had Felix taken it? Had Robin taken it back? Her hands clenched into fists. She wished she could bribe the guards with her wedding ring. Maybe she could have a simple gilded replica made. She would wear it and see if Felix noticed the difference, and if he didn't, she'd give her real one to the guards. Oh, but where could she find someone to make her a replica without word getting out?

"I had a feeling you would come. It's been a while since the Queen has visited the dungeon."

She spun around and searched for where the voice had come from. In a dark corner of the room on a dining bench sat Chef Ademar. Her future shattered like a rock turned to rubble in the mines, and Chef Ademar was the one with the pickaxe. Felix's biggest devotee knew her biggest secret. The room around her spun, causing her to grip the table to stay upright. She would hang for this, and that was the last thing that could happen. She couldn't leave her son alone in the world with Felix.

"Sit," Chef Ademar said.

It was a command, but the tone of his voice was anything but...it sounded defeated. Her mind spun—maybe she could make a deal. She took her time to sit down in front of him while she thought about how to make him an offer. Between his hands, she made out the shape of the goblet. *Funny how nothing has color in the dark, even gold,* she thought. "Chef Ademar, please—"

"My Queen, I have known a long time that you bribe the guards with gold to sneak into the dungeons." He slid the goblet along the table from one hand to the other.

She stilled; making no move for the goblet. Something did not fit. If he knew about her trips, why had he waited so long to reveal her? She studied his posture a little more. There was nothing about it that said he was a man who had rooted out a traitor. "Chef Ademar, what is it that you want?"

He sighed. "I want to make a deal."

"Continue," she said.

Ademar shook his finger at the swan dish still sitting on the head table. "I killed the bird with my own two hands. During the banquet I sat in the kitchen biting my nails until someone came back with news that it had been admired by your guests. I celebrated and gave each of my assistants a tart."

He pointed at his temple. "My mind is not well, Queen Magdalene. It is only mine again at night, if at all. The palace sleeps, my crew sweeps, and my thoughts are laced with the tone of my own voice once again. But every morning I wake and my thoughts are once again overtaken by a stranger I do not know, a stranger who makes decisions and controls the words I speak. A stranger who loves to bow at my King's feet. A stranger who skips to the sound of gold coins in my satchel. It will be a good day when I understand why and how I have done this to myself. But this is a problem for another day, one I doubt will come. However, tonight, I think about the swan before I waded into the water to capture it, before my hands wrapped around its neck."

Magdalene's eyes had adjusted to the dark and she noticed Ademar's were glazed.

"Tonight I will dream of it coming back. In my dream I have enough coins to have my very own pond, a place where I can sit in the tall grasses and watch my very own swan's grace and beauty from afar. My Queen, although I am ill in the head, I am well enough to know my dream will not come true, but in exchange for my silence about your matters, I ask for your help in my next best option."

Magdalene nodded. "Tell me, Chef Ademar. I will do what I can." She wondered what the man she had once only perceived as a simple, overjoyous worshipper, had conjured up.

"I wish to create a butter sculpture of a swan and present it to you and the King. I ask my Queen to say it is more awe-inspiring to the eye than any real swan may ever be, and that any future banquets must feature the butter swan as the main centerpiece."

"We have a deal." She reached her hand out. Ademar kissed the top of her hand. "Thank you, my Queen. I will let you gather what you need in the kitchen and you can rest assured that I will never utter a word." Ademar slid the goblet to Magdalene.

They stood together and walked side by side into the hall. Without another word, Ademar turned toward his quarters, devoid of the usual buoyancy of his chef's walk. Although he had threatened her to some extent, Magdalene had the feeling that she had made a true friend in the palace, something she had never expected outside of her ladies-in-waiting. *May your suffering ease, Chef Ademar,* she thought.

Chef Ademar's staff was busy working into the night, cleaning, and prepping for the next day, but gave their full attention to Magdalene as she entered.

"Two baskets with anything fresh you can find. And please, something sweet, as well, perhaps the marzipan," she said.

"We already had them ready," a man named Lowell, eyes red from lack of sleep, said and handed her two baskets.

They had even remembered to add a candle.

Magdalene thanked them and headed back in the direction of the banquet hall to the corner, where the hallways met. Two guards stood in front of a locked door.

Magdalene revealed the goblet. "It's pure gold. For your discretion."

The two guards eyed each other. "Be quick," one said and snatched the goblet and hid it under his surcoat. Magdalene sighed with relief, grateful that the guards' desire for gold was stronger than their loyalty to Felix.

Magdalene rushed down the cold, stone steps. They grew in dampness until she stepped into a puddle at the bottom, where the dungeons began. The place was dominated by the stench of mold.

Wary hands reached out for her from between rusted bars, and perverted comments were said as she passed the cells. There was still light from the torches, but it was difficult to make out the prisoners' faces.

At the end, where it was completely dark, was a large cell. A guard well aware of her infrequent routine opened it for her to enter.

"Please be so kind as to light this." Magdalene presented the candle to the guard and stepped into the space.

Her eyes needed a few more moments to adjust, and then she saw the children huddled against one another, shaking.

She fell to her knees, embracing the ones who came at her. "Shh. There, there. Only a few more days, I promise. I brought nice things for you," she cooed.

They didn't attack the basket like normal hungry children would. The amount of fear that had been instilled in them would forever make them hesitate about everything and anything, even kind offerings. They picked at little pieces of bread and shook as they tried to eat.

The soldier handed her the lit candle through the bars. While the children nibbled, she crawled around the space until she found a boy sitting alone in the corner. His hickory-brown hair fell in strands over his eyes, which were an almost-white light blue. Cold. He looked past her as if she weren't there.

"Movo, my son. Here," she said through tears as she placed the candle in his hands. She kissed his cheek, but he didn't respond.

She cursed the fact that the only place of power she had was as the Queen as she took in her son. When Felix was crowned King of Isolda after his father's death, never had she imagined he had the ability to create something as treacherous as the Dungeon Law, set into stone the day after his inauguration. Every child in his or her fifth year had to spend a month in the dungeons. Felix believed that fears instilled in a child lasted forever, and they would be less likely to act against him as adults if they knew the reality of the dungeons.

Everyone believed that the Dungeon Law would not apply to Felix's own son. Movo had turned five, then six, then seven, and Felix never mentioned it. Then, on Movo's tenth birthday, Felix had informed Magdalene over breakfast that Movo had been sent to the dungeons.

He sat there, testing her composure as he leisurely described the conditions under which Movo would be allowed to leave. She sat there, still and composed with grape skin stuck to the edge of her throat as he explained that his plan would be an important lesson for their son. It was the best training he could get before he began formal military training. After his time in the dungeons, he would forever be a leader and know everything it took to rule a kingdom. He would understand the sacredness of being a King, and what it would take to control his people, even if that meant having to sacrifice one of his own. In order to be freed, Movo had to take the life of another child. Magdalene had never excelled more at her composure than in that moment. She had smiled and congratulated Felix's wisdom knowing that she would be of no help to anyone, especially her son, if she spoke against Felix and got herself hung. After all, queens were dispensable. But now as she looked at Movo, she realized that even her visits, the little amounts of warmth she was able to give her son, had been meaningless. What had once been a sweet boy who played with toys and dreamed of riding a horse was now a stranger she no longer recognized, a stranger with a killer's glare. He would break. Soon.

The guard clanked a staff against the bars. The ringing scratched at Magdalene's ears. "Time to go," he said.

Magdalene's heart ached as she made her way back. When she reached the stairs, she could still see the candlelight from far away. Suddenly, it extinguished. She pictured Movo's face, its hard lines converging to blow it out on purpose, and shuddered. Movo, her only son and heir to the kingdom, was beginning his third year in the cell. Even if he did see light again, his own had been extinguished from his eyes. Felix would have his heir.

• • •

Felix ordered the harp player to attend to Robin with a pamper and massage. He didn't need him roaming the castle and spying on his private matters tonight. Then he retreated to his private chambers.

He leaned over his table and supported his weight with his hands as he concentrated deep in study. Each candleholder held a lit candle to provide enough light for him to study the intricate maps of Ipta. Every so often he glanced up at his portrait in which he sat wearing his crown and holding a staff. Underneath the portrait was a stand with a chessboard that had only one piece: the king, standing victorious in the center of it. As it should be.

Someone knocked on the door, two short taps followed by three consecutive ones. In came Dartharus, his highest military commander. He set several books, all with the name Ipta in their titles, on the table and began flipping through pages. Felix honed back in on the map.

"Nothing in this one." Dartharus leaned back and stretched. "Some have overheard talk that the Iptans speak of a war in the sky."

"Ha! I suppose I should begin training my cavalry to charge on imaginary winged horses from now on. And where was this rubbish heard?" Felix said.

"Traveling merchants on market days. One was selling a protective amulet for when the war comes."

Felix sneered. "Those fools will say anything to sell their hogwash."

"I agree. But, if I may say, the Iptans consistently study the sky. There could be some truth to it."

"Has anyone managed to intercept an Iptan message? Any sort of letter?" Felix asked, distraught.

"Not a single one. They only communicate verbally with their visitors."

Felix locked eyes with his portrait. Conquering Ipta seemed impossible. Every time he looked at a map, the desert surrounding Ipta only seemed to grow wider. If it wasn't for that damned desert. At least one month of travel would be needed to reach the city. Resupplying his army would be impossible at such a distance, and his soldiers would die of thirst and hunger before even reaching Ipta. How did the Iptans do it?

This question made him want to rip his beard hair out. He could not even find someone to torture for the answer. The only way into Ipta was through invitation, and never had he met one of these guests because they never returned. Arresting, let alone torturing, an Iptan was out of the question. He wanted his destiny, not suicide.

But the desert was not the only problem keeping him from his destiny of sitting on the throne of the world. It was also rumored that those who, by some magic, survived the journey to Ipta faced a barricade of pyramid structures that no ladder was tall enough to reach the top of. The methods used to seize places in Felix and Robin's world were children's toys compared to what would be needed to invade Ipta if this were true. He thought he could learn more by intercepting one of their messages. It was no secret that they could read and write, but when it came to important messages, they left no traces.

All he did know was that for as long as history had been recorded, an Iptan Emperor had always been the richest and most powerful man in the world. Iptans were also smart. They had medicines even the most educated alchemists in his kingdom could not understand.

At the beginning of Felix's reign, Iptan officials had approached him with a proposition. All they'd wanted was a small space in the city to build their headquarters, and in exchange, they would provide protection against crowpox to every being in his kingdom. Felix had wanted to decline but feared the crowpox and Ipta's reaction to a 'No'.

His father had been right about him being weak, and he'd succumbed.

Bottles filled with a milky, golden medicine were distributed amongst his people, and not a single crowpox outbreak was reported thereafter. Felix had had every one of his alchemists study the contents of the medicine, but not a single one could decipher its ingredients. Ever since, Iptans had resided in their headquarters, not bothering anyone, but their presence made it clear to everyone that Felix's power over the kingdom was not absolute. The truth was that Iptans could do whatever they wished at any given time, and had offered the medicine more so out of pity than a fair bargain with an equally capable ruler. And so here they were, sitting comfortably in his city, and only leaving once in a while with their ridiculous telescopes.

"Ha!" Dartharus placed an open book on the table. "Here it states Ipta was started by a people who could make their mirages become real. They would purposefully travel the desert until they saw what it was they wished for most in a time of desperation."

Felix flipped the book to look at its cover. "Some nonsense about children's tales and legends," he said, unimpressed, "As if this were all some magic trick."

Felix was about to throw the book into the fireplace when he froze. Could it be? Was that what made the Iptans so powerful? Some forces of magic no others understood? It was the absurd explanation that no one would ever delve into to study further. What would happen if someone tried to understand Ipta's powers by taking magic into the equation? It all unraveled. There were certainly more questions, such as what kind of magic and how they used it, but what was most important was to know that there *was* magic.

He reopened the book to the page and gazed at the words. Then he looked back at the map and, last but not least, he thought of all of the stories about Ipta that he had heard. Yes. There was magic, he was certain of it. "I know how I will conquer Ipta," he said.

Dartharus raised his eyebrows. "Your Majesty?"

"Magic," he declared. If Ipta could use it, why couldn't he?

Dartharus crossed his arms. "I do not understand, Your Majesty."

"They use magic." He crumpled the map into a ball and chucked it into the fire, watching it burn, and laughing before eyeing Dartharus.

"We will, too."

CHAPTER 6
The Whales

"MOTHER, ARE YOU *CERTAIN* that tonight the thunder moon will rise?" Herlot spun in a circle.

"Yes, child. And be careful not to spill the berries from your basket."

"It was the thunder moon when Enri and Mahtreeh came to visit last year, right?"

"Never in my years did I meet a child so obsessed with the moons. What is so special about the thunder moon?"

The thunder moon meant that it was highly likely that Devotio would appear tonight. Herlot and Ambro had snuck into the woods almost every evening since summer started. But tonight would be a full year since the last time they had seen him. If there was any day that it would happen, tonight was it. But she couldn't tell her mother that. Instead, she said, "Rudi said that fireflies usually come out around the time of the thunder moon. Ambro and I are going to look for them tonight." It was as close to the truth as she could get—fireflies were magical. Unicorn bugs.

"As long as your story is ready," Herlot's mother said.

Herlot bit her lip. Tomorrow was her first recitation—a rite of passage in Alonia. Each child, during the summer of his or her ninth birthday, recited a story or a poem he or she had written. They were given ink and a piece of parchment to use, which were strictly rationed and reserved only for the best stories. She had still not written a word.

"It is ready, right?" her mother asked.

"It will be."

"Herlot, what does that mean?"

"Ilvy, Herlot, come here!" Merle called, poking her head out of her home. Herlot released a sigh of gratitude for the interruption.

Merle's abrupt appearance had not startled the two birds in front of her dusty toes, picking at the seeds that had escaped someone's apron. Herlot side-stepped them as she entered. Everyone deserved to eat in peace. She only wished everyone also deserved to not have to recite stories if they didn't want to.

Merle unfolded an apron. "The trader said it will shatter if it falls, so we must be very careful."

Herlot felt the heat of the sun's rays sneaking through the doorway and gliding by her shoulder, the light landing onto the center of the porcelain plate. "Can I touch it?" she asked.

Merle nodded.

Herlot ran her finger over a crack from the center to the outside and then along the chipped edges. In the center was a picture of a large, stocky, four-legged creature with wide ears and a long nose that somewhat resembled the coral tubes in the sea. A magical creature.

"The trader said that it's called an elephant," Merle added.

Herlot's heart fluttered. *A real magical creature, just like, oh,* she could not allow herself to think it or she would blurt.

"Did he say where?" her mother asked.

"From what I recall, he said it was named Ipta," Merle answered, popping her lips on the P.

"If I remember correctly, we read about elephants in one of Bee's books." Herlot's mother leaned forward to examine the details. "They're a little different from what I imagined."

"Yes. Yes, they are," Merle agreed. "It's a shame I can't keep it in here to look at all the time."

"Why would that be?"

"Well, you see, I traded a pair of Rudi's shoes for it." Merle blushed.

"Where will you hide it?"

"I will bury it right outside our home with my other treasures."

Herlot's mother and Merle giggled into their hands and Herlot followed suit. "Herlot, since when do you understand the humors of having a husband?" Merle asked after both women had stopped laughing.

Oh no. She grabbed a blanket off the floor and held it to her face to muffle her words. "I needed an excuse to let my joy out! I'm meeting my friend tonight. He is a magical creature like the elephant and his name is Devotio." She dropped the blanket and skipped outside before they could question her anymore.

Next to Sira and Viktor's home, Manni and her friends were taking turns skipping over a rope. She quietly took her place in line behind Lara and watched eagerly as Manni and Rietta swung the rope from side to side while Coral, hair tucked into a cap, counted her jumps. *I don't know if I'll count when it is my turn. It will take away from the fun of jumping for the joy of it. Maybe I'll sing a song though.*

Coral stopped at a staggering fifty-one jumps, after which it was Lara's turn. After Lara got tangled at thirty-three, Herlot took her place on the left side of the rope. She eagerly awaited her first jump when an unwelcome impact met her from the side. Coral now stood in the ready to jump spot.

Herlot looked to the other girls, waiting for someone to announce the rules of playing fair jump rope. But no complaint was made, and Manni and Kristen spun the rope for Coral. *It's like I'm invisible.* She hugged herself, making sure that she really existed. Anything is better than this feeling. The sniffles. Head pain. Stomach upset. I would rather have all three at once than this lonely hollowness, she thought.

As quickly as her legs could carry her, she left the group of girls and headed toward her home where she could think about Devotio.

"Ah!" she exclaimed as she ran right into Rudi.

"My, young Herlot, what is the rush?" Rudi steadied her.

"Time for a nap." She did her best to keep her lip from trembling.

"A nap? Now this is the first time I hear of someone your age excited to take a nap."

Herlot was silent.

"Playing with the girls didn't go so well," Rudi said, nodding toward the jump ropers. He must have seen everything. She sighed and shrugged. "Well, I just gave Ambro and Elvin permission to take the new boat out for a row. If you hurry, you might still catch them at the shore."

It sounded like a nice idea, and she might have enjoyed it before, but right now she just wanted to be alone with the hurt in her belly and chest. It was hard to smile and enjoy things when these places hurt. "Maybe some other time."

Rudi picked up a stick. "I know you wish to nap and all, but in case you can't fall asleep, writing isn't only used for recording stories. I do it when there is too much happening here," he pointed the stick at his temple. "I like to write my thoughts out when I'm upset. Always makes a breath come easier."

Herlot took the stick from Rudi as he kissed her on top of the head. "Thank you, Rudi. I'll try."

Once home, she sat cross-legged and drew a circle in the dirt. She closed her eyes. At first, the swarm of thoughts was overwhelming and she could not pick one to write down, but she continued to travel through her thoughts and then she found herself in a new place. Instead of being stuck in them, here she was able to observe the thoughts. They were like a tall, disorganized stack of blankets waiting to be folded. There was a blanket of thoughts about Manni, another one about the other children, and at least three for loneliness. Of course, there was a magnificent collection of thoughts about Devotio. Those she really liked and wished to stack on the top of the pile. She continued on until she reached a black blanket on the bottom. This one she could not decipher but she started to write with her eyes still closed. She made the shape of an A, then an F, and when she opened her eyes she stared down at what she had written: AFRAID.

I am afraid of the black blanket. I don't know what it is and I'm afraid that even if did, I would not be able to run away from it—it's like it's already wrapped around me.

Eyes wide, Herlot whipped her hands over the letters. She stood and shuffled over them. Why couldn't her heart stop pounding? She hugged herself and sat down on her mattress. She did her best to slow her breathing. "No more writing out my thoughts," she said out loud, hoping to intimidate whatever had scared her so.

She awoke to the sounds of water boiling in the soup pot and her parents talking about the tide. She stretched and then poured herself a cup before having a seat by the fire. Something was missing. Usually Ambro chattered off into the night about his adventures with the boys, but he was completely quiet. She watched him stir his soup and poke at his potatoes without taking a bite.

"Are you sick, son?" Ernest asked.

"No. Just tired," Ambro snapped.

"What did you and the boys do today?" Ilvy asked.

No answer.

"Did you race? Did you beat Elvin?" Herlot asked. Usually, Ambro talked endlessly about the competitions he had won, such as rock throwing or tree climbing. He must have lost today.

"No."

How could he be so grumpy when Devotio was likely to appear tonight? Surely losing a contest couldn't spoil that.

After supper, her mother checked Ambro's forehead and tongue before setting out with Herlot's father to join the villagers at the hearth after telling them to stay together if they still planned on looking for fireflies. Herlot was grateful that she was allowed to go in the woods at night even if she was still not allowed to go alone. "Ready?" Herlot asked.

"I guess," he mumbled, shrugging.

"Don't forget your tug-of-war rope." All year he had talked about how he wanted to see if he could beat Devotio if he was willing to play.

All the way to the forest, Ambro dragged the rope behind him. He looked as if he had lost the most important game in the world.

"Sing a song so he knows where we are," Herlot said once they were a fair distance into the woods.

"He probably won't come," Ambro said.

"He probably will."

"Won't."

"Will."

"Won't."

"Will. Will. Willwillwillwill."

Herlot froze in her tracks and stared down at her shadow. Shadows needed light, but the moonlight was hidden by a cover of clouds tonight, yet there it was, defined by a glow coming from behind her. Goosebumps spread across her body.

A gentle breeze surrounded her ears. "Will," it said.

She spun around. "Devotio!" She wanted to hug him but had to take in his sight first. He was more beautiful than she remembered. Every part of him defined unlike the blurry edges of her memory.

"Devotio!" Ambro exclaimed, pushing his long, curly hair back. "You came!"

A breeze danced around Herlot's ears. "You can't imagine how delightful it feels to see you. I have thought about you all year. Oh, I just knew you would come," Herlot said. "What do we want to do first? We can't waste a single moment."

"Devotio, I brought my rope. I made it myself. Do you play tug-of-war? I was hoping we could play."

"I have never played the game, but if you teach me, there is nothing I'd like more," Devotio said.

Ambro unwound the rope while Herlot explained the rules. "Simple," Devotio said when she finished. He took one end between his teeth.

Herlot and Ambro tugged with all of their strength but they were no match for Devotio. Ambro flew forward each time, and then held his stomach as he laughed with joy. Herlot had never seen him so happy to lose. "Again?" Devotio asked each time he won.

Herlot played until her palms were sore and then sat against a tree to watch the dance between Ambro and Devotio. *If only it could be like this every night*, she thought as she clapped while Devotio raced in circles around Ambro until Ambro could no longer keep up. Sweat poured off of Ambro, but Devotio only seemed to have more energy.

Finally, Ambro collapsed on his hands and knees. "I give up. Holy Basil, unicorns are strong. Water. I need water."

They headed toward the stream. "Devotio, what have you been doing since we last saw you?" Herlot asked.

"Waiting to see you."

Herlot giggled. "Me, too. Oh, how I wish we wouldn't have to wait another year. It was too long."

"If only you didn't have to hide. I don't know what I'm going to do after tonight. Tug-of-war won't be fun without you," Ambro said.

"I will try to stay a few days," Devotio said.

"That would be a dream come true!" Herlot clicked her heels together. "Was your family upset with you last year?"

"Yes, but they can't make me come back."

"You're never going to tell us where you hide, are you?" Ambro asked.

"No."

Herlot elbowed Ambro in the ribs. "No more questions about that."

The last thing she wanted was Devotio to not come back because they asked too many questions. Herlot was certain that if Devotio ever thought his family was truly at risk of being discovered, he'd never come back.

Once they reached the stream, Ambro practically dunked his entire head in the water. Herlot scooped the water and sipped it out of her palms. As Ambro shook his head, sending water flying in all directions, "So refreshing," he said.

Herlot was happy that he was in a better mood. "What were you upset about before?"

Ambro's mood collapsed and Herlot regretted asking the question. His head hung low and he walked over to a tree and tapped it with the tip of his foot, causing a sprinkle of moss to fall down. "It's all my fault," he blurted. "I didn't bring it high up on the beach enough, and now, it's gone."

"Ambro... What's gone? You're not talking about Rudi's..." She gasped and covered her mouth with one hand. The new boat. Rudi had spent the entire spring and half of summer building it. Her stomach dropped at the thought of it floating out at sea, all alone, and lost forever.

Ambro's lips were trembling. "I'm sorry! I didn't do it on purpose! When we returned to shore, Elvin wanted to race to the tree line. I got caught up in the race and forgot to secure it on the beach. I ran back as fast as I could, but by then the boat was gone."

Herlot paced.

"We can find it," Devotio said.

"How? It's too dark, and the sea is too big. The boat could be anywhere," Ambro said.

"For you, it is dark and big, but not for others," Devotio said.

"Huh?"

Herlot pretended to understand. "Exactly. Now, let's go find the boat."

They trotted farther west than usual to enter the shore, near Enri and Mahtreeh's mother's pine tree. A row of rocks protruded from the sea, extending all the way to where the shallow water ended. Thanks to the alicorn's glow, the seaweed-covered rocks were easy to walk in the dark. When they reached the last rock, Devotio blew into the water. Ripples dispersed across the calm waves.

"They may not come," Devotio said.

"They'll come," Herlot insisted.

"You don't even know who *they* are," Ambro complained.

"Look!" Herlot cried. Off in the distance, a golden glow floated beneath the sea. Then, a gust of water sprayed into the air, tinted with all the colors of a rainbow.

Devotio treaded into the sea until the water reached his neck. "Come. They are safe," he said.

They left their clothing on the rocks and jumped into the water. Herlot took a deep breath and dove under. Several fish swam around her, showing off under Devotio's light. There were also plants that swayed and brushed against her calves. They seemed more colorful than during the day.

Then she looked ahead and almost swallowed water when she saw the three whales. They were pearl white with golden dorsal fins. A mother, a father, and a child. The parents were no less than five times the length of a person. The small one swam ahead, undulating and singing a melody in long, pleasant pitches. As he swam closer, she noticed he had a rope in his mouth.

She broke through the surface and took a gulp of fresh air, noticing the boat trailing behind the child whale. "Ambro! Look!"

Ambro splashed forward, crying, "Rudi's boat! Thank you!"

The whale broke through the water in front of them, and even the good news of Rudi's boat being returned was forgotten as they were mesmerized by the whale's beauty. Herlot and Ambro patted him and he squealed in pleasure.

"My! Look at you! You are so beautiful," said Ambro.

"Puff," Herlot sounded after he exhaled. His breath was so powerful it blew her hair back.

"He's a pearl whale," Devotio said, closeby. "His kind were here long before any of us, and they hold all the secrets of the sea. It's rare for them to show themselves to land creatures, especially humans."

The whale opened his mouth, releasing the rope until it floated into Ambro's hand. Then he disappeared underwater and they watched his golden glow until it reunited with his parents, after which they swam away singing their melody in harmony until all Herlot could hear was the whoosh of the waves.

Ambro wrapped his arms around Devotio and didn't release for a long time. "Thank you," he said against his neck. Ambro stepped into the boat, holding his balance perfectly as it teetered from side to side. "I need to get it back right away to Alonia. Herlot, I will meet you at home," he said.

"I will come with you," Herlot said.

Ambro shook his head. "This was my mistake and if someone sees me, I don't want you getting in trouble, too."

"But it's so dark. Aren't you afraid to get lost by yourself?"

"A little. But I can do this. All I have to do is row toward the shore and follow the coast." Ambro flexed his arms. "And if I get lost, I'll just keep rowing using my strong muscles and end up home eventually."

After watching Ambro row the boat back toward home, Herlot and Devotio treaded back into the forest.

"Will you tell me an Alonian story?" Devotio asked.

Herlot thought about it. She wasn't good at coming up with new stories, but there certainly were ones she loved. She decided to tell Devotio one of her favorites that her mother had written.

"Once upon a time, a sparrow visited a princess named Kira. It told her that an evil warlock sought her beauty to give to his wife. As long as she didn't tell him her name, he would never succeed, because in order to take her beauty, he needed an invitation to her soul. One day, a prince arrived at her kingdom. She recognized him from her dreams. He knelt before her and asked to know her name so he could ask for her hand in marriage. Her heart overflowed with joy. Her dream was coming true! But then she remembered the sparrow. She searched her heart for trust but couldn't find any for the prince. The prince's face sagged and half of his teeth fell out. No kindness was left in his eyes. It was the warlock, but he could do nothing because she had not told him her name. In the end, she met a prince she had never seen in her dreams but whom she trusted in her heart. They married and ruled the kingdom together, and the warlock was never seen again."

Herlot looked up from braiding Devotio's mane, noticing that every time he exhaled a firefly emerged from its hiding place and flew in the shore's direction. "What are you up to, Devotio?" she asked.

"Errrrr." A tortured moan sounded, and a stick snapped.

Herlot let the braid go, and it unraveled. "Run and hide," she whispered. "Quick. Before someone sees your glow." Then she hid behind a tree, not wanting to get scolded for being out in the woods alone.

The steps came closer and she dared to sneak a peek to see who it was.

Manni appeared from the shadows, marching in a zig-zag, and scratching her nails against the bark of trees in her path.

She must have a horrible belly ache, Herlot thought.

"Please," Manni groaned, "help me. I'll do anything," she said, pulling at the roots of her hair as she gazed up at the night sky.

Herlot was about to leave her hiding place to help, but then froze. Someone else was there—or some*thing*. She couldn't see or hear it, but she could sense it. It felt like the black blanket, back in her home. A lump of fear formed in her stomach, and waves of tension rolled down her arms. Blood pumped through her veins, shouting at her muscles to run, but she was too frightened to move. As Manni passed by, something about the air changed. It felt heavy and sticky. Herlot's ears began to ring with the pulse of her heart. Every instinct in her body was yelling at her not to move, as if her life depended on not being noticed by Manni. As Manni continued farther away, the ringing dissipated.

As soon as Herlot couldn't see Manni anymore, she wrapped her arms around herself and realized she was shaking. The heavy air she had swallowed sat heavy in her stomach. She felt it twist and churn. *Stop it. She just had a belly ache. You are imagining things.*

Devotio's glow approached once more, and she couldn't be more thankful that he had returned. His vast pupils widened and muscles tensed when he saw her. She still hadn't stopped shaking.

"Are you hurt?" he asked.

Before she could answer, he lowered his alicorn over her head and her entire body felt like it was being hugged by a warm glow. The shaking slowed enough for her to speak. "No, I am not hurt. Thank you, this helps."

"What happened?" he asked. "Or do humans get cold even when it is a warm night?"

She wanted to tell him about Manni and that she was speaking to something that was not there, and that the air had not felt right. But what if Herlot had imagined it and frightened him away for no real reason? She'd never see him again. And after tonight, the tug-of-war and meeting the whales, she didn't think she could survive if she never saw him again, even if it was just once a year. A realization swept over her as she realized Manni could have been practicing for her performance. Yes, of course, that was what it was. How could she have been so silly and allow her imagination to throw her into a fright?

"I was just cold. But now I'm better." Her belly was still churning.

"Herlot, if you are sick you need to go back home."

"No, please. It's just a belly ache. I will feel better if I can drink water. Maybe we can go back to the stream? Please, Devotio? I don't want our night to end yet."

Devotio's eyes softened as his lids closed halfway over them. "We can certainly go back to the stream."

They waded through the water, listening to the forest at night. Herlot had always preferred the stream to the sea. The sea was deep and vast, and it stretched out forever. The stream was shallow, and she could see what lay beneath. It was comforting after what had happened to Manni in the forest, especially because she could watch her and Devotio's reflection in the stream thanks to his alicorn's glow.

"Devotio, can I ask you a question? It doesn't have to do with your hiding spot."

"Yes."

"How does your alicorn glow?"

Devotio stopped and bowed slightly forward—her signal to climb off. She shivered when the water poured into her sandals, but it was more refreshing than discomforting.

Devotio seemed to be searching for something, his gaze intent on the landscape around them. Along the stream were tall, thin trees whose branches began high up. Purple fog floated between the trunks as an owl hooted.

Devotio exhaled in the direction of the hoot. Out of the fog, an owl descended with its wings spread wide. Herlot gasped as she settled on her head. She could feel the sharpness of her talons on her scalp.

"Close your eyes and look up," Devotio said.

Herlot followed Devotio's directions and felt herself ascending. She opened her eyes to a new night world, seeing through the owl's eyes. Everything was crisp and sharp. A spider sat in the moss of the birch trunk. Bristling sounded to her right. Her head pivoted. A mouse had caught her foot in a spread of weeds.

At the edge of her vision was Devotio's light, but she had to pivot her head again to center her vision on him. In a flash, his body began to blur and she could see through him. Below his shoulder, she saw his heart. And what a heart it was. It was gold and pumped a golden elixir. It looked like a golden stream flowing through his body where blood vessels would be. The elixir navigated to his forehead, filling his alicorn and transforming into a mist as it beamed outward.

The owl closed her eyes, and Herlot saw only black as she descended back into her body. The owl flapped her wings and lifted off into the fog.

Herlot, calm and content, traced the path from Devotio's heart to his forehead. "Your heart creates the glow. It is golden," she concluded.

"Everything magical originates from the heart," Devotio said.

Herlot swallowed down a lump in her throat. Her father always told her stories came from the heart. And she still had a story to come up with for tomorrow. The most important day in a little Alonian girl's life and she had struggled all summer to even remember that it was coming. Oh, how she wished writing a story were more important to her. It would take a miracle to make it a good one with only from now until the next night to write it. "If only my heart was golden. Then I could write a magical story for tomorrow."

"What is this story you have to write?"

Herlot explained to Devotio about Alonia's rite of passage tradition and how she still had a blank scroll for the occasion.

"Meet me here tomorrow at noon. We will ride farther downstream where your villagers won't see us and I will help you write your story."

Herlot clasped her hands to her heart. This was her miracle. If a unicorn's help couldn't make her write a good story, then she was eternally doomed. But she was certain that with Devotio's help she wouldn't make a fool of herself, and most important of all, she wouldn't disappoint her parents.

"Tomorrow. Noon. I will be there," she said.

When Herlot came home, Ambro stirred. "Are Mother and Father back?" he asked, yawning.

"No, not yet."

"You know, the nicest thing happened on my row back. All of these fireflies showed up and it was much easier to see. They stayed with me the entire time until I got home."

Herlot remembered how all the fireflies she and Devotio encountered in the woods began to fly in the direction of the shore. Devotio must have sent them.

CHAPTER 7
The Firefly Poem

HERLOT HAD A BEAUTIFUL summer day, a unicorn, and even that wasn't helping her story. Her scroll was as empty as it had been all summer.

How could she write anything when there was so much happening in the forest? The wind was unpredictable. One moment, all they could hear was the water running over the rocks, and then a strong gust would send a bristle through the trees, leaving the branches bouncing after it had passed.

"I am a prisoner trapped with no way out," Herlot said.

"You are free to move around as much as you'd like. It's not that bad. Just try to focus. Maybe try a story about birds."

Herlot gazed after the flock of birds that flew from a family of trees across the stream. A shiver went through her body at the feeling of freedom that the birds had to be experiencing. "Not as free as them, Devotio. They have wings. They can soar through the skies."

"You are right," Devotio said. She glanced over at him, her heart sinking at his sad expression of longing as he watched the flock disappear over the canopy.

"You miss your wings, don't you, Devotio?"

He bowed his head, as if ashamed. "I never had them. I was born during the massacres, after my mother and father had already lost theirs. I came into the world without wings."

Herlot was shocked at how willingly Devotio had shared this piece of information with her, but even more, she felt sorrow for how much he had lost, or rather, never even had a chance to lose. Once again, she was reminded of how much of a risk Devotio was willing to take. Humans and unicorns had once been the best of companions, but when the humans began their lust for gold, they didn't care about their friendships with the unicorns anymore. Hunting them for alicorns was horrifying, yes, but Herlot could imagine how awfully it must have hurt to lose a companion, a friendship that was supposed to last forever. In the legend, it had hurt the unicorns so much that they had lost their wings. She couldn't believe Devotio was interested in her at all knowing the level of betrayal her kind was capable of. Her hand flew to her chest and she pressed her palm against her heart. "I-I'm so sorry."

He nuzzled against her cheek. "No need to be sorry. It is better that I never had them. This way I don't miss them. Now focus on your story."

Herlot scratched the side of his jaw as she looked down at her empty roll of parchment. She raised her shoulders and huffed, trying to fight the tension that had been growing in her for the last few days. "I hate tradition," she said.

Writing letters was not Herlot's problem. Hers were neat and legible, although hardly anyone knew that, since Manni always managed to shuffle her feet over Herlot's writing when they practiced with sticks in the dirt. Once Simon walked by and complimented Manni on her dancing skills instead of scolding her. But that was the least of Herlot's worries.

The pressure was tremendous. Almost all of her father's stories had been written on parchment. The villagers had talked about Ambro's sea creature at each hearth gathering for a good three seasons after his recitation. Now, three years later, it was considered a classic, and it was her turn to show everyone that she was her father's daughter. After everything she had put her family through because of the ghost rumors, this was her chance to prove to the village that she was a true Alonian, not just a strange girl who had troubles playing with the other children.

Manni was performing today, too, and all winter, she had boasted about how much better her performance was going to be. Herlot didn't mind if Manni's performance was better; she was just afraid it would highlight the tragedy of hers.

Herlot focused on her reflection rippling back at her in the water. Her blond hair was tangled. The wind was never gentle to it, especially after riding Devotio. It left her hair in knots she had to rip apart, and then it looked like parts of it had been chiseled by the fire. She sighed, her closed lips vibrating as the sound escaped.

She would have to find some way to not look a mess for the performance compared to Manni. The last thing her parents needed on top of her horrible performance were remarks about how unkempt she was. Herlot tried running her finger through a tangle. "Ouch!" she exclaimed.

All of a sudden, Devotio pressed his alicorn against her scalp and twirled it in circles so a strand of hair came free. Untangled now from the rest, it lay in a gracious wave when she checked her reflection.

"It's a masterpiece!" she cried.

When all of her hair fell in waves, she shook her head from side to side, enjoying the strands gliding over one another.

For this Devotio deserved all the berries she had in her pocket. While he ate out of her palm, she shared her ideas out loud. "Let's see... How about a story about a farmer who is upset because the rain won't come, but then one day, it does and he lives happily ever after?"

She raised her eyebrows expecting Devotio's approval, but he dropped his head, pretending to sleep.

"Boring? But imagine if you were the farmer! I'm sure you'd find the rain very exciting." She crossed her arms. "It's boring. You're right."

Instead of trying again, she took turns winking her eyes as quickly as possible. "The new baby who was born wiggles her nose when she looks up at the sun. I wish I could do it, too." Herlot concentrated on her nose, looking at it first from one eye and then the other. "When I wink like this, it almost looks like my nose is wiggling!"

Devotio didn't react. "I know, I know. I should concentrate better," she said.

She continued to share her ideas until she felt utterly helpless, lying on the grass and looking up at the sky in defeat.

"I have no talent for storytelling," she said.

"You will be better off showing the Alonians your winking," Devotio said.

"Hey! You're supposed to be encouraging," she laughed. "Wouldn't that be a sight. Everyone having to watch me wink until the fire dimmed. At least I have our story, even though I can't share it with the village. It's the only story I really care about. Say, I have been thinking about the legend my father told me. He said that it was only after the boy came back without his unicorn that the humans began to change. What do you suppose happened to him? Do you know? Does your family?"

Devotio remained silent.

Herlot's face sank. "You don't trust me," she stated. She understood Devotio had secrets and the only reason he could spend time with her was if they remained secrets. But it hurt knowing she couldn't be a trusted friend for him, that she was a risk. Could it ever be a real friendship if they couldn't trust one another?

"I do...but my family doesn't. You knowing our secrets could lead other humans to us if you ever told, and you remember what humans did to unicorns in the legend, don't you? The stories my family tells are awful. It was like their human companions didn't recognize them anymore, as if they weren't real, and all that counted was our golden alicorns. These humans, not strangers, but our cherished companions that knew our hearts looked at us as if we weren't even real."

"Your family must think I'm awful."

"That is not true. My family just wants to be safe, and they worry about you," Devotio said.

"They...worry. About *me?*"

"They worry that us playing together in the woods will not be enough for you, that you will want to understand how my story fits into your world. They fear that our friendship has only one result—that you will become confused without answers to your questions. Confusion is a painful emotion, especially for someone your age, and it will be best for me to leave you alone. As much as I would like, I cannot give you answers, Herlot. The less you know, the safer my family is and the better it is for you. I trust you now, but what if you learn my secrets and then change as you grow older just like the humans in the past changed? You could tell other people that we still exist, and bring them with you to wait for us at our hiding spot to hunt us for our alicorns. Or perhaps you wouldn't be interested in the hunt, but you might drink the strong ale and tell someone who can't be trusted with the information, and then they would seek our hiding place."

She took a shaky breath. "You have to tell them, please, please, please, that I don't need to know any more as long as you don't go away. I will never do anything to put you in danger. You're safe with me. Tell them I promise."

"I will. But now you must get back to work," Devotio said.

"Right. Oh, and I won't ever, ever, ever change. Ever."

The sun continued to sink in the sky, but Herlot's quill still had not done any work. What would happen if she stood in front of everyone with nothing to recite? She dropped her head into her hands, pressing into the headache pulsing through her forehead. "I'd do anything to make them proud like they were when Ambro recited."

At that, Devotio dipped his alicorn into the ink and then glided it over the parchment. Herlot's jaw dropped as she watched the most beautiful, perfectly shaped letters form into a poem.

Herlot picked it up and held it close to her face. She soaked in its magic, reading every line twice. It was perfect. She hugged Devotio tight. "I am so lucky to have you. Thank you. You don't know how much this means to me."

She began reciting the poem, forming a bond with each word so that when it was time, they would roll off her tongue as smoothly as the curves of the letters.

At sundown, Herlot skipped into Alonia, her hands clasped behind her back, whistling a tune. Once home, she ate a quick supper and then her mother helped her change into her new dress. It was still made of plain, colorless fabric like she always wore, but it was clean and new—and without rips or holes. This dress would last her many years, and her mother had woven it especially for the recitation.

She reached into the old dress's pocket for the parchment, but her hand pushed through a hole at the bottom. Her heart beat faster and she tried the other pocket, hoping a miracle would be on her side. No parchment. She took a breath and checked the first one again, hoping that somehow magically the hole had disappeared and the parchment was still there. No luck.

"Mother, I must run. I'll see you at the hearth," she cried.

Herlot retraced her steps, but the parchment was nowhere to be found. She went as far back as the stream and then into Alonia's paths and even inside the chicken shack. The wind must have taken the parchment far away. It could be anywhere now.

"You can recite it from memory," she reassured herself. She did not have another choice.

• • •

Ambro and Elvin sat at the hearth, a cloth with acorns between them. Ambro leaned back on his hands, remembering his successful performance and how some of the mothers had covered their children's ears at the scary parts. That trick never worked.

He felt like a king—his story was now a legend everyone tried to beat, he was Elvin's best friend, and, he would get to watch Manni during her entire performance without the risk of him saying something stupid. But even though life was great, he couldn't help noticing that something felt empty, something he chose to ignore because a solution seemed worlds away.

Herlot took a seat next to him without saying hello. Her head bobbed around as she muttered undecipherable words. It was probably best not to distract her. Out the corner of his eye he caught Elvin watching her. There was something he recognized in that look, almost like—no, it couldn't be. For a moment Elvin had reminded Ambro of himself watching Manni.

He straightened the moment he saw Manni walk to the center—her walk was so graceful—smiling down at the people she passed. She pulled a piece of parchment out of her pocket, unrolled it, and then began the first phrase. At the same moment, Herlot grabbed his forearm and dug her nails into his skin. "Hey," he hissed as he opened his mouth to yell at her, but then heard her stomach churn. She was about to be sick.

"Go," he whispered, nudging her.

He squeezed his fist, hoping she could hold it while she rushed out, crouching so as not to block anyone's view of Manni, who had paused, causing everyone to watch Herlot. He sighed once his sister was out of sight, and turned all his attention to Manni who began her poem again from the beginning.

Ambro hadn't thought Manni would recite a poem. Somehow, it made her that much more enchanting. He leaned forward, supporting his weight with his elbows on the tops of his thighs, and listened.

Amidst the firefly flow between the leaves of a willow,
An enchanted world unveils below their illuminating glow.
Vagabond faeries rest upon blades of grass,
and children sleep in their mothers' laps.
Then come the working faeries singing celebratory chants,
Who, at the end of the day, wish nothing but to dance.
The one with the fiddle loves the one who whistles.
And the one who sings riddles,
Has a middle that tends to jiggle.
But, out of all the places,
Venture to the lake, where the fireflies have their races.
It is not enchanted faeries you will see beneath their flow,
But your very own reflection that makes the fireflies' hearts
glow.

Ambro clapped and cheered as Manni curtsied.

"One more time! One more time!" Simon hollered.

To Ambro's surprise, Manni didn't recite again, even though so many were asking for it. She seemed to be looking for someone in the crowd. She curtsied once more and ran off before anyone could get to her, strangely in the same direction Herlot had gone.

● ● ●

Herlot gave a final heave after Manni recited the last line of Devotio's poem, her supper spilling onto the thistles below. She leaned against the cool wall of Rudi's home, concentrating on how the stone conformed perfectly to the shape of the back of her neck.

Suddenly, cold fingers wrapped around her throat and her eyes flew open. Manni stared back at her. But these weren't Manni's eyes. Manni's eyes were teal—these were only black pupils that engulfed the irises. Herlot struggled to back away, but the wall stopped her.

"If you tell anyone," she hissed, "I will show them this." She displayed the parchment, pointing to the perfect writing. "This is not your writing. I will tell them the ghost possessed you."

A twig snapped close by and the black pupils retreated, revealing her teal eyes once more.

Herlot's hand went to her throat where Manni's hands had just been, as Ambro jogged out of the shadows. "What happened?" he asked, looking back and forth between them. "Manni, what are you doing?"

"Just giving a friend advice before her performance. Herlot, if you stand more to the left, Simon's whistle won't make your ear pop like it did mine," she said and left.

Ambro put his hand on top of Herlot's shoulder. "Did something happen between you two?" he asked, the worry clear on his features.

Her heart was still pounding. What was she supposed to say? That Manni had attacked her and that her eyes had been black? Would he believe her or just ask her if she had taken her shoes off again? And there was also the fact that Manni loved to talk about Herlot being haunted. If she told Ambro, or anyone for that matter, they'd think she was trying to get back at Manni. And what if Manni was just being her normal, cruel self and Herlot had just imagined her pupils? After all, she had had a daydream nightmare about the black blanket the other day...

She thought about telling Ambro that Manni had stolen her poem, but the truth was that it was Devotio's, and it wasn't her poem to have stolen. Part of her was glad the villagers had gotten to hear it either way. But all of this was aside from the real problem she had been avoiding.

"I don't have a story or poem," she said, "and I don't think I want to, either." Finally admitting it to someone felt even better than the cool stone against her back.

"Oh." Ambro leaned against the wall next to her. "I'm not sure what to say."

Herlot chuckled. "Nothing like brotherly advice," she said, swaying her shoulder against his.

Ambro chuckled and then seemed to go deep into thought. "You know what I would do?" he said, breaking the silence. "I'd go up there anyway and show them I'm not scared, and that I'm not doing anything awful by not reciting anything."

"That's easy for you to say. Your story was the best use of ink since Father's."

"True," Ambro said with pride, but then his face sank. "But do you really think that matters? There's a whole world out there, and we don't matter a single bit. There're people out there having real adventures on real ships. There are real princesses in real velvet dresses, dancing in real ballrooms. There're soldiers fighting real battles for things that have an actual meaning. And here we are, doing the same thing every day, and the only time we ever experience anything new is through a stupid story."

Herlot was dumbfounded. Ambro had never expressed these things before. He was clearly riled up—his chest rising and falling as if he had finished a race.

"Ambro—"

"So go out there, Herlot. How they react doesn't mean anything. Show them they can't get to you," he said. Then he wiped the sweat off his brow and headed back toward the hearth.

"Wait!" Herlot called.

Ambro turned and walked backwards.

"Out there, sailors sail ships and princesses dance in ballrooms, but only we have Devotio," she offered.

A sad smile spread across his face. "We do." He winked and walked off, leaving Herlot alone.

She took a few moments to gather herself. Ambro was right. She wasn't doing anything wrong by not having anything to recite. She might not be like everyone, but not telling a story or poem did not make her a bad person.

● ● ●

Back at the hearth, she felt every eye on her as she stepped over feet that didn't move aside for her.

"She was probably talking to the ghost," someone whispered.

Herlot didn't bother rolling her eyes. Silently, she dared every villager to make another comment. Her heart swelled as she felt her mother squeeze her hand when she passed by her.

Now by the fire, Herlot folded her hands in front of her and looked at firelight flashing across the faces of her audience. She was certain many of them were eager for her to make a fool of herself, but what was also true was that she had decided to be honest, and as nervous as she was about upsetting her parents, she knew it was the best she could do.

She cleared her throat. "Thank you, everyone, for coming to listen to my recitation. I'm sorry to disappoint you tonight, but I don't have anything to recite for you. I really love and enjoy listening to stories and telling the ones I like, but I do not wish to make up any of my own. I wish everyone a good night and congratulate Manni on reciting the beautiful poem," she announced.

Someone snickered, but it was overridden by Ambro, Elvin, and Rudi, who were standing, clapping, and cheering. To Herlot's surprise, Merle, Agatha, and Simon joined them. This was unexpected, indeed.

"I'd like this written on the best parchment in the village!" Elvin hooted.

Herlot covered her mouth to hide her smile, but when she looked at her parents, she had to suppress sobs. They were standing shoulder to shoulder, clapping the kind of claps that made one's hands hurt. They weren't mad. They weren't upset. Their eyes beamed with love and...pride? How could this be?

The other Alonians began to scatter, probably confused by the peculiar situation. But they didn't say anything unkind, at least from what she could hear. They resorted to circling around Manni, congratulating her, hanging necklaces made of seashells on her, and serving her a cup of strong ale.

Herlot stumbled through the crowd.

When she spotted her mother, she ran into her arms. "I'm sorry," she said into her shoulder.

"It's alright, my child. I'm not upset. I promise," she assured. Then she brushed a loose strand of hair from Herlot's face. "You're my daughter. I love you, with or without stories and poems," she said.

Her father patted her on the back. "With or without stories and poems," he repeated.

In that moment, Herlot felt ashamed for not realizing how much they really loved her and how she could have been honest with them from the beginning. They weren't against her, and based on the look in their eyes, she knew they were proud of her, too. She could be the least traditional Alonian girl in the village, and she'd still be their daughter. Even though she had caused her mother pain from worry, her mother still wanted her. And her father, someone who would go down as a legend of storytelling in their village, looked at her as if he saw his own self in her, even though she hadn't been able to write a single, original word. She didn't know if she was deserving of this kind of love. She didn't know what the future would hold for her in the village in not having completed her rite of passage. She knew where her heart was and where she wanted to be—in the forest with Devotio, but that she could only do once a year. Whatever it was that her future held, she hoped she would never take her parents' love for granted...or betray it.

● ● ●

The next morning, Herlot woke in high spirits. While helping Rudi and Ambro gather sticks in the woods, she picked blueberries for Devotio. After Devotio had written the firefly poem, he had said that he would stay one more day and that they were to meet after sundown by the stream. She wouldn't miss it for anything.

Ambro hummed a tune the entire time, only stopping once in a while to yawn. He had been awake the entire night with the other children by tradition to celebrate Manni's recitation. He worked slow, stopping every few beats to stare off into space with a hypnotized smile on his face. Herlot hoped he'd be able to stay awake long enough to meet Devotio one last time.

"Somebody's in love," Rudi said as he checked a wheel on Herlot's cart.

Herlot raised her eyebrows. "What?"

Rudi pointed at Ambro smiling up at a cloud. "That look," Rudi said and then chuckled.

Who could Ambro be in love with? Her stomach sank. She had seen that look a few other times before on Ambro, and each time he had been around Manni when he did it. She shook her head. No. It couldn't be. Yes, she was beautiful, but hadn't he heard how she treated Mahtreeh the year before? Herlot's hand touched the side of her neck. How she wished he could have seen how frightening she had been last night. No. Ambro couldn't be in love with Manni.

"Stop speaking nonsense. He's just tired," she snapped.

Rudi lifted his hands in front of his chest. "Alright, then. He is just tired." Then he chuckled again and went back to work.

For the rest of their time working, she tried her best to keep the awful idea of Ambro in love with Manni out of her mind. Instead, she thought about Devotio, Ambro, and her having another adventure in the forest.

Once they were out of the woods and pushing their carts alongside the wheat field, she caught up to Ambro. "We should tell Mother and Father that we want to go look for fireflies again. Do you have your tug-of-war rope ready?"

Ambro rolled his eyes. "I think it's time we stop playing games. We have to grow up some day, right?"

"Well, we don't have to play games. We can just go for a ride and look at the forest," she suggested.

"Just stop. I don't want to play the Devotio game," he replied, grinding his teeth.

She pushed her handcart in front of his, forcing him to stop. "Devotio is not a game. He is our *friend*," she hissed, trying not to raise her voice in fear of the others overhearing.

Ambro leaned his head over his cart. "Herlot, sometimes you take these things too far. It worries me and I worry that you really might think it's all real. Devotio," he articulated, "is not real. We made him up." Then he pulled his cart backward and went around Herlot's to catch up with Manni and Elvin working between a row of wheat.

Herlot stood frozen in place. Each word Ambro had said pounded against her forehead. Her head had never ached this much before, but the pain was the least of her worries. Devotio? Not real?

Her cart tipped and thudded to the ground, several pieces of wood spilling out onto the meadow as she raced toward the vegetable garden.

"Mother," she called out as she arrived.

Ilvy and the other women looked up from the cabbage they were picking.

"Where is Father?" Herlot demanded.

Ilvy looked around. "I don't know. What's—"

Herlot kicked her sandals off, one falling into a patch of carrots, and took off toward their home. She looked around, not noticing how her feet swiveled against the dirt ground. *The shore.* She didn't know where the thought had come from, but she knew she'd find him there.

Sand kicked up as she ran across the beach. "Father! Wait!" she called, running through the water, trying to catch up to her father, who was rowing away.

Seaweed wrapped around her ankles and held her back as she tried to kick up to swim. Thankfully, he had already turned the boat around and was heading toward her when she finally managed to slip away from the sea grass's grasp. As their paths intersected, she held on to the edge of the boat, the water up to her shoulders.

"Father...the legend you told us when we were kids, the one about the unicorns, do you remember it?"

"Of course." He balanced and reached his hand out to help her into the boat.

She ignored it. "Where did you get it from? Oliver? Cloudian? I need to speak to them."

Ernest frowned. "Well, you can speak to me. It's my story. I made it up before my first recitation. Now, please, come into the boat. The water is freezing today."

"You said it was a legend," she said, her voice having lost its urgency, "and that it could be true."

Her father looked down and shame seemed to engulf his features. "I never thought you would remember so well," he said. "I had only wanted to make you happy when you asked to hear about a real magical creature. I didn't have the heart to tell you then that there weren't any—"

Before her father could finish, she was already swimming toward shore.

Herlot wandered by the stream all day, calling for Devotio every few moments, but he didn't show up. "He's real. He has to be," she repeated, even though, deep down inside, she knew that Ambro had spoken her greatest fear out loud.

She sat, hugging her knees to her chest, watching the reflection of the sky until the day turned to night.

First, she felt him behind her, and then the area illuminated from his light.

"I have good news. My family agreed that I may leave once every moon. They took to heart your promise," Devotio's words wrapped around her ears.

She ran to him, sweeping her hands over his mane. "You're real, you're real," she repeated. "Are you not?"

But her thoughts spun. What if she was imagining this? How could she know if he was real? She could check his reflection in the water. That would assure her.

"Devotio, come to the water. I need to make sure," she said.

He backed away. She took a step toward him, reaching her hand out. He lowered his muzzle so his alicorn was pointing straight at her. His ears flattened, and a wild look came over his eyes as he swaggered back.

"Wait!" But he was already gone, having ran away faster than she had ever seen. She didn't understand. What had she done wrong? Why had he run away? And when would he return?

Every day and every night for the rest of the summer, Herlot went into the forest taking turns visiting the meadow, the pine tree, the western shore, and the stream. But Devotio never came. He said he could come once every moon. Why was he not coming?

One morning she snuck Rudi's carving knife out of his wooden chest. He wouldn't miss it while eel searching, and she'd return it before he returned. She marched to the stream, determined to follow through with her intentions. It was evident that the forest conformed to Devotio, but it didn't to her hair. It only helped her collect twigs, leaves, bugs, and an astounding amount of tangles. When he returned, it would be easier for her to go for a ride without having to worry about her hair. Just the other day while waiting for Devotio, she had climbed a tree to examine a bird's nest and nearly fallen out because a strand of her hair got caught in a branch and pulled her back.

She lowered to her knees and stared at her reflection in the water. She imagined the reflections of the villagers next to it, telling her to stop. "I know I'm breaking another tradition," she said. "But you would understand if you knew what it was like to ride a unicorn." She brought the knife several spaces away from the roots of her hair and cut. Within moments, golden strands fell into the water and floated downstream. She shook her head from side to side, delighted at how alive each strand felt, free of the weight it had carried for so many years.

She touched her reflection on the nose. "Good work." Then, ignited by the bounce in her hair, she skipped into the forest, calling for her best friend. "Devotio," she sang. Nothing.

As the leaves changed color, she visited less and less. The last day she went out to call for Devotio was when all the leaves had fallen. She wandered the stream, remembering the time he had shown her his golden heart.

"Sister." She turned to look at Ambro just as he began wading through the water.

She waited in silence until he reached her and then they began walking through the stream together, the only conversation between them that of the swishing and splashing their steps were making when coming in contact with the water. A breeze sent a dried leaf Herlot's way and it glided off her hair and into the water. It looked like it was desperately wanting to drink, but even being submerged in the stream wouldn't bring its colors back.

"You're still looking for him, aren't you?" Ambro broke the silence.

Herlot shrugged. She didn't really know what she was doing. She only knew one thing for certain, and that was that she missed her friend and that she was somewhat afraid of herself. How could she have believed in a figment of her imagination for so long? Was there something wrong with her? And why had Ambro allowed it to go on for so long? "Why didn't you say something sooner?"

Ambro sighed and stuffed his hands into his tunic pockets, slouching as if he was embarrassed of what he was about to say. His voice was quiet when he spoke, and she had to lean toward his side to hear. "Because you were happy."

"Happy." She was at a loss for words.

"Yes. Happy."

She stopped in her tracks and dug her toes into the muddy bottom to ground herself. "Happy? Ambro! You thought that allowing me to be—" she finally had to confront the word. "*Delusional* was a good idea because it made me happy?"

She put her hands on her hips, waiting for his explanation as he stopped to face her.

"Well, I didn't think you *really* believed it!" He raised his hands in the air. "I thought you were just playing. Sure, I thought it was strange when you wouldn't stop, but you've always been different and alone a lot. And skies forbid, yes, I thought it was alright if at least you had your imagination for company because being alone and happy is a lot better than being alone."

In a flash, Herlot's legs felt like porridge and she sank to her knees. She felt the water flow over her thighs and her dress clamp to her as she dropped her face into her palms. "The first night you met him. How did we make it through the forest without light if it wasn't for his alicorn's glow?"

"You had a candle and then the moonlight was unusually bright."

She pressed her palms harder against her face as she saw an image of Ambro, Mahtreeh, Enri, and her skipping through the meadow in a line. "How did we find Enri and Mahtreeh's mother's tree? How could we have known that?"

Ambro's voice was now nearer. He must have squatted down in front of her. "We didn't. It was a coincidence. We pretended he had something to show us and we just so happened to stumble upon a pine tree. Then Mahtreeh and Enri took over the pretending from there."

"The boat?"

"I knew the tide at that time of the year could have taken it there."

"How did we make it out on the rocks without being able to—"

"Candles," they said together. The skin on Herlot's cheeks sagged as she dropped her hands into her lap. She shook her head from side to side as she spoke. "And what do I do with myself now? I don't think I'm well, Ambro. How...how do I know what to trust if I can't even trust myself?"

Ambro's expression turned serious. "You can trust yourself. I've known you my entire life. You're different but you're healthy. Listen to me, Herlot. All of us use our imagination to make our lives better. That's what every Alonian story is for. I think it took a lot of courage for a little girl to imagine a unicorn to bring her back home safely when she was lost in the woods during a storm. She just stayed in her imagination a little longer than usual."

Herlot raised her eyebrows.

"Alright. A lot longer than usual," Ambro said. "But now you have a choice. You can forgive yourself and hang on to all our good memories of pretending and come home."

She nodded. Ambro helped her to her feet, put his arm around her waist and started leading her toward Alonia. She pulled away. "Actually, Ambro. I think I need a few moments alone. I won't be long."

Ambro winked. All of a sudden, he broke into a sprint, splashing water all over the place. When he reached the shore, he began mimicking a horse gallop. He lunged into the air, raised his fist toward a branch, and howled at the top of his lungs. "Come on, Devotio! Faster!" he shouted. Herlot waited, chuckling, until she could hear his cheers no more.

Herlot closed her eyes and stretched her hand out in front of her, imagining touching Devotio's golden heart. He seemed so real in her mind—she could still sense the softness of his coat. When she opened her eyes, a small part of her still hoped he might have appeared, but he hadn't. There was nothing there except for space and the forest around her.

She crossed her arms and took a deep breath of fresh air as her lips stretched into a sad smile.

"You're not coming back," she said, serenely, scanning the sky and the tree canopies. "Goodbye, Devotio."

CHAPTER 8
The Mound

VINCENT SAT HUNCHED WITH his elbows on his knees on a bench, disguised in a commoner's cloak. It was a crisp early morning, busier than most. An influx of people from outside the city were setting up for Damalathum's annual flower market.

Vincent had no interest in flowers, but this was an opportunity. For several years he had searched for something of a magical nature to present to King Felix, without success. Perhaps today he would discover something he could use. After all, the people outside the city had nothing better to do than chat about superstition. Most of it was rubbish, but he was desperate, and he hoped that a desperate yet determined man like him would eventually run into some luck. He could already see himself, wrapped in a cloak of luck, one that announced to all around that life had specifically decided to unfold in a way to favor him, to make him the one who found the magical tool that King Felix was searching for and would make Isolda the most powerful kingdom in the world. Much better than watching water bowls.

He searched through bits and pieces of the conversations around him.

"Don't drop that."

"Excuse me, Miss, do you know where the nearest well is? My roses need fresh water."

"He knew better. The space has been marked for ages and only fools go near dark magic during the night." Vincent raised his head.

"Look at the colors of those lilies. Even the queen would want those!"

"Will you save a garland for me? I can't pay for it right now but will at the end of the day."

"He made it three steps and dropped dead. They say his heart burst."

Vincent dropped his hood and marched toward the woman who had spoken of the dark magic and bursting heart. She held a vase of marigolds to her chest and took a step back as if protecting it from him. He realized she thought he was a thief, so he undid the clasp of his cloak to reveal his surcoat, which bore the Felixian Coat of Armor—a single chess piece: the king.

"Come with me," he said.

The woman's mouth dropped open, and others looked with envy at the marigolds, apparently believing she had been chosen to present her vase to the queen. Vincent withheld a sigh at how naïve they were. If only they knew how much work, but mostly luck, it took to get noticed by the royals. However, at least the woman did not put up a fight as he guided her to the garrison headquarters. She kept her gaze down at her vase and mumbled words of encouragement to the flowers. "The moment you bloomed I knew you were beautiful enough to be seen by the Queen. Don't worry, I am sure she'll find a good new home for you. Perhaps by a window in her royal quarters?"

It was evening when he finally escorted her back to her stand. He shouldn't have because it meant King Felix would wait that much longer for his news. He didn't understand himself. For years, he had climbed the ranks of Damalathum's garrison while hunting for the magic King Felix was seeking to use as a weapon against Ipta. He had developed an eerie patience, unlike the others in King Felix's private circle of special persons trusted with his plans against Ipta, who presented him with every nuisance under the sun, claiming it was magic. Vincent chose to be smarter and waited instead of striking too soon with something hopeless just for the sake of showing Felix he was trying. He wanted to ensure that if he did strike, it would be with gold: something with the potential to attack Ipta.

Now his goal was accomplished. He had imagined this moment differently—some glorious fulfillment or at least a celebratory atmosphere, but he felt only a hollowness. As for the woman, he felt sorry for her. All day he had questioned her until her throat was sore and her marigolds had wilted.

He observed her state when they reached her empty stand. Oily strands of hair had fallen out of her bun, and her cheeks sagged. The market was over, and she had not sold a single flower. She should have been enraged, threatening him in some way for the loss he had caused her. But she didn't. He may not have been a general like Dartharus, but she had no power next to him. Her only choice was to allow her emotions to boil over inside of her because if she spoke against him, he had every right to harm her in any way he pleased. Part of him wanted to tell her that he wouldn't do that. That he wasn't like that. But instead he took two gold coins from his pouch, placed them on her stand, and left.

● ● ●

King Felix slouched in his throne, picking at his nails and deciding which mistress would join him in a lavender-water bath that evening. He was not amused, because he could have been in his porcelain tub now had it not been for Dartharus's plea to wait because the garrison guard, Vincent, had news. Vincent. Felix was particularly fond of the guard, especially since the day he came out of the dungeon as a child. The first thing Vincent had done was get on his knees and kiss Felix's feet. Felix was a good king, hence why he would always reward those most loyal to him. Vincent's loyalty had earned him the place to be the only garrison guard trusted with Felix's plans for Ipta.

For four years, there had been "news." Palm readers, oversized or contorted body parts, and snakes controlled by music. Once Dartharus had proposed using a love potion on an Iptan woman in hopes that she would yield secrets, but she had shown no interest in anything except for a stray dog in the street.

The doors opened and Felix held a blank expression while listening to Vincent's boots pounding on the tiles as he approached. *Don't disappoint me now.* The man had confidence, he had to give him that. Most of the people slouched their shoulders and tapped their fingertips together when they neared him about magical findings.

Vincent knelt in front of Felix and bowed his head. A strong bow with shoulder blades pulled back, Felix noted. Confident in his submission to him. "Speak," Felix ordered.

For the next half hour, Felix listened to how in a village east of Damalathum people spoke of a cursed mound in the center of a field. Anyone who stepped past a certain point, toward the mound, died on the spot. For their safety, the people had marked the border of the field with stones, but once in a while, a drunkard or travelers who didn't listen to warnings stumbled in. There were plenty of skeletons scattered within the field.

Evidence and possibilities. Finally, information that sounded promising to Felix. And he had more than enough persons at his disposal to experiment with. "Gather the prisoners due for execution. We set out at once."

● ● ●

Sunrise was hours away when Vincent tapped his heels against the side of his horse. He glanced behind him at the disappearing city, noticing the group of horsemen trailing him and the rocking carriage where King Felix and General Dartharus sat. They had comfort inside there, but he had the fresh air and a leader's view in front of him.

Soldiers in training spoke often of the things they would see in their travels across lands only to learn that it was mainly a daunting journey of staring at a man's back or worse, a horse's, which made avoidance of stepping in droppings a higher priority over enjoying the scenery. But riding at the head was a different story. This was where Vincent belonged.

For four days they rode east, and he was always the first one people gawked at as they stepped aside to clear the path—mothers holding their children at their sides, men nodding their heads, and young women whispering in each other's ears as he rode by.

However, as they neared their destination, more and more commoners dared not to clear his path. "Near the village of Elfolk is a haunted mound. Mind the omens surrounding it if you wish to live," they would say.

They arrived near nightfall, climbing the hill to the field where the supposed mound lay. A hidden owl hooted in an isolated tree, the only sign of life nearby.

Vincent lowered his torch and saw the omens in front of his feet. He walked along the perimeter, careful not to near any of them. They consisted of simple things like rocks and worn shoes, but there were also skulls. Up ahead, where their torchlight could not reach, a shadow rose from the ground. Every instinct within Vincent urged him to leave. The wind blew at his back, enhancing the goose bumps that had risen.

"We will have to wait until morning to see it," Dartharus said, "Shall I arrange for your carriage to be accommodated for a night's rest, my King?"

King Felix just stared toward the shadow, his lips tight. They stood like that for what seemed like an hour waiting for a reaction from King Felix, but he didn't even stir. Eventually Vincent lowered himself onto the ground, leaning back on the grass and closing his eyes, grateful that he didn't have to look at the mound anymore.

The morning sun blared right through Vincent's eyelids, burning at his dream and jolting him awake. In the daylight, instead of a dark shadow, he saw the mound right at the center of the field. It rose a solid story from the ground in hill-like fashion and was covered in grass except for a wooden-plank-lined entrance at the bottom. He noticed how the sun and scattered clouds dissipated the place's haunting atmosphere that had been present during the night.

A distance away, he spotted King Felix and Dartharus. He jumped to his feet and jogged toward them. A garrison guard didn't need time to wake up. But then, a garrison guard should have been the first one awake or not have slept at all.

They didn't acknowledge him as he took his place behind them. The field was scattered with skeletons that he hadn't seen the night before. Based on their locations, Vincent concluded that some had made it farther than others, but not by much, and definitely nowhere near the mound.

Dartharus, his stance relaxed, bit into an apple he took from his traveling pouch. Thrashing his jaw to the right and dismembering the flesh from the core, he then chewed while pointing at the entrance with the hand still holding the apple. "Someone lives there," he observed.

"Mhmm," Felix responded.

Vincent wondered if Felix had taken his eyes off the mound at all since the moment they arrived. His eyes were dry and red. He seemed hypnotized, and Vincent noticed he wasn't blinking.

Vincent began counting to see how many seconds it would take for Felix to blink, when all of a sudden, Felix's body jerked. Felix raised his foot over one of the omens and his body seemed to yield toward the field.

"No!" Vincent shouted. He shoved Dartharus aside, stretching his arm out in front of Felix's chest, almost collapsing into the field himself.

For a split moment, Vincent was swarmed by thoughts of what he had been willing to do for his King. Had it been instinct? Was his desire to rise up in the military so strong that he was willing to risk his life for it? Or, most insane of all, was it because he genuinely cared for another being's life? Absurd. It was simply because he was good at what he had been trained to do.

Felix shook his head, as if he didn't know what had come over him. The hypnotized glare was gone, replaced by an irritated fire. King Felix was back.

"Bring the first prisoner," Felix snapped.

Within moments, Vincent was jabbing a thin man with tangled, long red hair and a mustache up the hill to the field. His name? It didn't matter. He was a thief sentenced to death and his struggle to hold his balance, most likely due to the muscle that had withered away while being held captive in a cell, irritated Vincent and he jabbed him even harder for it. Vincent hated this man's weakness, his inability to make a fortune in a dignified manner, and his withered state. This man was the last person in the world Vincent would ever want to be.

When they reached the field, the prisoner's legs froze, his head shaking from side to side.

"Walk," Dartharus commanded.

The man took a step backward.

"I said walk!" Vincent shouted and kicked him forward.

The prisoner fell past the omens, catching himself with his hands at which he hissed as a crack originated from the area of his stick thin wrists. He scrambled to stand, but before he could, he cried out and gripped his chest. His wide eyes protruded as blood vessels popped in the whites. He toppled over. Congested gags escaped him as his shoulder blades tensed together, raising his chest off the ground. Twinges of discomfort infiltrated Vincent's nerves as the prisoner thrashed against the grass in a wild attempt to fight off the mystery that was killing him with such ease. And then, finally, he was still.

Vincent looked away from the agony of the scene, only to see saliva trickling out the corner of Felix's mouth, as if he had been filled with an appetite for life.

"Pull him back," Felix said, his voice breaking at the end, suffocated by a joy that could be felt in waves coming from his body.

Vincent tugged at the rope still attached to the prisoner's ankle. The body glided over the grass, slippery from the morning dew, and then stumbled over a skull. The prisoner's limp head rocked from left to right. Once the body was past the omens, Felix knelt and ripped open the prisoner's tunic. A puddle of blood grew underneath the surface of his skin, right above his heart.

Dartharus poked at the spot. "I believe his heart burst," he said.

"Take the body down and bring the others. We'll take each one back and have him inspected by my physician," Felix said.

Vincent was more than happy to leave the scene. As he held his posture erect next to Dartharus, while they made their way to the carriage, it took all his strength to resist his nausea. He was proven weak once at the bottom of the hill, where he vomited in front of the wheels of the carriage.

"Hence why you're a guard. You wouldn't last a piss in battle," Dartharus snickered.

• • •

Still at the top of the hill, Felix stood tall, penetrating the mound with his gaze. "What is this exquisite power you possess?" he whispered as though to the wind. Never before had he been filled with as much pleasure as he was feeling now. Euphoria pulsed in his belly as if he had taken a sip of the most exquisite wine, while images of using this power against Ipta seduced his mind. He wouldn't need weapons; he'd be able to kill them all from a distance. This magical power, it was like reaching out an invisible hand and squashing the heart of your enemy. It was better than any magic he could have imagined previously. Now all he needed to do was to meet whoever lived inside the mound. Destiny had brought him this far, and destiny would bring him the owner of the power. "You hide yourself well, but I promise you, one day, you will have to come out. And I will be waiting for you."

CHAPTER 9
The Sailor

ERLOT'S EIGHTEENTH SUMMER arrived in Eraska. She was walking with Ambro and Elvin through the village with ropes of fish hanging over her back. Her line, as usual, had the most.

"Back so soon?" Bee asked, dumping dirty water outside her home.

"Would have been sooner if it hadn't been for these two! You would think they were Ruelderian sheep herders the way they fish," Herlot said.

Bee shook her head. "Herlot, your complexion shines health like nothing I have ever seen. Are you sure you don't wish to grow your hair out? You'd be beautiful."

"Perhaps if I get tired of feeling the breeze on the back of my neck." And besides, long hair was a burden that constantly got tangled with pieces of thatching when she was busy fixing a roof.

She could plow and fix roofs along with the men, milk and gather with the women, and massage Agatha's feet, which no one else could do. Tell stories? Absolutely not. Find a husband? Absolutely not. But she was happy for she had a future brewing on the horizon, one she couldn't stop thinking about.

That evening, she sat alongside Ambro and Elvin, listening to stories, each of them hiding a cup of the strong ale underneath their blankets. They were celebrating because next time Cloudian's stewards arrived, Ambro, Elvin, and she would show them their muscles and ask to become one of them. Being a steward meant living at the fortress and helping deliver supplies to the villages of Eraska. Whenever they could, they would talk about their future. Greeting sailors, meeting people from all the villages, and seeing the mountains that bordered Eraska from the south near the village of Bundene.

"And they lived happily ever after," Bee concluded.

Herlot smiled as the crowd clapped. Every story ever told in Alonia ended in a happily ever after. All except those of one storyteller—her father.

"Share," Rudi said, sitting next to them with her father. "No hogging ale, especially from us."

Ambro and Elvin handed them both their cups and laughed as Rudi and Herlot's father tapped the cups against one another before finishing the drinks. Rudi wiped his mouth with his tunic sleeve and burped. Herlot pressed her forehead against Elvin's shoulder, trying not to display her guilty smile.

"You, too. Hand it over," Rudi said.

Herlot pulled her empty cup out from underneath her blanket and tipped it upside down. "Too late! All gone," she sang.

Rudi patted her on the shoulders as the others chuckled.

"Ernest, there is something I've always wanted to ask you," Elvin said as the laughter subsided. "You have never ended your stories in happily ever after. Not even one of them."

It amazed her how sometimes Elvin and she would think the same thoughts. She poked at the fire with a stick. "He doesn't believe in happy endings," she offered.

Her father ran a hand through his beard. "Ah...that is not the reason, by far. I just don't believe anyone should wait until their burdens are resolved to be happy."

"Now those words of advice call for a toast," Rudi said and stood up to refill their drinks. Returning with overflowing cups, he said, "To happy nows."

"Wait to drink to that," Ambro said. Herlot watched as he walked to where Manni was sitting with her family. He took her hand, and together they stood. Oh no. This looked like they were...no, it couldn't be.

"My fellow Alonians!" Ambro called. "I would like to share the best news I have yet had the honor to share in my life. Manni has agreed to be my wife!"

Herlot dropped her cup. It rolled off her lap and into the dirt. She stared at it in horror. Dropping an empty cup was a sign of bad luck in Alonia. She scrambled to pick it back up. *I don't believe in omens. It doesn't mean anything.*

She looked back up at her brother. It couldn't be, but it was. Ambro was engaged to Manni.

Time slowed down for Herlot as she watched Alonia's response. Every barrel of strong ale was rolled out. Ambro and Manni were hugged and kissed by each villager at least once. The women huddled around Ilvy and Sira to offer how they could help with the wedding, and the younger girls crowded Manni with wonder and questions about what flowers she wanted in her hair.

Her brother was getting married. Of course, it was supposed to happen. She just never expected it to be so unexpected. He had not said a single word about it to her or Elvin. And married to *Manni*. Nonetheless, his eyes shone and his smile was wide, exposing his teeth amidst his beard. This was a good thing, at least she hoped. She hesitantly made her way toward him and Manni. She felt like she was looking at a stranger when she reached Ambro.

"Congratulations from the bottom of my heart, my brother," Herlot said. As she hugged him, she could feel the joy radiating from him. "We will still be stewards, right?"

Ambro beamed. "Of course. I will be a steward and bring back the most precious treasures for my love." He planted a kiss on Manni's cheek.

"Congratulations, Manni. You will be a beautiful bride and I know my brother will love you forever," she said, opening her arms wide to embrace her.

Manni had been awful to Herlot as a child. It was because of this, Herlot thought, that she had once imagined Manni speaking to something that was not there when she really had been rehearsing for a performance, or Manni's eyes turning into wide black pupils. Even now, she shivered to think of it, but reminded herself about the dangers of imagination. Manni had never been a friend, Herlot was always just grateful that the worst Manni did was ignore her rather than talk about Herlot being haunted by a ghost as she had when they were young. But now it seemed that they were to be sisters, and Herlot was determined to make this peaceful. For Ambro. Even though hugging her made her want to shudder.

Manni returned a quick, one-armed hug and murmured a thank-you before being swooped away by Coral and Kristen. According to Alonian tradition, the woman soon to be wed was to spend the night of her engagement with her closest friends, where they would tell stories of good luck for her marriage. Herlot didn't even need to wonder. She was definitely not invited.

"Herlot, would you like to go out on the boat with me?"

"Oh! Father, you startled me. The boat? Now?" Why was her father wanting to go fishing when Ambro had just announced his engagement?

"Why yes, on the boat, on this beautiful night."

She smiled. "Why?"

He poked the dimple on her right cheek. "I thought it might make you smile."

"I'd really like that, Father."

Once at the shore, they worked together to push a boat into the water. They wrapped wool blankets around their bodies and sat on the two benches within. Her father rowed farther and farther from shore, past the cove.

Eventually, he pulled the oars into the boat and laid them down in the crevice, patting the space next to him for Herlot.

"Holy Basil!" she gasped. "There are so many stars! And not a single tree to block the view. It feels like I'm going to fall into the sky!"

He must have noticed her hold on to the side of the boat. "You won't fall in. It feels like that at first, but it goes away," he said.

She released her grip.

"Is it true that you are thinking of joining Ambro and Elvin in becoming one of Cloudian's stewards?"

Herlot sighed. "Yes. Now before you say anything, Father, it really is the best place for me. I'm good at the work I do, but it would be good for me to be away from Alonia every so often. I mean, like tonight, I wasn't even invited to spend the night with Manni. And the stories, I love stories. Listening to them, that is. Falling in love with a hero, and the anticipation of him fighting a villain. The innocence of the children's stories. The passion of the adventures. The absurdity of some of the comedies..." She chuckled as if remembering a particular one. "I never want to stop listening to them, but I am still the only one with no story to tell. I-I'd like to be more useful, somehow."

"I wish you would have told me sooner," he said.

"I would have. I didn't want to make you and Mother upset. I feel like the last thing you both need is a daughter trying to become a steward."

Her father shook his head. "Do you remember the day we spoke about the different creatures in the world?"

She squeezed her eyes shut and shook her head as the image of a white horse with a golden alicorn danced across her mind. *Stop.* The image dissipated and she opened her eyes again. "Of course, I do. I remember a lot of things from when Ambro and I were younger, you'd be surprised, Father. All our moments, they're important to me. I think about them often, so I never forget."

"I do, too," Ernest said.

"I even remember the mist in the morning of that day. You took us out on the boat, Ambro kept talking about how he was going to catch more fish than ever before." She laughed.

"And how the other day he had collected more rocks than ever before," Ernest added.

"And how the next day he would run faster than ever before," Herlot said.

Her father grinned. "You do have a good memory."

"When you said it was time to go back, Ambro got upset because there were still so many fish to catch," Herlot continued. "Every time we looked over the edge of the boat, the shoaling fish flickering underwater were mesmerizing. They seemed infinite. You told us that it was a bad idea to catch them all, that if we tried hard enough, we probably could, but then the fish would cease to exist. Every lifeform plays a special role in our world."

Herlot yawned and stretched her arms above her. "And then I told you that I thought the world would be better without snakes and wanted to know why they were created if all they did was bite and scare people."

"Do you remember my answer?" her father asked.

She nodded and repeated what he had said word for word. "I suppose it's much like a story. There are heroes, villains, companions, and monsters, and they are all important to the story, even though they may not be your favorite. A hero would not be a hero if he did not have a villain to overcome, and what good would a companion be if he did not have a hero to help."

"And Ambro's trick with the fish?" her father asked.

She giggled. "I would rather *not* remember that." Ambro had held a fish near her cheek and nearly fallen off the boat from laughter when she had turned her head and pressed her lips right into the fish's mouth.

"You scolded Ambro for it but then played the same trick on Mother when we came home."

Her father's laugh started with a quiet humming and grew to a full-out belt.

The wind picked up and the boat teeter-tottered in the rising and falling waves.

Then Herlot spoke seriously. "Aren't you afraid of what the others will think of you for having a steward as a daughter?"

"Let me ask you this, Herlot. If it weren't for me and your mother, would you be worried or afraid of what they think of you?"

Herlot sighed and just like he would, took her time in thinking about the question before answering. "It's difficult imagining a world without you or Mother, but, no, I wouldn't be worried or afraid of what they think of me."

Her father reached over to squeeze her shoulder. "Then, one day, you will be the one people are telling stories about."

Herlot was shaken out of sleep as someone barged right through their door. "Ernest!" her mother cried.

The intruder whistled, and she heard Ambro shuffle toward the wall.

"Bear! Oh, please! Someone help!" he cried. Herlot could hear his teeth chattering.

Luckily for their nerves, a familiar voice spoke. "King Fog has taken command of Eraska," Elvin announced. He pulled at each of their blankets, throwing them into a pile at the foot of the mattresses. Herlot shivered from the morning cold. "Everyone plays," he articulated and then left.

"You heard what he said—everyone plays. To your feet, family!" her father said, pulling his tunic over his head.

Herlot slipped into her leggings while trying to eat a slice of bread. She would need the energy for the best game of hide and seek in all of Eraska, only possible to be played in the fog.

"Ernest, don't you believe we are getting too old for this?" her mother asked.

Herlot opened the door to be greeted by Merle and Rudi, who had his arm raised ready to knock. "Too old? Ilvy, nobody is ever too old to play King Fog and King Cloudian," Rudi said.

"You say this as if it was your idea," her mother muttered.

Herlot recognized a glimmer in Rudi's eye; "It was!" she exclaimed.

He wrapped his arm around her neck and squeezed her to him. "As a matter of fact, yes, indeed it was! Your short hair makes you clever," he said. "And you know what that means—I choose the first King Fog. Ambro, it is my honor to give you the crown."

Ambro finished tying his boot. "Ha!" he exclaimed. "I promise to work hard and give you back the honor. Come on, family and friends, let's be the ones to wake the birds for a change!"

Soon, she and the Alonians were in the forest, playing a village game where one person was deemed King Fog and had to search through the mist and tag someone. Herlot loved the game although it was difficult, only being able to see a footstep or two ahead because of the dense fog. At least it made it impossible for Ambro to cheat.

"Cloudian!" Ambro called.

"Here I am!" she and several other voices answered.

"Cloudian!" he called again.

Oh no. Somehow he had managed to find his way so close to her that if she reached her hand out into the fog, she'd touch him.

"Here I am!" she squealed as she shuffled to the side. But she wasn't fast enough. Soon Ambro tackled her to the ground, belting out a laugh.

"Herlot is King Fog!" Ambro called. His face and figure receded into the fog and she was left in a place of feeling that she was either completely alone or completely surrounded.

Herlot brushed the leaves off her dress and tugged down the cuffs that had scrunched up on her leggings. "Cloudian!" she called. "You can't hide forever!"

The responses returned from farther away. This was going to be a challenge, especially with all the tree trunks they could be hiding behind. Her toe got stuck underneath a tree root, causing her to trip. Without a thought, she kicked off her sandals. "Cloudian!" she called.

There. Instinctually she whipped her body around to the right. She was certain someone was there who wasn't answering her call. A cheater. Her feet squiggled against the earth.

Where do you think you're going? She closed her eyes and listened to the cheater's footsteps receding away from her. Just as quietly, she followed. She had to wait for the perfect moment to strike. It would be best if he, or she, didn't even know she was after them. A bead of sweat trickled into her eye. She blinked for the stinging to pass and then realized how warm she had become. It felt like her chest had turned into a clay oven. Probably because of the excitement of the hunt.

She heard a boat rock in the stream. *Tricky place to hide,* she thought. She leaped, pouncing at the cheater in the boat.

The fragile body fell forward, and a choke escaped the person. Right away she was attacked by an unfamiliar, rotten stench and once she was close enough to see through the fog, she realized the boat wasn't Alonian. Neither was the person. He was wearing a blue vest over white, puffy sleeves and loose pants tightened below the knee by long, leather boots.

Then she saw his face and gasped, stumbling out of the boat, causing it to wedge out of the mud.

"Stay away," he croaked as blood trickled from his mouth. What should've been white around his pupils was entirely red, and his skin was splotched a dark purple.

The man collapsed right as the current took the boat downstream.

I have to help him! She ran ahead to cut the boat off, but the dense fog made it impossible to spot it. Then she realized that her legs weren't working as they should be. Her knees wobbled and she felt the need to sit down. She thought she was dizzy, but couldn't tell if she was walking in a straight line as there were no surroundings. The fog was too thick, and she had nothing to compare her position to.

She lowered to her hands and knees and felt sweat drip from her face onto her knuckles. The heat in her chest expanded to her entire ribcage. Sharp aches spread throughout her lungs making it difficult to breathe. It felt like she had inhaled spiders. Then the heat focused entirely on her lungs, pulsing, as if burning the intruders. Her lungs contracted and spasmed like never-ending waves arriving at the shore. The violent coughs sent her to her knees. Finally, her lungs relaxed and her body cooled, though each new breath hurt, almost like trying to stretch a piece of wood.

"Cloudian! You can't hide from me!" Maurice's voice rang across the forest. They must have continued on without her, thinking she might have gone back to the village for something.

She was exhausted and it was not even full morning yet. She didn't even know if she had the strength to make it back home to sleep. She sat on her behind and rested her forearms on her knees. She felt weak, as if she had just broken a days' long fever. The fog was dissipating at a quick pace now. The trees allowed the purplish colors of the sunrise to shine through, barely visible over the stream as the fog blurred the scenery, contrasting the deep shadows of night that still resided in the forest. Far off in the distance, she saw the boat disappear around a bend. She'd never see the man again, but the ravaged, diseased face of the sailor would never leave her memory.

King Felix took the last sip of his tea. He rested his head back against his pillow and handed the cup to his mistress. "Take that with you. And add another log to the fire on your way out."

She climbed out of the bed obediently and closed the drapes that hung around his bed. Satisfied with having his needs fulfilled, he closed his eyes and drifted to sleep.

In his dream, he found himself standing in the middle of the field right outside the doorway leading inside the hill at the center. A giant owl flew across the entrance and then settled on top of the mound. It stared at him, cocking its head from side to side.

He walked inside and followed a tunnel until it opened up into a room. He saw two figures. The first one was a woman, who rested on a bed as she twirled her black locks between her fingers. The other had the shape of a man; however, he wore a cloak that covered his face.

"Ahhh..." the cloaked man moaned. His hooded head fell back. There was no trace of tone in his voice as he moaned, only a crisp purge of air.

"Master?" asked the woman. She walked over to him. "What is wrong?"

"Someone has attempted to escape my hold."

The woman seemed disheveled as she rearranged the foldings of her dress. "Someone new?"

"They are too far away for me to determine. I can only distinguish one thread from another if they are close by."

The woman paced. "The ability could be spreading."

"Calm yourself. I am not pleased, but I have a solution. We must act now. Follow me," the master said, and walked the dark tunnel toward the mound's exit.

Felix followed after them. He saw his own soldiers posted outside, visible at the edge of the field.

The woman and her master stopped just before the exit to the mound. "Whoever it was, the man, woman, or child—" the master tilted his head to the side, "escaped my grip, but not for long. They are weak. Furthermore, during that time, he or she fought off the crowpox.

I could taste the battle against the disease as soon as I resecured my grip on the heart."

"Did it happen for long enough for you to sense the person's location?"

"Yes. He is somewhere south, beyond the sea."

"I'll ready to go," she said.

"No. I will have King Felix do the work for me."

"Why?" she asked.

"We will not go near the sea for the time being."

The woman nodded. "The sea...that's right. And how will King Felix find this person?"

"The person will be unsusceptible to crowpox. The crowpox never strikes again where it has lost a battle."

A sly grin grew on the woman's face. "It is my understanding that very few in the southern lands have taken an elixir to ward off the illness. Our hunt is now easier than I ever expected. Simple. This Felix will spread the crowpox, sort out the survivors, and then bring them back to us. We'll make them live nearby, at Elfolk, perhaps. Then, if this person were to escape your grasp again, he will be right in your reach." She shook her head in delight. "Ah, solutions make me hungry. Is there any news of the one who is like me? The caller who seeks you?"

The master's hand wrapped around a space in front of his chest, as if there were a string there, and tugged. The woman stared at the space and spoke. "It is beautiful how the caller threads reach for you, unlike any of the others. I wish I could see how my thread wove into your hold when I first called. I didn't know who or where you were, but I could feel your power." She glided her hand up the master's arm. "I remember every moment of how our bond grew, until it was so strong, I finally knew exactly where to go to find you, to serve you forever."

The master brushed her hand aside. "She'll be ready soon."

The woman put her hands on her hips. "You didn't tell me the caller was a woman."

"Yes. She has your spirit, too. Hungry, willing. So... easy... to sense. If she were closer, she'd be with me right now."

"Has she given you her name yet?"

"Tell me your name, beautiful one." He slid his finger back and forth along the space in front of his heart as if he were running his finger along a taut string that began at his chest and spooled out to somewhere off in the distance. "Not yet. But soon, the more her thread weaves into my hold, the more I will know."

Felix watched the woman and her master walk back into the depths of the mound. Felix continued to stand and observe, unseen by these people. The master ordered the woman to set the cauldron above the fire and disappeared into another room. He returned with a crystal-clear stone and a glass vial. He held the stone to his mouth and blew on it for what seemed like five regular breath cycles. Felix watched the stone turn from clear to midnight black in fascination. The master then dropped the stone in the cauldron. A sizzling sound filled the space as the stone melted. Once the sizzling ceased, he scooped the liquid into the vial.

"Now what?" the woman asked.

"Now...it is time for King Felix to get what he has wished for."

● ● ●

King Felix startled awake in his four-bannister bed, gripping his chest. He slid the curtains aside, causing them to fall on top of him as he thudded onto the floor. The pressure on his heart diminished, and he realized how dark the room was. The fire had completely gone out, and no embers were left.

Someone chuckled.

"Who's there? I shall have you hanged by morning," Felix said. He scanned his quarters but couldn't see anyone. Climbing back into his bed, something caught his attention out of the corner of his eye.

A dark, shadow figure was sitting in the corner, facing him, not moving a muscle.

Cold, sharp pangs of fear raced up Felix's spine and his arms. He was petrified, waiting for the figure to budge. He blinked once, twice—it was still there. Then it shifted as if readjusting its posture.

Felix blinked again, and this time, the shadowy figure was not in the seat anymore. It was standing a few steps closer. He made out a black cloak with no face visible inside it.

166

Felix cleared his throat. "Who in the damned world do you think you are, coming into my chambers?" His voice cracked.

He opened his mouth to call for his chamberlain, but his chest tightened. It felt like a hand was squeezing his heart, trying to make it pop. He bent forward, crying out.

"For years you have waited for me and posted your soldiers outside my home. I thought I'd be much more...*welcome*," it said.

The pressure released.

"It—it's you," Felix managed. This was the man—was it a man?—who lived in the mound.

"It is my understanding that you seek my art to conquer Ipta," the figure said.

"Your understanding is correct. But, please, do that again," Felix said. As painful as it was, he was exhilarated by the dark power. This is what his enemies would feel when he attacked. This is how the Iptan Emperor would die before Felix took his destined throne.

The figure lunged forward in front of Felix, who fell back onto his bed. His heart ached as it shook inside his chest, threatening to detach. Then his senses began to disappear.

After a moment, the clench released, leaving him gasping for breath.

"I have a proposition for you," the figure said, looking down at Felix. "I seek your assistance in accomplishing a particular task for me. I need you to invade the southern lands and find somebody for me, someone who is not susceptible to crowpox. If you are successful, I promise you Ipta."

"I accept," Felix said without a moment's pause.

CHAPTER 10
The Wedding

THE WEDDING WAS JUST two days away and Alonia was overcome with summer heat. Even so close to the sea, the village fields and woods were dry, the stream shallower than it had ever been before. As Herlot hiked along the sea cliffs, her skin seemed to soak up each spray of water the waves sent her way.

"Need a hand?" she asked once she spotted Ambro. He was looking for the finishing stones for the home he was building for Manni.

"Do I ever. I'm starting to think the seagulls could do a better job wedging this one loose."

"I know a trick father showed me. Here, let me show you."

As she hoisted herself up next to him, she paused to take in the dark blues of the water colliding with the vivid greens of the sea grasses. The sea was agitated, and waves crashed furiously against the rocky shore, which made it impossible for the seagulls to find a landing.

"Lucius must have lost control of his pet today," Herlot said, referring to one of their father's stories about a giant who lived under the sea with his pet seahorse. Whenever the seahorse would escape to the surface, the giant would swim after him, causing the waves to grow wild.

Ambro's chisel slipped and the side of his palm slammed against the rock. "Lucius," Ambro said, "Would do good not chasing after his pet and instead capture a storm cloud that he could throw our way. Or, at least give the hunters a hand. They were supposed to be back two days ago. It's starting to look like we might not have a meat dish at our wedding."

Herlot couldn't agree more. Let alone the endless trips to the stream to bring back water to water the crops in the excruciating dry heat, she longed for the simple pleasure of falling asleep to the sound of rain on the roof. But there was something else agitating Ambro. He had every reason to be happy—he'd be married to the love of his life in a few days and the home would be finished today. "I'm sure the hunters will be back any moment. Is something burdening you, brother?"

"Manni and I were supposed to eat breakfast in the forest together. She didn't show. Sira and Viktor don't know where she went. They think she's just *nervous* about the wedding. Why would she be nervous? Does she not want to marry me? And if she is nervous..." he pounded the chisel into the rock, "why can't she tell *me* about it instead of her parents. We're not children anymore."

"Oh." Herlot was at a loss for words to comfort her brother. Not that she cared much for understanding Manni's reasoning for doing things, but she couldn't imagine getting married, or how she would feel if the day ever came. "She'll come back."

Ambro raised an eyebrow, then chuckled. "What a meager attempt to lift my spirits."

"I know."

"It will have to do for now. Say, have you thought of marriage?" he blurted.

"Not at all." Herlot continued to dig, using her nails to loosen a stone. The stone came free and she held it up in victory. "This one is perfect, isn't it?"

"I know for a fact that Elvin is fond of you..." Ambro continued.

"I'm fond of him, too. He will make a great steward. As will we." She winked at him before getting to work on another stone.

"Have you ever thought about him differently?"

Herlot sighed. "Do you want my help with these stones or not? Because if you do, the only marriage we are speaking about is yours, agreed?"

Ambro rolled his eyes. "Agreed. But only for now. I'm your brother, I'm allowed to break these kinds of agreements."

Lovely. As if it wasn't enough that Agatha and Bee bugged her about it every day. She thought becoming a steward would get her away from the marriage questions. Now she could look forward to trying to avoid the tedious discussion on her travels across Eraska when Ambro and she became stewards.

Once their handcarts were filled with stones, they headed back toward the village.

"Look! Sailships!" Ambro pointed down the coast toward the fortress. "Just imagine—soon we'll be there and get to see them up close. Ah, all of those people travel the world and we'll be the ones who get to talk with them and look at all the things they bring. We'll get to trade. I'll always have something exquisite to bring back home for Manni."

Herlot nodded. "Soon, Cloudian's stewards will arrive and I will have a chance at having a future, of being useful. I can't tell stories, but I am strong. They will see that I'll be a great help, right?"

"I'll be the first one to tell them, Sister."

Once back in Alonia, they secured the last stones to the home. Ambro wrapped his arm around Herlot as they stared at the masterpiece. It was by far the nicest home in the village. The clay for the interior finish perfectly suited the curvature of the stones that comprised the home's walls. The hay roof had been arranged so that the ends of the stacks created a wavelike pattern where they met.

Nearly every villager stopped by to admire the work. Agatha asked where they had gathered the rocks, and then scolded Simon for not having searched the same area. The previous spring, Simon had rebuilt his home, but Agatha believed that even the new and shiny stones of their home were dull and old compared to Ambro's. "After the wedding we will have a lot of work to do," she said, pointing a pudgy finger at Simon.

When Agatha wasn't looking, Simon shared his thoughts on the matter. "Your home is a tragedy fueling her passion for improvement, which she claims is just as nutritious for the spirit as berries are for the complexion," he said. Then he shook his hands toward the sky. "Just once, I wish that, just once, I could eat the berries while she and her well-nourished spirit do the work."

The only person who didn't show was Manni and the hunters. It was taking them longer than usual, and Herlot was beginning to worry. Was this a bad sign? Two Alonian traditions were not going as planned—the husband presenting the home to the wife, and the hunters arriving with meat for the wedding. As the day passed, it became more and more difficult for Ambro to remain calm. Herlot was still at a loss for words, but the least she could do was follow him as he paced around the village for a sign of Manni. It was unusual for Manni to be out in the woods this long—trees, plants, and animals of the forest were not particularly forthcoming with compliments. Manni usually preferred to be surrounded by people so she could put herself on display.

Just as the sun was setting and they were forming a search party, Manni entered Alonia from the north. "I'm fine!" she called as she approached the group. She seemed flustered and tripped over a rope two children were playing snake with.

"Oh, Skies. I will never forget why the birds sing in the morning," Ambro said and then rushed to scoop Manni into a hug.

"I'm sorry," Manni said when he put her down. "I just needed to spend some time alone to calm myself before our day. I'm sorry to have made all of you worry."

"Come. I think this will cheer you up," he said, guiding her by the hand to the home. Herlot, along with the others followed, eager to see Manni's reaction.

"Do you like it?" he asked when they reached it.

Manni nodded. "I've had a long day. I'm going to go rest now," she said.

Herlot's heart felt as if it had been broken in half like a branch seeing Ambro's defeated composition as Manni rushed away. She could feel the disappointment swooning off of him while no one else said anything. Herlot waited for the crowd to disperse and took a seat next to Ambro. Her shoulders relaxed to see that her father and mother were heading in their direction. Someone needed to comfort Ambro, and she needed her parents to help her do it.

"May we sit with you?" Herlot's father asked.

Ambro dropped his head in his palms. "Yes, since my soon-to-be wife doesn't want to be near me."

"Son," Herlot's mother said. "It's normal for women to be overwhelmed before getting married. I remember not eating for three days before our ceremony, and your father thought I would rather starve myself to death than marry him."

Herlot smiled. She had never heard this story. It was strange imagining her parents ever not married.

"You'll see. Tomorrow you'll feel silly for worrying about any of it," her father added.

"Very well," Ambro said, and ran his fingers through his curls. "I hope you're right. Skies, I just wish those hunters would return."

They spoke with such confidence as if they had joined Manni on her walk and learned her deepest thoughts. Herlot wished she could have done that for Ambro. Why couldn't she? Why couldn't she tell Ambro that he had nothing to worry about when it came to Manni? That they would get married and everything would be fine? She clutched the collar of her dress as she imagined Manni in the woods surrounded by a blanket of darkness, and Manni with her hands around Herlot's neck with those wide, black pupils. She poked her stomach and told its nervous pulsing to hush. She was imagining things again.

Just as she calmed, cheers emitted from the woods. The hunters had returned.

Ha! See? Bad signs don't exist. They arrived just in time. Everything will go perfectly.

• • •

The morning of the wedding, Herlot awoke happy that the sun was shining and new patches of wildflowers had appeared overnight—a good sign for the ceremony. Rain still had not arrived, and she hoped it would hold off at least for another day, no matter how dry the air was. Her brother deserved the sun shining on his special day.

She joined her mother in Sira's home to help weave flowers into Manni's hair. Agatha had been practicing her singing since sunrise, and every so often Simon would walk by and they would laugh at the blades of grass rolled into balls he had tucked into his ears.

While they worked, children would enter to recite good luck poems to Manni, and Herlot's mouth watered at the delicious food she saw people carrying toward the center of the village as they passed the doorway of Sira and Viktor's home. There would be fresh breads, berries, nuts, potatoes, and, of course, fish. A special roll of parchment had also been set out on which the Alonians would write a story of Ambro and Manni.

"Hoot-hoot. Hoot-hoot," an owl sounded.

Herlot stopped prepping her flower stem. How strange. The owl never hooted in the day. Something felt heavy in the pit of her stomach, as if she had swallowed a nut in its shell.

She stepped aside to allow Sira to fasten Ambro's necklace around Manni's neck. All of a sudden, several children shrieked outside and wildflowers rained to the ground as Manni rose from her knees.

"What in the world is going on out there?" Herlot's mother said as she rushed out the door. Manni stood frozen, her fist clenched around and suffocating a flower at her side.

"I'll be right back, Manni. I'm sure the children just spilled something. Everything will be taken care of," Herlot said. *I hope she manages a smile by the time the ceremony starts. She's acting as if today were a funeral*, Herlot thought on her way out.

Herlot gasped, then rushed to her mother's side. A group of about twenty strange men stood near the hearth. Behind them were several horses with wagons. They looked as if they had come right out of an Alonian story. They were wearing leather boots that reached above their knees with black breeches of rough texture tucked into them. Each had a thick, brown belt with many types of tools around his hips. Their dark shirts had loose, long sleeves that gathered at the wrists. Some were wearing straps that wrapped and crossed around their shoulders, chests, and backs. They all had swords.

A gush of safety embraced her as her father appeared.

"Ernest, who are these men?" her mother asked.

"I don't know. Let's see what they have to say," he answered, pulling her and her mother close as they joined the crowd.

Herlot glared at one of the men standing near the feast table, circling his fingers through a bowl of berries until he found one suitable to eat. Whoever they were, they didn't have manners, but there was also something eerie about them that made even the thought of scolding the man unacceptable. Then her attention was brought to another, who had strayed from his group and was looking inside their homes. He was wearing a wool cloak that reached just below his chest, its broad hood so deep his face was lost in shadows. Herlot's voice got stuck in her throat and she wished she had the courage to tell him, "Nobody said you could walk into our homes as you please. Leave." But his lack of hesitancy and his confident stride as he stepped into each home told her that words would have no use.

Then the one who was taller than the rest stepped forward.

Herlot watched Kristen's daughter crawl to him and touch his sturdy, leather boot. Kristen hustled to grab her, but he picked the child up and sat her on the crease of his elbow.

"What a dear, little, button nose you have," he said, tapping her on her nose. "My daughter has one just like yours. But now is no time to wander off. Stay with your mother."

The girl nodded as he gently set her down, and Kristen apologized, struggling to take her away as the little one stretched her arms toward him.

Herlot relaxed. Maybe they didn't have manners, but they couldn't be bad if they were nice to children.

The leader cleared his throat. "King Cloudian sends his regrets for disturbing your wedding celebration. We are Eraska's allies, sent by your king to protect your village from danger."

"Danger?" Simon asked.

"Eraska has been invaded and we are here to protect your village. Since you are not trained to fight, it is best you are secured in a safe place. You are all to enter your homes without delay. Your village must be secured until King Cloudian arrives and we are certain the danger has passed."

Panic. The women cried out while the men did their best to calm them. A strong, dry wind blew, bending the trees. Wildflowers were swept along the ground, and Herlot watched the parchment scroll fall and unravel, exposing its blank surface. Two soldiers, one of them the one with the cloak, stormed past her, the cloaked soldier's broad chest knocking her to the side away from her parents.

"Just make sure they're paired with their families so they don't get chaotic," the hooded soldier said to another.

"...that simple we could send the support troops out now and get this over with," the other said.

"No. We have strict orders in case of a rebellion. Stop your suggestions and round up the children in a separate home."

Get what over with? Herlot thought. *Why a rebellion? What is happening?*

She barely noticed her father leading her into her home. Ambro rushed after them. "Have you seen Manni?" he cried. "I searched for her through the entire crowd, and I can't find her anywhere!"

Her father held him back. "Ambro, it's important to get to safety now. Wait here, I am sure she is fine. We don't want to create holdups for these men as they try to help us."

The gathering winds found their way in, lifting the hay that covered the dirt floor. Herlot watched from their doorway as soldiers ordered families into specific homes, until blowing dirt stung her eyes. She felt so disoriented, as if she couldn't pick an emotion to feel.

"Why are they putting so many families together?" her mother asked, covering her mouth with a scarf.

"It will be easier for them to protect a smaller area," her father replied.

"Thank the skies," Ambro said. Herlot followed his gaze. A soldier guided Manni and her parents to their door.

Two soldiers followed, lowering a large chest to the ground while Ambro embraced Manni. Their leader appeared, eyeing Herlot and each person in her home. "In the chest you will find blankets, food, and water. We have more if necessary. Please do your best to remain calm. Oh, and the one with the black hair comes with me," he said.

"No!" Ambro shouted, but before he could take a step, one of the men pressed the tip of a blade to his chest and ripped his tunic to the skin. Herlot wanted to cry out, but she seemed to have lost her voice. Ambro fought forward, nevertheless. "Get out of my way!"

The other man grabbed Ambro by the shoulder and struck his head with the hilt of his sword.

"Ernest!" her mother shrieked.

Her father caught Ambro as he toppled over, unconscious. All Herlot could do was watch Manni being taken from their home and listen to Sira cry. *What is happening?* cried a voice inside her head. *Move. Do something.* But her legs felt as if they were stuck in a frozen stream.

"Close them off!" the leader called. His voice rang through the village, cutting through the wind that carried the cries of frightened children and adults shouting questions.

Their home was engulfed in darkness as soldiers placed a heavy, wooden plank in front of their doorway. Herlot searched the wall and found a narrow crack between the stones to look out of. She watched the other homes being sealed. The soldiers wedged large beams against the wooden planks, anchoring them with what looked to be heavy, squarish stones. Upon hearing a pounding against the plank that closed them in, she ran to it, pushing against it with all of her strength. It was impossible to move. "Why are they doing this?" she asked.

"It will be harder for the attackers to get to us," Viktor said.

Or for us to get out, she thought. Something about this method didn't seem thought through. True, if there were people attacking Alonia, moving the rocks, beams, and planks, would make it more difficult for them. But she didn't like the feeling of being trapped either. Where would they hide if these men didn't succeed at fighting off the invaders?

For a long time, the only noise inside was Sira's sniffling. The eerie quiet grew as they tried to listen to what was happening outside while Herlot sat next to her mother who was holding a washcloth to Ambro's forehead. Then, without exchanging any words, her father and Viktor started a fire.

Ambro's eyes opened lazily, and he gripped his forehead in pain. "Manni!" he cried. "Don't!" he shouted, resisting Herlot's help to stand. He shoved her to the side and threw his body against the plank, pushing and kicking, and when that didn't work, he proceeded to pound his fists against it.

"That's enough now," her father said calmly, resting his hands on Ambro's shoulders and guiding him away. "You're only giving yourself more bruises."

Ambro gripped his hair. "What am I supposed to do, Father!? Sit here while a stranger has my wife in his hands?"

"I know you are upset about Manni, and I am, too. We all are." He stood in front of the plank. "I suggest we remain calm until we learn more. Cloudian would not put us in danger. I am sure he had the most important reason to send these men. We have all experienced a shock, and it's a good idea that we eat. Herlot, will you bring water for our guests? Ilvy, will you bring us some of the bread you baked yesterday?"

Her mother fetched the bread while Herlot served cups of water. They sat in a circle, passing the bread between them, each tearing off a bite until it was gone. They were all still hungry. Though each family had prepared many dishes of food for the wedding, it had all been left outside.

Sira crawled to and opened the chest. Herlot stared at a selection of breads, vegetables, fruits, and smoked meats. There was water, as well.

"See? These people plan on taking good care of us. Let's each pick one thing for now," her father said.

"Taking good care of us," Ambro repeated with sarcasm. "Father, have you seen my forehead?"

"Enough already," Herlot said. "It was your own fault. They're just trying to do their duty and prevent chaos. Now, stop making everyone more nervous than we already are."

Ambro stared at her for a long while, but she didn't break eye contact from him. Then he shook his head and sat in the corner on his mattress.

After eating, no one felt like telling stories. Her mother shook out the blankets from the chest and handed them to Sira and Viktor. Dust sprinkled from them and landed on their clothing and skin.

Sira stroked the blanket. "It's so soft. I've never felt this type of fabric before. It's about time Cloudian sent us something of better standards," she commented.

Herlot let out a disgusted sigh. "Your daughter was dragged out of here by a complete stranger and you're marveling at a blanket?"

Sira's mouth dropped open.

"Herlot, apologize," Ernest said.

"Sorry," she mumbled—although she was not—as she stood and went to her mattress, covering herself with her own blanket.

It was impossible for Herlot to sleep. She wanted to know who these soldiers were. They called themselves allies, but no one had ever seen them before. Something serious must have happened for Cloudian to have sought help from them. Even though they were here to protect Alonia, they didn't seem like good people—what kind of a person could strike a defenseless man like her brother with such ease? But then again, the leader had been nice to Kristen's daughter. Is this how soldiers behaved?

The night went by with no further news. As did the next day. And the day after that, too. Every night after everyone went to sleep, Herlot heard her mother waken and sip her healthy spirits tincture. Her mother didn't like being asked questions about it, but her father had once explained to Herlot that it helped keep her mother's cases of the nerves at bay. However, she seemed to be drinking more of the tincture than usual. Instead of a sip, it sounded more like two large gulps.

"I'd give anything for a breath of fresh air," Herlot said on the fifth day. She lay holding one of Rudi's figures in her hands, keeping herself occupied by running her fingers over the wood.

"Me, too," her mother wheezed.

Herlot dabbed her mother's forehead with a damp cloth. She and Sira had been coughing all day and had troubles swallowing their food. If her mother and Sira were sick, they would need medicine. Most of it was in Agatha's home. What if they needed Oliver? She had a feeling they all were worrying about the same thing but were too afraid to say something out loud, because what could they do? They were locked in.

Still, she did not begin to worry until the evening her father and Viktor began coughing. That night, she awoke to muffled sounds of panic outside. Ambro was already at the crack in the wall, switching between looking through it and holding his ear against it.

"They're begging for help and to be let out," he said dryly.

Herlot knelt next to him, and they looked at each other as more and more cries echoed through the night while their and Manni's parents lie barely conscious between fits of coughing.

By morning, her mother's cough had turned to a pained heaving, and blood trickled from her mouth. Her body was trembling and covered in sweat. She needed help fast.

"Help!" Herlot screamed. Her throat was raw from shouting. Then she noticed her father reaching to help her mother, but he fell short as a fit of coughing led to spasmed heaves. His eyes were blood-stained and black bumps were growing on his skin. She pounded even harder. "Please! I beg you! Someone, help!"

"It's no use," Ambro said, pressing his forehead against the plank.

Ambro crouched forward, his hands on his thighs as he caught his breath.

Herlot knelt by her mother and pressed the back of her palms against her forehead. "It's burning hot."

"So is Father's," Ambro said before checking Sira.

Herlot worked frantically, drenching cloths in water to cool the adults' foreheads and wipe blood away. Outside, the cries for help didn't cease, yet the soldiers didn't respond.

"I don't think they know where they are anymore," Ambro said. He wiped tears from his cheeks as their parents mumbled incoherent phrases.

"Help me. We need to turn them on their sides," Herlot said, noticing more blood flowing from their noses. "It's alright, Mother. I'm here. We are taking care of you," she whispered as she rolled her on her side.

Then she headed over to Sira. "No," she whispered. "No. No. No. Ambro." Herlot held her hand above Sira's mouth, and Ambro pressed his ear against Viktor's chest.

Her hand trembled as she covered her mouth and squeezed her eyes shut, releasing a trail of tears.

"They didn't even know they had taken their last breath," Ambro muttered, his eyes wide.

They covered the bodies with blankets.

"Once we're out, we will find you a good place to rest," Ambro promised. "I'll take good care of Manni forever."

Ilvy and Ernest worsened. Herlot could hardly recognize her mother's face, which had turned a dark purple.

In quiet spells, they paced back and forth like trapped animals. Herlot pinched herself when she felt close to breaking down. She had to hold herself together. As good as she had become at blocking her imagination, she had to do the same now with her fears. She pinched herself until she bruised whenever an image of lowering her mother or father into a grave crossed her mind. She couldn't break down while her parents were in this state. She needed to be calm and strong for them and be able to get them help the moment the soldiers let them out.

As the day went on, the shouting outside ceased, perhaps because they realized the soldiers didn't care. Or because there were fewer people left to scream. She knelt next to the crack in the wall and held her ear against it. She could hear two sets of footsteps a short distance from their home.

"They are not surviving. We'll have five, at the most," a man with a low, hoarse voice muttered.

"You're right," another answered. "Ahh... This is more boring than the siege of Radinburg, and we waited close to a year until Luther surrendered."

"You don't feel your time is wasted?"

"Sometimes. But when I do, I think of the gold I was promised. Then it is not a waste anymore."

Herlot sat back against the wall. They had said they were here to protect them but there had been no signs of a threat outside. The only real danger was the illness that was spreading inside. Herlot thought through her knowledge of illness. People in Alonia rarely felt unwell. Eating ill-preserved fish might bring a few days of stomach upset and the air at the shore helped to feel better. A hearty broth and rest eased the discomforts of a cold. To prevent fever, village women knew how to clean and stitch small cuts, which happened often enough in their fishing village.

She considered how everyone was fine and well when the soldiers had arrived. Since then, no one had been outside. Could it have been lack of fresh air? Or the change in foods? They all had been eating and drinking only the supplies from the chests.

She looked up just as Ambro ripped off a piece of stale bread. "Don't touch that!" she cried, slapping the bread out of his hands.

She examined the contents of the chest. The water was a shade darker than normal water. How had they not noticed this before?

Were these men poisoning them somehow? Were they doing this on purpose?

She shared her thoughts with Ambro, and he looked at the supplies in horror.

"Why would someone do this, Ambro?" she whispered.

"No human would do this to someone," he replied.

A commotion arose outside.

"Get back in your home!" a soldier yelled.

They looked through the crack in the wall. Simon had broken through the hay roof and was about to jump, when a soldier chucked a dagger into his back. He fell from the roof, his head splitting on a rock.

"You ignorant fool! He was well!" roared the voice of the leader.

Ambro sat back on his heels, panting. "They killed him...Simon tried to escape, and they killed him."

A numbness enveloped every fiber in Herlot's body. The horrors happening around her were impossible to comprehend. It had to be a dream, or rather, a nightmare. She hugged her knees to her chest and tried to stop her teeth from chattering as she fought to not think of the dagger in Simon's back.

As night fell, Herlot held her father's head in her lap while Ambro held their mother's in his. They stroked their hair, just as their parents had for them when they were young. By the time the moon had fully risen, her parents' breath came in ragged fits. Their pulses were beginning to slow, their hands cold to the touch. Deep down inside she knew their lives were fading. Herlot held her father's hands between her own, hoping her warmth would keep the cold of death from spreading. She squeezed her eyes against the tears threatening to spill. She could not be weak because already her emotions were making it difficult to feel the ground beneath. She had to be strong. What if the men took the planks away now? She had to be ready, even though there seemed to be no hope.

"I love you, Mother, Father. Every kind act you've ever done for me, every memory, your smiles—I'll never forget," she whispered.

Her father's lips moved, and she leaned in close to hear.

"Cry, Herlot. Always cry. Just like the rain. The clouds break after a rain to let the sunshine through," he struggled to say. "Tears free your sorrows...to open the way for your love to shine through," he finished with a weak smile.

And then, Herlot and Ambro felt the final, erratic flutters of their parents' hearts.

A mute humming rubbed away at Herlot's nerves until the only thing she could feel was hollow. She was a corpse able to breathe, but not alive. Ambro covered their parents' bodies with blankets and guided her to sit next to him near the crack in the wall. Overcome by loss and gutted of any hope, they held one another and listened for any sign of life outside.

● ● ●

Ambro awoke from his hollow trance to the sound of voices outside. The words were blurred, or was that his vision? With the raindrop amount of strength he had left, he dug his elbows into the ground and pulled himself forward until he reached the crack in the wall. Body shaking, he pressed his ear against it.

"No one here," one soldier said.

"One here," another said.

He shook his head, trying to distinguish his hearing from his sight as footsteps approached their home. The plank locking them in vibrated. They were coming in. What were they planning? Would they kill him and Herlot if they saw that they were alive? Should he pretend he was dead? No. Manni. He had to find out what happened to Manni, and the last time he had seen her she was taken by them. But what about Herlot? Shaking, he crawled to his sister and covered her with a blanket.

"Pretend you are dead, and when they are gone, run. I must find Manni. Go into the forest. I know you can survive there. Herlot, I love you." He kissed her on the forehead, then crawled to the sealed doorway.

• • •

Ambro's words drifted down, finding Herlot through her stupor. She stirred, feeling his kiss on her forehead, and tried to whisper, "I love you, too" but did not know if she had spoken or only thought the words. All of her senses seemed paralyzed. Just trying to feel the texture of the blanket over her was like a foot that had fallen asleep for too long and was expected to walk.

"One here," someone said as fresh air found its way into their home.

She didn't budge, still too paralyzed to move. After a while, she heard more footsteps outside their home.

"What do we do with the dead?"

"Burn them. Burn everything," another answered. "Dartharus's orders were to not leave evidence."

Before she could move, a bundle of burning hay was thrown into her home. It landed across her body, catching in the blankets. It was as if lightning had struck her. Her body buzzed with chaotic energy. Herlot rolled away, squelching the flames that had found her dress. She sat up, struggling to see through the smoke, holding her breath against it and the searing heat. The fire blazed, feeding on the dry straw and grasses that covered the floor. Flames leapt upward, catching the roof afire. Burning thatch fell, blocking her path out. She was trapped. She eyed the blanket-covered bodies of her parents and she thought of throwing herself into the fire. She didn't want to live. Not without them and not in a world where something this horrific had happened.

Through the din, she heard a thumping at the wall of the home that faced the forest. One stone fell in, and then another, until she saw a beautiful golden alicorn pierce through. With another thump, a clatter of stones fell away, revealing—

"De-Devotio?"

Herlot staggered backwards. Impossible. He didn't exist. Yet there he was, and a toppled wall as evidence of his strength. Was she with fever?

A long time ago she had wished for the happiness of seeing him again. Happiness was gone from her. She would neither feel it again, nor did she want to. This was just a trick her mind was playing on her, an illusion to help her when she was frightened.

"Herlot, listen to me. Don't think. Don't try to understand. If you want to live, climb on my back right now."

She took a step back. "But..." She shook her head. "No, you're not real."

She yelped as a bundle of the roof fell right behind her, sizzling her dress.

"Herlot!" Her eardrum banged from the magnitude of Devotio's voice. "Look at me. I am real. I knocked the wall down."

"No. No. I am imagining it. I need to go out the front."

If she ran fast enough through the fire there'd be a chance she could make it. Just as she was about to leap, something gripped her by the back collar of her dress and she flew on her back. Devotio's head bowed over her. "When is the happiest you have ever felt?"

She wanted to ignore the illusion but then she looked into his eyes. The answer was so clear, even after so many years. Herlot's senses cleared and the light that Devotio had once brought into her life as happiness was now a light to ignite her survival.

"When I saw your golden heart." she said. She stared at the toppled wall and his defined features. "You're real. You have to be."

"Climb on, hurry."

Herlot squeezed through the wall after Devotio and then threw herself onto his back. Her strength surged as she held him, settling herself as he ran. The fires from the village leapt behind them, ignited by the wind and the dry grasses. Herlot glanced behind her in horror as her history burned in flames. She could practically smell the death of the stories of her village family that the fire radiated into the air. She and Ambro were the only story left.

"Devotio! Faster!" she urged. Her story, the only trace of their story, had to survive.

The unicorn stretched his head forward. Each stride came faster than the one before. They came to a place Devotio had never taken her to, yet she remembered it from the day she and Ambro had gone to search for unicorns. Devotio ran toward a chestnut tree, but the moment before they collided with it, heat pulsated through Herlot's chest and the sides of the trunk lifted up as if a curtain were being raised.

CHAPTER 11
The Chestnut Tree

A REFRESHING MIST DRIFTED through every fiber of Herlot's being. Waking slowly, she found herself in a meadow of long, waving grasses and bright wildflowers. She sat on the side of her leg, supporting her weight with her arms as she looked around. To her right was a tunnel lined with intertwined branches of chestnuts and white, pink-frosted bunches of flowers.

Ahead was a basin of shimmering golden water. Chestnut trees lined the meadow's edge. The place felt so alive, its vivid colors full of mirth. There were colors that Herlot had never seen, yet within them, she could see every color she had ever known. Every part of her body felt as if it were breathing...her toes, her belly button, her nose, her cheeks, her arms, fingers, everything. A vibrant pulse hummed around her—even the air seemed to be breathing. Within her veins, she sensed a tree's roots stretching against soil, and that same soil arranging itself to make space for the root. For a moment, she thought she was the roots, and then the soil.

She remembered the fire, the soldiers, her parents, yet it seemed like a story written ages ago. Every painful memory seemed to be hugged by the life swarming around her. So much life, it was impossible for anything to die. Even though she couldn't see them, she could feel the life of each Alonian, of her parents. They had to be here somewhere. Had she died, as well? Was that why she was in such a beautiful place where death seemed impossible?

"Herlot," someone with a light voice spoke.

A girl with curly, wheat-colored hair down to her waist stood next to Devotio and a group of unicorns. Her eyes were closed, her eyelashes resting on her cheeks. She was wearing a green dress made of sea grass that flowed from her chest down to her thighs. A mellow light emanated from her body.

There was also something very different about her and the unicorns. Their shape was defined yet also intermingled with the elements around them. One moment they were a strong, vivid white. But the next, whenever a breeze moved through, their appearance spiraled into a vast array of colors.

"Devotio, am I dead?" Herlot asked.

"No. You are in my family's hiding place."

Herlot dropped her head. This place was so beautiful, so alive, and so real, of that she had no doubt, but her parents were not here.

"I-I wish I could see you," the girl said, reaching her hand out, then pulling it back. "It's been so long since I've seen someone like me."

"Emrys, we have to hurry. The fire rages toward us," Devotio said, standing at Herlot's side.

A sad smile formed on her face. "We do," she agreed. "Herlot, I know you're hurting. If I could, I'd hold your hand, embrace you, cry with you. But I can't do that. What I'm about to tell you will be confusing, but you must listen carefully because the unicorns' survival is in your hands now."

Herlot used Devotio's support to stand. "I don't understand what is happening."

"Listen to Emrys, follow her," Devotio said.

She followed Emrys toward the basin. It looked like Emrys was painted into her steps, as if a brush were smearing her color forward and then recombining to redefine her shape. Once at the basin, Devotio stepped between her and Emrys, who still had her eyes closed. She felt comfort with him next to her, but also sensed that he was protecting Emrys.

Herlot did not know how she was capable of even being upright. Her heart wanted to shout and cry in grief, but every time the grief rose to the surface, it was met by the invisible hugs of the air in this world, soothed and quieted into peace.

"I'm not allowed to look at you." Emrys knelt and put her hand in the water. A golden liquid pooled from her hand, and she moved her hand back and forth to disperse it. "I'm going to tell you the story of my people and how they lost their golden hearts. A long time ago, there was a boy named Brom who met a man who took the gold from his heart. When Brom ran to his family for help, the light around their bodies extinguished, too."

Brom. Why did Herlot feel like she had heard that name before? And the golden hearts. "Wait," she said. "Are you saying that people once had golden hearts?"

"Yes. However, they had lost their gold by simply looking at Brom. All over the land, golden hearts extinguished and babies were born without them. Soon my people didn't want to greet the sun anymore. They had lost something they had never fully understood but couldn't live without."

"So all it took was for someone to look at someone without a golden heart for their own to extinguish?" Herlot asked.

"Yes. Or a touch."

"And if you were to look at me?"

"I would lose mine." Emrys rested her chin on her fist. "Before, they'd lived rich lives and, like me, could blend their gold with life around them to create new things. We had so many ideas. Flowers. Herbs. Butterflies. Games. I once blended a daisy with wide petals big enough for my sister to jump on, and at night, we would sleep on them with our unicorns."

Emrys took a shaky breath.

"Sometimes we had so many ideas we didn't know what to do with them. The trees were a great help. Their roots connect them to the earth, yet their branches reach toward the sky where the dream world resides. When we touched the leaf of a tree, it would hold our idea for us in the world of dreams until the time came for it to fall in autumn."

Herlot remembered the one leaf on the chestnut tree. It had been so vivid and strong even though it had been winter.

"Eventually, the people found other sources of gold, and it helped them to feel whole again. But this type of gold was different. Some were lucky and found a lot. Others didn't. They couldn't live with the idea that another could have more gold. And the ones who had the most, hated the fact that they could not be the ones with the most forever—another person could always steal theirs or find more. They did horrible things to each other to gain more. Soon, the unicorn massacres began. Many were killed for their alicorns."

Herlot shuddered at the thought of someone hunting Devotio. Especially now, with a group of strangers in Alonia capable of doing nothing while an entire village begged for their help, strangers who could throw a dagger into someone's back, Herlot had no doubt there were persons capable of the evil described in Emrys' story.

"I met Brom when I was returning to Eraska from the desert lands with Seliria, my unicorn. I knew something had changed because there were no others in the sky that morning to greet the sun. Brom found me in the forest and warned me of everything that had happened and made sure to keep himself hidden so I wouldn't see him and lose my gold. He had gathered a hundred unicorns that had escaped the massacres. He needed me to blend an idea of a place that could hide them into a leaf."

"So we are inside the chestnut tree's leaf right now?" Herlot asked. She looked around at the beautifully mysterious world she was in.

"Yes. This world is my idea that the leaf has been holding onto for ages. And the tree is our link between the physical and dream worlds." Emrys pressed her palms into the soil. "Listen carefully, Herlot. Everything is at stake. The fire races toward us, the tree can feel it. It will burn the chestnut tree, the leaf along with it..."

Herlot's eyes widened in understanding. "Emrys, you have to leave! Now!"

The idea of more death made her head spin. Sharp pains jabbed at her temples as memories of her parents clamored to the forefront of her mind, too quickly for the invisible hugs to catch. She grasped an image of the heavy planks and used it to block the memories.

"We can't. There's not enough time to blend the unicorns outside."

Herlot paced back and forth. "You have to try! If you start now it might be possible and you can find them a new tree."

The water in the basin lowered a hair, and Emrys held her hand in it, once more filling it with more gold liquid.

"Even if Emrys could blend each of us out in time, we would need someone to create a new hiding place before any humans saw us," Devotio said.

"Can't Emrys do it? All you have to do is find another leaf," Herlot said.

"I could have many ages ago. But it is only in this world of memories and ideas that I exist now," she stated helplessly. "Someone else who has mastered the art of blending would have to do it. I can't leave."

"I don't understand. If they can leave, why can't you?"

"This world is an idea. In the beginning, we realized we were forgetting what our bodies felt like. It felt like wandering far away from home and forgetting where it was. We learned that the unicorns had to step outside once every twelve moons to not separate from their physical bodies. Every summer, I blended them out one at a time. We also faced another problem. To prevent the leaf from wilting, I had to pour gold into the basin every few moments like I still do now. If I left, the leaf would crumble with the unicorns still inside. My only option was blending them all out first and going last, but there were too many risks. A human could have spotted them, or once I joined them, I could have looked at a human and lost my gold, unable to provide the unicorns with a new hiding place. I only had one choice— to let my body go so we could stay here."

Herlot understood Emrys' sacrifice. She would have made the same decision without a doubt.

Emrys approached Herlot with her eyes closed. Her face looked as young and fresh as a child's. Her lips had a gold shimmer, and her lashes a gold frost. Being in her presence felt like a lullaby.

"Herlot, your heart sparks gold. I don't know how, but after the spark, gold runs through your body and you're able to blend. The chestnut tree felt you blend through the oak tree the day you met

Devotio. You can do this. Once you and Devotio are out, you will climb the tree and take the leaf. All you have to do is find a way to ignite your golden heart, and then you will blend the leaf on to another branch. As long as you find a way within twelve moons, Devotio's family will survive."

"Wh-what?" Herlot choked. "I-I can't do that. You're mistaken."

"I know you have been through tragedy, and this is the last thing I would wish to put on your shoulders, but if there's anyone who can help them, it's you. You must try, for them."

Herlot was at a loss for words. If what Emrys said was true, she could save Devotio's family. She was the *only* one who could save them. Today could not be the death of Alonia and the death of Devotio's family, too. This world, this magnificent world, had to live. Its story had to continue, because out there, the world with daggers, planks, and death was a story that never should have been written.

Emrys's toes curled into the ground. "The fire is almost here. Devotio, are you ready?"

Devotio bowed and Emrys scooped water from the basin, pouring it over his alicorn. Water dripped from his forehead, his eyelashes, and his velvet nose, but not from his alicorn. There was no alicorn anymore. Only a patch of golden hue upon his forehead remained.

Emrys kissed him on the forehead. "You will forever remain a unicorn in our hearts."

Herlot swallowed, understanding the severity of Emrys's words. "You won't be able to blend the alicorn back again..."

"No. But he wants to come with you, and the only way he can do that is if he looks like a horse."

A unicorn lowered a branch into Emrys's hands. She ran her hands over it, molding it into a shape of a handle. She lowered the handle into the basin for a flutter of a butterfly wing and then blew. Water fell in droplets while it hardened into a blade. She had created a sword.

Then she reached her arm into the water and pulled out a scabbard and baldric made of sea grass.

"This sword is for you, Herlot. It will defend you if trouble comes your way. Protect Devotio and yourself, but never strike first or take a life with it. If you do, you will abuse something that is pure and good, and it will turn against you in one form or another."

Herlot firmly gripped the hilt.

Emrys presented a string of seaweed. "Use this to pierce the leaf and wear as a necklace. Now go."

Herlot pulled the baldric over her head and put the sword in the scabbard on her back before climbing onto Devotio. She paused. "How will I learn to blend with the gold in my heart? I can't even control when it happens."

Emrys took a deep breath. "I do not have a good answer for you, I'm afraid. Once you find a way to ignite it for long enough, the blending should come naturally. You must find a way to hold onto it for long enough when it happens."

"I'll find a way. Twelve moons. I promise," she said, her heart thumping wildly within her chest.

Without looking back, Devotio raced toward the tunnel.

They leapt into a blackness of suffocating smoke. Acrid and dry, it seared Herlot's throat, lungs, and eyes. Hauling herself onto a branch, she climbed higher, reaching for the branch with the leaf. "I can't see!" she cried.

"Sense it with your hand. It will feel different." Devotio's advice arrived jagged, his breath interrupted from the gusts of smoke.

Herlot brushed her hand along the leaves until she sensed a vibrant pulsing from the five petals of a leaf. It had to be that one. She plucked it and fought her dizziness as she tucked it in her dress pocket. A thick cloud of smoke engulfed her. She lost her grip on the branch and slipped from one darkness into another.

CHAPTER 12
The Soldier

HERLOT AWOKE TO THE blur of the ground and Devotio's hooves leaving imprints in the dirt. She tried sitting up, but then felt the soreness in her arms, realizing that they were tied behind her. Using her belly muscles, she managed to curl up straight without falling forward.

Sunlight filtered through the forest greens as her vision cleared. A soldier walked alongside them, holding a rope tied around Devotio's neck. There was a belt around his waist and two more wrapped diagonally across his back, crossing at the middle. She saw several knives and three swords—one of them hers, gifted by Emrys. She recognized the soldier as the one who had bumped into her in Alonia; he was still wearing the wool half-cloak, so it was impossible to get a glimpse of his face.

Devotio wasn't resisting him at all, the rope around his neck hanging loose. How long had they been walking? The last thing she remembered was the black, heavy smoke. It was surreal. But not as surreal as....

The memories rushed to the surface, no longer dulled by the magical world inside the leaf. They were just as real as when she lived them. Alonia. The illness. Her parents' heartbeats fading. The sorrow in her heart bloomed and rose up her throat.

"Father! Mother!" Her anguish split the silence and birds took flight in all directions from a family of oak trees. She fell forward, her cheek against Devotio's mane and her chest tight with sobs. Her tears fell and carried her pain into the hoofprints along the path. That's all there was. Pain, as if she had been stripped of her skin and left out in the sun, and a tiny glimmer of light—Devotio's mane under her cheek and the sound of his pulse beating under her ear, all enveloped in the smoke that had infused his coat and her clothing and hair.

The soldier grabbed her by the back of her dress and practically threw her off Devotio, her glimmer of light ripped from her as if her arm had been torn off her body. From his belt, he grabbed a piece of cloth and tied it around her mouth.

"I'll take it off when you stop wailing," he snarled and hauled her back onto Devotio.

She recognized his low, hoarse voice. He was also the one she had overheard talking outside her home. However, she couldn't catch a glimpse of his face, hidden in the shadows of his hood, except for the sharp lines of his jaw. She wanted to see it, see what the eyes of someone who could cause such torture looked like, and if there was even the slightest glimpse of regret in them.

They walked until sunset, the cloth drenched in tears that she hadn't been able to stop, every memory of her parents' death piercing her. The pain was so much she could not think of anything else. She barely noticed the soldier tie Devotio's lead around a tree trunk near a clearing in the forest.

"We'll stay here for the night," he said.

Something about her surroundings not moving anymore, to be stable above one spot in the forest helped the memories slow down to a point where she could take regularly paced breaths again. While the soldier gathered wood, she thought about the magnitude of their situation. What was he planning to do with them? How would they escape? Why was he alone? Thankfully, Devotio did not have his alicorn.

She noticed a slight limp in the man's walk that she hadn't spotted before. Was he injured? If so, would it slow him down enough for her to attempt an escape?

Once he started the fire, he approached her with the dagger in hand. Panic seized her as she took in the sharpness of the blade and his overwhelming size. He reminded her of a buck she had once seen, with strong, defined muscles that rippled beneath his coat. She was capable of wrestling with Ambro and Elvin, but wouldn't stand a chance against this man. But she might be fast enough. *Run,* she urged her body. She swung a leg over, but he was right in front of her when her feet hit the ground. *He's going to kill me,* she thought, turning her cheek away from him, the most pathetic attempt at defending herself she could think of. He grabbed her by the side of her arm and turned her around so that her back was to him. Sharp pains fired across her back in anticipation of where the blade would make contact. Then, she felt the dagger against the rope around her wrist. Her hands were freed, and soreness shot through her wrists, elbows, and shoulders as her arms fell at her side.

Then he untied the knot of the cloth around her mouth and put it back in his pocket. Next, he took the rope off Devotio's neck. She stood in place, not sure what to do, not understanding why he would make it so easy for both of them to get away.

"Sit," he ordered.

Something about the relaxed way he said it, as if he was sure attempting an escape would be foolish on her part, smothered any thoughts of her running. When she took her first step, he had the dagger pointed at her chest. "Don't run." Her instincts had been right as she now clearly understood his intentions and the consequence she'd face if she didn't abide. She felt his glare on her every move as she sat on her bare heels by the fire. Somewhere along the path of her soul shattering, she had lost her shoes.

He opened a pouch and handed her a roll of bread. She stared at it in her hands. She hadn't eaten in days. Just feeling the crisp crust in her hand made her stomach grumble, but she remembered the poisoned food.

He sighed, then crouched down next to her, taking her bread away. He took a bite, swallowed it, and handed it back to her, chuckling while returning to his seat. The chuckle burned her veins. How dare he attempt anything close to a laugh after what he had just done to her Alonia?

She pondered throwing the bread at his hooded face, but her body's cravings overpowered her. She took a nibble. The bread was stale and flavorless but the moment she swallowed, her belly called for more and she took a large bite, this time chewing with urgency.

"What's your name?" he asked.

Herlot remembered Princess Kira's story and how names were an invitation into one's soul. She would never let this monster know her name. "You want to know mine?" he asked.

"No." She didn't want anything to do with his soul.

The fire crackled between them.

"You know how to use that?" he asked, waving his bread toward where the swords were in their scabbards, seemingly not bothered by her previous lack of response, which made her feel small, as if none of her actions or choices could have an effect on him.

"Is he your horse?" he asked.

"Where are you taking me?" she demanded. If he wanted to talk, she would be the one asking questions.

"Oh, so you do speak. The fortress of Eraska. But, first, I'd like to explore the land a bit."

Set a village on fire one day and explore the land the next. Who *were* these people? "My brother. Your men took him. Is that where he is?"

"Yes."

Good. At least she knew where Ambro was. "Why are you here? You weren't protecting us like you said, you liar."

The soldier grunted sarcastically. He wasn't going to answer that question, but maybe she could find out other things. "Where are you from?"

"Damalathum."

"I've never heard of it. Where is it?"

"It's a city about a week's sail north. Could fit hundreds of your village in it. Thousands of people. Buildings taller than the trees here."

"I don't have a village anymore," Herlot said, her words measured. The way he boasted about his land made it clear that he thought nothing of hers.

His head lowered, and she guessed he was gazing at his hands. An army of ants carried breadcrumbs across the dirt. Some moved around him, while others climbed over him. One scrambled back and forth between his knuckles. He set his hand on the ground by his boots, but it still would not leave his hand. Clearly frustrated, he shook it off.

"Maybe if you had been more patient, he would have found his way," Herlot said.

He stood and broke several dry branches in half against the thigh of his leg with the limp. *It won't slow him down,* she thought.

"Go to sleep. I warn you—I'll hear if you try anything." He chucked the pieces into the fire, grabbed his belts and pouches, and sat against a tree. He crossed his legs, folded his arms in front of him, and dozed off.

Devotio chewed a thistle before lying down behind Herlot. Resting against his side, she softened, comforted by his warmth. "Devotio, why did you disappear for so long? I really believed that I had imagined you for the longest time," she whispered.

"The look in your eyes on the last day we saw each other. The same look that has haunted my family for ages. It was the same as the humans who hunted my kind. Friends who overnight no longer saw us as real, only a means to acquire gold."

"I-I didn't want your gold. I was afraid that you were a figment of my imagination."

"I thought so, but I couldn't be sure. You frightened me."

"But you saved me anyway. You came back."

"I came back every year. I just kept my distance."

Herlot's throat tightened. She had no tears left to cry, but pressure built behind the backs of her eyes all the same. Even though she had scared Devotio, the few times they had spent together when she was a little girl had been just as important to him as they had been to her.

She curled up closer. "You're real."

Herlot realized Devotio was the only soul she had left in the world aside from Ambro. She looked to the stars, visible through the forest canopy, and thought of her parents. She imagined her father's laugh and her mother's caring touch. Without them, the world was a cold and unfamiliar place with no place for her. Just like Emrys had lost her body, Herlot had lost her home. How could she navigate anywhere without a place to come from?

It felt like the only story that could be told from this point was one of loss. It was everywhere, leaving no space for an adventure, a comedy, or a romance. She had lost her parents, her village, and Ambro. Devotio had lost his alicorn. Emrys had lost her body. Humans had lost their golden hearts. But, though she had once lost Devotio, he'd come back. Maybe there was hope.

She lifted the leaf out of her dress pocket and traced her fingers over the ridged petals. She pierced it with the seaweed string before wearing it around her neck. She thought about the unicorns and how much they had given up. They could have fought back against the humans but had resorted to centuries of waiting, in hopes that the humans would change. She couldn't let their sacrifice go to waste. She had to learn to control her golden heart and blend with its magic. She stared down at her chest. She couldn't imagine anything like the beautiful golden heart she had seen in Devotio having anything to do with her, let alone her having a heart that could spark gold occasionally. Yet it did explain how she escaped from the willow tree. She hadn't climbed out. She had *blended* through.

"What if my heart doesn't spark gold anymore?" she whispered, thinking of her dying parents, her ruined town. Surely that had the potential to break any magic she had hidden within. "I need that in order to save your family, or else I can't blend the leaf onto another tree."

"You did it twice today. First when we entered the chestnut tree, and then when we left. Emrys would have lost her gold if she had blended you with and out of the tree."

Herlot swallowed, digesting Devotio's words, feeling like even her body had become an unfamiliar place. How could she have blended without knowing it? Could it even *be* controlled? Herlot shifted, causing the soldier to stir. She waited to speak until she was sure he was asleep again.

"First," she said, "we'll have to find a way to get away from him. He's a light sleeper, that's for certain. Hopefully tomorrow will bring an opportunity for escape."

As she dozed, she thought of her father and her promise made all those years ago to explain to him what it was that happened when she had disappeared in the woods so long ago. "I found the word, Father. It's blend."

• • •

Herlot had heard few curse words in her life. In the morning, she awoke to a slew of so many she couldn't comprehend what was being said.

"... ill-bred strumpet..."

He was holding on to a branch, and each time he put weight on his foot, he spat another curse.

"You're hurt," she observed.

He told her to stay away, but she ignored his admonition and knelt before him. She lifted his pant leg and cringed at the sight of a swollen laceration weeping a yellow pus. Rage engulfed her as memories of her parents' swollen faces resurfaced.

"I'm going to leave you here. You will see for yourself what it is like to wait for someone to help you." She stood with the intention to push him off balance and walk away, but froze when she met him face to face.

Cold eyes glared back at her from the shadows of the hood, making her feel as if she had slid across a patch of sharp, cracked ice. They were a crisp, light blue, so light they were almost white. She had never seen anything like them. She felt intimidated by their fierceness and coldness, and even more so, afraid.

Her confidence plummeted and she backed away. "Come on, Devotio. Let's go." She seized the pouches and the weapon holders.

She didn't make it far before sensing that Devotio was not with her. When she turned around looking for him, he was still standing next to the soldier, his head tall. This wasn't a time for games. "Devotio. Let's. Go."

"He burned his leg rescuing you from the fire," Devotio said, his words wrapping around her. "Help him."

Herlot startled, afraid that the soldier had heard Devotio, but then exhaled, remembering how precisely Devotio could direct his breath.

"After what he did to my family, he doesn't deserve anyone's care."

She couldn't believe Devotio would dare to ask something like this of her, and this soldier should have been the last person to be allowed near Devotio. This soldier was the enemy and Herlot knew he'd kill him as mercilessly as his people had put a dagger in Simon's back if Devotio were still to have his alicorn. She realized Devotio had one major fault. Just like her, he was naïve and too trusting. Of course, he was. After all, he risked being exposed to help her when she was cold and wet from the storm, and he even took a chance on Ambro, Enri, and Mahtreeh. Well, no matter how magical he was, she was the one making decisions now, and helping a murderer was the last thing they were going to do. She marched down the path at a fast pace. He would follow, eventually.

"Help him," Devotio said.

The way he said it sounded as if he truly believed her heart had some magical capabilities that would show kindness to someone who killed her parents. His family needed her to blend the leaf, which seemed impossible enough, but this, this was really asking for the impossible. She still couldn't hear Devotio following behind her, and the confidence drained from her legs.

She spun around and glared at Devotio. "Give me one good reason," she said.

"I like him."

This was what it felt like to be emotionally slapped by a unicorn. He *liked* him? As much as her thoughts were racing with rage, she found her glare softening the more she looked into Devotio's eyes. She looked at the path ahead of her and it was as if one of the planks dropped right in front of her, making it impossible for her to go forward. Each step forward, no matter where she went, was a step into a territory of uncertainty and hollowness. The truth was that she didn't care about the soldier's leg or anything about him, for that matter. But she needed a friend more than anything in the world; she was too afraid to be alone. If helping the soldier meant Devotio coming with her, then that was what she had to do.

"I need another reason, please...a better one," she said, already defeated.

"He feels different. Like you did when we first met. I don't know if he's good, but he's different from the others."

"Feels different," she mumbled to herself as she glanced back at the soldier. "What do you want me to do? I can't heal a burn."

"You climb trees in the middle of a fire and talk to horses. I'm sure you can come up with something," the soldier said.

Herlot pressed her lips together. She would have to be more careful when she spoke to Devotio. He could control who heard his voice, but she didn't have that ability.

She rested her hands on her hips, walked in a circle, and looked about as if an answer of how to help the soldier might be seen. A bird flew by carrying a sunflower seed. An image of Enri with a sunflower in her strawberry-blond hair crossed her mind. Oliver. Lorfin. They were already heading south, and based on her knowledge of Rudi's travels to the other villages, they could make it to Lorfin by sunset.

"I will take you to a healer. Can you get on the uni...horse?" she asked.

Without hesitation, the soldier gripped Devotio's mane and pushed off with his good leg, swinging the injured one over. He extended his hand to her. His palm was callused and scarred, and strong veins rose up his forearms. With the amount of weapons he carried, she wondered how many deaths that hand had been responsible for. No. She would never give him her name and would definitely never take his hand. Thankfully, Devotio knelt his front legs so she could climb on with ease.

They rode in silence, following the path north. Herlot's emotions somersaulted from numbness to rage, despair, sadness, and loneliness. Sometimes hope appeared, but then she crashed down into hollowness once more. She tried focusing on the trees, but that made it worse. These weren't the Alonian trees that felt like family. These were strangers. Strangers she had once looked forward to meeting when she became a steward. That dream was from a different world now.

She tightened her grip on Devotio's mane, hoping to hold her current feeling of despair in place. She didn't care which emotion she felt as long as it didn't switch. But it was no use.

"Stop." She slid off and stumbled toward what sounded like water flowing over rocks.

The trunks and foliage spun and closed in on her as she struggled to reach the climax of inhalation. *Mother, help me. I can't breathe, I'm afraid.* She fell to her knees in front of the stream and plunged her head into the water. The cold shocked her thoughts, and the water running over the back of her neck froze them in place. The spinning came to a still. She stayed there until her body fought for breath. *Ha! Now you want to breathe? If you ever choke me again, next time, I won't come up.*

When she finally came up, she indulged in the feeling of air spreading all across her lungs. Success. Water dripped from her hair and mud covered the dimples in her reflection. There was a disoriented wildness in her eyes that reminded her of her mother's state after Herlot came home that first night she had met Devotio. She didn't care to clean off the dirt and returned to the main path.

The soldier lifted an eyebrow when he saw her. "Thirsty?"

"Something like that," she mumbled as she climbed on. She lifted her chin high as they rode on, but the soldier's eyes seemed to penetrate her from behind, as if he knew she was barely holding herself together.

They turned left at a fork in the path where a sunflower symbolizing Lorfin was carved into a trunk. On the other path was a trunk with a circle carved into it, symbolizing Temes. From what Herlot knew, Temes was surrounded by a wall and Cloudian's stewards never traveled there at night because of how dangerous the animals that lived there were.

After hours of riding, her back muscles began to cramp as the soldier's weight bore more and more onto her. Heat smoldered from his body, a sign that his fever was dangerously high.

"You need to stay awake. We are almost there," she said.

Black clouds masked the sky above the sunflower field that appeared at the end of the path. At the horizon, it looked as if the clouds had touched down where the rain had begun to pour. A flash rippled through the clouds, magnifying their layers.

Herlot slipped from beneath the soldier, and he slumped forward. It was strange how their roles had reversed. She almost did not hear his whisper, swept up in the crescendo of rustling leaves. He uncoiled a clenched finger to point at her dress.

"Blood...will spread the illness," he said.

She looked down at the skirt of her dress. The center was blood-stained. The illness that had killed her mother now tainted the wool she had woven for her daughter's gift. Herlot understood that if she wore it into Lorfin, it would infect the people just like the food in the chests had poisoned her family.

She took the dagger and cut above the stains, remembering the day of her recitation and how proud her parents had been even though she had failed. Parts of that dress had been used to weave the one she had on now. This dress was the only evidence she had left of those happy days, and she would salvage as much as possible.

She dug a hole with her fingers and covered the fabric with soil, exactly the same way her Alonians should have been buried according to tradition.

CHAPTER 13
Lorfin

HERLOT GUIDED DEVOTIO BETWEEN two rows of sunflowers outside of Lorfin village. Several birds were more interested in picking at the seeds than seeking shelter from the oncoming storm. The wind continued to pick up, and the sunflowers wavered above Herlot's head.

The field opened into a meadow that slanted down toward the village. Women balanced baskets against their hips while men guided livestock into their enclosures. A tall, thin man, unable to rush a cow chewing grass, turned as if sensing newcomers. Herlot recognized him right away by his delicate frame, even though a decade had gone by since they met. Mahtreeh.

Thunder rumbled and the others picked up their pace to their homes. But the man smiled and ran through the rain driven by the fierce wind pelting the meadow.

"Herlot? Is that you?" He embraced her but let go when she began to shake. He eyed the soldier, now unconscious, then did a doubletake on Devotio. "Is that Devotio? What happened to his—"

He turned to face her and studied her for a silent moment. His eyes widened. She must have looked a mess—the ripped dress and dirty face. "What happened to you?"

Herlot's cheeks quivered as she tried to still her trembling lips. She knew she had to get the soldier to Oliver, but the little piece of human warmth she had felt in Mahtreeh's embrace was all that mattered. She threw herself against his chest, too weak to hold back her tears.

"It will be alright. Whatever happened, all will be just fine," he said, enwrapping her in his arms. "Come. We'll get you inside where you'll be safe."

"Mahtreeh, this man needs help. His leg is badly burned, and he has a fever," she said.

"Who is he?"

"Alonia was invaded by soldiers who claimed to be protecting us. They locked us in our homes and gave us poisoned supplies. Everyone fell ill. The few who survived were taken away. The dead were burned in their homes," she choked out. "He's one of the soldiers."

He looked at her, eyes widening even farther. Finally, he held two fingers in his mouth and blew a loud, clear whistle three times that had no difficulty traveling through the wind and rain. "That's our signal so Father knows someone needs his immediate attention," Mahtreeh explained. Then he held Herlot by the forearm as he guided her into the village.

Lorfiners stared at her from their doorways. She was not upset that they didn't greet her, and she was too exhausted to care to make a good impression. To them, she probably looked like a strange girl wearing only half of a dress with her wool leggings, traveling by horse with an injured man dressed in odd garb.

Oliver stood outside the doorway of his home. With Mahtreeh's help, he lifted the soldier from Devotio and carried him inside.

Herlot followed as they settled him onto a wooden table while Mahtreeh stuttered, recapping what Herlot had told him. Her gaze found Enri, who was faced away, crushing plants in a mortar. A purple wildflower, now wilting, held her hair back. It seemed she hadn't broken her tradition of wearing flowers in her hair. How nice it was to have something as simple as wearing a flower, something that could remain stable throughout one's entire life. As long as there were flowers, Enri could wear them in her hair every day for as long as she wanted.

Oliver examined the burn as Herlot and Mahtreeh waited for his response to the news. She was surprised to find that what remained of his hair was now a pure white. How things changed, and there was nothing one could do to stop them. Just a few days ago there had been an Alonia, now there wasn't. She was grateful she hadn't seen the ruins after the fire. Had Ambro? He was still out there in the hands of the soldiers, and she had no idea what they intended to do with him.

Nervous whistles escaped Mahtreeh, piercing the quiet. "Father? What do we do?" he asked.

"Take the horse to the stable. Herlot, help yourself to the water. When Enri and I finish here, you must explain to us everything that has happened, and I send a prayer now that I have misunderstood my son." His lips barely moved as he spoke, his hands steady as he cleaned the wound.

Herlot scooped a cup into the water bucket and then took a seat on the floor. She took slow sips of the water while she watched Enri and Oliver work.

Several chests with their lids open were filled with all sorts of plants, pouches, cloths, and small, glass bottles of oils. She recognized several herbs hanging from the ceiling. Marjoram. Vetch. Valerian. It was like an upside-down garden. She also noticed two clay tablets hanging among them. In Eraska, it was a tradition to make clay tablets of a child's handprints if he survived his first year. She couldn't remember the last time she had seen hers. Would she find it beneath the rubble that had once been her home if she ever returned to Alonia?

She watched Oliver spread Enri's mixture over the burn. Then he wrapped the leg in cloth while Enri poured a liquid into a cup. Oliver supported the soldier's head and brought the cup to his lips, but the soldier moved his head to the side.

"Please, son. A peaceful dream is the best medicine," Oliver said.

Herlot almost snarled at Oliver's words. The soldier didn't deserve his kind attention or a peaceful dream. Son? How could Oliver call him son? He was a monster, a monster that deserved to have nightmares for as long as he lived. And Herlot had brought him here. At least he was too weak and outnumbered here to do any damage. By no means could they let him near his weapons.

The soldier yielded, drinking the liquid in one gulp. He was asleep by the time Enri and her father had cleaned the materials, only to begin work on another mixture.

Mahtreeh returned and placed his arm around Herlot's shoulders as he sat down next to her. She drew a ragged breath and rested her head against him. With a worried glanced her way, Oliver reached up for several basil leaves. "Add these."

Enri took them and crushed them in the mortar.

Herlot closed her eyes, listening to the crackling fire, boiling water, and Mahtreeh's heartbeat. Hers finally found a steady rhythm, using his as a guide.

"Here, drink this, Herlot. Something special to soothe. Not heal, but soothe," Oliver said.

Herlot opened her eyes and took a clay cup from Oliver. "Soothe is such a nice word," she said through chattering teeth. She was warm so it had to be from exhaustion or shock. Probably both. "It sounds exactly like what it means."

"Indeed, it does. That's why storytellers can be great healers, if they know how to use the right words."

If only there were a word that could make time run backwards to the morning of Ambro's wedding. That was impossible. But perhaps there was a word that could help her wake the gold in her heart and blend the leaf onto a new tree. She eyed the contents of her cup. The liquid smelled of soil and grass with a hint of ashes. She took a slow sip. When she swallowed, it felt like an anchor had dropped into her belly, strong and stable, and she didn't have to fight against the spinning of her mind anymore.

"Herlot...can you tell us what happened?" Enri tucked a short piece of hair, dirty and weighed down by sweat, behind Herlot's ear. Herlot was grateful that none of them seemed disgusted by her state.

"If you just want to rest, we understand. You don't have to speak about anything if you don't want to," Oliver said.

Herlot swirled the remaining liquid in a circle. Her body was too exhausted again to cry, so she was certain she could speak without breaking into tears. And for her own sake, she needed other humans to know, ones she knew cared about her. She didn't want to be alone in her awful memories, as selfish as that might have sounded. Finally, she said, "I will tell you."

As storm winds raged outside, bursts of rain were driven in harsh rhythm against stone and thatch, and elements sought their way through any gap while Oliver's family listened to the horrors that had befallen Alonia.

Oliver leaned forward when Herlot explained the chests, the blankets, and how the illness had spread. He held her hand, not breaking eye contact when she spoke of her parents' deaths and how Ambro had been taken while she'd managed to escape. She was surprised at how easy it was to talk about it, how quickly it spilled out of her, as if it were just a story that couldn't be real. Thanks to Oliver, the Herlot in the story had a hand to hold through the entire tragedy.

"He said he was from a place called Damalathum. That is the only thing I know about them," she concluded.

"He could be lying about that, too," Mahtreeh said. "It makes no sense. There is no reason for them to be here. Whoever they are, they lied about being there to protect Alonia. They would've helped the sick if that was so. They had to have known the supplies were poisoned, too."

"What if they didn't let them out because they were afraid to get sick, too? If they had wanted to kill and poison the Alonians, why did they not kill Ambro on the spot when they saw he was alive? Also, the soldier did help Herlot get away from the fire," Enri said.

As exhausted as Herlot was, the unanswered questions swirled like a storm inside her chest, one of anger and frustration. This was what it had to be like to be pulled under by the sea and thrown around, the path to light nowhere in sight, just darkness. Each comment by Enri or Mahtreeh only added to the power of the sea, to the confusion in her chest.

"I do not know who these people are or where they came from. But there are several things I know for certain," Oliver finally spoke. "Herlot, you and Ambro are lucky to have been spared the fate of your parents. The illness is called crowpox."

Crowpox. What had killed her parents had a name. Oliver had given her a drop of understanding about what had happened in her home, and it didn't make it better, just more real. Her hands shook as the word *crowpox* repeated in her mind. Oliver's soft hands pressed on her elbow and then he guided the cup to her lips.

"Recently, on one of my trips to visit Cloudian at the fortress, a ship arrived. The captain spoke of an illness called crowpox that had taken many lives in the kingdom he came from. It begins when someone gives birth to the spirit of the crow, which then ravages through the body from the inside out, destroying anything in its path. Black blisters form where it has managed to escape. Anyone in the vicinity of the victim, especially those who come in contact with the body, will ingest the spirit offspring of the crow and be forced to go through the same. A very small few, if ever, are spared. Herlot, you and your brother were two of the lucky ones."

While Oliver spoke, Mahtreeh had traced a crow in the dirt. Never had Herlot been afraid of the bird, but now just a dirt drawing of it made her uncomfortable.

"Father, didn't the captain also speak about a golden elixir? One that can protect people from it?" Enri asked. She reached for a bucket and placed it behind her where drops of rain were falling through the roof.

"Yes," Oliver said. "There is no stopping it, unless one drinks a golden elixir before the illness occurs. Which is why I have no doubt that the soldiers did this on purpose. The food and blankets must have been tainted with crowpox offspring. The captain explained that staying away from the sick was the only way to survive. When one of his sailors became ill, he had to be put on a boat and abandoned. These soldiers would not have handled the tainted food and blankets, let alone enter the homes after had they known they'd be at risk. They must be protected by having ingested the elixir."

"But...why?" Herlot remembered the sailor she had collided into while playing King Fog. Had this been the same sailor that the captain had spoken of? If so, Herlot had not succumbed to the illness back then either.

Oliver stared into the distance. "I fear I do not want to know. What these foreign men have done is evil beyond anything I have ever heard."

"What of this soldier?" Mahtreeh asked. "He said he wanted to take Herlot back to the fortress."

"Ha! It will be all of Lorfin against him. We won't let him take Herlot," Enri responded.

"He's been through immense stress," Oliver said.

Herlot huffed. "A burn is nothing compared to what Alonia suffered."

"Not just the leg burn. I am guessing that the man is around your age, possibly five or so years older, but..." Oliver went to the table where the soldier slept and parted his hair. "Look, some of his hair is beginning to gray, and these frown marks between his eyebrows normally would not appear for at least another few years."

Herlot walked over to have a closer look, allowing herself a longer glance that she had been too intimidated to risk with him being awake. His eyes were closed and there was no threat of seeing the ice-cold blue of them. He had hickory-brown hair that layered itself at random lengths, reaching to the center of his neck. His strong jaw, covered in stubble, was tensed even in sleep—as was the rest of his body and his breath. His thick eyebrows seemed to be attracted to one another, because they sought to touch even when at rest, bringing a scowl to his face. "He's a monster, Oliver, no matter what he has been through."

"He's a monster we can get more information from. It is good that you didn't leave him," Oliver said, taking Herlot's hands in his own. "There are no words that can express my grief for the losses of Ilvy, Ernest, and Alonia. No words that may ever fill the emptiness you feel. But I open my home to you, Herlot. You are part of our family now."

Herlot almost attempted a smile. Oliver had given her a drop of something else now, a glimmer of a future, of family. If there was any place she could find some semblance of peace to focus enough to learn to blend, Lorfin, especially with Oliver, Enri, and Mahtreeh would be it. "Thank you, Oliver. This means the skies to me." She kissed his hand.

Instead of sleeping, Herlot listened to the wind outside. She heard Oliver awaken several times to check on the soldier, and Herlot watched his figure in the dark as he changed the bandage.

Oliver had not seemed to give the matter of helping the soldier a second thought. He still took care of him after hearing her story. The soldier was a monster and he did not deserve Oliver's care. And she hated him even more for making her think that, because it was just another way his kind had broken her.

Herlot was no longer the girl who had instinctually felt the need to help the sailor with what she now knew was crowpox. She thought of the rage that had taken her over earlier that day, when she had almost left the soldier. She hadn't told Oliver's family about that part. But no matter how hard she tried, she couldn't hide it from herself, and she knew that she would never be Herlot of Alonia again.

● ● ●

A warm, moist breeze stirred Herlot awake just in time to see Oliver close the door behind him. She shot upright—but Enri, Mahtreeh, and the soldier were still asleep. Sighing, she fell back down onto the hay.

The breeze had stirred some of the keepsakes hanging from the ceiling to swing, and her attention was brought to the two clay footprints she had noticed before. "H" and "A" was written underneath the prints. Letters. Only Alonians wrote letters. A for Ambro and H for Herlot. Why were their tablets at Oliver's? She slowly rose to her feet doing her best not to bump into Enri or Mahtreeh and avoided looking over at the soldier. Just the thought of having slept in his vicinity for the second night made her stomach churn.

When she stepped outside, she approached Oliver to speak with him, but something about the way he stood made her withhold her words. Turned to her, his back was straight, his palms open and hanging at his side. She could hear him take a deep breath through his nose and she noticed the aroma of the rain-drenched soil that lingered heavily in the air. He clasped his hands and stretched them above his head, the sunlight illuminating his face. He turned and smiled at her. "There is never a reason to not appreciate the first breaths of the morning air, no matter what sorrows lie behind or before us."

"I like this advice," Herlot said. It reminded her of something her father would have said. Grief flooded her, but she kept her voice from cracking when she spoke. "Oliver, may I ask you why our tablets hang in your home?"

"They were a gift from your mother. I hope you know how much you and Ambro helped my children back then." He lifted his chin as if he was taking another sip of sunlight. "There was a light in them again after our trip to Alonia, one I didn't expect to see in them for a long time after my wife passed. Your mother saw it, too, and she wanted them to have a gift to remind them of your time together."

Herlot swallowed back a lump in her throat. A piece of her mother's story she hadn't known about, a fingerprint of her kindness marked into the story of Oliver's home. She found a piece of her mother after she thought nothing was left of her in the world.

They hadn't had a private-enough place to talk about Devotio, but Herlot knew that Enri and Mahtreeh would want to spend time with him. Since they knew what he really was, and believed what he really was, she could tell them about the leaf, and she hoped with all of her heart they might be able to help her. This was the last thing she wanted to or could do alone. And Devotio would need them, too. They could feel a pure happiness about him, something she had lost, something that was now in the ashes of Alonia and possibly getting scattered by the wind.

She was about to go check on him in the animal enclosure when a rustling inside the house grabbed her attention. She and Oliver eyed one another and hurried inside to be met by the view of the soldier sitting up on the table and beginning to lower his legs to the ground.

"You must not stand just yet," Oliver said.

Listing to one side, the soldier lunged toward his weapons.

Herlot rushed in front of Enri and Mahtreeh, who had scrambled to their feet. "We should have hidden those," Mahtreeh said.

The soldier fastened the belted weapons around his body. Herlot eyed the doorway, only Oliver stood in its entrance, blocking the soldier's path out. She had to intimidate him, somehow, before he tried anything on her new family.

"You're outnumbered here. There's at least a hundred people outside. If you hurt us, you won't get away with it," she said, her voice cracking at the end.

In one stride, the soldier slid a sword from his belt and covered the distance to her. Oliver was ready to step in front of her, but the soldier was quicker, his limp barely noticeable.

"If you want the people of this village to live, I suggest you take your sword." He shoved the hilt into her hand. Her fingers weakly wrapped around it.

"Want us to live?" Mahtreeh asked, his eyes wide.

The soldier turned to Oliver. "A troop will be arriving in your village at any moment. Find anyone with fighting experience and anything that may be used as a weapon," he ordered.

"What? *Here?*" Herlot cried.

The soldier shook his head. "Yes. Here. Are you that naïve, girl? Please tell me it's because you're conceited and not stupid to think your village would be the only one."

Herlot's jaw dropped open.

"Every village of Eraska is being invaded. Temes. Ruelder. Noray. And Bundene. Right after they finish here."

Herlot gripped the hilt of the sword with rage as the walls of the home seemed to cave in. The same horror that had befallen on her village was to spread all over the land, her new family now the new victims.

"Do your people have weapons?" the soldier asked Oliver.

"No. But I do. A sword I received in exchange for helping a sailor a few years ago." Oliver shuffled through a weathered chest and pulled a rusted sword out.

"It will have to do. Gather anyone willing to fight and meet me in the field. You don't have much time."

"You expect us to *fight*? We don't stand a chance!" Herlot nearly screamed. With all her courage she stepped as close to him as she could get and glared into his eyes. "This is some sick part of your plan. With me here the monsters you travel with won't convince the Lorfiners to go inside your crowpox traps. You just want to get rid of anyone able to resist."

"We should hide in the woods," Enri said.

The soldier snarled, his face twisting in derision. "And they'll send a message by pigeon to the fortress! By the end of the day the troops controlling the fortress will arrive, as well, to help hunt you down. With me, you have a chance to fight them off without anyone noticing. You'll have *time* to run, at least a week, enough time to warn your other villages, too."

"How many of your men are arriving?" Oliver asked.

Herlot whipped around to face Oliver. Was he really thinking of trusting this man?

"Twenty."

"And you think my people stand a chance against trained soldiers?"

"We don't. We need to go now; run and hide in the woods like Enri said," Herlot said.

"Not everyone will live. You'll have losses," the soldier said. "But you have the advantage of surprise and numbers. Your sunflower field will force them into single formation as they walk through it. We will set barricades to force them to disperse even more. You will hide in the field until I tell you, and then you will attack them in groups."

It was a good plan, Herlot had to admit, if only the soldier wasn't here. "He will warn them the moment he has a chance," she said.

Oliver, calm and sturdy as a sunflower in a breeze, folded his hands in front of him as he stared at the soldier. "My people's lives are at risk. How do I know your word can be honored?"

"You gave me your honor by healing my leg when you had no reason to. I'd like to return it. Sir, this is your only option. If your people try to run or hide, they will be found if my men are set on searching for them, I guarantee you that. This is your only choice." The soldier looked straight into Oliver's eyes, not breaking eye contact.

Oliver nodded. "We will trust you."

● ● ●

Herlot and Oliver's family ran to each home, shouting and pouring water buckets onto those refusing to wake. Like many others, a resistant older couple questioned Herlot as she flustered to get them to move. "Who are you? What are you doing in my home?"

Herlot felt her impatience spill into anger. Fortunately, Oliver followed behind her and called, "Carl, there is an emergency. Do as this young woman asks." *If only they would listen to me like they did to him.*

Herlot jogged ahead to emphasize the urgency to those who were walking at a slow pace while frustrated shouts were expressed around her.

"Who is she?"

"There better be an explanation for this ruckus!"

Impatient thumps stirred from the barn as she passed it, the animals ready to start their day.

"Devotio, I'm sorry, but you have to wait. You'll be safe with the other animals. I have to help Lorfin," she said under her breath, trusting Devotio's keen sense of hearing.

Soon she felt the familiar breeze around her ears. "I understand," Devotio said.

She waited in silence as Oliver guided his entire village into the largest stone structure in Lorfin, the one that housed food stores and tools.

Once the Lorfiners were settled, sitting on sacks of grain, baskets of potatoes, and sheaves of hay, Oliver addressed them, explaining what had happened in Alonia and that the soldier was going to help protect Lorfin.

"I'm going to fight, and I do not ask this of anyone else. But, if you happen to have a weapon and are willing to take the risk, please join me right now," Oliver said.

"I have no weapon, but I have my pitchfork and I will fight at your side," Carl said and took a stand next to Oliver.

"Thank you, Carl," Oliver said.

Several other men began to make their way toward Oliver.

Herlot joined the group. "I will fight." She adjusted her baldric where her own sword now sat fastened, ready to be used for the first time.

"I can throw rocks better than any Lorfiner." Herlot turned around, surprised to see Enri and Mahtreeh right behind her. Enri turned her palm upright to present a rock.

"Don't be ridicul—" Oliver started.

"I'll throw them from afar where they can't get to me!"

About ten women joined. "We can help Enri," one of them said.

Herlot barely made out Mahtreeh's muttered words to his father. "No matter what awaits us tomorrow, we will do it together. Remember when you told us that? We survived Mother's death together. This will be a whistle during harvest compared to that. I need to fight alongside my family."

A pained expression covered Oliver's face. "Very well, my son. Together."

In a deadly silence, they followed the soldier into the sunflower field, where the bird songs and bee buzzes seemed oblivious to what lay ahead of them. Herlot could barely look at the people around her. Some of them wouldn't be here anymore when it was over, and she could easily be one of them. She could only hope that the sword would defend her as Emrys had said. Never before in her life had she had to risk her life at something she had no idea how to do, but there was no chance that she could not try and help the Lorfiners. They were all in this together, no one trained to use a weapon, nonetheless fighting trained men. Their strength in numbers was their only advantage.

The soldier stopped and handed one of his swords to Mahtreeh, after which he took a wide stance. "We'll disperse the barrels and carts along this part of the path. My group will attack them from the front. Do not move until we do. You," he said, lowering his gaze at Enri and the rock throwers. "Once the fight begins, aim for the ones farther back. It will slow them, spread them out, and give us more time."

"Do not attempt to fight with your pitchforks. Your goal is to strike them once to slow them down before I can reach them. Their swords will break your wooden handles in half and find themselves in your stomachs before you know it. You have a slight advantage of distance due to the length of the pitchforks, so your best strategy is to aim at their feet and trip them. Then, and only then, will you attack, and you have to be quick. They'll be back on their feet quicker than you'll expect. If you don't think you have time to finish it, run."

As everyone got into their hiding places, Herlot followed the soldier back up the path, closer to the village. It would be up to Oliver, Mahtreeh, and her to fight alongside the soldier and prevent anyone from reaching Lorfin's homes.

Herlot's hugged her belly in shame when he looked at the lot of them. His gaze focused upon their sword-holding hands and he looked like he was embarrassed for them and ready to laugh. Had it been her decision, she would not have trusted him, but Oliver had. She didn't know enough about these matters, but Oliver was the most educated Eraskan man in matters of the outside world, so she would have to put her faith in his judgment.

"It takes years to learn to use a sword." He raised his eyebrows as if expecting them to run. "Hold it right below the hilt. Keep one foot slightly in front of the other. These men have orders not to kill you. That does not mean they won't if they're provoked, but they might hesitate. We need to use that to our advantage. Work together to attack anyone who gets past me. Try to stay relaxed when your opponent strikes and focus on his entire body, not just the sword, it will give you clues from which direction the strike will come. Aim for the neck or below the ribcage."

The sound of wagon wheels rolling over rocks from afar broke his speech. Herlot clutched her sword. "They're here," she whispered.

Herlot took her place behind one of the sunflowers. She tried to calm herself by focusing on the place where one of the stems met the sturdy stalk. The incoming soldiers advanced leisurely, obviously not sensing a threat.

"What is your name, soldier?" Oliver whispered.

"Movo." He turned and extended his hand to Oliver. "Your healing skills are unlike any I have ever experienced. Thank you."

Oliver took his hand in both of his. "We thank you for helping us," he said, giving the embrace a shake.

"Thank me later and only if we succeed at protecting your people."

Herlot snuck a peek at the soldiers through the stalks. She didn't recognize any of them. The leader was different, too. Much shorter than the one who had led the troop into Alonia. How many had come to Eraska? How many more would arrive?

Herlot studied Movo. Strands of hair hung in front of his face as he stared at the ground, his body tense, one arm hovering above the hilt of the sword in his belt. If only she could read his mind and know if his plan was genuine. The only good sign was that he still had not attempted to warn the soldiers.

As the soldiers neared enough for her to hear them complain about the numerous objects that had been left on the path, Mahtreeh's breaths quickened next to her.

"Slow your breath, it will help," Movo said without turning around. "Get ready. They're almost here."

Herlot closed her eyes. *You have to survive this. You need to stay alive to blend the leaf. Now focus.*

Next to her, Mahtreeh was a mess. "This is it. This is it. This is it," he huffed, his hands shaking.

"I'm right next to you, son. Herlot, we do this together," Oliver said.

"Now," Movo said.

In a motion as quick as a lightning strike, Movo had his sword in a guard in front of his body. Herlot tightened her grasp on hers with sweat-glazed palms and followed him out into the path, toward the line of strangers, poisoners, and villains, far more dangerous than any Alonian story could ever prepare one for.

● ● ●

Movo pounced ahead to meet the leader, Peter, and the soldiers wavered back. Peter braced, his eyes focused on Movo's sword, which teetered above. *He's too focused*, Movo thought, and skidded his heel, kicking loose earth and pebbles into Peter's eyes. Blinded, Peter lost his stance and Movo shouldered him onto the sword of the soldier, Cerec, behind him. Never before had his opponents been ones whose names he knew so well. He wasn't surprised to learn that it didn't make a difference. It never did during a fight. It was how he had been trained. With his free hand, he pulled his dagger and slit Cerec's throat.

Movo intercepted the third soldier with a slice of his sword. There was something different about this fight. In previous battles he felt numb after taking someone's life. Now he was feeling a quiver of satisfaction, as if there was actual meaning behind what he was doing. He didn't have enough fingers to count the castles he had besieged, yet a single, meager village had made him feel something for the first time. He could speak several languages and calculate ship speeds in his sleep, but for the life of him, this, he could not understand.

He took down two more men, snaking the sword in swift motions around his body as he turned in a circle to block and counter their strikes simultaneously. However, several broke his defensive line and he prayed that Oliver, his son, and the girl were smart enough to follow the directions he had given them.

• • •

Every instinct in Herlot was screaming at her to run. She saw the blur of Movo's sword and a figure lunging toward her. She squeezed her eyes shut.

"Relax." Devotio's voice enveloped her. "The sword will help you."

She opened her eyes just in time. Her sword pierced the ground and blocked a strike at her legs. The two blades shrilled against one another as she hoisted her attacker's sword from his grip. Oliver deftly stepped in, piercing the soldier's throat. Another soldier made it past Movo.

Herlot's senses sharpened, and her heartbeat stilled. She felt the footsteps on the meadow drumming below her feet. She felt air parting toward Mahtreeh as iron slid through it.

With a swift leap, she skidded in front of Mahtreeh, blocking the attack with her sword. "Now!"

Mahtreeh plunged his sword into the soldier's torso.

A storm of rocks pounded at the soldiers and pitchforks swiveled through the air.

Herlot raced in front of Movo, blocking the path of two more soldiers. Their attacks railed against her, but her sword met their strikes with the rhythm of a master. It seemed to propel itself to the spaces around her, sensing the path of each attack before it occurred.

Don't let go of the hilt! she thought as a rapid movement by the sword twisted her shoulder.

Mahtreeh snuck under her shoulder, slicing the neck of one and the other in the groin.

All of a sudden, Oliver cried out and Herlot's heart throbbed in pain. It was as if she could feel the iron pierce Oliver's heart. "Don't look!" Herlot yelled to Mahtreeh as they faced the oncoming soldiers. He couldn't see Oliver now—not if they wanted to survive. It would break him.

However, her feet sensed the thump of Mahtreeh's sword against the earth. At the same time, she watched three men with pitchforks taken down in their attempt to run. Aside from Movo, she was the only one with a sword left.

Herlot charged, allowing the sword to take over again. She was all heartbeat, senses, and movement. She was dancing, and her new opponent hated it. Frustrated grunts escaped him. Between her blocks, she sensed moments of opportunity to strike, but remembered Emrys's warning to only use the sword as defense.

"Mahtreeh!" she shouted. She needed his help, desperately, to finish the soldier.

Out of nowhere, an ax soared past her ear. Instinct pressed her eyes shut for a flash as the crack of her opponent's splitting skull rang out and he thudded to the ground.

A gigantic man dressed in black leather from head to toe, with a long, copper-red braid and beard, ran ahead of her, catching a soldier by the hips, and hurling him over his shoulder into the sunflowers. Grabbing the next two by their collars, he cracked their heads together in one fluid movement with deadly force.

He whipped his braid behind him, squatted, and held his interlaced fingers low to the ground. Once again, a formidably huge man shrouded in black leather raced by her. This man, though still towering in height, was lean and young. His black hair was tied back in a braid. With a sword in each hand, he charged toward the red-haired man, setting his foot in his hands and leaping high into the air. As he arced, he curled his body in a ball, bringing his feet over his head, landing in a crouch behind two soldiers before his swords sliced through the backs of their legs. Herlot watched in horror as blood splattered the sunflower petals.

The remaining soldiers approached with faltering confidence. The ax flew with perfect aim at another's soldier's chest. Blood flung from it in all directions as it spun through the air. Herlot watched the vivid greens around her get tainted in red as the two strangers disarmed the remaining soldiers with ease.

It was over. Any care for what had just happened or who the strangers were disappeared, her heart had only one place it wanted to be and that was alongside Oliver. She couldn't see his face from where she stood, for Enri and Mahtreeh were crouched over him, but she didn't need to in order to know that his eyes wouldn't open again. She made her way lifelessly toward them. She was alive enough for Devotio. Most of Lorfin's people were alive, safe in the village, but the darkness that had shrouded Alonia had arrived here, as well, even into the flower heads under which numerous Lorfiners lay, their blood still spilling onto the soil. Not even the birds and bees could escape it she realized as she watched a bird peck at blood-stained sunflower seeds. The only thing in her power now was to help Mahtreeh and Enri not feel alone in their loss, but just as she was about to reach them, Movo shoved past her. She turned and watched him pick up pace into a spring toward one of the wagons, one with what she made out to resemble a pigeon cage from far away.

This had been part of his plan all along. Almost everyone able to fight for Lorfin was now either dead or injured, and Movo was going to send a message for more men back to the fortress so they could capture the Lorfiners at their weakest. She had to stop it. With the little strength she had left, she pushed her legs forward, nearly stumbling over a pitchfork and the limp arm still holding onto it.

He was too far ahead of her. She'd never reach the wagon in time to stop him from making Oliver's death meaningless. She slowed her pace and almost laughed at her pathetic attempt to stop him, as pathetic as she had been to get herself locked inside her own home. As evil as Movo and his men were, they were smarter, stronger, and her land would succumb to them.

"Stop! Please!" she yelled. The wind blew the futility of her words back in her face. She was weak, the only thing in her power was to beg.

Then, a miracle happened. Movo toppled to the ground.

Herlot picked up a pitchfork from the ground and sprinted again. The closer she got, the more grateful she was because he was still not able to get up. His injured leg must have been hurting him.

It wasn't until she neared that she realized he was fighting someone—another soldier—whom he had tackled to the ground. They both had their hands wrapped around each other's throats. Herlot's mind raced to figure out what to do. To her left, the pigeons sang in their cage. They could suffocate themselves to death, the only thing important to her was making sure no pigeon sent a message back to the fortress. She hauled herself over the side of the wagon and practically ripped the cage door open. "Go! Fly!" The pigeons sat, motionless. Of course, they were trained to serve. She returned her attention to the fight.

"Vincent!" Movo shouted, shaking the other soldier by the collar. "You don't want to do this! I know you don't!"

Vincent let go and pressed his palms to his forehead. Movo took a moment to catch his breath, then extended his hand to his comrade and helped him to his feet.

"You either help me or die here. I can't let you run back to Dartharus," Movo said.

Vincent nervously rubbed his arm guard against his blond-bearded cheek. "It's treason, Movo. Even for you. What you're doing... That's the end. You'll be running forever and can never go back."

"You want to go back? For a few pieces of gold? What we're doing here is not a siege. We aren't forcing these people into taxes, we're killing them. You have no family stuck in Damalathum for Felix to torture if you disobey. You can be free."

Vincent frowned, biting his lip. "What is it, exactly, that you plan we do?"

"Warn the other villages. Then get as far away from Damalathum as we can."

Herlot listened intently for any clue for the reason why they were here, but even more so, she was beginning to question her belief about Movo. Not only had he really helped them protect Lorfin, here he was trying to convince another soldier to do it, too. He didn't need to keep up his act anymore, the pigeons had been right there in his reach, and instead he had tackled one of his own men to the ground.

"There's no time. Dartharus already sent the others—"

"The bastard's orders were to wait!" Movo shouted.

"The Valentina docked yesterday at Eraska. The villages they were heading for no longer exist, so they were given orders to help us speed up matters in Eraska. Dartharus and the rest of your troop will stay with the prisoners at the fortress. My troop and two from the

Valentina were each ordered to head to a different village, they are still on their way to Temes and Ruelder."

"I don't understand, what is happening?" Herlot asked.

Movo looked at her. "It means we don't have time to warn the others. My troop was supposed to wait for Vincent's to return with any survivors from Lorfin before they headed out to Temes. Now we have enough men to invade three villages at once."

Herlot gripped the edge of the wagon. Their situation had just grown worse. The darkness was strong, able to squander any light of hope. She couldn't believe what she was about to suggest, especially with the dead lying all along the sunflower path. "We can try to fight them."

"They were still prepping the palfreys when we left. You might still reach Temes before them. But Ruelder, I doubt it," Vincent said.

Movo gritted his teeth and breathed heavily through his nose. He hit the side of the wagon and Herlot jumped as it reverberated through the wood. "I forgot about that."

"About what? And what are palfreys?" Herlot asked. She couldn't imagine the situation any worse than it already was.

"The Valentina is a larger warship with more space for horses. Palfreys are the horses we use to travel longer distances, unlike the ones that just pulled the wagons to Alonia and Lorfin. The supply wagons will slow the troops down, but each soldier will have a horse. Even if you had a year to train your people to fight, they wouldn't be ready to face a soldier on horse."

Herlot's attention lingered to the two strangers dressed in black who had joined the fight. Who were these strange men? They were crouched over a dead soldier, inspecting a weapon, and she thought she heard one of them laugh.

"You care to explain to me how you came to treason against your kingdom *and* managed to find two Iptans to join your cause since the last time I saw you?" Vincent asked.

"No. As for them, I don't know where they came from."

"Iptans?" Herlot asked. The name sounded familiar. She was certain she had heard it once before.

Vincent smirked. "They really have been isolated from the rest of the world. Thought it was an over exaggeration when I heard."

"They are from an empire named Ipta. They have the most riches and powerful armies of any place in the world," Movo said.

"Elephants," Herlot said. "They have elephants, don't they?" She remembered Merle's plate now.

"Yes," Vincent said. He and Movo eyed her curiously.

They had elephants, but what was most important was that she had watched with her own eyes as they took down half of Damalathum's troop on their own. She jumped off the wagon and came face to face to Movo. "You really wish to help the people of my land?"

Movo nodded.

"What about you?"

Vincent crossed his arms. "I'll think about it. I'd rather be on my way, but I won't interfere with your plan, if that's what you want to know."

Fair enough. She held her fist in front of her heart, unsure of whether she was making the right decision or not. Slowly, hesitantly, she extended it toward Movo. He wasn't a monster like she had imagined him to be like the warlock was in the story of princess Kira. "I'm Herlot," she said. "Of Alonia."

He didn't break contact with her eyes as he slid off the glove of his right hand. His large hand wrapped around hers. "I've overheard, but it's nice to hear it from you. Movo." For a moment she was afraid he might crush the bones in her palm, but his squeeze was gentler than she had expected. "Of Damalathum. And this is my friend, Vincent."

Herlot nodded toward Vincent and returned her gaze back to Movo. "I need you to help me protect the other villages, and I also need to find a safe place for my people to hide from yours. And most of all, I need to get those two Iptans to fight on my side."

Movo nodded. "Vincent, send a pigeon to Dartharus letting him know your troop's work here has gone as planned so he has no suspicions. If we keep Dartharus in the dark and manage to stay ahead of the other troops, we might get these people to someplace safe."

"And I need you to tell me why you're here spreading illness in the first place," Herlot said.

Herlot noticed Vincent and Movo exchange quick glances. Vincent pulled a coin from his pocket. A gold coin. Herlot took a step back as he flicked it in the air. "We're here for these. What else? King says invade the southern lands, we invade the southern lands."

She crossed her arms in front of her chest. "Your king asks you to kill hundreds of innocent people and you don't ask questions?"

Vincent laughed. Herlot winced at the sound. It felt like a hot stick from a fire nudging her in all of the raw, painful places inside her. "My king has a most prestigious torture chamber if I happen to question him. Even if he were to order me to kill my own family, which I luckily don't have, I'd do it. So please, little girl, don't think you're the only one with hardships in this world. You've just gotten your first taste of it."

Herlot clenched her fists. "Maybe if you had a better king—"

"Had a better king?" Vincent draped his elbow over the wagon and raised his eyebrows at her. "What have you been doing, listening to fairy tales your whole life?"

Herlot cringed. That's exactly what she had been doing.

"As if I had a choice what kingdom I'm born into. Or are you going to blame me for not having been born into your little sheltered adobe, looked over by the humblest of humble King Cloudian? Good it did you, he barely lifted a finger against Dartharus when he killed him. And he certainly could not help you when we invaded your village from his new home on the seabed."

Herlot fought to stop her tears from flowing. King Cloudian was dead, too. No stewards would arrive at a village again with toys from their king for the children, especially the fairy tale books for the children in Alonia. Vincent leaned in closer and she turned her cheek.

"So spare me your righteousness, little girl. What you saw here today, and in your village, I see as often as a flower market in summer. The only difference between you and me is that I've found a way to survive in this world, and I'm actually thinking of giving that up to assist your helpless lot—"

"Vincent." Movo pushed Vincent away from Herlot. "That's enough for now."

Herlot managed a breath in the newly created space between her and Vincent. "No, he's right."

Herlot took a moment to look into Vincent's eyes, not expecting to see something she could relate to—rage, desperation, pain. What these soldiers had done would never have a good enough excuse, but she had never thought that they might be toy figures controlled by someone much more awful. Whoever their king was, he was the one who had ordered them here. He was the real enemy; however, that wouldn't stop her from doing everything to protect her people against the men this king had sent to Eraska. Temes and Ruelder needed all the help they could get, and right now she needed to get Vincent on her side. "I hope you decide to join us," she said. "Will you both come with me to speak to the Iptans? I want to find out why they're here, and then we need to convince them to help us."

She led the way to the strangers, and it wasn't until she was hovering directly above them as they inspected a weapon that they stopped their conversing and stood.

"Asm of Ipta. Pleasure to meet you," the older, red-haired one said. He clasped each of their forearms.

Herlot noticed the different accent he spoke in and the tan color of their skin. The younger one had stray hairs falling against fierce, high cheekbones and sharp, green eyes. They were wearing leather vests that cut off at the shoulders and were buttoned down with gold buttons. The elder's ax handle was gilded in gold, and so were the younger one's two sword hilts. But what really caught her attention were the black designs outlined in gold color and etched into the skin of the younger's arms.

"And this here is my son, Seum. We thank you for the good time. I hope you don't mind us claiming our spoils, and then we will be on our way," Asm said."

Seum eyed her up and down. Had she not been devastated, traumatized, and at wits end by the current events, she probably would have felt uncomfortable. She wished his inspection were the largest of her problems. Then he bowed and met her eyes. "I must know the name of the woman who wields her sword defensively better than any man I have yet to meet in battle," he said.

"Herlot. And please, don't go. We need your help," Herlot implored as she watched a group of villagers help Enri and Mahtreeh carry Oliver's body back toward the village. "Follow me. Please."

Once in the village, she slid the door to one of the enclosures open, revealing the frightened Lorfiners inside.

"Our land is under attack. The people of my village were locked away and infected with crowpox. Most died and were burned. The soldiers you helped us fight planned the same for this village." Herlot drew a deep breath. "They intend this for all of Eraska."

Asm nodded toward Movo and Vincent. "These two—they are dressed like your enemies. Why?"

"They want to help. Movo warned Lorfin and prepared us to fight."

"Never trust a man who changes sides," Seum said.

"Seum—" Asm warned.

"Who sent you, and why are you spreading the crowpox among innocent people?" Seum demanded.

"King Felix," Movo answered. "We have orders to search for crowpox survivors."

Herlot noticed the same silent and quick exchange between Vincent and Movo.

"I have reason to believe the king is seeking a way to create a crowpox medicine," Movo said.

So there was a reason. This king wanted to create a medicine for his own people and was willing to sacrifice hundreds of others for the cause. Herlot couldn't grasp the reasoning. This king had no right to deem others less worthy of life.

"Such a noble cause your king has undertaken, squandering the helpless for the benefit of his own," Seum said, his sarcasm evident.

And there it was, a slight drop in Movo's shoulders. A sign of relief. Was it because he had lied and Seum had not noticed? Something still did not feel right. They were still hiding something.

"Felix. The name sounds familiar. What kingdom did you say you were from?" Asm asked.

"Damalathum."

Seum snickered.

"Ah, yes, yes, I believe the history books write your king as the fourth or was it fifth most-powerful king in our world?" Asm said.

"Third," Vincent.

"Third, it is. Never traveled there myself...my son and I have always been stationed in the eastern lands. However, I do remember... my, this must have been even before Seum's birth. An acquaintance of mine was sent there. That's right! We were building headquarters in your city. I'm surprised to learn that a king kind enough to open his doors for us would do such awful things to these people," Asm said.

"Say, didn't the emperor offer Damalathum elixirs in exchange for the headquarters?" Seum said. "Makes sense why they're not afraid to spread the crowpox. Now that's a real piece of filth, good ol' King already has the medicine but is greedy enough to try and make it on his own instead of asking our gracious emperor for more. And then he orders fools as yourselves to do the ugly work. Don't know which is worse, the leader or the followers."

Vincent got right in Seum's face. "Does it look to you like I'm following?"

At that, Movo and Asm wedged themselves between Vincent and Seum.

Herlot paid keen attention to Movo. His belly expanded, as if able to take a full breath, even though he was trying to stop Vincent from fighting. Another sign of relief, even though his king was being accused of barbaric crimes, and him for following such orders. If only she knew why. Was he trying to hide the real reason for why they were here? If only she knew more about the world and these people whom she would have to rely on.

"If you agree to help, we must set out now," Movo said. "General Dartharus has prompted the invasions. Two troops on horses are headed for Temes and Ruelder as we speak."

"How far away is Temes?" Asm asked.

"According to the maps I've studied, Temes is a day's travel by foot south, and then another half-day west from where we are. Ruelder lies a similar distance west of Temes," Vincent said.

"We saw the Ruelder village on our travels here," Asm noted. "Right after the two closest to the mountains, Bundene and Noray. These villages are not part of the plan, or are they being saved for last?"

"The troop headed for Ruelder has been ordered to wait for reinforcements and then invade Bundene and Noray once the mission in Ruelder is complete," Vincent said. "And why is it you are here and not in the east as you mentioned?"

"Sometimes a father and son need to go on an adventure of their own." Seum winked.

Herlot wondered if that was true, as well. Again, if only she knew more about the world outside of Eraska, she might have been able to know what questions to ask and then determine if their responses made sense.

"Is that why you decided to help us? Because it's an adventure?" Herlot asked.

Asm frowned. "I promise you, our intentions were genuine, as they will be from now on. We heard the fight once we arrived and saw what kind of people made up both sides —weaponless untrained villagers should never be at the mercy of armed, trained men. My people, Iptans, can be gruesome but we don't take advantage of the unarmed, hence why I see it as a personal responsibility to get you to safety."

"We must go to Cloudian!" a Lorfiner proposed.

"He's dead. His stewards, too. Their bodies now rest at the bottom of the sea, and General Dartharus has taken control of the fortress," Vincent said.

The crowd erupted in sorrow and complaints.

We were supposed to meet him when we became stewards. No. Don't think about that. Don't think of Elvin. Pressure began to form at the front of Herlot's forehead as the villagers continued to sound their opinions.

"You want to pull us from our home? To where?"

"I refuse to go anywhere."

"I stay."

"If you stay and no scout returns to the fortress within the week, Dartharus will send more soldiers and you can face them on your own. Now, shut your foolish traps!" Vincent shouted.

More insults were exchanged between Vincent and the people.

"Stop!" Enri pushed past and faced the Lorfiners. Her chin was high, her shoulders relaxed. She spoke with a clear and steady voice. A knot the size of one of Ambro's tug-of-war ropes formed in Herlot's stomach. Enri had just lost her father and had the courage to address her entire village. Her strength was nothing but admirable. "Lorfiners, do not look at these men with blame. They saved us from Alonia's fate. They fought for us. Movo even fought his own. My father trusted him. We can trust them. We are wasting time arguing when we should be searching for a safe place to hide."

More admiration pulsed through Herlot. Enri's words had subdued the tension in the air.

"My son and I explored a labyrinth of caves behind a waterfall, right by the river that separates Ruelder from Noray and Bundene," Asm said. "It's a short walk along the river from Ruelder. We can easily hide several hundred people there, fresh water...and a cliff for lookouts."

"We will go there," Enri decided.

"Gather your food and anything you can use as a weapon," Asm said, "We have two wagons and four horses for the injured and weak. If luck is on our side, we'll manage to travel through the night, and arrive at Temes before the soldiers. We meet at the path to Temes."

"Five horses," Herlot said. "I have one, too."

● ● ●

With a heavy heart, Herlot watched Enri unroll a cloth for wrapping Oliver's body. "Mahtreeh, gather as many herbs and supplies as you can fit in our pouches. We will need them."

Herlot's admiration was now outright shock at how well Enri was handling Oliver's death. Mahtreeh, on the other hand, resembled a sunflower neglected by the sun—his head hung heavy and low. Herlot recognized her own numbness in his eyes.

Enri put her hands on Mahtreeh's shoulders. "We still have each other. Father would want us to fight through this."

Feeling that it was an important moment for them to be alone, Herlot quietly slipped out and headed toward the livestock enclosure. Someone had already opened it, and chickens were running loose while a girl cried as her mother explained that some of the animals would need to be left behind.

"Devotio." Herlot sighed, seeing him waiting for her. She pressed her forehead against his. "I haven't forgotten," she whispered. She touched the leaf resting on her chest. "But it might have to wait."

"I know," Devotio's voice wrapped around her.

"As soon as we are safe in the caves, I'll start trying, I promise."

She stroked his mane. "The sword worked, just as Emrys had said," she whispered. "I was able to fend off every strike. The sword practically did all the work for me, all I had to do was not let go of the hilt. We're going to have to fight again if we don't arrive at Temes on time. It can defend me, but I'm afraid I have to strike back, Devotio."

"Not with that sword, don't ever forget what Emrys said about it."

Herlot nodded. "I'll need to make sure that I have someone at my side who can go in for the killing strike when I fight..."

She overheard a group of people who were gathering chicken eggs inside the barn wondering out loud about how an Alonian girl had come to own such a beautiful horse and how she had learned the art of the sword. She scanned their faces, expecting to see scowls at how different she was, but it wasn't criticism she saw. It was...inspiration? Impossible.

"He is magnificent," Seum said, appearing at her side and stroking Devotio's coat. "His coat puts Iptan horses to shame. Not a spot of discoloration. But can he run?"

"I haven't met any horses in my life. But I promise you Devotio can outrun any one of them," Herlot said.

Seum chuckled, the green in his eyes flashing. Sunlight glimmered off the designs on his arms as he circled Devotio.

"Where is his saddle?"

"Devotio will never wear a saddle as long as I'm standing."

Seum dropped his arm over Devotio's back. "You ride the horse bareback and have mastered the sword. I saw the way you fought. My father and I can do what we can to help your people, but they will need leaders of their own to trust. They will need someone like you to be their leader when they have to fight. We can only help to a certain extent. Our assistance will be worthless if your people don't have a leader whom they trust and who inspires them."

"If we hurry, we might avoid any more fights, as long as we arrive before the soldiers," Herlot reminded him. "You are well aware of the plan. First, we go to Temes and then to Ruelder, and then we hide while some of us go to gather the people of Noray and Bundene. It's simple, and we have nothing to worry about as long as we stay ahead of the troops."

"Temes, yes, but I doubt we will reach Ruelder on time."

"Which is why we have you, your father, Movo, and Vincent. I saw you fight, too. You are who my people need to trust, you need to lead."

"It never ceases to amaze me what morale is capable of. Once, in the eastern lands, I had the pleasure to observe a battle between two tribes from my ship."

Herlot shook her head. Pleasure was looking at stars from a boat. How could a person find pleasure in watching a battle?

"The one side had at least five-hundred more men than the other—and they were professionally trained soldiers. The other side consisted of farmers and craftsmen. Guess which side won?"

Herlot couldn't believe he would even ask her that question, for the answer was so clear. "The side with five-hundred more soldiers."

A sly smile spread across his face. "Wrong."

Now he was having fun fooling her. "I don't believe it. How?"

"Morale. Not enough to face my empire's abilities, of course, but enough to win against the tribe they were facing." As he spoke, he played with a dagger from his belt, flinging it, spinning it into the air and catching it by the handle. "Very similar to your situation with this Felix's—is that his name?—soldiers. And I guarantee you, the only reason your people can't fight his is because they are afraid. It won't help them to see me or my father fight. The only way they'll gain confidence is if someone as skilled as you takes the lead."

Herlot opened her mouth to protest but he continued.

"Do not fool yourself. Yes, first you will hide, but for how long? They won't simply leave you be. These men don't like their egos curtailed because that is all they have. They'll keep coming...you'll keep hiding...perhaps running, eventually. But, if your people had a leader like yourself," he swiveled the dagger until the tip of the blade pointed at her, "it just might be an equal match. You could ignite a passion in your people which would send Felix's rats scurrying back to his nest."

Herlot gently pushed the dagger aside, careful not to cut her finger. "It won't come to that."

"It already has."

• • •

Movo ignored the humidity, dirt, and sweat clinging to his body as he gazed up at two pine trees hovering over the grave he had dug for Oliver. Alonia's dead had burned. Lorfin's would receive a proper burial.

Enri, Mahtreeh, and Herlot arrived, carrying Oliver's body. Movo extended his arms and took a gentle hold of Oliver, then lowered him into the damp soil.

Movo knew many skilled physicians. Thanks to them, he had survived numerous wounds and infections from past battles. Each time he had been required to listen as they raved about how much work and how many special ingredients they had invested into their salves. They pestered over him for hours, each of his wounds a blessing that promised them gold. Once he had taken the risk of wearing worn chainmail and an arrow had pierced him during the battle. He had spent weeks in the infirmary waiting for his abdomen to heal. Since then, all it took was the thought of one of the medics' voices to make him doublecheck the state of his armor.

But Oliver had been different. His simple mixture had worked better than the prestigious ones he was accustomed to. For the first time in his life, he had felt someone mend a wound for no other reason than for it to heal.

"Oliver, my land would be a good place if there were more people like you. I hope you're at peace," he said.

He kept a fair distance from the others as they mourned. Even if he could channel that emotion, he wouldn't know how to express it, just like he didn't know how Herlot had been able to fall apart in front of him, yelping like a child when she awoke after the fire. Yelping, just like the young boy on Movo's last day in the dungeon had.

The daughter, Enri, slipped a wildflower from her hair and dropped it on Oliver's chest. The villagers covered the graves, each person setting a stone on the mound before trailing into the forest path to Temes.

His thoughts wandered back to the girl, Herlot. Had she not felt any shame displaying her pitiful weakness in front of him? Every reflex in him had fought to smother her every time she had called for her parents. He had had to resist his father's voice hammering through his mind, urging him on. *Do it. If you want to see the light, you have to do it.* Light was the biggest temptation for someone who had spent years in darkness. If only these villagers knew what he was capable of doing for a mere glimpse of light, they would refuse his help.

He had fought many opponents, some skilled, some not, but as strong as the urges had been, something about Herlot had made it impossible for him to attack her. His father had trained him to be a master of sensing people's weaknesses to his advantage. Herlot's cries after he rescued her from the fire displayed anything but strength. However, never had he imagined that a disgraceful wail had the ability to silence his father's voice in his head.

● ● ●

Enri cried out as one of her sandal straps broke when she stepped onto the path to Temes. She felt her heel sink into the mud.

"Are you hurt?" Movo asked.

"No. I forgot something. Mahtreeh, stay with the group. I'll catch up."

Enri barged through the door of her home. She rested her hands on her hips and breathed in the smell of the herbs and plants. She could still feel her father's spirit here.

"I'll stay strong for Mahtreeh, Father."

Mahtreeh was fragile. He was holding himself together, but she didn't know how long he could keep it up. She could not allow herself to break down. She had to be a strong wildflower so Mahtreeh would know how to be one, too, until they were in a safe place to grieve.

A breeze rushed through the doorway and swayed the herbs and keepsakes that hung from the ceiling. Enri's attention was drawn to Herlot and Ambro's clay handprint tablets. She tapped each one and watched them swing. She didn't understand that symbols carved beneath the prints. Only Alonian tablets included written names. She was sure Movo, Vincent, and the Iptans would be baffled if they learned that the Alonians had been able to read and write. Maybe they would have spared them had they known that they were more special in this sense, possibly closer to their own kind than the rest of the Eraskans.

Herlot and Ambro were alive. It felt like her father wanted her to remember this. The breeze tickled her side and she startled, realizing it had not come from the direction of the doorway. She turned toward the source of the breeze and saw her father's sandals on the ground facing the table, as if he were standing right there, tending to a sick person. Enri slipped her other sandal off and stepped into her father's sandals. To her surprise, they fit.

CHAPTER 14
Benyamin

EVERY STEP FORWARD WAS one of uncertainty. Two afternoons ago, Herlot had begun the day as a hostage to her enemy with only Devotio at her side. Now she was walking a path to Temes with an entire village of Eraskans and her once enemy, Movo, was an essential guide in their journey to safety. They had lost more Eraskans in the sunflower fields of Lorfin, more violent death on their once peaceful land, yet at least they were together and had a plan to stop more death and illness from occurring. Each step forward was an eerie mixture of horror and elation. Herlot could only hope that their plan would make it certain that there would be no more horror in their homeland.

A glade in the forest revealed hillsides shaded in variants of green and rocky peaks. Bandy trees still grew out of the steepest hills. It was beautiful. How she wished she could be experiencing the miraculous landscapes of Eraska under different circumstances.

"Not like one of our usual walks, is it now?" Enri said to Carl, who was breathing just as hard as Herlot was in the humid air.

"Not by far. You can even feel it in the air—the heaviness of our future sinking in," he answered.

"I feel it, too. We might not return home for a long time," Enri said.

Or in Herlot's case, never. Could the rubble that was all that remained of Alonia ever be called a home again?

Enri's footsteps fell in harmony with Herlot's. She pointed at a tree trunk that leaned the farthest away from the hillside compared to the other trees. She spoke quietly, so only Herlot could hear. "I used to love climbing out on it and would let my feet dangle over the steep drop beneath. This one time I dared Mahtreeh to climb out, too. He tried, crawled toward me as slow as a turtle, but turned around as soon as he made it halfway. He's doing better right now than I expected him to but, Herlot, our journey ahead won't give Mahtreeh the option to turn around. When that halfway point comes, I'll need you to help me."

Herlot nodded. "Of course."

A young girl named Tulia skipped in front of Herlot and Enri. "Can we go out on the tree?"

"Not today. But would you like to ride on the horse?" Enri asked.

Tulia nodded, and Enri lifted her to sit in front of the other two children already on Devotio. Somehow, thanks to him, the journey was a happy experience for the children, easing the morning's trauma.

"Makes me want to be young like them again." Carl said.

"They have been through the same trauma as us. They heard the fighting and saw the graves. Thank the skies a ride may ease it a bit," Enri said.

The children occupied themselves by pointing out bugs they spotted along the path. As soon as the bug was identified, it would leap and land between Devotio's ears, which brought about yelps of delight from the children. Enri and Mahtreeh exchanged amused looks each time it happened and even managed genuine smiles. A grasshopper stayed especially long, showing the children how he cleaned his antennae with his forelegs.

"How is it that you have such a beautiful horse?" a woman, Arlette, wearing a straw hat, asked Herlot.

Herlot smiled. "My brother and I found him in the woods. A wanderer must have lost him. We have been taking care of him ever since."

The truth is that he is the one who takes care of me, thought Herlot. He had saved her from a thunderstorm and a fire. It was her turn now to save him, and his family, too. The leaf felt heavy on her chest. Devotio's family's future all depended on whether or not she could learn to control the gold in her heart and use it to perform magic.

"Maybe Devotio came from King Cloudian's castle in the sky?" Tulia asked.

"Huh. I think you're right," Herlot said. There was no castle in the sky and King Cloudian was dead, but she preferred the child's idea even though it was impossible. It was beautiful, and there were many more beautiful things in the realm of imagination than in the real world.

Enri spoke in her quiet voice again. "I remember a different story. Mahtreeh and I never forgot that night. I know that now is not the time, but we have questions, especially about why Devotio no longer has an alicorn. But tell me, just yes or no for the time, that sword, is it also magical?"

Devotio's voice wrapped around Herlot's ears, as if he had read the question that was on her mind. "Yes," he said. "You can tell them about my family and the leaf."

The weight on her chest became a bit lighter. It would mean the world to her if Mahtreeh and Enri could know about her mission to blend the leaf. More elation—she wouldn't be alone in attempting something that had never been done before.

"Yes," Herlot whispered. "I'm not allowed to attack with it, though."

Enri nodded and smiled. Herlot returned the smile. She was beginning to feel hope that all she had to do was continue to take steps forward, one at a time, and somehow all of this could be possible to accomplish. Maybe she could get more and more used to the idea of uncertainty this way.

Herlot's thoughts turned to Movo, who was walking at the front of their line carrying extra loads of sacks he had taken from the elders that could not fit onto the wagon. How had he become a soldier? Did he have a family back home waiting for him? She wanted to know more about the stranger who had sided with her, and any more information she might get out of him about Ambro and his whereabouts.

She caught up to him, trying to match his long stride.

"You have something to ask me?" he asked, still looking ahead.

"My brother. He survived the crowpox. What are they really going to do with him?

"Right now you do not need to worry. There are strict orders to not hurt the survivors. He is safe. Eventually, they will take him back to my father's kingdom. You do understand that going back for him is too dangerous, right? It would be suicide. Don't think about it."

She nodded. As long as Ambro was alive, that was what was most important. The crowpox couldn't threaten him anymore like rest of the villagers in Eraska whom the soldiers were heading for. She knew her brother. He was smart. He might find a way to escape. How much she wanted to try and go back for him, but Movo was right. Her death in making such an attempt right now was unacceptable. She had to remain alive to blend the leaf. For now, all she could do was learn more about Movo and his world, the world where Eraska's invaders came from.

"The other night by the fire, you said you wanted to explore before taking me back to the fortress. Do you not get to explore when you're home?"

"Something like that."

She wanted to ask for details, but at that moment Seum stepped in front of them.

"What kind of a soldier has the luxury to leave his troop to explore? Where I come from, a warrior stands naked in the blistering sun for three days for treason like that. That is, unless you're the son of a king who can get away with it."

"You're right." Movo lifted his chin in challenge.

Son of the king? Son?

In a flap of a hummingbird's wing, Seum reached for the hilt of his sword, but before he could free it from the scabbard, Asm had him by the collar.

Seum struggled forward, but Asm lifted him up so only his toes touched the ground.

"Enough?!" Asm shouted.

"Enough, dammit," Seum choked.

"Good." He let Seum go.

Seum pointed his finger at Movo. "He's leading us into a trap. Puny prince, that's what he is." He spat at Movo's feet.

"The soldiers attacked him just as much as they did us!" Mahtreeh shouted in Movo's defense.

Asm kept his chest facing Seum, but he turned his head to address Movo. "Are you leading us to our deaths, soldier?"

"No."

"Then we carry on. Seum, let this be the end of it."

Seum stormed ahead, swinging at a nearby bush, which startled a group of wasps that charged after him.

"Serves him right," Asm muttered.

They continued walking, Herlot afraid to ask any more questions. She had more information on Movo, but it had only opened new doubts about him.

He was a prince. The king was his father. Could she have turned against her parents even if they had done the wrong thing? She wanted to say yes, but the truth was that she would have done anything for her parents if that meant having them back. On the other hand, she couldn't imagine her parents ever planning something like what Movo's father was doing. Either Movo was the strongest man she knew, a hero in an Alonian story, or Seum was right and he was leading them into a trap. And Seum had made a very strong judgment earlier—Movo had switched sides, so what was stopping him from doing it again? If anyone were most likely to change his mind, it would be the son of the king, after all.

As they carried on in silence, Mahtreeh began to whistle. Although the tunes were happy, she doubted they were a reflection of how Mahtreeh felt inside. She was grateful he was doing it, though. Not only was it probably distracting his mind away from the morning's deaths, but distracting everyone else, too. He seemed to know a language only the birds could understand. He chirped at a family of crossbills and trilled to a hawfinch in a cherry tree. It was nice to listen to. Something beautiful in the real world.

Enri hooked her elbow with Herlot's, surprising her by the gesture, and asked, "What's your favorite bird song?"

"The nuthatch," Herlot answered.

At that, Mahtreeh whistled three rapid and connected chirps. Herlot's lips parted when the first nuthatch appeared alongside them. Enri handed Herlot an acorn, and she rolled it along the ground to the nuthatch, that snagged it when she backed away.

"It depends on the kind of day the bird is having, but sometimes one will sit on Mahtreeh's shoulder," Enri said.

"It's astounding," Herlot said.

Enri and she started a game. They took turns giving Mahtreeh the name of a bird to call. Surprisingly, humor began to slip through Herlot's melancholy fog.

"That's annoying!" Seum called each time Mahtreeh sounded a new chirp.

"One of my first lessons about men from the outside world—they come with an awful temper," Enri said.

"Great idea... Travel with the enemy and a bunch of peasants who've never touched a sword..." Seum said. "Bird calls! That's what we'll fight with—mewling bird calls."

A robin dipped over Seum, causing him to flail his arms in the air and grunt.

Asm let out a cackle that resembled a crack in a fire.

"Mahtreeh, do it again," Asm said.

"Nightingale." Herlot barely heard Movo's lulled request.

Mahtreeh sighed. "That's a tough one."

Herlot watched intently to see how he would manage it. He puckered his lips and sucked air through the space between his front teeth, followed by a gurgle in his throat. He ended with warbled, high-pitched whistles, but the nightingale did not appear.

"There might not be one around. We'll try again though. She'll come sooner or later," Mahtreeh said.

After sunset, they made fires and ate some of their rations. For Herlot, there was something about sitting around the fire with a group of people, doing a simple thing like eating, that was comforting. Everyone's normal life had been taken away, but at least not every moment was chaotic. At the beginning of the summer, she, Ambro, and Elvin had complained about the boring routines of village life, their hearts set on their plans of becoming stewards and having adventures.

But now Ambro was missing and Elvin—she had to set her bread down and place her palm on the earth to stop the spinning—Elvin was dead, his life, like everyone else's in Alonia, stolen from him by the crowpox. She examined the breadcrumbs in her lap remembering how much Elvin and the seagulls didn't get along. She smiled to herself as a strange jolt of playfulness and curiosity swarmed through her heart: Elvin would still find the routines boring. Elvin would still seek his adventure. His kind of spirit could never be broken.

"Not only does he sound like a bird, he eats like one, too," Seum said, his eyes on Mahtreeh.

Herlot tipped her head back and poured a bunch of sunflower seeds from her palm into her mouth. "And you're a browbeater," she said. "Bernard the Browbeater. It was an Alonian tale. All Bernard did was frown and tell the fishermen they were too weak to fight a sea monster, yet he never was brave enough to try to fish himself."

Seum's chewing slowed. "Browbeater, you say? Huh. Maybe you're right. Mahtreeh, my friend, let me share my drink with you as an apology." He handed Mahtreeh his flask.

Mahtreeh took a bite of bread and a large gulp from the flask. He dropped the flask and spit the liquid and bread chunks into the fire, which sent the flame higher. Seum collapsed on his back, holding his belly, laughing. So much for putting him in his place—she had only provoked his teasing.

"Holy Basil! What was that?" Mahtreeh cried.

"Rum. Traded a pirate for it a while back," Asm said.

She thought about Ambro, wondering what he would say seeing her with people who had met real pirates and drank real rum.

Vincent took a swig. "How is it that your travels brought you to Eraska?"

Asm set his dried meat on his lap. "We first set out working aboard ships headed to the southern lands, wandered the lands until we came upon the mountain range to the south of here. They all told us it was impossible to climb. Too tall. Too much fog. Too dangerous, is what they said. It was exactly what we were looking for. And that's how we landed on Eraskan land and now find ourselves in your company."

"What was your role in the eastern lands?" Vincent asked.

"We are warriors. My son trains infantry."

"Ah, a trainer with the luxury to leave his empire for several years," Movo stated.

"My business is no matter of yours, prince, unless you'd like to explain why your father has not put his son in command." Seum leaned on his elbow and threw a seed in the air, catching it in his mouth. "I understand it is a custom among all kings, including my own emperor, that only the strong and *trusted* are given positions of command."

"Movo's talent would be wasted there. We need him in the front lines," Vincent said.

Herlot didn't know anything about military organization, but she had seen Movo tackle his own men. There was no doubt he had talent, and Vincent's explanation seemed sound.

Vincent changed the crossing of his legs. "Is it true that an Iptan warrior is trained within a day?"

"Ha! A day. We begin at sunrise and are finished by noon," Seum said.

"How is that possible? Our soldiers require at least six years of training before they are knighted," Vincent said.

From what Herlot had observed of Asm, she thought his main focus was to maintain politeness and peace. But something about what Vincent had said made him smirk. "Six years..." A no-pitched guffaw escaped him. "Could teach a camel the spear in less time!"

Herlot sat dumbfounded as Asm and Seum continued exchanging comments and slapping their thighs as they laughed.

Vincent maintained a straight face, clearly offended by their reactions. Movo just gazed into the fire, chewing.

"I can't imagine what it must be like to have seen so much," Enri said as their laughter subsided.

"You see good things and bad things, my dear. And, usually, they come together." Asm's eyes squinted as he smiled.

Herlot restrained a gasp. There was something about Asm that reminded her of her father. He had a big beard that seemed to muffle his speech and a spark in his eyes when he smiled. His words even reminded her of her father's wisdom.

"My father once said something similar," she said. "He never ended a story with happily ever after because he believed people didn't have to wait to be happy until the end." To her surprise, it felt good to talk about her father.

"Wise man. Did he teach you the sword?" Asm asked.

At that, Movo leaned forward, his gaze intent on her.

"Yes." It was a good enough explanation. She hated lying, but it was impossible to tell them the truth.

She noticed Mahtreeh and Enri exchanging glances. To them, she could tell the truth. She would tell them what happened in his hiding place in the tree and how she got the sword, but not now.

"He only taught you to defend yourself with it," Movo stated.

Herlot was at a loss for words at how observant Movo was. How could he have noticed that when he had had so many men to face on his own? And how could she explain that it's not that she didn't know how to attack with it—it's that she wasn't *allowed* to attack with it?

Enri huffed, causing short hairs to lift off her forehead. "Of course, he didn't. But then you wouldn't know because you're not an Alonian. It's a cursed sword and only the Alonians know the true legend behind it. It is the greatest story they ever told in Alonia. Only Herlot knows its secrets out of all of us, right?" She winked at Herlot.

"Right," Herlot said, nodding at Enri in gratitude. Enri had saved her with the fib, though her intuition was strikingly accurate. "The sword is only to be used for defense or else its curse will be released, and we would never want that to happen."

Movo sneered.

"Laugh all you want, but in Ipta we have many stories like this, and only fools don't listen to them," Seum said. "She is wise like her father. And, out of all of you, the only one capable of Iptan training."

Herlot avoided his gaze, remembering what he had said about her being a leader.

Devotio, that had been scavenging along the path with the other horses, lazily grazed near their group.

"Blimey, that's a white horse. His coat shines like a lantern!" Asm exclaimed. "We'll have no trouble following the path with him leading."

"It's time we move," Vincent said.

"That we should." Asm jumped to his feet, swift for his size.

"We'll gather the others," Enri said. "Herlot, Mahtreeh, come with me."

When they finished their rounds, Enri pulled Herlot and Mahtreeh behind a brush off the path. Devotio followed along. "Can you tell us now about what happened?" Enri said.

"Yes, what happened to Devotio's alicorn?" Mahtreeh asked.

Herlot's eyes moved rapidly. Her mind felt as if it were the center of a tug-of-war game. Why was she all of a sudden so frightened to tell them about the leaf? It was one thing for them to believe in unicorns and magical swords. What if her mission to blend the golden leaf with the gold in her heart was too much for them and they deemed her mad? *What if they don't believe? What if they don't believe?* A small, fragile voice inside her head repeated. Of course, they would believe. After all, they remembered their night in the woods with Devotio as children. If anything, Mahtreeh and Enri's memories were proof of that.

Her temples pounded and she rubbed at them to ease the pain. "Ouch," she cried.

What if their imagination is just as ill as yours? An image of her father holding the scroll with the legend of the unicorns written on it crossed her mind, followed by her swimming toward his boat and asking him where he had gotten it. She swallowed the memories and squeezed her belly, ordering it to hide them far, far away. A voice screamed at her as the memories began to dissipate from her awareness more and more. *You're ill! He's just a white—*

Herlot covered her ears and squeezed her eyes shut. "Stop. Please, stop," she mumbled.

She heard Enri shuffling in her pouch for something. Suddenly, Herlot had a glass bottle in front of her nose. "Sniff," Enri said.

A bitter smell filled Herlot's nose and within moments she was able to take a breath again.

Enri smiled at her. "Better?"

Herlot nodded. "A lot. What was that?"

"A medicine for head pain."

"It worked like magic."

"Magic, like Devotio." Enri ran her hand over Devotio's mane.

"He's a unicorn. We kept our promise and never told a soul. But something happened. He doesn't have his alicorn anymore," Mahtreeh said. "If there's any other trouble you are in, we can help you, but you must tell us." He pressed his palms together at his heart.

Herlot's eyes softened and all of the conflicting voices in her head stilled. "Can you promise that you will believe me?"

"Yes, of course," Enri said.

Herlot steadied her trembling hands. She put her hand over her chest and felt the leaf press against her skin. "It's a long story, though, and there's not enough time to tell you all the details, but Devotio rescued me from the fire. He took me to his home, where the other unicorns hide. There're many more unicorns. There was a girl, Emrys, and she gave me the sword. They need my help to save them, and—"

The group began calling their names.

"We have to head back," Herlot said. "The rest will have to wait until later."

"Can he still talk?" Enri whispered as they slipped back onto the path.

The familiar wind of Devotio's voice danced around Herlot's ears—and based on their expressions, the siblings heard it, too.

"No. Horses don't speak," Devotio's voice said.

At that, they all laughed.

"It's good to hear you, Devotio," Mahtreeh said.

● ● ●

Movo slipped from the shadows by the brush. He was at a loss for words. True, the horse was unusual, especially its coat. He knew that the people of Eraska were isolated, but after the story about the sword and having overheard the words exchanged between the three just now, he was certain they wouldn't survive—only children resorted to imaginary stories about unicorns to help them through traumatic times. He feared they were no less insane than his father, who sought a non-existent magic in his delusional dream of conquering Ipta.

There had been a time when he had been as foolish as they were. Movo thought about the wooden statues he had received for his birthday from his mother when he was young. One had been a horse with a horn and wings. He had loved playing with it and had imagined it having the ability to come to life. Then he remembered throwing it into the fireplace after he learned that he was to be sent to the dungeons.

The weight of the weapons on his back gave him comfort. Grounded him to this world, his mission. There was much involved in creating a sword—searching for ore, hammering, smelting, and grinding. Magic was not part of the process, and what a sword was used for was nothing but. The girl would be better off learning that sooner than later.

He frowned as he heard footsteps nearing and hid again, dreading what the group of friends could possibly talk about next. When he did not hear anything else for a bit, he stood, only to be taken aback. The horse, Devotio, stood a few steps away, his gaze focused straight at him. It was almost as if he wanted to communicate to him, that he had known he was there all along.

"Hurry up. Everyone is waiting."

Movo was on his guard before the sentence was finished, eyes darting around for the source of the voice. He looked at the horse. *Nonsense*, he thought. Through the leaves of the trees, he did see someone stepping back on the path. It must have been them, and they had walked by him after relieving themselves in the woods. He found himself walking side by side with Devotio all the way back to the group, fighting the urge to ask if he had been the one who had spoken.

● ● ●

Enri gazed up to see the night sky covered in stars between the tree canopy. She yawned, thinking how nice it would be to fall asleep looking up at them, like one of the children taking turns sleeping on the horses' backs.

All of a sudden, Devotio halted, and their parade came to an abrupt stop.

"Go on, Devotio," Asm said.

But Devotio didn't budge. Enri followed Asm to see what was causing the holdup. "Steady, steady," Asm chanted, tipping back on his heels, having almost fallen into a giant hole in the path.

"Enri, I think there is someone in there," Mahtreeh said, peeking over her shoulder.

There was, indeed, someone there. A man lay holding a strange gadget above his face. His knee was twisted and jutted out to the side. He moved the gadget aside, revealing his face.

"Apologies if I'm being rude, but please move aside, you're blocking the view," he said in a high-pitched and scratchy voice.

"Old man, do you realize you are injured and stuck in a hole?" Seum asked.

The man looked around. "My! Seems I may have walked right into my grave."

"We need to get him out," Enri said. A person in his condition needed tending to immediately, not humorous exchanges with Seum.

Movo lowered himself into the pit. "Hello there," the man said. "How nice it is to have some company in here."

Movo knelt on one knee and examined the leg. "It's broken."

She had feared that was the case. "Careful when you lift him," Enri said. "Mahtreeh, find a sturdy stick."

Movo excavated the man, lifting him up above his head toward Seum. Meanwhile, the man continued to aim his gadget up at the sky. "I wonder how long you can hold him up, prince," Seum said.

Enri was about to shove him but Asm beat her to it, knocking Seum out of the way with a grunt.

Enri began adjusting the stick she would use as a splint. Thankfully, someone had thought to light a candle and hold it near her workspace.

"What's your name?" Herlot asked.

"Benyamin of Bundene." He extended his hand straight up for a handshake to those around.

Enri carefully lowered his arm. "There will be time for handshaking later, now please be still."

"How did you manage to fall into a pit of this size?" Seum asked. "You must be blind."

"My eyesight is very well, thank you very much. Much better than my wife's. I was watching the sky and forgot to look in front of my feet." He chuckled, not showing any signs of pain while Enri worked.

"And what is this bronze object you carry around?" Movo asked. He tapped the gadget Benyamin held tucked against his body with his other arm.

Enri had never seen such a strange object. It had many circular gears that attached to one another, and engraved markings.

"That's what I would like to figure out. I traded all of my food stores for it."

"Where is your wife?" Herlot asked.

"She passed. I reckon she's blind as a bat now." He winked. "Ah, I miss her..."

Enri finished securing the splint, then brushed the dirt off her dress. Benyamin, as if he had no worry in the world about his condition, smiled as he turned one of the gears. She caught Seum tapping his temple. "He may have slept with a chicken in his home and suffered a mind pecking," Arlette, standing behind Enri, muttered.

"We need to find a way to keep his leg stretched out," Enri said.

Herlot began to lift one of the sleeping children off Devotio.

"Oh, you don't have to do that. Continue on and let him sleep. I will be fine on the wagon," Benyamin said.

"Nonsense," Herlot replied. "You'll be much more comfortable here than on the wagon with all that jolting and rocking from side to side. Right, Enri?"

Enri nodded. These wagons that belonged to the soldiers were not like the ones Rudi had built. It would be too much of a bumpy ride for Benyamin. It was a miracle that he was not feeling pain now. It would definitely get worse once his leg swelled more.

Movo set Benyamin on Devotio so his back leaned against Devotio's neck.

"Could one of you be a dear and hand me my sack?" Benyamin asked.

Once Vincent had retrieved the sack from the pit and set it on Benyamin's lap, Benyamin shuffled through it, leaning in until his head was halfway inside.

"Here it is!" His voice echoed from within. "For you, Enri, as a thank-you for fixing my leg." In his palm was a string of seashells. He pinched a shell between two fingers and the rest unraveled.

"It's beautiful." Enri smiled at the seashell doll. "Thank you."

The seashells were of all different shapes and colors that shone in the candlelight, the face shell engraved with markings for the doll's eyes, nose, and lips. The breeze made it sway in wavelike motions, and the shells clinked together.

"I'll take good care of her."

"I'm glad you like her. My wife used to make them. Everyone waited for Alonian seaweed to arrive, but she only waited for the seashells. She never got too old for dolls—and magical creatures, too, for that matter." He winked at Herlot and shooting stars of wrinkles extended from the corner of his eye.

Huh, Enri thought. *If I didn't know any better, I'd say he was referring to Devotio. But that's not possible.*

The sun rose as they continued on. A boy who had been too stirred awake to fall back asleep sat on Movo's shoulders. The others helped carry the sleeping children of the weaker parents—Asm had one in each arm.

Enri looked back at the sleepwalking Lorfiners. She had to do something before they toppled over. Luckily, she spotted a patch of wild mint and made them all pick a leaf to chew on. A refreshing breeze swooshed through her body the moment the mint leaf touched her tongue. Next to her, Asm plugged his nose with two leaves. She laughed as he entertained the children by opening his eyes so wide when he inhaled that it looked like his eyelashes stuck to his eyebrows, almost as if he had covered them with a sticky tree sap.

The mint leaves helped for a bit, but they still had a long way to go. Soon she felt as if she were walking through a swamp. She had to squeeze her eyes together every few steps in order to clear her vision. Only Movo, Seum, and Asm maintained a wide-awake state as the day continued, and she wondered at their stamina. Enri was out of options to help the others stay awake. Her father would have known what to do. There were so many things she would never get to learn from him. They would just have to push on to Temes and she prayed to the skies that her knowledge would be sufficient to help in the days to come.

CHAPTER 15
Temes

E VENING WAS A SLIP of the sunset away when Arlette fell to her knees. "Thank the skies!" she cried. Herlot looked ahead and spotted a group of Temesian villagers gathering sticks in the forest. *Looks like we made it before the soldiers. So far luck is on our side. I hope the skies know we will need much more, though.*

Herlot waited at the front of their group as a woman who looked her age jogged up to them. Her hair was knotted in intricate knots on top of her head. Both her eyes and her lips were narrow and serious.

"By the looks of all of you, I am certain it is not good news you are bringing," she said in a monotone voice.

"You are right, unfortunately." Herlot stepped forward. "My name is Herlot, and these are the villagers from Lorfin."

"Lucinda, pleased to meet you." They shook hands. "And this is my brother, Hans."

Hans looked Mahtreeh's age and nothing like his sister. His cheeks were a ripe-raspberry color, and his blue eyes were decked in long eyelashes. He had long, brown hair tied at the nape of his neck.

"Lucinda, we come to warn you of invaders," Herlot said. She pushed her shoulders back, determined to look brave—like someone worthy of following—but she was too conscious of the mud flecking her torn dress. "They come from a distant land with weapons and chests holding poison. My Alonia was destroyed, all my people are dead, but these Lorfiners escaped with a fight. Your people must come with us to safety. Temes is going to be invaded next."

Lucinda looked up at the sky, where only a sliver of the sun's light remained.

"We will go back to Temes," she said, "and you will tell us this history in detail. But we must hurry. Believe me, an equal threat will burden us any moment if we don't get inside the wall."

Another threat? Herlot was sure Lucinda hadn't heard her right. *What could be worse than the soldiers invading?*

"These men could really arrive at any moment. Even tonight," Enri emphasized.

Lucinda's raised her eyebrows. "Let's hope they do because then the beasts that roam our land at night will solve the problem for us. Come on, follow me."

"So the stories are true? Temes really is surrounded by dangerous beasts that come out at night?" Mahtreeh asked.

"I would bet my entire carrot garden on it," Lucinda said. "Faster pace, Lorfiners!"

Herlot huddled next to Enri and Mahtreeh as they followed Lucinda.

"Hurry," Devotio's voice wrapped around Herlot. "I know what these beasts are. They were once unicorns."

"Impossible," Mahtreeh said. Herlot glanced over at him and Enri. Devotio must have been speaking to them, too.

"They were the ones that turned against their companions, they fought back and killed them with their alicorns, after which they turned into dark, spiritless beasts. Herlot's sword works the same way, it will protect her, but if she ever kills someone with it, she will have the same destiny as these beasts. It is important that you don't let her do that."

"We won't," Enri whispered.

Herlot placed her hand on the side of Devotio's neck, which he was still holding upright to support Benyamin. "I won't," she whispered. "You don't need to worry about that."

"We have warm food, ale, and plenty of room to rest," Hans said, turning to look at them. His tunic and leggings were plain and dirty like all Eraskans', but his hair was tied with a sheer, shiny, red ribbon. Herlot had never seen such nice fabric and wanted to reach out and touch it. "You will all be safe the moment the sun sets as long as you are inside Temes's walls. The beasts will tear apart anyone who comes near."

Lucinda pulled a camouflaged piece of wood up from the ground, revealing a tunnel. "This way!" she called.

"These beasts you speak, are they not wolves?" Vincent asked as he helped a Lorfiner into the tunnel.

"Not exactly," Hans said. "We have never seen them, but we can hear them, and, well…"

"Oh, then they must be wolves," Vincent said.

"Perhaps. They're the reason we have a wall around our village," Hans explained, "They come out only at night. Many Temesians have overestimated their time outside in the past…and, well, I'd rather not say how they were found."

"Our father mentioned the wall and the beasts a few times after his travels," Enri said.

"Who is your father?" Lucinda asked.

"Oliver, the healer," Mahtreeh said.

Hans stood on his tiptoes, bouncing up and down as he looked at the group of Lorfiners. "Where is he?" he asked.

"He's not with us. Our father died defending Lorfin." Mahtreeh said. Herlot noticed his lips quivering.

Lucinda pressed her hand over her heart. "Oh no, not Oliver. It can't be true."

All of a sudden, a loud noise sounded as if it were coming from the trees. Herlot lunged into a protective stance in front of Devotio. It had sounded like a heartbeat and a growl and had made her eardrum vibrate. "What was that?"

She wasn't the only one who had heard it. Seum and Movo had removed their swords from their scabbards.

"They're awake. Run!" Lucinda shouted into the tunnel.

Movo grabbed Benyamin off Devotio and slid down the slope. Asm yanked one of the four horses by the reins, but it backtracked, afraid to go in.

"No time. Leave him," Lucinda said as Hans slid in.

"Come on, Devotio, show them the way," Herlot said, leading him inside, knowing instinctually that the horses would follow after if Devotio went first.

Once they were all in, Lucinda pulled the camouflage over the opening.

"We're not safe yet," she warned. "They can still smell us in here."

At the end of the tunnel, a wooden ramp led them up into the center of the village where a crowd gathered around Devotio and the horses. "Take a look at this one's coat. Looks like it was painted on by snow faeries."

Herlot was pushed aside by several Temesians to make room for a heavy log of timber being rolled on top of the tunnel's opening. She looked around at the village. Unlike Alonia and Lorfin, Temes only had one large, stone cottage. "Where are everyone's homes?" she asked.

"We sleep and eat together inside this one. Once you hear the beasts scavenging, you'll understand. We feel safer together," Hans said.

"That sound..." Herlot shuddered.

"Never heard a growl that loud before," Vincent said.

"I don't think it's a growl. It was like a heartbeat," Mahtreeh said.

"That's impossible," Vincent said.

"Awful sound, isn't it? You'll hear it many more times throughout the night," Hans said.

"What is it exactly? And why is it so loud?" Vincent asked.

"Well, none of us know, to be honest. To understand that, someone would need to get close to one of them. But don't worry. They have never made it over the wall."

Was there any place left in her world that didn't have monsters? At least the Temesians knew how to protect themselves. What if Alonia had had a wall? Would the soldiers have had a chance? Nausea swayed within her belly, not from regret of not having a wall around her home village, but because the answer to her question was yes. Yes, even if there had been a protective wall around Alonia, the soldiers would have invaded. Because her people would have allowed it. Because her people had been naïve.

She followed Hans inside the cottage, wondering at the thatching skill and the beams holding the long roof up. It was a risk. If ever a storm came and it collapsed, they would have no place to go until it was fixed.

"Where do you keep your animals?" she asked.

"We have a walled-in meadow a short ways from here. It's large enough to fit all the cows, pigs, and chickens and has enough space for them to graze. We have a few vegetable gardens, but anything we've tried outside the walls gets destroyed overnight by the beasts."

Inside, Herlot found herself holding dried meat, two chicken eggs, and a cup of ale, offered by a Temesian woman who was already onto another guest before Herlot could thank her. Bales of hay were rolled inside and spread out along the edges of the structure. Travel sacks thumped against the ground, some of their contents spilling out, followed by sighs and moans as the Lorfiners sat and stretched their legs. Herlot noticed a few people already asleep still holding their half-eaten food in their hands. Others were conversing with the Temesians, sharing bits and pieces of information about the invasions.

Lucinda stood and clapped her hands. "Before the story gets misunderstood, I'd like someone from Lorfin to stand and share what happened for all to hear."

All Lorfiner eyes turned to Enri. She rose, wiping what Herlot guessed were tears of exhaustion from the corners of her eyes. Herlot hadn't been able to stop her own from watering.

"Yesterday morning, Lorfin was attacked by soldiers of King Felix. But their first attack happened in Alonia..."

Herlot, sitting on a haystack in the corner, rubbed her forehead as images of her last days in Alonia accompanied Enri's telling. It didn't take much for the late summer breeze to lure her outside. She had lived the story—she didn't need to hear it again.

Outside, she saw Movo walking the perimeter of the wall with Devotio at his side. They weren't interacting, but Devotio seemed content with him. Movo didn't seem to give Devotio much attention, probably treating him as if he were another horse.

Every few moments, she heard one of the frightening heartbeats. She wondered how Movo could be so close to the wall knowing they could be on the other side. She cringed as Movo shoved against the stones at one spot, imagining them toppling and leaving them exposed, but she knew what he was testing.

She crossed her arms in front of her chest, careful not to crunch the chestnut tree leaf, and walked over to him. "Is it strong enough to keep the soldiers out?"

"At first, and only if we had arrows. Without those, they'd build ladders and climb over eventually." He patted a stone. "We'd be caged pigeons in here."

There were three heartbeats beating now. A deep, rumbling growl echoed, followed by scratching against the ground outside the wall.

Herlot backed away, but Movo held his ear to the stone.

The creature slammed into the other side of the wall, but Movo didn't budge. Herlot dug her nails into her arms, imagining it circling outside. Then, a high-pitched shriek sounded that felt like long, sharp nails scratching up Herlot's neck and across her head.

"They call to one another when they find food." Hans explained, stepping out of the cottage. "We are ready to start planning our escape. Enri told us to wait until you both are back."

"It will work," Movo announced. He spun on his heel and headed back inside.

"What will work?" Hans asked.

"I don't know. Let's find out," Herlot said.

Once inside, Herlot was surprised to see all the Lorfiners wide awake, some shaking from fright.

Lucinda broke away from the conversation she was having with Enri. "Everyone, stay calm. They have never made it through the wall," Lucinda assured. "Now, we need to make preparations to leave our home first thing in the morning—"

"What will the soldiers do if they find our village empty?" a Temesian man asked.

Herlot hadn't thought about that. *What would they do?*

Movo stepped up next to Enri and Lucinda, towering over them and making some people put their heads back to see him better.

"I'm afraid that because of our spending the night here, we won't be able to put enough distance between us and them. They'll send a pigeon to General Dartharus and to the troop headed for Ruelder. It will raise suspicions and they'll search the area on horses, increasing the risk of finding us before we warn Ruelder or reach our hiding place behind the waterfall," Movo said.

"Is there anything we can do?" Hans asked.

"I have a plan," Movo said.

"We're going to kill them," Seum said with an air of enthusiasm. Movo didn't say anything to negate Seum's suggestion, and just nodded. Movo knelt on one knee and used the tip of a wooden spoon to trace a map of the village and its surroundings on the ground. The man whom Herlot had deemed a monster was about to share a plan that he had devised on his own to kill his own people. She was grateful, of course, but it worried her at how easily he did it. True, he was not happy about it, but there was something about him that seemed detached, and she worried about what would happen if he did change his mind again.

"Mahtreeh, can you mimic the beasts' call?" Movo asked.

"If I have time to work on it a little, yes."

"How long is a little?"

"Less than a nap's length," Enri said, and winked at her brother.

"Perfect."

Herlot and the villagers crowded around Movo as he explained the plan. It was risky beyond all reason, but its main advantage was that no villager would have to use a weapon and fight. On the downside, Temes's fate would lay in Movo and Mahtreeh's hands. Had it not been for Movo fighting for Lorfin, no one would have agreed to it. Once again, they would have to trust him.

"There's nothing more we can do until sunrise when those pups go back to their homes," Asm said. "We sleep."

Herlot, Mahtreeh, and Enri settled themselves against Devotio on a pile of hay. There were too many people around to continue their conversation about Devotio from before. As the heartbeats and shrieks continued outside, fear threatened to keep them awake, even in their exhausted state. But, to their surprise, the opposite happened.

Hans sat at the center of the dwelling with his ankles crossed, holding a wooden instrument that resembled a miniature harp in his lap. Herlot had seen these instruments in some of the books in Alonia. Several Lorfiners sat up and asked what it was.

"A psaltery," Hans said.

An older woman with features resembling Lucinda's spoke up. "When Hans was just four years old, he climbed into the stewards' wagon. He found the psaltery and taught himself to play it. Cloudian heard him on one of his visits, and since then, once a year, he asks Hans to come to the fortress to play for him. Well, that's what he did until now, at least."

"This song is for our King Cloudian, a king who only had the good of his people at heart. My friend." Hans started to play, and a lullaby drifted to comfort each soul. Before long, Seum was grunting and complaining about the music as he tossed from side to side. Herlot couldn't fathom how such beautiful music could be irritating to someone's ear. Maybe Iptans did not like falling asleep to music? Yet Asm was already snoring like a giant.

To Herlot, the music felt like drops of water falling from the tips of leaves, and for that moment, all of her worries dropped away with them and she closed her eyes.

One after another, images of her mother and father's blood-tainted eyes and blackened skin crashed against her skull, paralyzing her in pain. She wanted to shout but couldn't find her body, just the pain in her head. All of a sudden, it felt like she was drifting away from her body, as if her mind had found a way to escape the pain. Somehow, she knew that if she drifted far away enough, she'd never have to return. *No. Devotio depends on me.* She put all of her attention on where her fingers should be, and when she thought she could sense them, she pinched the side of her leg with all of her might. Just like that, she was back, as was the headache. She wished she could go outside and dunk her head in the stream because of how hard it was to take in a full breath. Slowly, tauntingly, the pain dissipated and all she could feel were the tremors arriving in waves down her arms and legs. She stared at the roof, unaware if she was blinking or not, until somehow darkness succeeded and she drifted into nightmares of the crowpox.

● ● ●

Herlot stepped aside as Asm slammed his ax into the crevices of the wall the moment the first sliver of light appeared through the woods. He swung again, and some of the stones came loose. Herlot grabbed a tool and helped chisel at the cracks between the stones. Movo ordered Devotio and the other horses to buck their hind legs against the wall. After a while, Vincent and Seum arrived with a heavy log to ram into it. By mid-morning, half of Temes's wall lay in rubble. They were ready for the next part of Movo's plan.

Herlot, Hans, and Enri covered Mahtreeh's body with honey and pasted foliage onto him. He then held onto Seum's back as Seum climbed onto the top branch of the highest tree near the village. Seum tied a rope around Mahtreeh's waist and fastened it to the trunk. Mahtreeh hugged the trunk as Seum glided down and jumped off a lower branch.

Herlot bit down on her lower lip as Movo approached. She glanced at Devotio, who stood proud and ready for Movo. She knew Devotio would never put her in harm's way, but was she putting his life in danger by allowing him to do this? Before she could think about it anymore, she kissed Devotio between his eyes.

"I will be fine," Devotio's voice sang in her ear.

Herlot winced. She couldn't believe she was allowing Movo to ride Devotio to meet the troop. He was the only choice, for if anyone in the troop noticed one of the horses that should have been at Lorfin, their plan would fall apart.

"Take care of him," she told Movo.

He nodded. "Don't forget to take all of the horses to the enclosure." He tapped his heels against Devotio's side and raced down the path.

When she couldn't see them anymore, she faced the Temesians by the rubble. "Whatever happens, do not touch the chests."

Then she turned to the Lorfiners, ready with their sacks to head to Temes's livestock enclosure. Enri and Asm both held on to the reins of Lorfin's horses. "If everything goes well, we will see each other soon," Herlot said. "Now go."

Then she turned to Seum. "I'm ready."

CHAPTER 16
Monster

HERLOT STOOD NEAR THE stream, her hands balled into fists at her sides, waiting for Movo and Devotio to appear on the path. She looked to the blue sky, which blended into a bright orange toward the horizon. It was nearing sunset, and they would soon be out of time.

"He should be here by now," Seum said as he examined yet another plant in the riverbank.

"I know that!" she snapped.

"He'll come," Vincent said.

A branch snapped in the distance, and her shoulders relaxed.

"He's coming," she said.

A squirrel shuffled across the path. No Movo or Devotio.

"No!" Herlot gripped at her short hair and walked in a circle. She went over their plan trying to predict where Movo could be based on how the events *should* have unfolded. Movo and Devotio were supposed to have met up with the troop after circling around behind them, at which point Movo was supposed to explain that he had met up with the troop at Lorfin, realized they didn't need help, and then decided to find the troop from the Valentina headed toward Temes. He was supposed to help them get the Temesians enclosed in their home, fooling the troop that their plan was a success. By now the soldiers should have had all the planks situated and had the Temesians locked in the enclosure and made camp outside, exposed to the beasts because of the torn-down wall, while the Temesians waited safely inside. Movo was supposed to have offered to bring Devotio and the other horses to the stream to drink where he would meet her, Seum, and Vincent, after which they were going to take Devotio and the horses and meet the others inside Temes's livestock enclosure. Once the sun set, Mahtreeh would sound the beasts' call, luring the beasts to the village. The only problem was that the sun was about to set and Movo was still nowhere in sight.

She went through the plan again. Had the troop been farther away than expected, they could just be planking the Temesians inside their home. But Movo would have been aware of the sunset, he could have offered to leave even while they were still at work. What if he had decided to betray them? Would Devotio be able to get away? All it took was an image of Devotio, helpless and unprotected in the path of the beasts, for her to decide that she had to go back to see what had happened. However, upon her first step, the image of Devotio worsened. She saw him dead, torn apart. Her body froze with emotional pain as the image was now accompanied by her mother and father, their bodies torn apart by crowpox. The pain was too much to take. She had to escape.

"Herlot!"

She blinked her eyes several times and Seum's face sharpened into focus. "Blessed emperors, are you well, girl?"

Her entire body was trembling. "I-I think so."

"Have you heard a word I said?"

She shook her head. She couldn't help thinking of her mother, how she seemed to have disappeared that one night, and her constant sipping of the healthy spirit tincture. Was Herlot becoming like her?

"Here, sit down. There you go, hold on to my shoulder."

Seum held a flask to her lips. "Drink."

She took a few sips of water. "Better?" he asked.

"I suppose. Thank you."

He sat down next to her. "Bad memories?"

She sighed and nodded. "Yes."

"They go away with time."

"I don't know if I want them to go away, to be honest. I feel like I'd be living a lie if they did."

"They won't ever go away, but the pain will, not completely, but it will."

She couldn't ever imagine seeing the last moments of her parents' lives without feeling pain.

"Their faces—their faces were unrecognizable at the end. It wasn't them. The crowpox was so powerful—" She wiped a tear from her eye. She couldn't believe she was talking about this to a stranger. "It was so powerful and bad, and they were so good, and it killed them so easily."

"Warrior girl, tell me what made them so good?"

The corners of Herlot's lips naturally raised up a sliver. "They told beautiful stories. And they loved. A lot."

"That's how it fades. You need to remember the good, too, then the crowpox loses power because their good lives on in memory."

Herlot took a deep breath. By some magic it had come easier than any breath since the fire. "Thank you, Seum."

"My pleasure."

"And please, don't call me a warrior girl."

He chuckled. "Very well, then. I'll just have to wait until you decide to become one."

She shook her head. "You think I have some profound skills just because you saw me fight *once*?

"Yes. You see, you weren't fighting, you were dancing freedom. There's a difference."

Whatever that meant, it was the sword that had done it, not her.

"Someone's coming. Hide," Vincent said.

They each lunged behind a shrub, flattening on their bellies. Horse hoofs and heavy boots trampled against the ground. Herlot inched forward to get a better look. She saw Devotio's white hooves, and her heart raced as she counted four soldiers—none of them Movo.

Out of the corner of her eye, she saw Seum slithering toward the soldiers, a sword in each hand, not making a sound. "We have to go back for Movo," Devotio's voice wrapped around her ears.

The moment the men passed Seum, he lunged and caught them by surprise from behind. Groans of pain and choking sounded. Then it was over.

Herlot ran at Devotio, holding his mane as she swung herself on top. "Head back to the meadow! I'm going back for Movo!" she shouted.

"Wait!" Seum yelled.

But Devotio charged ahead, leaving a cloud of dust behind.

"Why didn't he come?" Herlot shouted into the wind as the last ray of sunlight disappeared.

"He was ordered to stay. They didn't trust him to go off by himself again," Devotio answered.

"Did he resist?"

"No."

He hadn't fought the order. He chose to stay. Why hadn't he tried harder to bring the horses to the stream? Was that his way of betraying them? For all she knew, since the time Devotio had left with the other horses to head for the stream, Movo and the other soldiers were safely inside the enclosure and the Temesians were left outside as bait for the beasts. She didn't know what had come over her when she made the rash decision to save Movo. But it was too late, because at that moment, she heard the heartbeat that meant that the beasts had awoken. Mahtreeh's call reverberated through the forest, the same one the beasts had emitted the other night as a signal of having found food.

Another shriek answered from behind her, followed by a gargled growl. Herlot squeezed her knees against Devotio's side and put her weight forward while holding onto his mane as he extended his neck to gain speed.

She could hear their claws behind her, and an image of the few blades of grass on their path springing back to life after being flattened under Devotio's hooves, only to be shredded as the beasts' claws dug into their roots crossed her mind. "Faster," she urged. Or else they'd be like the dismantled blades of grass.

They passed the camouflaged tunnel entrance. Almost there. Temes came into view, the cottage barricaded with the plank and beams. Felix's men were patrolling the structure while others sat around fires. She picked out Movo's figure, taller than the rest of them, outlined in the shadows as he leaned against part of the wall that remained intact. His arms were crossed, and his head hung low. How was he not afraid of the fate that awaited him? It was almost like he was waiting *for* it.

"Movo!" she yelled with all of her heart.

His head lifted, and then he sprinted toward her. She had one chance to do this right, or else he'd be torn apart. She extended her hand. Their palms touched. She held on with all of her strength as he kicked up and swung his body before landing right behind her.

Devotio raced north, and they ducked under a branch as he leaped over a bush while screams and sounds of shredding echoed from Temes. Herlot's stomach churned with the relief for having saved Movo and escaped the massacre with the horror of what was happening to the soldiers. As the guilt rose, she told herself that she had to mix the good with the bad, like Seum had said. More lives had been saved because if they had fought the soldiers, they would have either lost the fight and everyone would have ended up in a crowpox enclosure, or they would have won with heavy losses just as had happened in Lorfin's sunflower field.

Movo cursed as Devotio swerved left and right between the trees. "I've never met a horse that can run like this. Someone must have been a fool to lose him. I wonder where he was from, never been to a place that has horses like this."

That's because you have not visited a chestnut tree leaf that has been hiding unicorns since ancient times.

The full moon greeted Herlot as they leapt into the meadow, its light pouring relief onto her face. The rolling hills of the meadow fluctuated and Devotio pushed forward like a wave undulating toward shore. A laugh rippled through her, and another because she realized she really had just laughed. It was like she was back in the past, her second night with Devotio when they had ridden through the meadow near Alonia.

She felt like that young Herlot on the horizon again. The moonlight penetrated her dimples as she threw her head back and spread her arms wide, howling at the moon. Ambro was right there with her, cheering each time Devotio leapt from the top of a hill. They, with Devotio, were free again. Free to be alive. Free to not worry. Free to be wild. Free to know magic. But then she realized something. It wasn't Ambro who was cheering behind her. It was Movo.

• • •

Herlot slid off of Devotio right into Enri's embrace. "You cannot imagine how happy I am to see you three," Enri said. "Did you see Mahtreeh?"

"No, but I heard him," Herlot said. She swallowed. "You don't need to worry about him. The beasts will have enough to keep them busy most of the night."

"I just can't wait for morning to get him out of that tree. What if he falls and is left hanging upside down all night? Oh, don't answer that. I need to stop. He's an adult, he can do this."

"He'll be fine even if he does fall. Seum said he used the best knots he knew how to tie," Herlot said.

"Right. Right." Enri picked a petal off the flower in her hair and rolled it between her fingers.

Vincent appeared after having untied the last of the horses he had brought back from the stream and started to help Movo roll a log to cover the tunnel when sounds of hooves and a battle cry blew through the entrance, sending them both tumbling to the side.

Herlot's mouth dropped open. For the night, Enri's wishes had been answered—Seum cheered, his fist in the air while a frightened Mahtreeh clung to his back.

"I told you to go back! The beasts were right on my heels. You could have killed yourself!" Herlot charged up to Seum before he could dismount.

"Don't be upset with him. He went after you. We didn't know what was awaiting you and Devotio," said Vincent.

And he had brought Mahtreeh back. "You're right. Just, how did you—oh, thank you Seum. Thank you for going after me and getting Mahtreeh."

"At your service." He winked and slid off the horse, Mahtreeh still clinging to his back. "I found him hanging upside down from the tree," Seum said, as he peeled Mahtreeh's hands off him. At that, Enri practically threw herself on to Seum.

He lifted his arms in surprise, then patted her back as she thanked him over and over again.

Poor Mahtreeh was a sight to see. His cheeks were bloated like a bullfrog's, probably from all the blood that had rushed to his head. A pink rash covered his hands, which were gripping his chest in martyrdom as whistles escaped his lips. And on top of all of this, he was covered in foliage and honey.

"My time has come. I wish to find a place to rest in peace," he said. He raised his chin and dragged his toes as he walked forward.

"Will he be alright?" Herlot asked.

"He thinks he's dying. This might be worse than the time he was bitten by a turtle. He lay in the sunflower field and wouldn't move until Father agreed to organize his burial," Enri said. "It will pass, though. Now, tell me what happened?"

"Movo was ordered to stay and guard. They didn't trust him to not...*explore* again. He didn't expose the plan to a single soul. He...he was willing to die for us."

Movo seemed caught off guard. He frowned as he addressed Herlot. "How do you know about my orders?"

Herlot's mouth opened and then closed again. This was information Devotio had shared with her. She gave Enri a look, clearly pleading for help.

"Ouch!" someone shouted.

"Well, let me tell you what has been happening since the Lorfiners and I arrived here," Enri said. "We decided that we want to learn to fight. Asm has been teaching us. Many of us were afraid that the plan might not work, and if that were the case, we wanted to be more prepared to fight the troop in the morning." Perfect. A distraction. With relief, Herlot hadn't noticed the sounds of metal on metal emanating from the far end of the enclosure.

"Argh!" another person cried from the other end of the field, followed by a clank and a grunt.

"That didn't sound pleasant," Herlot said.

"It's not going too well," Enri said, and began leading Herlot and the others toward the area where the lesson was taking place. "I don't think Asm is a good teacher, although he is trying his best. He just swings his sword and grunts a few times and expects us to understand. Seum, you said that you are a trainer. Will you help?"

"No."

"Why?" Herlot asked. If she were a military trainer, she would do anything to help these people.

"They wouldn't understand my way."

"Then change your way so that they understand!" Herlot said. "They want to learn to fight for their lives and are scared to death of what our future holds."

"That's exactly why I can't train them. It's futile. They won't win until they're ready for my way."

Herlot crossed her arms. "And what is your *way*?"

"You don't understand yet either."

This was ridiculous. "It can't be that hard. You go up there, show them how to swing a sword and tell them what they're doing wrong."

Seum chuckled. "Exactly. Futile."

Before Herlot could make another remark, Enri placed her hand on her shoulder. "Seum, I'm grateful you rescued Mahtreeh so he didn't have to sit in the tree all night—or, rather, hang from the tree all night—but if you have something you believe is more important than training these people right now, I don't wish to see you any more tonight... Movo? Will you and Vincent help?"

Movo nodded. "They won't need to fight tomorrow but should know the basics if we plan on going to Ruelder."

"What news do you have of Ruelder?" Herlot asked, alarmed.

"We received a pigeon from the troop that was headed toward Ruelder. They are on the outskirts of the village and are waiting to invade Ruelder until morning, before the villagers scatter out to tend to their sheep herds."

So that was it, Herlot thought. Ruelder would succumb to the same torture Alonia had. If the soldiers invaded in the morning, by noon the villagers would be locked in their homes. By the time her people arrived, they would have opened the chests already. There was a chance that some would not open them, and for those who did, would it still be possible to save them from the crowpox?

She followed after Movo as he headed toward the group. She folded her arms in front of her and listened intently as Movo interrupted the lesson and shared the news with the group.

The Lorfiners' faces dropped when they understood their fighting skills would be needed for certain at Ruelder. Instead of giving them time to fret, Movo and Vincent ordered them into formations and started the lesson by directing them to pair up.

"Partners?" Enri asked Herlot.

Herlot smiled. "Partners."

While she and Enri practiced, Herlot was well aware of the tension growing once again between Seum and Movo. Seum sat against the wall, shaking his head along with a cow and her calf, that obviously weren't fond of guests who refused to sleep this late at night. Every so often he would belt a laugh whenever a villager made a mistake. It was distracting.

"We could use your help," Movo said. He adjusted the angle of Carl's block and then rushed to catch Arlette stumbling backward after her partner had thrown her off-balance.

"I'm used to training people more...capable." Seum's attention fell on Herlot, and no matter what she did, she couldn't stop glancing at him as he sat swishing the loose tip of his braid against his chin.

"The nerve of that man," Herlot said. She put her hand on her hip and faced Seum. "What? What could possibly be so interesting? Do you plan on watching me the entire practice?"

"Absolutely not." In a flash, Seum was on his feet, broad shoulders swaying as he approached, taking Enri's place in front of Herlot. He raised one perfectly symmetrical eyebrow and pointed the tip of his sword at Herlot's chest.

Herlot's body tingled, as if it could sense a new, more challenging opponent. She blocked his first attacks with ease. Then, as each strike increased in speed and power, she fell into a trance, all her senses becoming more alive. Her bare feet avoided a cricket in the grass caught in the action while sensing echoes from Seum's steps. She could even feel the moonlight dance over his skin as he lunged.

Eventually Seum walked away from her, his sword limp at his side, breathing loudly. Everyone else had stopped practicing. Only Benyamin's cheering for more from his spot against the wall could be heard.

Out the corner of her eye, Herlot saw Asm nudge Enri with his shoulder. "It's not every day I see a barefoot peasant woman cause my son to wipe the sweat off his forehead."

Then, without warning, Seum extracted his second sword and rushed at Herlot.

The attacks came at her from all directions and at twice the speed as before. Surprisingly, the second sword did not make it more difficult. She enjoyed it, cheering as her sword guided her body to twist, turn, bend, and leap.

Seum stopped, his eyes glimmering. "Now, you attack. Take one of mine—we would not want to release the curse." He winked.

Herlot faltered. There was no possible way she could fight without her sword. Without it to guide her, she felt helpless facing someone like Seum, and just the thought of feeling helpless was making it difficult for her to hold her balance. Planked-in doorways, dirty blankets, blood spilling underneath skin, the images kept coming.

"I'll do it," Enri said, eyeing Herlot.

"No, I asked her to do it," Seum said, his voice firm.

"That's enough," Movo interrupted. "Herlot, walk with me."

He pulled her by the forearm until they were a fair distance away from the others. "Where did you really learn to fight like that?"

His tone was serious, expectant. Demanding. When she didn't answer him, he spun her to face him. "That sword will do you no good if you can't strike and kill someone with it."

She struggled against his grip.

"I heard you talking with your friends behind the brush about how you believe that your horse is a unicorn and that some woman gave you a magical sword. Your tales won't help them. Right now, they need to face their reality, not hear stories about unicorns and cursed swords. Had your Alonians realized that, they wouldn't be ashes today. Only fools could have made it so easy for us to lock them in their own homes. Now next time you pick up that sword, you will strike and make sure the Lorfiners see it."

He gave her no chance to respond. He turned on his heels and left her alone with his harsh words.

She pulled herself up on the wall and lifted her arms for balance, placing one foot in front of the other. Although his words had been painful, there was truth in them. She and the Eraskans were ignorant of the world around them. No village had weapons, let alone training on how to defend themselves.

She touched the chestnut tree leaf, frightened by how impossible Movo had judged her stories to be. He, on the other hand, hadn't been sheltered from the world like her people. What if she still didn't know the difference between imagination and reality? No. It couldn't be. Enri and Mahtreeh remembered and believed, and they could hear Devotio speak.

When she awoke from her thoughts, she wasn't alone. Enri walked behind her and Mahtreeh alongside, riding Devotio.

"Will you tell us now?" Mahtreeh asked. "We are far away enough for no one else to hear."

Movo's words pinched at her—she wasn't doing them any good by telling them about unicorns and magical swords. Even though it was true, maybe he was right in that it would distract them from the seriousness of their current situation with the invasion. But she wanted to tell them. She needed to. For her own sake and sanity, as selfish as it was.

Herlot sat on the wall, allowing her feet to dangle while she examined Devotio's golden patch where the alicorn had once been. Could he be just a horse she had imagined to be a unicorn? Then where would she have gotten the sword? It was clearly magical, and it was impossible for her to be imagining that, after all, she did not know how to fight. Devotio was real. There was nothing that supported otherwise. Her stomach clenched a bit and then relaxed again.

"Devotio rescued you and took you to his home..." Enri said.

"His home is inside the leaf of a tree. This leaf." Herlot pulled the leaf out from beneath her dress.

Mahtreeh's mouth dropped open a few times as if he wanted to say something. Enri loosened her hair out of the wildflower and pulled it back again, gathering the strands that had fallen loose. She rested both palms on her lap and straightened her back.

"Devotio. Unicorns. Home inside a leaf. And then what?" Enri asked.

"Wait. How do you fit a unicorn inside there?" Mahtreeh pointed at the leaf and then bit his nail.

"Well, you first need someone with a golden heart to perform the magic." Herlot took a deep breath and explained everything. "So it's all thanks to Emrys," she said halfway through her story. "Since she still had a golden heart after everyone lost theirs, she was able to blend her idea of a safe world for the unicorns, into the leaf. For centuries, they have been hiding there, waiting until the world is safe again for their return."

"What was it like inside the leaf?" Enri asked. Herlot couldn't believe how easily Enri had believed everything she said. She didn't question a single part. Instead of seeking evidence that a hidden world inside a leaf was possible, she wanted to know what it was like to be there.

Herlot took a moment to find words. "Safe. And alive. Blurred and defined. Fresh. And so, so colorful."

"I want to go there," Mahtreeh said.

"That's where it gets complicated." Herlot ran her fingers through her hair. "The tree burned, and without the tree, Emrys can't blend the unicorns in or out—it is the link between our physical world, and the dream world, which holds the idea of the unicorns' hidden world. Once twelve moons go by, the unicorns will begin to lose their bodies, and if that happens, all of these centuries of waiting will have gone to waste. They will never return again even if people change. In their world, there is a basin Emrys pours her gold into to keep the leaf from crumbling, and she lost her body to keep it intact. I managed to save the leaf, but in order to save them, it has to be blended onto a tree. There's only so much Emrys can pour of her own gold into the basin to keep it alive while it is not attached to a tree branch. And the only person who can blend it—"

"Is someone with a golden heart," Enri finished.

"Herlot can do it." Devotio's voice wrapped around them. "Her heart sparks. All she has to do is learn to control it between now and twelve more moons."

"Eleven." Mahtreeh's voice cracked. He pointed up at the full moon.

Herlot's temples began to pound again. She slid off the wall. "I don't know what to do. Eraska is under attack. We're not strong enough. We have no experience. Eventually, they'll win. And I'm afraid that what Emrys asks of me is impossible. If my heart really can spark gold, how is that anything compared to an ancient human who has had it all the time and knows how to perform magic with it? And... and...everything hurts. It hurts to breathe. It hurts to smell. It hurts to see. It hurts to hear. But, most of all, it hurts to feel. There are icicles behind my eyes, wedged in my throat, tearing through my stomach... My heart is turning into ice, and there is nothing I can do to stop it. Gold can't flow through ice."

Sharp pains pierced all over her head, like ice cracking. Herlot's head spun, whirling her in memories of her parents. She remembered her mother humming while working on Herlot's dress, weaving the wool yarn through the loom. But, when her mother looked up, her eyes overflowed with blood. She continued working, red drops falling onto the fabric and staining it. Herlot grasped for another memory.

She and her father were in the boat. It was a good memory. Nothing could harm her there as long as she held on to his laughter. All of a sudden, her father's warm chuckles turned into chokes. Blood trickled from his mouth, and crowpox marks spread down his arms

All of her muscles cramped and she cried out in pain. A sharp ringing buzzed inside her head. She stumbled forward and grabbed the wall, slamming her forehead against the stone. She had to shatter the ice.

● ● ●

Seum took off at a sprint as soon as he heard Mahtreeh's shouts and Herlot's body thrashing on the grass. Movo was just paces ahead of him.

"Hold her down," Movo called, racing toward Herlot.

"I can't. She's too strong!" Mahtreeh shouted.

"I've got her." Movo tucked his ankles under her knees and pinned her arms down. He brushed the hair from her face while her head thrashed.

"I'm sorry," Mahtreeh cried. "I wasn't strong enough."

Enri returned with a medicine pouch. She opened a small, glass bottle and instructed Mahtreeh to hold it to Herlot's nose and then pour it in her mouth. "Father once helped a delirious man after he'd fallen into quicksand. I am missing an ingredient, but I hope it will work anyway." Within moments, Herlot's body stilled and her eyes drooped, and Movo released his grip.

Devotio lowered himself next to Herlot and she curled toward him. Seum jogged to a pile of supplies stacked against the wall and grabbed a blanket sticking out of a sack. He headed back to Herlot.

"I'm sorry I won't be able to blend the leaf, Devotio. I don't have a golden spark, I'm turning into ice," she muttered.

Mahtreeh covered her with the blanket that Seum had brought over. "You don't need to worry about that, Herlot. We'll help you." He leaned forward. "And, if it helps, I feel the icicles, too."

Enri and Mahtreeh settled against Devotio's other side as Seum pulled Movo aside.

"Do you have any idea what they were talking about?" Seum asked. "Something about blending a leaf?"

"She's delirious from losing her village," Movo said. "The other two lost their father and seek magical nonsense to make sense of their world."

"Magic and nonsense don't mix." Seum looked up at the night sky. "Magic is too complex and mysterious for most to understand. And it doesn't like to be studied. It might leave a trail for you to follow, but only for the purpose of witnessing your reaction when you discover you have been walking in circles. It will break laws one day and follow them to a precision the next. It makes a mockery of us all, but it is not nonsense, Prince. I also have a feeling that it likes the girl, and my guess is that it has a plan for her."

● ● ●

"How much longer will I let this go on?" Seum wondered out loud.

Everyone had formed a circle around Asm, who was sleeping on his belly, which raised his body off the ground so only his forehead and toes touched the ground. A calf practiced his balance standing on Asm's back, clearly curious of the new surface he had discovered that rose up and down in harmony with Asm's belly breaths.

"Ahh...I have not had a lady massage me in years!" He smacked his lips together, as if attempting to chew a delicious dream he was having.

"That's because the last one tangled her fingers in your back hair and told her friends to stay away from you," Seum said.

The others snickered, but there was only one person whom Seum cared to entertain with the scene. He felt a sense of accomplishment when he noticed a small smile spread across Herlot's face.

Seum had avoided waking his father sooner specifically for Herlot. After she awoke, her head had hung low, and she had avoided making eye contact with anyone. He knew she was ashamed of her delirious state last night.

When he had watched Herlot fight the soldiers at Lorfin's sunflower field, he had recognized a wild freedom in her spirit that only Iptan warriors possessed. Other kingdoms had it all backwards—they spent years learning techniques and repeating the same motions endlessly. The method was a futile hope for a lucky moment of harmony. However, his warriors were trained to harness their power from within first, hence avoiding tedious years of repetitive torture. *This wild freedom is what the Eraskans need. Yes, they are passionate and determined. But they are fearful, not free. Herlot could show them the way, but she has to see it in herself first. Starting the day with a smile was a step in the right direction, and what better way than my father's absurd sleep state to make that happen?* And more than anything, he knew that laughter was a crucial medicine for her now, because as much as he hated to admit it, her delirious state was not a good sign. He feared that her only choices from here on were to either become the leader she was destined to be...or lose her mind. For the sake of his empire and the dark future predicted by Iptan divinations, the real reason why he was in Eraska was that he needed to tip the odds in favor of Herlot's health.

● ● ●

Movo couldn't take his eyes off the dismantled soldiers, men he had trained and traveled with. Some he had known his entire life. Their work in Eraska was wrong, but he wondered if they really deserved what had happened to them. Most of them had fought for the few pieces of gold to take back to their families. It was his father who had planned and ordered this meaningless mission, destroying innocent people for the sake of chasing an illusion.

He tried his best to not step on any of his men as he followed Asm toward the Temesian home, and he was grateful that Asm was doing the same, as if he understood that it was the least they could do. None of them would receive a burial. Movo doubted anyone would feel the need to even if they did have enough time.

The Eraskans were innocent. His men were guilty. That was as simple as telling the difference between wool and satin. But where did that leave him? He had harmed and killed both sides. What he looked at now was only his fault. He was the one who had come up with the plan to trick his own men into being torn apart by monsters. No. The beasts weren't monsters—they were hunters. He was the real monster.

"Thanks to you, the innocent were protected," Asm said. He wrapped an arm around his shoulder and squeezed.

If only you knew how many innocents I have murdered.

Movo's memories choked him by the throat while Asm swung his ax at the plank, splattering it into pieces, just like Movo had done to a young boy's leg so many years ago. He could still hear his father's words as if it had happened yesterday. *Look at his knees, son. Look at how weak they are,* his father had said. *If you hold him at the right angle it will only require one stomp to get it over with. Come on, son. Do it for the light.* Movo would never forget the sound it had made— like stepping on a cluster of seashells on a brick road, but with a lot of screams. A child's screams. The screams of a boy who didn't live to hear what his voice would sound like when he became a man.

Asm pushed the door open and light cascaded onto the white faces of the Temesians. The Temesians shook as they climbed over the pile of splattered wood, just like the other boys in the dungeon cell had shaken while Movo had followed his father's orders. Each and every single one. And there had been more after the knee. Temesian fathers pressed their children's faces against their chests, shielding them from the horrendous scene their village had transformed into overnight, and Movo almost warned them to do the same against him.

Movo's attention focused on Hans, who mimicked the same gesture with his psaltery, as if afraid that his music would forever be tainted if the instrument saw the scene. Movo spotted a blanket and flung it over the psaltery. "Close your eyes and don't open them until I tell you to," he said to Hans. Movo then led Hans outside by the hand.

CHAPTER 17
Ruelder

MOVO ADJUSTED LUCINDA'S GRIP on the hilt of the sword. Then he wove between her father and Hans in time to catch Arlette as she stumbled over her own feet.

"A prince charming they must call you in, how do you say it—Damalathum?" Arlette said.

He whipped around and headed toward the front of the formation before she asked anything else.

"Did I say something wrong?" he heard Arlette say.

He was nothing resembling charming. If she knew about his past, she'd be busy keeping her children away from him instead of calling him a prince charming.

Once he arrived at the wagon where Vincent and Asm were demonstrating sword-fighting techniques as the wheels glided across the ridged path, he asked Asm if he had noticed anyone who needed more help. Asm pointed at a girl in the far back. Movo turned back toward the villagers, who walked in formation while attempting to mimic Asm and Vincent's sword maneuvers. Two advances forward, retreat, and block. Repeat.

Sacrificing speed for training had been a difficult decision for the Eraskans to digest, but rushing to Ruelder would be a futile attempt.

The Ruelderians were already trapped in their homes. By evening, hunger and cold would lure them to open the chests.

Movo had struggled with the fact that bypassing Ruelder was the logical decision. Even if they won against the soldiers, crowpox could not be fought. It would run its course and kill, and no weapon stood a chance against it. But the Eraskans were a different breed of people. They barely knew their neighbors but thought of them as if they were their closest family. It was something no invader could take from them, unless they were robbed of an opportunity to help Ruelder.

Movo weaved through the formation, sometimes not having to look to spot mistakes. He could sense weaknesses as if a hidden instinct pulled him right to them. It was a skill his father had taught him.

"Keep your guard up. Never leave your front unprotected." Movo held a boy's wrist and navigated the guard across the vulnerable areas of his torso.

Movo believed his plan would be a success. His father's men would be weak in numbers and unaware of any approach, let alone peasants who knew how to hold a sword. His calculations of those capable to fight left him with four Eraskans to each soldier. Similar to the plan at Lorfin, he, Asm, Seum, and Vincent would lead, followed by the Eraskans organized according to ability.

One of the horses neighed as Asm ordered the wagon to halt. "Seum, they need a water break."

However, there was one problem. If only foot soldiers were awaiting them at Ruelder, Movo would have felt confident fighting with only Vincent, Asm, and Seum at his side. But the Valentina ship had not only carried people. The ship had space for more than enough horses for each man to have his own for the journey to the villages farther away. If the Eraskans really wanted to fight for Ruelder, most of the soldiers would find a mount within moments of spotting the villagers come onto the field. The Eraskans were willing, he didn't want to shatter that since it was one of the only attributes they had, but he feared that they did not understand what fighting a mounted soldier entailed. Facing an opponent head to head was difficult, but facing an enemy on horse meant that they would have to defend against greater speed and force, and because of the height of the horses, getting close enough to do any significant damage was an overwhelming obstacle.

He spotted a man bracing, holding the hilt practically against his belly. "Maintain the distance of the length of the swords between you and your opponent, but keep your elbows slightly bent," Movo said. He stood at his side, demonstrating the footwork. "If he steps forward, you take a step back, if he steps back, you step forward."

Next to Movo, Asm was giving one-on-one instruction, as well. "Be aware of the entire sword. If he gets too close, sometimes you won't have space or time to maneuver the blade, but the hilt of the sword will be at your disposal. And remember, the sword is not your only weapon. If you're in a bind, use your legs, your head, or even your teeth."

"What would you use?" a Temesian woman asked.

Asm patted his belly. "This. And then I'd find a way to sit on him."

She giggled. Movo never thought humor had a place in training, but with this group, the rules had to be changed. It helped ease their fear. He wondered if what he had said to Herlot the other night had been too harsh and that it had triggered her break down. He looked over to her and Mahtreeh and immediately decided he had done right—humor was one thing, believing in fantasies was a threat that could bring the entire group down.

He watched, appalled, as Herlot blocked Mahtreeh's quick advances, not once attempting a strike. But something else was wrong—her blocks were weak and mindless. Her eyes drooped, her face long and expressionless. She hadn't once tended to her horse—normally, she barely left his side.

He wouldn't allow her into the field when the time came, unless something changed. But he doubted that. If she continued on this path, she would only spiral down more. *Crowpox tears apart the bodies of men and women, but it ruptures the spirit of those who witness it murder their families.* He had seen it in lands outside of Damalathum in the few people who had survived. They'd sit, mind lost, and stare into space, barely able to chew their porridge if they were lucky to have someone to feed it to them. *Herlot has the same look in her eyes as they did.*

"Are we ready to practice the dismounts?" Asm asked.

"Yes."

"Eraskans, time to make camp. Then meet me back here," Asm said.

He hated to admit it, but he wished Seum would agree to help train the villagers. Seum was an Iptan trainer, which meant that he'd be the most skilled at teaching a dismount. However, like everything about Ipta, nothing made sense about their training methods. How could one train an army in as little as a day? That was an over-exaggeration, he was certain, but one thing was true—Iptans were the most skilled fighters in the world. From what he had seen at Lorfin, if his father's men were ever to face an equally sized army of Iptans, they would stand no chance. Having Seum and Asm on their side at Ruelder was going to be their biggest advantage. If only Seum were willing to teach even a minimal amount of his skills to the Eraskans, their chances of success could increase even more.

They practiced long into the afternoon. Asm was becoming a better and better teacher, evident by the bruises Vincent now fashioned from having been dismounted from his horse repeatedly.

Hans and Lucinda stood shoulder to shoulder, each holding a branch to mimic a sword, one foot in front of the other and knees bent. Vincent charged at them on a horse. Lucinda was promising, as were many of the Temesians. Earlier Movo had found out that they often practiced finding the tunnels blindfolded in case they ever found themselves in the woods at night. Like Lucinda, they were more aware of their footing and balance than the Lorfiners.

The moment Vincent was several paces away, Hans and Lucinda divided, concentrating to determine which of them Vincent would decide to strike. He swung at Lucinda, and the moment she blocked it, Hans jumped from the opposite side, attempting to jab Vincent in the side when he was at his least-balanced moment on the horse, but missed. This was Hans's fifth failed attempt.

"Enough. Tomorrow Hans will stay behind to help Enri. Lucinda, you will fight in the first formation following Vincent, Movo, Seum, and myself," Asm said. "Movo, Vincent, come here, I need to speak with you."

Movo followed Asm to the side of the path. "I suggest we fight on foot tomorrow, as well," he said.

"I thought our intent was *not* to die," Vincent said. "With Seum, we are the only ones who can fight on horse, why would we even think about fighting on foot?"

Movo rubbed the stubble on his chin. "I agree with Asm," he said.

Vincent pulled his chin back, as if appalled by the agreement.

"It will give the villagers more confidence," Movo said.

"Pardon me, but I don't understand this philosophy if you care to explain."

"Fear will be the villagers' worst enemy tomorrow," Asm said. "I worry that if we were on horses and they would see the first dismount, they'd question what they have learned to do on foot."

"I understand your point." Vincent sighed and turned to Movo. "I have to say, packing my sack and heading for the mountains sounds awfully tempting about now."

"You know you're free to go whenever you want. I know you have not made your decision yet."

Vincent started to walk back to the practice area. "Nah, I made my decision already."

"When was that?" Movo asked.

"Several years ago. An incident involving vomit, your father, and his precious Dartharus."

Movo frowned. That had to have been the time Vincent led them to the supposedly cursed field.

"Not to mention that while you were sieging castles, I spent a good chunk of my years cooling my heels around some poisoned ground. With only an occasional delivery of one of Ademar's butter sculptures to look forward to may I add," Vincent said.

"At least you got a butter swan," Movo said.

"There were several aboard the ship. Too bad you didn't think of grabbing one before you decided to betray our kingdom."

Movo chuckled.

"We won't see Ademar again."

"We won't," Movo said.

"His meals were the only good thing about Damalathum anyway."

And my mother, Movo wanted to add.

"Herlot! Mahtreeh! No more hiding in the crowd," Asm pointed at the spot where he wished Herlot and Mahtreeh to stand in guard.

Once they were positioned, Vincent began his approach. Movo studied Herlot, who was looking back and forth between her hands as if trying to understand which one held the branch. Mahtreeh nudged her. She looked up, squinted, and shook her head. Vincent was a mere amount of paces away, but she wasn't budging and neither was Mahtreeh. Vincent's horse skidded to a halt in front of them, its hooves touching the tips of Mahtreeh's sandals and Herlot's toes.

"Both of you will stay behind with Enri," Movo said.

"That's not fair. We only get one try?" Mahtreeh asked.

The Lorfiners were just as dumbfounded as Mahtreeh. Herlot, who had fought off the soldiers at Lorfin and escaped the beasts at Temes, walked off the path as if Movo's decision didn't mean anything to her.

• • •

The next morning, Enri awoke with what felt like ale fizz running through her veins. Fear of the battle mixed with relief that by tonight it would be over. Today, they would learn their fate at Ruelder.

Enri picked up an armful of plants she had gathered over the last few days and hauled it onto the wagon. "Can I help?" Herlot asked. "Since I'm not allowed to fight, I hope I can be of some use helping make the salves."

"Of course," Enri said. She tried to catch Herlot's gaze but she kept avoiding her eyes.

"Where's Devotio?" Enri asked. Last night, Herlot had gone to sleep away from the group, even away from Devotio. Mahtreeh had suggested going by her, but Enri had disagreed. Herlot needed time to rest her mind, and they could keep a watch on her from far away. On top of that, she must have been embarrassed about her breakdown. Enri's father taught her that whenever someone was suffering, it was important for them to have some time alone, although not too much. Herlot hadn't had private time for herself since being trapped in her home, since her parents' death.

"With the other horses, I think."

Everything aside, it did worry Enri that Herlot had seemed to have distanced herself from Devotio. Enri's last memory of the night was Devotio's longing look as he stared at Herlot. She couldn't imagine having a task like Herlot had taken on—find gold and blend a leaf to save a family of unicorns. Enri hoped that Herlot didn't think that she had let Devotio down by having had a breakdown. Oh, how she wished she could do something to help her friend, but she knew nothing about gold, especially about how to find it in her heart and use it to perform magic. When this all started, Enri had been worried that Mahtreeh would be the one who would need the most support. She had been wrong. It was Herlot. "Herlot, you can talk to me, you know, if anything is pressing on your mind. I mean, *if* you'd like someone to talk to."

Herlot gave a faint smile and nodded. "The tincture you gave me to drink last night...what was it?"

"It was a form of a healthy spirits tincture. It is meant to calm and soothe."

"Oh." Herlot seemed to fall into deep thought. "It's used for people with nerve illness, too, right?"

"Why yes, it is. There's a stronger form of it for that, though," Enri said.

Once the wheels started turning, Enri got to work crushing leaves in her mortar while Asm ordered everyone to walk and practice. She hoped she wouldn't need as many salves as she was planning to make, but she thought it better to be safe. If only she had her father here to tell her how much to prepare for battle wounds.

"Wouldn't it be best if they didn't exert themselves?" she asked Asm when he neared the wagon. "Surely a walk without having to practice the maneuvers will help them preserve their strength."

"I want them to keep their bodies warm. Won't allow the fear a chance to send its cold breeze and stiffen the muscles."

"Aha. Makes sense," she said.

"Mahtreeh," Enri called and waited for her brother to arrive. "Can you find some more of these comfrey leaves? If you do, I'll need the root, too." Enri held up a vivid green leaf longer than her palm.

"Of course," Mahtreeh snagged the leaf. It seemed like he was also looking for a way to be of help. Like Herlot and Hans, he was also not allowed to fight. She knew it saddened him, but she was glad knowing he'd be safe and by her side.

"What is it used for?" Herlot asked.

"Lots of things. Today, it will be to stop bleeding and to ease the pain of broken bones," Enri said.

Herlot's mood seemed to have lightened, asking the occasional question about the plants while prepping them. Enri noticed Herlot glance Devotio's way several times. Devotio seemed to be at peace with keeping the children entertained, although Enri was certain he was hurting, too. He had to be worried, or whatever it was that unicorns felt when the person they depended on to save their family seemed to have broken down. It was a huge task, but until Herlot found a way to believe in herself, there was not much Enri could do besides be patient. She guessed Devotio understood this, too.

She spotted a plant she had been looking for a little ways into the woods from the path. "Mahtreeh, can you grab that comfrey plant, please?"

"Yes," Mahtreeh said, and hurried into the woods. He bent to dig at the soil around the comfrey plant. He pulled it up by the roots, and waved to Enri signalizing success. She waved back with a smile. But then he dropped the plant and a look of horror crossed his face. "Movo! Movo!" he shouted and raced back to the path, his arms flailing. "They spotted us! Oh, Holy Basil, they spotted us! There was someone on a horse and they sped away in that direction when they saw me." Mahtreeh pointed up the path.

Enri jumped off the wagon and stood next to Mahtreeh, who was now biting his nails. She watched Movo gallop ahead, holding the reins with one hand and shielding his forehead with the other to scan the premises.

He sped back to a frowning Asm. "It was a scout. He's going to inform the rest."

"We've lost our element of surprise. Is there time to run for the caves?" Asm asked.

Lucinda pushed past Enri. "No. We can do this," she said.

Movo nodded. Enri knew that there was no time to second-guess decisions now. They had to attack now or never. "Eraskans!" Movo exclaimed. "Take your formations!"

"Mahtreeh, I'm going to need more of those comfrey plants," Enri said. A lot more than she had expected now that her people had lost their element of surprise.

● ● ●

As Asm dashed onto the field, Ruelder was as he had expected. Two pigeons flew over the stone homes leaning against the cliff—each one planked shut, trapping its inhabitants inside along with the crowpox chests. Each pigeon had a tiny scroll tied to one of its feet. Asm had no doubt that on the scrolls were written messages to Dartharus informing him of the rebellion.

Asm jumped and kicked his leg back and swung his ax at his first target. The ax spun through the air and then plunged into the chest of a soldier. He fell backward off his horse.

"Father!" Seum scolded. He pointed at the cliff, seemingly not worried about a soldier charging at him. "Stop shaking the ground!" He laughed as he extracted the ax from the soldier's chest and chucked it back at Asm.

Asm caught his ax with a firm grip as he blushed. Once he had caused an avalanche with that move when they had fought their way through a mountain passage.

He fought with ease next to his son. Ironically, this was the only time he did not worry about Seum. Seum's braid had now unraveled, and it was a wonder that his long hair was not ripped to shreds by his own maneuvers. In Ipta, Seum was referred to as the Jack of Spades. Iptan children played a game where they would try to spot the Jack of Spades while rifling through a deck of cards, which bore a striking resemblance to attempting to spot Seum as his two swords buzzed about him and his opponents.

Three men were currently attempting to intimidate Seum from afar with their ruthless stares. Seum crouched low and pounced forward before skidding to a halt a few steps away from them. As they stumbled back, their ruthless masks fell.

"Should have tied the strings tighter," Asm said under his breath as he knocked a soldier off his horse. Most ruthless masks, he had learned, were fake. He turned his attention back to Seum as he waited for another mounted soldier to charge at him.

Seum stretched his neck by rolling his head in circles, then sprinted at his opponents, spinning both of his swords at his sides.

Wherever their swords swung, one of Seum's was already waiting.

Then they stood with baffled expressions, for Seum was nowhere to be seen.

The Jack of Spades card was also used in Ipta's version of the game hide-and-seek. Children would hide gold coins and the Jack of Spades in a room or outdoor area; however, in this game, the one who found the Jack of Spades lost.

"Behind you!" Asm hinted as he ran past the men to retrieve his ax from a victim, but his clue came too late. They hadn't noticed Seum crouched right behind them.

"No!"

"Herlot!"

What sounded like Herlot and Mahtreeh's voices rang from across the field. They were supposed to be with Enri. Asm shielded his eyes from the sun to get a better sight of what was happening.

He cursed.

● ● ●

"Dammit," Movo said under his breath as the pigeons flew into the sky, headed toward the fortress. He raced onto the field after Seum and Asm. Several mounted men charged at them. Movo and Vincent positioned themselves at angles behind Seum and Asm, ready to block any attempts to break their line toward the villagers behind them. Asm swung his ax and Movo took his on-guard position.

He held his sword with both hands, ready for his first opponent. He ducked just as the soldier swung. It was enough to force him off balance.

He watched long enough to know Lucinda and Carl had a handle on him.

Then he raced ahead and slashed the throat of a soldier Asm had dismounted, not a hint of remorse in his being. He had fought this way ever since his last day in the dungeon as a young boy. As much as he had resisted, he had learned Felix's lesson after the years of being locked in that trap of torment.

"You want to leave?" his father had said. "Sense out his weakness. It's the only way. Ahh...do you feel it? He's afraid. Won't even fight back."

The city boy flashed across Movo's memory—the little boy whom Felix had ordered him to kill in exchange for finally getting to leave the dungeon. To see the light.

"Anything you feel for this boy is your flaw," his father had snarled. "It's what makes you weak and will trap you in a dungeon for the rest of your life. If you want to see *light* again, you must slaughter all your weaknesses by using his to your advantage. Look, he is so weak he won't even attempt to fight back. Come on, son. It will be quick and you will see the light again, I promise. As long as you listen to me, there will always be light."

Through his years of training and battle, Movo had learned that weaknesses were strong and required a heavier and heavier weight to be subdued and kept from rising to the surface. His own were proving stronger than he, rising from where he had squelched them below his feet that last day in the dungeon. They were taking charge of the steps he took. He could imagine it being turned into an Alonian story. In the story, there would be a soldier whose shoes forced him to run after a girl to save her from a fire and then take the steps to fight his own people. He almost faltered, almost, as he caught a man in a chokehold when he realized that even though he fought his opponent with no remorse, it was because he didn't want anything to happen to the people he was protecting. Never had he cared for the reason of the killing before.

"No!" A chill pierced through his spine as he heard Herlot's voice. She was supposed to be with Enri.

"Herlot!" Mahtreeh's voice followed.

The second Movo turned to see the mounted soldier racing at full speed toward Herlot, the weight holding his weaknesses down dissipated completely and he raced toward the edge of the field. He launched his dagger into the back of a soldier, then fought his way forward, caring more than he had ever cared before to reach his destination.

● ● ●

Herlot plugged her nose as she and Mahtreeh paced back and forth in front of the wagon. The mixture Enri was boiling over the fire reeked. She didn't understand Enri and how she was able to focus all of her attention on the salves not knowing what was happening at Ruelder.

"They might need us," Herlot said. That had to jar Enri out of her serenity.

Enri didn't flinch. "Yes, soon. That's why we need to wait here so we can help the injured."

"Is there anything else I can do?"

Enri pursed her lips to one side. "I have firewood. I have plants. Unless you can make me another mortar, there's not much else. I'm sorry, Herlot."

"Let's check on the horses?" Mahtreeh offered.

Shame already started to build on top of Herlot's shoulders at the thought of seeing him again after her breakdown. This was who had been chosen to help him and his family—a broken girl who hit her own head against a wall. How would he ever trust her again? How could she ever trust herself again? She wiped a drop of sweat off of her brow. She must have been standing closer to Enri's fire than she thought. "Yes, let's check on them. Let's go."

The heat didn't dissipate as Mahtreeh and she walked. "It's hotter today than yesterday," she said. It was so hot that she could feel it inside of her. What she wouldn't give to take a dip in the stream.

"Hmm...I would say it's a bit cooler. Holy Basil, Herlot, you're really sweating."

The toes of her right foot curled and anchored into the ground.

"Why did you stop?" Mahtreeh asked.

"I don't know. It's—"

"You're ill. I'll go get Enri."

"No, Mahtreeh, I'm not having a breakdown. Come here, there's something different about the ground here. Take off your shoes and put your foot here and tell me if you feel it, too."

She watched patiently as Mahtreeh bounced around on one leg trying to free his foot from his boot. Herlot kept wiggling her foot around, digging it deeper into the soil. An image of a footprint underneath her foot flashed across her mind.

All of a sudden, the warmth in her chest burst and travelled down her leg and out the bottom of her foot and into the footprint she had imagined underneath. The footprint was warm, as if someone had just taken it. It was a different kind of warmth, as if warmths had a flavor. It flowed into her, growing like a vine up her spine until it reached her head.

The trees around her began to spin. She gasped for breath. *I'm blending!* she realized. She saw willow tree leaves, then she was hiding behind a bush seeing a girl with a blue dress, then she was walking straight through the hollowed-out oak tree.

Focus, Herlot, focus. Remember everything. How are you doing this? Think, think, think. At any moment she would become the person who had made the footprint centuries ago and see their story. Who was it the time she had seen the blue dress? Brom. Holy Basil, she remembered his name, she had been Brom, the same person who had taken Devotio and the unicorns into hiding. It had to be him. She had been his memory before and not even remembered. What if she forgot this time as she had every time this happened?

Everything went black. She felt like chickling fuzz. She smiled internally at her first time feeling like this. How wonderful it was to remember.

May I share a memory with you? A voice, not her own, asked within her mind. *My name is Brom. You stepped on my footprint that I made long ago. You must have a golden heart. Please, may I share my memory with you?*

Yes, she thought.

Wonderful.

Just as quickly as her senses had disappeared, they reemerged, now completely blended with Brom's warmth, his memory.

Her eyes blinked open. As if possessed, her attention whipped to a unicorn that stood on the path before her. She had a golden alicorn, and the corners of her eyes rose upwards. Upon seeing Herlot—or Brom, she realized dizzily—the creature ran away up the path. Herlot-Brom had to stop her and bring her to Emrys to hide in the chestnut tree before a human could harm her. She raced after her.

"Wait! I won't hurt you, I promise!" she shouted in what did not sound like her own voice.

Herlot emerged onto the empty field, searching for the unicorn when, without warning, the bright colors around her faded and her surroundings morphed back to the present.

Ruelder unfolded in front of her. No—a battle scene unfolded in front of her.

What just happened? Where was I? How did I get here? Her heart pounded as she recollected. She could remember this time. She had blended. She had chased after a unicorn. A unicorn from the *past*. How could that be possible? Could she have traveled back in time? Had she seen a memory? Had she imagined it?

She would have to mull it over later. A soldier on horse had just spotted her and was galloping in her direction.

You will be fine, she told herself, but her arms shook as she unsheathed her sword and gripped it in front of her with both hands. She was all alone, and all she would be able to do was defend herself.

"Remember, keep your eyes on his sword and I'll get him from the side," Mahtreeh said, appearing at her shoulder.

Herlot felt a wave of relief pass through her. "Thank the skies you're here."

"What? Did you think I'd let you fight by yourself?" Mahtreeh asked, his hands visibly trembling.

Herlot managed a laugh. "We seem to shake an awful lot these days, don't you think?"

"Nothing new for me. Soon you'll barely notice, you'll be so used to it."

Side by side, they braced as exhaust steamed from the horse's nose with each gallop, its owner flaring his nostrils just as wide.

Herlot bent her knees to stabilize her balance. Blood dripped from the soldier's sword—blood of one of the Eraskans who lay lifeless on the field.

And then Herlot saw her—the unicorn. She was galloping toward the cliff, her coat shining bright. But where had all the soldiers gone? Herlot squinted into the distance, watching as several ropes lashed out from behind the cliff, tightening around the unicorn's neck. The magnificent creature jolted back and then came crashing down on her back with her legs in the air. More ropes wrapped around her legs as a group of people emerged. One carried a sharp knife, which sparked where the sun's rays hit it. The man kneeled on her neck and brought the knife down toward her alicorn.

"No!" Herlot exclaimed.

"Herlot!" Mahtreeh's shout rumbled through Herlot's mind.

She blinked, and only the herd of Ruelderian sheep remained near the cliff where the unicorn had just been. "What is happening to me?" she gasped, whirling in disorientation. She was back in the present moment, the soldier just paces away from her. *My sword. Where is my sword?* She gaped at her empty hands in horror as she realized that she must have dropped it.

The soldier leaned down the right side of the horse and raised his sword.

Out of reflex, she raised her right arm to shield her face and winced at the thought of the impact.

The soldier's sword grazed her cheek, and it stung. Instinct urged her to cover it, but she couldn't feel her hand. Something felt different. Something felt very off balance.

Where are my fingers? she thought. Then she realized she couldn't feel her wrist or her elbow, either.

All she could hear were Mahtreeh's screams repeated in short bursts. She had to help him. She turned her head, surprised to find herself on the ground. The horseman lay several paces away from her with an ax in his back. She wanted to sit up to find out what was frightening Mahtreeh, but her balance was off and her right shoulder felt as if it were sinking into quicksand.

"Get her to Enri now!" Asm yelled.

Mahtreeh appeared above her, his face and tunic covered in blood. "My cheek, I'm so sorry," she croaked.

"It's not your cheek. It's your shoulder." Mahtreeh's hands moved frantically over her until he had them tucked under her back.

And then, as her body rose off the ground, Herlot felt the most excruciating pain she could have ever imagined. It felt as if the moon were hanging from her shoulder and pulling everything out of her. As the pain stabbed at her, she slipped into a world of half-consciousness. She was aware of nothing but the pain and the image of blood spilling onto Devotio's white coat as Mahtreeh hauled her on to him.

• • •

Movo watched as Devotio raced off with Herlot, her blood spilling from where the soldier had severed her arm. Weaknesses ascended up his legs, as if climbing a vine from the place he kept them smothered below, but he clenched his stomach muscles to prevent them from climbing higher. He examined his father's remaining men on the field. Then he charged again, determined to fight the last few remaining, almost by himself.

I'll always outsmart you, he warned his weaknesses.

With each life he took, he drowned them back down before one could reach his chest. But, when the fight was over, they began to rise again, like ghosts of vengeance awoken from the dead.

CHAPTER 18
Fairy Slumber

THE WATERFALL'S POWERFUL HUM was all Enri heard as the water crashed onto the rocks below. She raced after Seum, who held Herlot tight against his chest, up a path naturally carved into the ledge. She hoped his heartbeat would motivate Herlot's weakening one. About halfway up the waterfall, the path turned inward into the mouth of a cave in the ledge.

The waterfall splashed upon her as they entered the cave, as if it were sending a refreshing greeting to its guests. But, to her, it was only a reminder that she was entering a place far different from her village home.

Sharp formations resembling carnivorous teeth protruded from the ceiling. It was as if she had entered the mouth of a frozen beast. At any moment, the sun would shine upon it, freeing it from its frozen state, and the beast would snap its jaw shut while she was stuck inside its mouth.

The moment Seum set Herlot down, Enri pushed her capabilities to stop the bleeding and save Herlot's shoulder from infection. It was not working. She knew how to heal wounds, but never had her father shown her how to take care of someone who had had their entire arm cut off. Her stomach churned at the sight of it and she was fighting against the spinning. Herlot's face was so pale and she was barely breathing. All Enri could think about was how horrifying the shoulder looked—the jagged bone and torn muscle, the veins, the blood. So much blood. Her hands were shaking as she unrolled the cloth. Bile rose into her mouth. *Skies, I can't do this. I'm not a healer like my father. I can't do this. I just can't.* The blood kept flowing. Enri's wool dress was drenched in sweat and blood, the harsh fabric scraping against her skin at the slightest movement. *Please live, my dear friend,* she thought over and over, desperate for something to help her. She was wrapping Herlot's shoulder in new cloth when Asm knelt behind Herlot's head, wedging a piece of wood between her teeth.

"What is that for?" Enri asked.

"In case she wakes up, she won't bite her own tongue off." He lowered the blade of his ax into a fire that had been started. "I've seen many of these types of severs and performed the procedure myself more times than I can count on both hands. She already lost the arm—the heat will stop the infection. Enri, there are many others who need tending to. Go to them. I will care for Herlot."

Enri looked away the moment she heard the hiss when Asm pressed the blade of his ax to Herlot's wound. "Enri. Go," Asm said.

I'm sorry, Herlot, but I can't look. I'm sorry.

There was an eerie silence among the people as she worked her way from one patient to the next. Only mothers lulling their agitated children could be heard between the sounds of excruciating pain from the wounded. Anyone not wounded helped bring supplies inside, only mumbling quietly amongst themselves, as if anything loud would break the fragile composure everyone was trying to uphold. By the time Enri reached her last patient, not a single fit person had left a blanket for himself before every wounded person had one beneath his back and covering his body. Her father had always said that even though he was the one who knew the recipes for the medicines, it took an entire village family to heal someone. A warm touch. A kind word. A loving gesture. These were all healing ingredients, too.

Enri spread the comfrey salve across a Temesian woman's leg wound.

"Bless you, child. If I weren't looking, I would think you were your father," she said.

"Thank you. Everything I know I learned from him." And there was so much, too much that she had not had time to learn. Enri held the woman's hand as she drifted to sleep.

"Is there anything we can do to help?" Hans asked, Lucinda at his side.

Enri sat back on her heels. "Hmm... Will you play us a song on your psaltery? It would help calm the children. It would help calm us all, actually."

"I would be more than happy to do so," Hans replied and bowed.

"And, Lucinda, can you help some of the men fetch more firewood?"

Lucinda crouched down to Enri's eye level. "Is there a plan for Noray and Bundene yet?"

"No. Movo and Vincent are setting up a camp for the Ruelderians as we speak. We were going to wait to set any plans until they return. Why do you ask?"

"We saw the pigeons and some of the soldiers escape. Dartharus will know soon if not already of our rebellion. They will begin searching for us and we should go get our people from Noray and Bundene back here before the invaders get to them. I'd like to volunteer to travel to them."

"I'll let Asm know." She took hold of Lucinda's hand. "Thank you, Lucinda."

Hans unwrapped his psaltery from a blanket. He plucked his finger against each string and closed his eyes as he tuned the instrument. Each time the note came closer to a perfect pitch, he tilted his head ever so slightly.

"Hans, do you think music is magical?" Enri asked.

"Hmm? What do you mean by magic?"

"I don't know. I guess it's when good things happen even though it's not likely that they will."

"That's what it feels like when I play a new song. I never know where it comes from, all I know is that I like it."

Enri looked over at Herlot, her face a haunting white. "Hans, will you try and play a song for Herlot? I-I think she needs the magic."

Hans nodded and closed his eyes. His eyebrows rose as if he were smelling the tune of the mellow melody ascending from the psaltery. It was a sad tune, yet it was perfect. Had he played a happy one now, many wouldn't be able to hear it. A sad mellow was in their reach, though. Enri hoped that it would blanket the trauma they were feeling and shield them from nightmares.

It was working—their bellies rose and fell as they drifted to sleep. She even thought that she saw Herlot take a deeper breath, but it could have just been her wishful thinking. There was a special emotion layered into the notes Hans strummed, one that made Enri also think of the Ruelderians. The wool of the fabric she was wearing had once been held by a Ruelderian, as was every piece of clothing worn by the Eraskans in the cave.

She prayed some had not opened the chests. Movo and Vincent had led them across the river and were setting up a camp of tents using hides. It couldn't be risked, bringing them in the cave, for fear of the crowpox spreading and they could not stay in a village of where Dartharus knew of the location. Movo had explained that they'd be safe from Felix's men across the river for the time being. But what would happen if the Ruelderians were discovered?

"I just remembered something, about King Cloudian," Hans said, his long eyelashes fluttering open.

"What's that?" Enri asked as the tune continued.

"I can't believe I had forgotten about this, it's just that this melody is similar to the one I played once for him. This was many years ago, my first or second visit to King Cloudian. I was so young, the memories are so blurry from that time. I remember crying in the middle of the night, though. I was scared and missed my parents. I wanted to go home. King Cloudian showed me a ring that he wore. It flashed when he clapped his hands, I was mesmerized by it. It wasn't gold, but he said it was considered a special stone, yes, that's what it was...some kind of stone. It was reddish. Argh, what was the name..."

Enri blinked her eyes several times. King Cloudian sat cross-legged in the center of the cave among the sleeping Eraskans. He had a gentle smile on his face and rocked side to side to the music. She blinked again and then he was gone. She probably needed sleep just as much as everyone else did.

"A ruby. Yes, that's what it was called. Anyway, King Cloudian then told me a story about a group of people who live in the mountains on Eraska's southern border. He said they were very kind, good people who watched over Eraska, and that if something were ever to happen, all he had to do was send someone with the ring to them and then they would come to his aid. Could the story be real? These people, they could be some sort of allies to us. They might be able to help us."

Enri hated to smash Hans's hope, but after everything that had happened, this sounded too much like a fairy tale. "Hans, King Cloudian was a good king, probably the best and only good-hearted one in this world but, well, he did everything to make us think we were safe, when really we were not. How do you know this is not just a tale he made up to make you feel safe here?"

"I know. I know. It probably was. Still, maybe it's an idea worth exploring?"

At that moment, Movo and Vincent returned, water dripping down their faces. "Perhaps. Let's see what they think. Come," Enri said.

They met Movo and Vincent as close to the waterfall as possible, ensuring their conversation would stay muffled by the rush of the water and not wake the others. Mahtreeh, Seum, and Asm soon joined, as well.

"How are the Ruelderians? Are they sick?" Mahtreeh asked.

"Most of them are already coughing. They all opened the chests. Enri, I need to speak with you later," Movo said.

"Alright..."

"How is Herlot?" Vincent asked.

Movo looked down and sideways upon the question.

"She should wake," Asm said. "If it were only a physical injury, I'd imagine her to wake soon. But the girl has been through an awful lot. It might have been too much..."

Enri swallowed. She should have been a better friend. She was so focused on Mahtreeh, how could she not have realized that Herlot needed more comfort? She had thought leaving her alone would be for the best, but what if she had tried harder to talk to her? She could have said something to ease her pain, although she didn't know what, there must have been something. She could have had Herlot hold the herbs over the fire, maybe then Herlot would not have run off.

"If she does wake, she will wake strong," Seum said.

Enri hated herself for doubting Seum's statement. She wanted Herlot to recover, but she could not see how a girl who had lost her entire village to crowpox, had to learn magic to save a family of unicorns, and on top of everything now had lost her arm, could be strong. She would need all the support friendship could give her.

"I-I have something to share," Hans stuttered.

"Please, Hans," Asm said.

Hans began to tell the story of King Cloudian's ring and the people in the mountains.

"Hmm... This is very vital information, Hans. Thank you," Asm said. "Movo, is retrieving this ring possible based on your knowledge of the circumstances at the fortress?"

"If the ring is a ruby, it is most likely in Dartharus's possession now. From what I understand, no Eraskan aside from Hans has knowledge of these allies, and there's no certainty they still exist, if they ever did. Right now, our focus should remain on staying hidden," Movo said.

Anger tickled through Enri's fingers at the thought of Dartharus taking King Cloudian's ring.

"Seum and I saw no sign of human life in the mountains," Asm noted. "But *if* they exist. Huh."

"They'll be strong," Seum said.

"Used to hard conditions," Asm said.

"Easy to train," Vincent said. "We'll need them if it comes to war."

"War?" Mahtreeh and Enri said at the same time.

"Shh." Hans pointed at the sleeping villagers.

Scum cleared his throat and looked at Enri, Mahtreeh, and Hans. "It's time your people understand the consequences of winning. If you manage to stay hidden, if you manage to fight off your attackers, one time after another, more will keep coming."

"So it's just a matter of when it's smartest for us to give up," Enri said. "That's just wonderful. Why not march to the fortress now."

"That's not what Seum is saying," Asm said. "He's saying that we need to think further into the future. He's right, more will keep coming and you will need more people on your side to fight them. One of us should ride out and see if there might be any sign of these mountain people."

"I'll go," Vincent said.

"What can we expect from Dartharus?" Asm asked, directing his gaze at Movo.

"Knowing Dartharus, he will do everything in his power before notifying Felix, so as not to make himself look weak," Vincent said. "And when he comes searching for us, which will be soon, his men will be more than ready to fight. If one of us is caught, he will use torture for information on our whereabouts."

"How many?" Asm asked.

"It depends on whether or not he will send for reinforcements from nearby ships. But my prediction is that Dartharus will want to handle the situation himself before resorting to that. Forty men, at the least, is my guess." Movo replied. "Vincent, how many were on the Valentina?"

"Four troops."

"Then we're looking at eighty," Movo said.

Enri looked at her patients. This is what only twenty soldiers did to them. "Seum, look at them," she said. "You know just as well as I do, they'll have to fight again, and like Vincent said, this time we won't have the advantage of surprise. They have to learn to defend themselves. You say you can train your special people in a day? I'm begging you to train mine for however long it takes."

"Seum...she's right," Asm said.

Seum sighed. "I will try, but my method may do more harm than good."

"Try is all I ask for now," Enri said.

They continued outlining their plans. Lucinda would set out on horse for Noray and Bundene in the morning. There were enough rooms in the caves to keep the horses and some of the sheep that had been brought from Ruelder, but they would have to be taken outside to graze and they would have to give special attention to covering their tracks near the area of the waterfall. They had brought what they could on handcarts from Ruelder's food stores, but some of them would have to leave to fish for extra sources of food.

First thing in the morning, Asm and Seum would lead the training. Movo and Vincent were in charge of looking over the Ruelderians. As for Enri and Hans, salves and music. Enri could only hope that would be enough to help Herlot.

"Enri." Movo nodded toward the outside. "Let's speak."

A night rain drizzle fell as they walked down the path and then away from the waterfall.

Movo put on a pair of gloves and opened a pouch attached to his belt. He pulled out a star-shaped flower that shone pink under the moonlight.

"A riadonna," Enri observed. "It's poisonous even to the touch."

"Correct. In Damalathum, there is a potion with the riadonna as its main ingredient. It is mixed with other plants so the drinker does not feel any pain."

Enri cleared her throat. "It's called fairy slumber. The name is misleading. It is a death potion."

"I need you to make enough of it for about a hundred people."

"What? How dare you to ask me such a thing. No. Never."

"Crowpox will tear the Ruelderians apart in front of each other's eyes! Do you not understand that?" His fists clenched. "Once the crowpox starts, there is no stopping it. Do you want them to experience what Herlot did in Alonia? Do you want their last memories of their loved ones' faces to haunt them into their death sleep? If we give them the potion, they can die peacefully with their families. Their last memories won't be their family's faces ravaged by pox."

"No matter what you say, I will not kill the Ruelderians."

His arms rose in their crossed position as he took a deep breath. He spoke through gritted teeth. "They are already dead. You won't be—"

"Yes, I will!" She looked up at him, her shoulders pulled back. "Maybe we can study them, like your king intends to do. We can try learning to make the elixir from Ipta—"

"My father's reason for doing this has nothing to do with the elixir! And even if we had this medicine, it is too late for the Ruelderians. It only works to protect those who have not been infected." His eyes turned cold.

"Why are your people really here, Movo? Tell me the truth and I'll think about what you asked me to do." She pierced him with her gaze and pretended it was a sword to penetrate the truth out of him. She had to speak his language.

He glared back with such coldness she regretted ever having looked his way. There was nothing there, no soul, no warmth, just pure hatred. She looked away, hugged the sides of her arms and took a step back.

He spun on his heel and walked over to the stream, his back to her.

Her belly expanded in relief. She hadn't realized she had stopped breathing. Yes, Movo had helped them up until this point, and although she knew he had participated in the attack on Alonia, she hadn't feared him. Now she didn't know what to think. There was something outright frightening about him.

"All of my men and everyone in my kingdom is protected from crowpox, like you know," Movo said. "We were all given a medicine that was provided by Ipta years ago, and in exchange my father gave the Iptans permission to build headquarters in Damalathum. Ipta gave us enough medicine to last for many more generations to come."

Enri tucked a loose strand of hair behind her ear, trying to appear unafraid.

Movo picked up a rock and chucked it into the river. "My father is a sick man. He shouldn't be a king. He's nothing like your King Cloudian was—at least, from what I have heard. For years my father has been seeking some magic that might make him more powerful than the Iptan Emperor."

A chill passed over Enri's skin. "What magic? Like the Alonians speak of?"

Movo shook his head gravely. "My father is convinced that a sorcerer visited him and promised to give him power if he brought him people from the southern lands across the sea who were unaffected by crowpox. My father believes that the warlock's power will help him invade Ipta successfully."

That she had absolutely not expected. "What does this sorcerer want the people for?"

"Enri, think about what I just said to you. That's the problem with you and Herlot. You believe these things and don't see what harm they do. There is no sorcerer. No one aside from my father saw him. He could have been a sick man who had found his way into the palace, for all I know. The problem is that my father is powerful and desperate. I don't need to explain to you what happens when those two qualities mix with the lust for magic. What happened at Alonia, Lorfin, Temes, and Ruelder is evidence enough." Movo's eyes glowed. "He is willing to kill anyone and everyone because the idea of magic has pushed him into madness."

Enri could not imagine what it would be like to have an outright evil father. She understood now why Movo had been so harsh on Herlot and her magical sword. His story of magic was one of outright evil.

"I lied because a real man would have burned his father's ships at the onset before following the orders of a lunatic. I couldn't let you know the truth, especially after Oliver treated me without question."

He was ashamed. His anger came from that shame. Without thinking, Enri put her hand on Movo's shoulder, but he brushed it away. He squeezed the flower in his other fist and dropped it into the river. "I'll come back tomorrow night. I hope you change your mind."

Enri watched Movo leap into the water, landing on a rock, and continue on until he disappeared into the night mist of the waterfall.

She climbed the path back into the cave and knelt by Herlot. She squeezed a wet cloth above Herlot's dry lips.

She wondered what the people of Damalathum were like. How did they spend their time? Were they very different from her? Would they find her life boring and meaningless? She loved life as a Lorfiner—seeing the sunflower heads open in the morning, sharing seeds with the birds, and watching the numerous competitions of who could weave between a row of stalks the fastest. But maybe they were all missing something. King Felix obviously saw them as people who could be used to his disposal, as if they had nothing to offer, no value.

She changed Herlot's bandage while listening to the psaltery.

She thought about Herlot's hysteria the other night. Ilvy and Ernest's deaths had broken Herlot. Crowpox had broken Herlot. Movo was right in wanting to prevent the trauma, but could she make a fairy slumber mixture and give it to that many people? She had seen it used on one person in her entire life. Mahtreeh didn't remember because he had been asleep, but she had been awake when her father prepared and served her mother the fairy slumber.

"Please, Oliver," her mother had begged. "You know it's over."

Her father had held her head while pouring the fairy slumber into her mouth and then told her about when they had met for the first time, when he had mended her sprained ankle during a visit to Alonia. Her mother had died with a smile on her face, but Enri had never stopped wondering if she would have lived had she not drunk it.

"Will she live?" Devotio's voice wrapped around Enri's ears. She turned to see him and Mahtreeh approaching.

"Her heartbeat is so weak. What if she doesn't make it?" Mahtreeh whispered.

"She will. She has to," Enri said.

"And if she doesn't?" he whispered. "Who will blend the leaf?"

Enri thought about King Felix and the suffering her people were experiencing at the hands of a delusional man. "It might be for Devotio's family's own good to never lay a hoof in this world again."

• • •

Seum despised every ridiculous part of the psaltery and every ugly sound it produced.

"Thank the Emperors," he mumbled when Hans finally stopped.

"One more, please," Arlette said.

He groaned into his travel sack. Never in his life had he experienced such irritation. The psaltery songs were worse than Mahtreeh's birdcalls. Those were the second most irritating sounds he had ever heard. He tossed and turned. He pressed his palms against his ears, which worked until he began to drift, but then his damn hands would slip and the melody would poke at his eardrum once again.

Enough was enough. He lit a candle in the fire and then headed down the tunnel into the cave's labyrinth. The melody followed him, bouncing back and forth off the cave walls like the candlelight. He walked what seemed like a journey through the desert when the light extinguished at the exact moment when he could no longer hear the music anymore. Perfect. This was where he would finally get his beauty sleep.

When he awoke, he found himself in a chamber he and his father had not explored when they first arrived in Eraska. Faint light from the cracks in one of the sides of the walls streamed in.

"Thank the Emperors indeed..." he said as he stared at the paintings on the walls. The moment he saw Herlot, a peasant girl fighting with the skill of a warrior, he knew there was reason to stay longer in this land. But this, oh, *this* he had not expected. He took a seat and rested his elbows on his knees. Then he laughed.

"Ah, now that is really something," he said as he studied the paintings, all of winged creatures with horns coming out of their foreheads—creatures like the Iptan watchers of the dark star in the sky had seen, except white, not black. It could not be a coincidence that he had found Herlot with a magical sword in the same land where these paintings existed. True, it was not a clear solution that the emperor had ordered Seum and his father to seek, it definitely was not a weapon, yet it was a sign that he and his father were in the right place to prepare for the war the dark star watchers predicted. He would continue his strategy of patience, the last thing he wanted to do was scare Herlot away before learning her secrets. But as soon as he would get the chance, and if she woke up, he would bring her here. He needed to see how she would react. *Wake up, Herlot*, he thought. *There is a war in the skies I must prepare for, and I need to know if you're to play a role in it.*

● ● ●

"Oh, come on, whatever your horse name may be!" Enri tugged on the horse's reins, but he whipped his head back and shook it from side to side. Apparently, the last thing the horses wanted to do was to go back in the cave after their short grazing session. "Listen. I'd rather stay out here, too. But the only way I'll ever get to spend more time out here is if I hide in there, if that makes any sense. Once this is over, no more caves ever again, I promise."

"Enri! Get that horse up the path! What are you waiting for?" Asm shouted.

Enri looked down the ledge and at the line she was holding up. "Here, you go ahead of me," she said to the boy behind her.

It turned out that she wasn't the only one with the problem—the horses were becoming more and more agitated as they bumped into one another. One even stepped on a villager's foot. Of course, Seum was voicing his complaints from his look-out position at the end of the line, which only made the villagers more tense.

All of a sudden, Devotio gracefully weaved his way between them, his white coat sharply contrasting their browns, blacks, and greys, his posture relaxed as he climbed the path, seemingly not giving anyone his attention. Soon the other horses, without the need of anyone's frustrated tug on their reins, obediently followed.

"Devotio, thank you, but maybe you're bringing too much attention to yourself," Enri muttered under her breath. She wasn't worried about the Eraskans who always had a comment of awe about him, but she was worried about Seum and Asm's speculative looks. Unlike the Eraskans, they had spent much time around horses, and she was sure they knew there was something different, if not special, about him. If only she knew what they were whispering about.

Training began the moment they were inside. Asm and Seum chose a large room that branched off the main tunnel, with light that punctured through the crevices.

Now that the immediate danger was over, they had more time to familiarize themselves with the weapons. Enri had never thought swords could be so complex, but then again, she had never thought about them much in the first place. From the handle designed to protect her hand, to the crevice that ran down the middle of the blade to make it lighter, she couldn't help thinking of Damalathum's people as intriguing. She would have liked to meet one of their sword makers, to have a conversation with a mind who had thought of so many solutions to perfect a tool. If their weapons were this advanced, what were their homes like? And their crop fields? And, was there anything the people of Damalathum would have found worthy to learn from her? She doubted it.

Once they were a good ways into practicing, Enri began wishing for Asm to show some sign of parental discipline on Seum, who'd had it out for Hans since the beginning of the lesson. Seum seemed to have an awful habit of picking on the weakest. First it had been Mahtreeh's whistling, but he had softened to him after the ordeal at Temes. Now all his cruel attention was aimed at Hans.

She, like the rest of the students she observed, could barely focus on their maneuvers while having to feel the embarrassment Hans was surely experiencing. She wished she had never asked Seum to help with the training. "This! Is not an instrument. Don't worry about breaking it!" Seum belted.

Hans' sword clanked against the cave floor. He shook his hand as if attempting to shake off the pain. Seum did not even try to hide his laughter.

"Why don't you kick him while you're at it, since you obviously can't teach him!" Enri shouted.

Seum raised an eyebrow at her, then kicked Hans in the calf, sending him hopping on one foot.

She could not watch or listen to Seum's bullying anymore. She knew it was a childish move, but she stomped over to Asm to complain.

"If he could just be a little nicer… That's all I ask. Like a pat on the back or a, 'Good work, soldier.'" She puffed her chest and her cheeks, attempting to make her voice low.

Asm wiped the drops of water falling from the cave ceiling off his forehead. "Don't want to look like I'm sweating doing nothing in front of my students," he said. "Aggravating Seum will only make it worse. Seum won't change for anyone but himself. And it has to be his own idea. I'm his father. Trust me, I have tried, and I've had camels less stubborn than he."

Enri waved Hans over and massaged his beet-red knuckles. His cheeks were flushed with embarrassment.

"Hold it in a bucket of cold water for a bit before you continue," she said and turned back to Asm. "I understand. I do. But I remember clearly both of you saying how in Ipta he could train a warrior in a day. I can't imagine that that's how he did it. I know what you must think of me. I'm not a soldier, and the only thing close to a weapon anyone in my village has ever used is a pitchfork. But my father was a healer, and he said no matter how many recipes and salves you knew how to make, you could never heal anyone without caring for them. Well, I don't think you can teach anyone to fight without caring enough about them to hope that they will stay alive."

Asm seemed to fall into a moment of reflection. "Our world lost much the day your father died, not only because of his talents, but because of his heart and the good he's instilled in his children—"

Asm's focus whipped to a Temesian who had been cornered into a crevice in the wall by his opponent. He was attempting to suck his stomach in to back away from the tip of his opponent's sword. Enri followed after Asm as he intervened.

"No matter how hard you pray, that wall won't swallow you," Asm said. Then he pulled a glove from his belt and handed it to the Temesian against the wall.

He had him hold the blade with the gloved hand and the handle with the other to resemble a fighting staff, explaining that, this way, he could defend attacks closer to his body if he ever was cornered. The man thanked Asm and started to return the glove, but Asm told him to keep it. Enri wondered how it was possible for a father and son to be such complete opposites.

"I promise you, Enri, Seum cares," Asm said as he observed the students. "He wants all your people to live, I assure you. But he is Iptan, like I am. An Iptan trainer only trains those with a passion for fighting, not merely staying alive. We Iptans have everything with no threat of ever losing it. It makes us free. Free to die, even. We're not afraid. Your people hate the fight and are very afraid, so his only option is to toughen them up."

"That is our *only* option? To toughen up?"

"For a time, but not forever. No, definitely not forever, because then you'd be like us. You don't want to be like us. It's a lot like with these caves. If you were to stay here too long, everything would smell like filthy murk. You have to remember that there is fresh air outside. For us, it's too late. Sometimes, it doesn't matter where I go. Even in the most peaceful of places with fresh springs and lavender water, I only smell blood."

"And what about Seum?"

"Seum..." Asm looked down, nodding as if coming to terms with an unpleasant truth. "Like most Iptan warriors, blood smells like fresh air to him."

● ● ●

Most of Enri's patients were awake, slurping from a few shared bowls of warmed sheep's milk as Enri applied salves to their wounds. It was a pleasant surprise to find her patients in good spirits after she had been away at the lesson.

"Will I get to play with the kids from Ruelder soon?" a young girl asked. She was sitting with her mother's head in her lap, combing through her hair using her fingers.

"I don't know, darling. First, their families have to be well before they can play."

Enri handed the mother a pouch of dried lavender to sniff for easing her headache from the bump on her head. Then she stood and walked over to the mouth of the cave, looking at the waterfall rushing down. If there were only some way she could make the Ruelderians well again... Then she wouldn't have to make the difficult choice. If her father had been alive, he would have found a way.

She pondered the waterfall and reached out her hand until her fingertips touched the water. She pulled it back right away, afraid the weight and rush of the water would take her down with it.

"Anything that meets your path has only one destination—the rocks at the bottom," she mumbled.

"Powerful, isn't it?"

Enri jumped—but it was only old Benyamin, who had limped closer using the crutches Giffard, Hans's father, had given him. Enri tilted her head to the side and nodded. "That it is."

"I've seen the rapids above us. All it would take is one trip or stumble into the water and the current would take you down the waterfall. There is no stopping it. That is, unless someone found a way to reverse the current." He chuckled. "I suppose even our Asm isn't strong enough to do that."

"Hmm," Enri said. Benyamin's words reminded her of what Movo had said about crowpox.

Bidding goodbye, she walked down the path to examine the waterfall from below. In the daylight, it looked even taller than at night. The crest looked as if it poured from a fluffy cloud in the sky. At the bottom, the water plunged into the rocks that jutted out, whirling and throwing anything that fell. She pondered heaving the water back up the fall and beyond the rapids that crashed under the power of the current through the rocks above.

"Impossible," she whispered. Enri crossed the river and wandered aimlessly, trying to get a sense of where Movo had set up camp for the Ruelderians, when Devotio appeared.

"Ah! Devotio, you startled me," she said, clutching a hand to her heart. Second time she had been caught off guard that day. She realized that she was thinking so hard that she was not aware of her surroundings. She would have to be more careful. The last thing she wanted to do was walk into a group of soldiers when they began to search the area near the waterfall. At least the Ruelderians seemed hard enough to find. Movo must have hid them well.

"I wonder... Do you know where I can find Movo?" she asked.

Devotio nodded his head. "This way."

He led her through a part of the forest where patches of bluebells grew between the trees. "Do you think Herlot is feeling better?"

"It's hard to say if she is feeling anything at all. That's good, though, her mind needs the rest and the injury may be too painful. I am hoping that that is why it is taking her so long to wake up."

"Do you think she wants to wake up?"

Enri stopped. "Herlot would never want to leave you, Devotio. And if you're worried that it may be your fault that you put too much pressure on her by taking her to your family and having them ask her to blend the leaf, don't. There is nothing more she'd want to do than help you. I think we all need to remember who is really to blame for our suffering, and that's King Felix."

Devotio stayed silent. She hoped he would take her words to heart.

"I almost forgot!" Enri exclaimed as she picked a bluebell. She twirled the stem between her thumb and her pointer finger "It's so strange. It's only been about a week since we left Lorfin, but it feels like a lifetime ago. I've forgotten to put flowers in my hair. I can't imagine what it must be like for you. You left a whole different world. I bet you miss your family terribly, Devotio."

Enri wrapped the stem around her hair so the string of flowers hung on the outside.

"Not as much as I miss Herlot. I missed her for ten long years and now she's gone again."

"She will wake up. Maybe even today." Enri did not know whom she was trying to convince more—herself or Devotio.

The bluebells grew denser as they walked farther. Soon she saw clothes and hides hung over tree branches to form tents. She also noticed something different about the air. It didn't have a particular smell, but something was inhibiting the aroma of the bluebells. Then, she heard the coughs emanating from the camp.

She observed Movo making rounds between the tents. When he spotted her, he dropped the bowl of water he was holding and ran at great speed. "Get out of here right now! What do you think you are doing?" he roared.

"I want to see," Enri answered with determination, "and I'm not leaving. I'll be fine if I don't touch anything."

"The ones coughing will send it your way—"

"Then I'll hold my breath," Enri said, shoving past Movo. She ripped a strip of cloth from the bottom of her dress and wrapped it around her nose and her mouth. "You can't expect me to kill people I haven't even had the chance to see."

"You can't return to the cave until I know you're not sick," Movo warned.

"Fine." As they neared the camp, Enri noticed Vincent was nowhere to be seen. "Where is Vincent?" she asked.

"I sent him to scope out the mountains for any sign of the people Hans spoke about. He used to be one of Damalathum's garrison guards and is trained to detect anything out of the ordinary."

"So you believed what Hans told us?

"I don't know. That's why I sent Vincent."

Movo slowly pulled back the cover of a tent. Enri resisted the urge to tear her eyes away to avoid the scene before her. In front of her, a family lay surrounded by blood-soaked cloths. Their bodies were oddly colored all over. One woman groaned in pain before a coughing fit shook her body.

Seeing her distress, Movo let the cover drop. "The colors you see are blood spills where the crowpox has managed to rip through. It happens everywhere—their organs, legs, arms, faces..." He lifted the cover of another tent.

Enri teared up. A mother with a child in her lap held a red cloth to her mouth. The child's face had no normal skin color left, and she was not breathing.

"Her daughter died this morning. She refuses to let go of her," Movo explained. "You can still help. These are the worst cases, where it progressed quicker than normal."

Enri staggered back. She could not look any more. Her stomach churned in all directions, her breakfast moving up toward her throat. "This is your mess, not mine."

"True. But that doesn't change the fact that you can help."

● ● ●

Back at the river, under the moonlight, the crashing of the waterfall made it difficult for Enri to focus on thinking of every combination of medicinal plants possible to stop the crowpox. After leaving Movo, Enri had marched deep into the forest where she spent the day searching for every known healing herb, flower, and mushroom she could find. *At the end of all of this, when we all go back to our normal lives, the Ruelderians will return home and make wool while their sheep bathe in the sun.*

The waterfall seemed to get louder, as if laughing at her. "That's enough!" She sprinted toward the bully until it came into view, water foaming around the base.

"You think this is funny?!"

Enri kicked her sandals off and stepped into the water until it reached her knees. Then she pushed off the edge and dove under. Her ears rang as she swam toward the waterfall. It took complete control of her, swirling her around in all directions until she didn't know where the surface was.

Movo is wrong. There has to be a way to stop the crowpox, she thought to herself, thinking of crowpox's power and how it could not be reversed, just like Benyamin had described the current of the water being too strong to stop anything from going over the waterfall.

Enri stretched her hands out as she slammed against the bottom of the riverbed. Her fingers clasped a rock, the only thing she could hold on to for dear life as the current continued to throw her around.

Any thoughts of finding a way to stop the crowpox disappeared as her body convulsed for air. She kicked her feet and paddled her arms, but the water was so strong. Luckily, a current, as if it had been destined just for her survival, trailed her away from the waterfall and to the surface, where Devotio was waiting.

"I can't stop it," she called as she swam to the brink and climbed out.

Water dripped from her dress and hair as she extended her palm and showed him her souvenir.

"But I can remove the rocks." A sob shook through her. "I can make the fall less painful."

She waited a long time for Asm to leave the cave for his nightly patrol. Keeping her distance, she asked him to have Mahtreeh come outside.

"No, stay there!" she called when he appeared at the bottom of the path to the caves. "I just wanted to tell you not to worry. I need to spend a few days with Movo."

"Why?" Mahtreeh called.

"We need to make sure I'm not sick. But I'm well. I promise! Send Devotio if Herlot awakes, understood?"

Mahtreeh nodded.

"And make sure everyone gets their wounds cleaned at least once a day. Asm and Hans will help you!" She blew Mahtreeh a kiss.

Back at the camp, she found Movo resting against a tree. She slid her back down the trunk and sat next to him.

"I'll do it. I'll make the fairy slumber." She took his hand in hers.

Movo released a deep sigh and let his head fall against the tree. "Thank you." He squeezed her hand. "And they will thank you, too."

Herlot was surrounded by a dense mist that made it impossible to tell in which direction she was walking. She could have been walking in circles for all she knew. She also had no idea what she was walking on because she could not sense a surface beneath her feet. Mist. That was all that existed where she was. No sounds. No tastes. Not even a breeze. It felt like ages since she had experienced anything else and she was beginning to wonder if for the rest of her existence that was all she would ever be—a wanderer in the mist. The idea didn't frighten her. In fact, it comforted her more than anything. This place was peaceful and she could be at peace as long as she remained here.

All of a sudden, she covered her ears, irritated by the first sound she heard in what felt like forever. *Could it be? Did I hear something aside from my own voice?* She slid her hands away from her ears.

"Ding...ding...ding..." a beautiful, soft, feminine voice sang.

Mother? Mother? Is that you? Herlot quickened her pace toward the direction from which she had heard her mother's voice. The further she went, the less dense the mist was, and she was beginning to see colors other than gray.

Finally, the mist disappeared completely and Herlot found herself on Alonia's cliff.

"Ding...ding...ding..." her mother's voice sang.

Herlot looked ahead. Her mother stood at the edge of the cliff facing the fortress of Eraska, teeter-tottering her shoulders back and forth. Her long, wheat-colored hair whipped around her in the wind.

At first Herlot wanted to run into her mother's arms and tell her how much she missed her. But even more than that, she wanted to act like this was normal. That the past had not happened, that this wasn't just a dream, and that it wasn't the last time she would see her mother. She wanted it to be a normal day in Alonia where she could be certain to see her mother again in the evening for supper.

"What game are you playing?" Herlot asked, walking toward the edge of the cliff with a bounce in her step.

"I am the bells of Eraska."

Hearing her mother speak made Herlot realize that she was already forgetting what she sounded like. "But, Mother, there are no bells in Eraska."

"Hmm... But there can be. I'll show you." Her mother wrapped her arms around Herlot, and they looked toward the fortress, cheeks pressed together. Herlot was taller and more muscular than her mother, but her mother's warmth made her feel safer than anywhere else. "Now, close your eyes. Ding...ding...ding..." her mother hummed. "See?"

Herlot watched, enchanted by the heavy, golden bells swinging and ringing, pushed back and forth by the wind.

"It's time to wake up," her mother whispered.

• • •

"She's waking up." Mahtreeh squeezed Devotio's mane out of joy.

It was late evening, and he had been cleaning wounds while the others trained, when Devotio had told him to come by Herlot.

He watched Herlot's breaths grow deeper as he held her wrist, feeling her pulse grow stronger. He was sure he saw the corners of her lips stretch the tiniest bit into a gentle smile as a sweaty group of villagers made their way back into the main chamber. They were in good spirits, giving one another compliments and discussing the techniques they had learned during their evening training session.

Mahtreeh waved Hans, Asm, and Seum over as he bounced up and down in his kneeling position. He couldn't wait to see their reactions.

"She smiles," Seum observed.

"Yes! Yes. I see it, too," Mahtreeh said, rubbing his hands together.

To his surprise, Seum frowned. "When she awakes, it will be in more ways than one."

"I don't understand. How many ways can a person wake up?" Hans asked.

Mahtreeh was wondering the same thing, but Seum didn't answer. Instead, he leaned forward as if he wanted to be the first thing Herlot saw when she opened her eyes, but Asm nudged him out of the way.

"The last thing she needs is to wake up thinking she went down under and not above," he cracked. Mahtreeh couldn't agree more.

And then, finally, Herlot spoke in a hoarse voice. "If I open my eyes, I won't see my arm, will I?"

Mahtreeh remained silent, trying to think of something motivational to say. No one around him seemed to have a reply for her.

Finally, Devotio spoke up. "What *will* you see?"

"Your friends," Mahtreeh whispered.

"What was that, son?" Asm asked.

Right then, Herlot smiled wider, her dimples appearing.

● ● ●

As Herlot's eyes fluttered open, she saw her friends kneeling over her. Mahtreeh was already holding a bowl of warm water to her lips while Hans held her head up. Herlot took several sips before clearing her throat.

"Thank you," she said, her voice closer to its usual state. "I'd like to stand up."

Asm carefully and swiftly stood her up like a puppet, supporting her around the waist while she tested her balance.

"Thank you, Asm. I think I can stand by myself," she said.

When he let go, she leaned slightly to the left but didn't topple. She inhaled, exhaled, and then looked down to her right, bandaged shoulder. "Strange... It's like I know where my fingers, palm, and elbow should be, but then they just...aren't there," she said. She caressed her fingers through the empty space below her right shoulder.

"I've met many soldiers who have lost parts of their bodies. It will take some getting used to, but you will," Asm said.

"What happened at Ruelder?" Herlot asked. She continued to look at her invisible arm as though enchanted by it.

"We won," Mahtreeh said. "Movo is certain that they will be back, searching for us, ready to fight. Vincent, Enri, and he are on the other side of the river, taking care of the Ruelderians. Many of them were exposed. Movo and Vincent are working on keeping the people who haven't shown any signs of pox yet separate from those who are already sick. Lucinda set out to Noray and Bundene. And the rest of us, well, we are hiding. And training."

"I suggest you start training with us as soon as possible," Seum said. "Even with the newcomers from Noray and Bundene, we will need every fighter we can when Felix's men return."

"I put Mahtreeh in danger last time. I won't fight." She would never forgive herself for what she had done. The magic she had within her, the magic that was supposed to save Devotio's family was also the magic that had the power to put herself and those around her in danger. Eraska was better off without her.

Before anyone could respond, Herlot attempted to walk away, but each step was difficult. Her body was weak from blood loss, and the truth was that her shoulder hurt. Lying down had felt like her shoulder was being held too close to a raging fire. Standing upright and moving felt as if bees kept stinging her over and over again—and then again in the places they had already stung.

She pressed her back against the wall and winced as she bent her knees to slide down.

"Give it time," Asm said.

Her throat was dry and she played around with holding the bowl without spilling the water, becoming irritated thinking about how much easier it would be if she had both of her hands.

She was ashamed for being upset. She was lucky to have her life. The villagers of Ruelder were suffering much more than she. Aside from the pain, she felt good and strong on the inside. Her vision had sharpened again, and she could hear distinct sounds.

She set the bowl down and leaned against Devotio.

"Let's let the girl rest," Asm said. "Mahtreeh, Seum, help me check on Enri's patients."

"Will you be fine for now?" Mahtreeh asked.

"Mhmm." If anything, she'd be better. It hurt to look at Mahtreeh. He could have been the one without an arm now, or worse, dead. She was lucky that this time her uncontrollable golden heart spark had only hurt herself.

Once Mahtreeh left, she leaned toward Devotio's ears. "Can you ever forgive me? I was awful to you after leaving Temes. I'm so sorry," she whispered.

"You will never have to ask for my forgiveness, Herlot," he said.

"As soon as I'm healed, we will go far, far away, and I will blend the leaf if it's the last thing I do," she said.

Devotio did not respond. "Why are you not saying anything?" she asked. She had expected him to be happy.

"I need to think," he said.

● ● ●

The next morning, Movo and Enri sat at the river's edge under the gray sky, crushing ingredients next to a tall pile of plants and herbs they had worked hard to gather since sunrise. Earlier, Devotio had told Enri the news of Herlot awakening in the night. She was a jumble of emotions. Between each tear for the Ruelderians was a smile for Herlot.

"He's a very smart horse," Movo said as he cut the riadonna into small bits with his dagger.

For the tenth time, Devotio had brought over the plant Movo had been looking for, even though Enri kept muttering under her breath for him to stop as she sniffled.

"Yes, he is," Enri said. She scolded herself for the slight chirp in her response. They had an awful task ahead of them, but she couldn't help feeling happy about Herlot being awake. There were good things that could happen even during the darkest of times.

"Are you well? If you tell me what to do I can finish preparing the rest of the plants while you rest."

"No, I'm not tired. I'm just so relieved that Herlot woke up in the night. I did everything I thought my father would have, but she was taking so long to wake up. I really thought she might not make it. Well, but that doesn't matter now. What's most important is that she's awake."

Movo stopped his cutting. "I told you not to go back to that cave," he said.

Oh no. There was no chance Movo would not catch her slip. How could she have let her guard down? She was always extra aware of anything she said in front of Movo, about Herlot or Devotio, or in front of anyone else aside from Mahtreeh, for that matter. Yet the way he had asked the question had seemed so natural, as if she were talking with a close friend.

"I didn't! This morning, Devotio told—I mean, yesterday Mahtreeh and I called back and forth to each other."

Movo frowned. "I thought you said she woke up in the night. You were with me all night."

"She did! Oh... Well, you see—alright. I did go back. I'm sorry. I did it while you thought I was in another part of the woods picking herbs. But I didn't get close to anyone."

"Another lie." Movo shook his head, clearly annoyed. "Enri, unicorns aren't real."

Enri's jaw dropped open. What did he know?

"I told you the truth about my father. How about you tell me the truth about what you and your friends believe about the horse. You think he can talk, right? You think that he's the one that told you about Herlot waking up, right? I overheard you that night when you and your brother talked with Herlot behind the bushes. You think he is a unicorn. You know, for now, believing that a unicorn told you that she awoke might make you feel better, but you are setting yourself up for disappointment if she hasn't. I hope coincidence is on your side," Movo said.

"If you really think you know so much about what is real and what is not, how do you explain Herlot knowing that the soldiers did not allow you to take the horses to the water?" Enri knew she was approaching dangerous territory of Devotio's secret, but she could not stand Movo thinking he had the right to tell her what to believe or not. He would not take away from her the magical night of when Devotio took Mahtreeh and her to their mother's pine tree.

"That's easy. It was the explanation that she wanted. She didn't want me to be a traitor," he said. "How can you be so blind? Thinking that anything magical in this world could be real only causes damage. It's not real. All of it can be explained by reason. My father stationed a troop at a field for *years*. All around the field is a giant circle filled with rocks, skulls, and boots to warn people not to step past a certain point. Anyone who walked into the circle died. My father believed someone powerful was hiding inside a mound in the center of the field, someone who was responsible for killing the people from afar. What would be your reasoning?"

"I would say that there was magic there, a bad form of it," Enri said.

"That's a great guess until someone actually tries to explain it with reason. You know what I found in the library of my kingdom? I studied numerous diaries of travelers and explorers. This field is not as uncommon as my father wished it was. There are some caves that even trick people to believe that they are breathing fresh air, and everything is fine until they collapse. Many things in the world look safe, yet their real behavior is far from friendly. You must know this very well. Think about all the poisonous plants, mushrooms. Animals, birds, bugs. There is an endless list of things. How could anyone reason that a piece of land that behaves in an awkward manner can only do so because someone is controlling it with magical powers? Among all the poisonous things in the world, why can't a field have the potential to be so, as well?"

"I'm sure it can." Enri twisted her pestle into her mortar with extra strength. "But some things don't need explanations. Some things are about a feeling, something you sense in your heart. What we *believe* is the truth, too. Think about how much wonder in this world you might be missing out on because you don't have the ability to believe something just because you're not used to it. That's the difference between you and me. I believed you both times when you told us why your father sent soldiers into Eraska, even though the first time was a lie. You're right. I might be naïve and believe too much. But you, you don't believe me even before I've said or explained anything. You can't even give something wonderful and unexplainable a chance to be true."

"You're right."

• • •

That afternoon, from the fringe of the camp, Enri watched Movo go inside each of the tents. A few had declined the fairy slumber, but most took it gratefully. After they finished drinking, he ducked out so they could go in peace with the comfort of their loved ones at their sides. When he left the last tent, he broke out into a jog when he saw the villagers from the cave crowded around Enri.

"What are they doing here?"

"We want to be here with them," Hans explained. "Seum and Asm checked the area before we left. It's safe."

Hans and Mahtreeh climbed a tree with a long branch that reached out toward the site. Hans pulled his psaltery out from the sack that hung over his back, and Mahtreeh wetted his lips. Together, they played and whistled a melody while the villagers hummed along. They did not know any mutual songs but strummed, whistled, and hummed their goodbyes from the heart.

Enri closed her eyes and imagined the journey that the fairy slumber was currently taking the Ruelderians on. The Ruelder families drifted along the tides of the song as they held on to one another. The pain in their bodies dissipated, and their hearts felt warm. They sank into a dream of hummingbirds, morning dew, and fresh, long grasses as they waved goodbye to their physical world. They were at peace. She could be, too.

CHAPTER 19
An Iptan Warrior

"WHERE IS EVERYONE?" Herlot yawned, her body already calling for another round of sleep. It was all she wanted to do since she had awoken.

Benyamin was strolling through the main chamber as if he were in an enchanted forest. He never seemed to bore from looking at the cave's formations. His mouth would drop open and then he'd limp to study a new spot.

"They went to say goodbye to the Ruelderians," Benyamin said, taking a seat next to Herlot. Stretching out his leg, he tapped her right side with his crutch. "It's not so bad," he sang. "You only need one hand to perform magic. Or none at all if you're good with your feet."

Herlot's eyes widened, and she struggled to sit up, using quick jolts to drag her arm closer until she was upright. What had he meant by performing magic?

Benyamin smiled at her, blinking his beady eyes. She searched them for deeper meaning, wondering if he was wise or just a little mad. It was hard to tell. Yet, she was the last one to judge anyone's mental state.

"Maybe that'd be the case if I could perform magic to begin with," she said at last. "But I can't. I am nothing. And it's even beginning to show." She pointed at her side.

Benyamin swooshed his hand through the empty space along her shoulder. "Nothing has no limitations. Nothing is everything. Out of nothing came the stars. Out of nothing came the planets. Out of nothing came the moon. And out of nothing came the sun."

She watched intently as he spoke while swirling his hands. Then he closed his hand into a fist.

"Now, you can be a star, planet, moon, or the sun—which one do you want to be?"

Herlot bit down on her lips, deciding to humor him. "A moon."

Benyamin stretched his fingers from his fist, exposing a wooden pendant shaped like a crescent moon in his palm. "It will look nice with the leaf on your necklace," he said, handing it to her.

Herlot gasped. It was like he had conjured the pendant out of thin air. She struggled to untie the knot of her necklace with one hand. Benyamin helped her and slid the crescent moon down the string before retying it and lowering it around her neck.

"Now, dear Herlot, you are a moon," he said.

"How did you know?"

Benyamin chuckled. "Next time you howl at the moon, don't forget to howl at yourself, too."

• • •

Over the next few days, Herlot did nothing but sleep, eat, drink, and walk around. She listened to the clashes of swords in the training chamber, but never walked close enough to be seen. She took pleasure in watching Devotio entertain the children. There were numerous places to explore in the caves and to play out imaginary stories. Parents even trusted them to go off alone as long as Devotio was with them. The adults, on the other hand, would leave the training chamber complaining about being stuck inside the cave. They fought over who would get to go outside to let the animals graze and gather firewood. Over dinner, they talked about their villages and how they could not wait to go back.

Enri eventually returned, having not shown any signs of the slightest cough, fever, or a sore muscle. She informed everyone that

Movo was still waiting with a few Ruelderians who had not taken the fairy slumber. Only four had shown no signs of crowpox thus far. It was a humbling realization for those who had been complaining about being stuck in the cave. They were lucky to be safe from the illness and soldiers.

The first thing Enri did was wrap Herlot in a hug.

"I have some interesting news," she whispered as they sat down in a corner away from the others.

Enri unwrapped Herlot's bandage, examining the shoulder and applying more salve. "It looks well but you have dark circles under your eyes. Are you sleeping well, or does it hurt too much?"

"I'm sleeping too much." She didn't know how to answer the question about the pain. Nothing in her life had hurt her body more than the moments after the soldier slashed her. She did not know how to classify the constant ache that pulsed in her shoulder since she had awoken. It hurt, but she didn't feel right trying to stop it.

"I think it hurts a lot more than I think it does," she said. "If it had happened before Ambro's wedding, I probably would not be able to stand it. Now it's almost welcome compared to...everything else. Enri, I'm sorry I put Mahtreeh in danger."

"I'm sorry I was not a better friend to you after what happened at Temes. I want you to know that I want to help in any way I can. You might be the only one whose heart has a golden spark, but you don't have to learn to work magic alone."

Herlot shook her head. "Absolutely not. Enough bad things have happened each time it has happened randomly, I won't allow people near me when I am purposefully trying to do it. As soon as I am better, Devotio and I are leaving."

Enri's jaw dropped. Then she pursed her lips and frowned. "How can you say that? Herlot, I know what you're going through is hard. None of us can imagine what it's like to carry a responsibility such as the one Emrys has asked of you, but running away is not the answer. We are family now. You, me, Mahtreeh, and Devotio. Going off and being alone after everything that Felix has taken from us—your parents, my father—is never going to be the answer."

Herlot didn't know what to say. She wanted this family more than anything, but how could she be a part of it if she knew she could hurt them?

"And you *do* have magic. If you just believe in yourself, who knows what else you can do? If anything, we're going to need you now more than ever when the soldiers start searching for us. And there's something else you should know. Movo lied to us about why his father sent the soldiers."

Herlot rested her elbow on her bent knee and leaned in. This she needed to hear.

"King Felix isn't looking to make his own crowpox elixir—he's looking for a way to invade Ipta. But I've been thinking about the golden elixir, the one the Iptan Emperor gave to Damalathum. I just can't help thinking it has something to do with golden-heart magic. What if there are other golden-hearted people out there and they're the ones blending these medicines that can protect people from crowpox?"

"If that's true, they could blend the leaf!"

Several heads turned in their direction.

Herlot hushed. "I never thought there might be some who still exist. I'm sure Emrys and the unicorns didn't think of that option either. Do you think Seum and Asm know?"

Enri shrugged. "They have secrets, more than Movo does, and it seems they want to keep it that way." She finished wrapping the bandage. "That's what I believe, at least."

"How does making us sick help Felix invade Ipta? And why didn't Movo just say the truth?"

"It's...complicated. I think it'd be best if you asked Movo about it yourself. I just want you to know that he was not trying to manipulate us, it's more to do with his relationship with his father, at least, I think. It will help you understand why he was so harsh on you. But what this all really comes down to, and you'll understand when you speak to Movo, is that King Felix may be more dangerous than we thought. He won't act reasonably. He won't leave us alone, no matter what cost. We will need fighters. Every single capable Eraskan who can fight, we will need them."

Herlot did not know what to say.

"Anyway, if you want, you can join the others in training, but take lots of breaks, and if it gets to be too much, stop for the day. And I swear to the skies, Herlot of Alonia, I will not let you run away. You just need to believe in yourself a little more, and if it helps, I want you to know that Mahtreeh and I believe in you."

Herlot took a deep breath. Oh, how it felt good to be wanted. Maybe Enri was right. Maybe if she believed in herself, she could train *and* learn to blend the leaf. There was one thing she remembered clearly about blending—her chest had felt very warm before it happened. If her chest ever got warm again, she could warn Enri and Mahtreeh so that they could be prepared to stop her from doing something dangerous.

However, the thought of being around swords again was torture.

"I don't think I can train. All I see is the soldier racing at me," Herlot said. She bowed her head.

"Tell me what happened at Ruelder. It was like you were there one moment and then it was as if something took over you. No matter what Mahtreeh, Hans, and I yelled, you wouldn't stop running. It was like you couldn't even hear us."

Herlot swallowed at how much the description reminded her of her mother. She gathered herself and looked down at her chest, then pulled out the leaf from under her dress. "That's because I *didn't* hear you. I was somewhere else. Enri, I blended."

Enri's eyes widened.

Herlot nodded. "At least this time I remember more. I don't understand what causes it to happen and most of the memory is blurry. My chest got very warm, that I know for sure. And my feet were drawn to a footprint. That's the sign that it's about to happen, I think, and if it ever does again, you need to be ready to restrain me when I tell you."

"Good. This is more than we knew of before. Then what happened?"

"The rest is somewhat blurred—I sensed a footprint in the ground, then I saw a unicorn with an alicorn. I chased after the unicorn. Next thing I knew, I was on the field in Ruelder, back in the present moment."

"And then? They say you dropped your sword and practically ran at the mounted soldier. It happened again, didn't it?"

"Yes." Herlot's lips quivered as she continued. "In a flash, I was back in the past, but it felt so real, like it was really happening. I saw other humans capture the unicorn. It was awful. And then, again, just like before, it stopped, and, and..." She dropped her head into her palm as a sob escaped her. "Because of me, Mahtreeh could have died."

"You can't think like that, Herlot. Mahtreeh is alive and you're alive, that's all that matters. And, think of all the people who are alive *because* of you. They look up to you, even after everything that has happened—you're the best fighter. A lot of them are struggling, and it's mainly because they're intimidated. If they could see an Eraskan fight the way you do, they'd gain more confidence," Enri said. "I know you have been through a lot. But I remember their faces when they watched you with your sword."

"But my arm—"

"You still have your left. I'm not saying it won't be hard at first, even with the sword's magic. But imagine if they see you try even after everything that has happened. Herlot, you have to do this. All of us do. No matter what trauma and loss is in our past, we have to put it aside."

Herlot swallowed. "I have to think about it," she said.

• • •

That evening, Hans played his psaltery after dinner, as he did every night. Herlot was staring at the ground, listening, when her scenery was invaded by a set of black leather boots.

"Come on, I want to show you something I think you'll like. And, if not, at least it will get you away from this annoying noise," Seum said. He reached his hand out in invitation toward Herlot's empty right side. "Oops," he teased, and then he extended it to her left.

She grabbed Seum's hand, and he used his strength to stand her up. He did not let go of her hand as he guided her into the tunnels.

The candle Seum held in his other hand illuminated the ancient cave. The deeper in they headed, the more the psaltery's music faded.

Soon all Herlot could hear was the sound of the flame, water trickling down the walls, and their footsteps. Eventually, Seum turned into a tunnel that opened into an enormous space.

Herlot gasped.

The walls were covered in paintings of all colors. Paintings of unicorns—so large one would need a ladder to reach the top of some of them. And they looked so real. The gold in their alicorns sparkled. And they had wings! She spun in circles, moving her head up and down, exclaiming sounds of delight.

Seum leaned against a wall, crossing his ankles and his arms. "Go on, have a closer look," he said.

She ran up to one of the paintings and stroked her hand over it. There was a man on top of one of the unicorns, and they were up above the clouds. Their faces smiled at a vivid, yellow sun. *Holy Basil. These had to have been painted by ancient, golden-hearted humans.*

The next painting was a group of small unicorns playing with human children. Something caught her attention near the bottom right of it. There was a perfectly square crevice in the wall as if someone had carved it out on purpose. It was about the size of a hand. She took a step to examine it, but froze when a buzzing sensation tickled her foot. A fire ignited inside her chest. *Oh no, please, no,* she thought. *It's happening again.* Enri was not here and she could not tell Seum. *Herlot, focus, you're going to have to try and control it on your own.* She felt warmth at the bottom of her foot, and then it dispersed through her legs, torso, arm, and then into her head.

My name is Brom. May I share my memory with you? A voice in her head said. She remembered him from the last time she had blended. He was the one who had chased after the unicorn. She had to try and remember his name after the blending stopped this time. He had to be the same man who had asked Emrys to create a hiding place in the leaf for the unicorns.

No, she said.

There's something very important I need to show you. Please, do reconsider.

She couldn't. Not after what happened before. But now that she remembered Brom, she wanted to know why it was him whom she kept seeing. What was so important that he had to share?

Make your decision soon, I cannot wait forever. These memories are fragile. Please, do consider.

What if she didn't get a second chance? Yes, she said.

Herlot stared down at her hands. She had two of them again. She had certainly blended with Brom's memory now. He was dying and desperate to communicate something important. He poured ink over his palm and pressed it against the wall. Suddenly, Herlot was overwhelmed with a collection of indistinguishable thoughts, and she imagined that this was what it felt like to be struck by lightning. She lost her balance, and in that moment the vision and the pressure faded, and she found herself in a squat, her palm pressing into the crevice. *At least this time it ended quickly and I didn't do something dangerous. Don't let Seum notice.*

"Are you well?" Seum asked.

"Yes. Fine," she answered. "I just had a small case of dizziness. Enri told me it might happen for a while," she lied.

She examined the crevice. She focused hard to remember what had happened a moment ago. Heat in her chest...then what. There was something about this crevice. An image of a handprint ran across her mind. She pressed her palm to the space between her eyebrows. *Think harder*, she urged, but it was no use.

She continued to make her way around the room, wondering if one of these times she would understand what exactly it was that caused her to blend. Was it the footprints? It couldn't be, for there was an infinite amount of footprints all over, and if that were really the case, well, she would be blending without end. Either way, understanding why it happened was still not enough to complete her task. In each scenario, even if she had been standing right next to a tree where she could blend the leaf, she had no control of her body while it was happening.

But at least she had hope. She was still able to blend after her injury, and there would be more opportunities for her to understand how to control it. She was wondering about when the next opportunity would come and hoping it'd be a safe experience, like the one she had just had, when she approached a painting that took all of her attention and brought tears to her eyes.

Several unicorns were running through a forest with children on their backs. They looked so happy, and the children reminded her of Ambro, Enri, Mahtreeh, and herself on that magical night that they had all shared with Devotio. The children felt so real she wanted to reach out and kiss one on the cheek—so she did, just to get an idea of what such a happy cheek felt like.

When she finished the circle, she skipped to Seum, hugging him. "Thank you, Seum. Thank you, thank you, thank you. How did you know this would mean so much to me?" she asked.

"I figured you might enjoy something nice to look at. I found this place while I was trying to find a place to sleep, and it made me think of you," he explained.

"Can we stay longer?"

"Of course."

They settled down, side by side in the center of the chamber, and looked up at the largest painting on the ceiling. It was of a group of people up in the sky on their unicorns, forming a circle. They had golden hearts that emitted a golden string, connecting them together.

"Seum, will you tell me about Ipta?"

He chuckled. "There are many things about Ipta I could tell you..."

"Are the people very...different there?"

"Yes. There are no peasants in Ipta. People spend their days eating fresh fruits from trees, bathing in lagoons, dressing in riches. It's a lazy paradise. The emperor cares for his people, too, much like your King Cloudian did. He is nothing like Felix. He is a busy man, of course, but he makes time to bless every man or woman who has died. They are carried into his palace, where he gives them a place in forever."

"A place in forever... What does that mean?"

"Ah, Eraskan. There are so many things you do not know. My emperor is the most powerful man in the world. Every emperor of Ipta always has been. Not only does he rule his empire, he gives life to those who have passed. We live on in his empire of forever after our time ends here."

An empire of forever. It reminded her of how Emrys had talked about the ancient humans who had lost their gold and how frustrated they had been because the gold they did manage to gather could not last forever. What kind of man could have the power of forever? A man who still had a golden heart, perhaps. It seemed more and more likely that the Emperor of Ipta could work golden-heart magic. "Have you ever met him?" she asked.

"No. He does not show himself often."

It would make sense that he wouldn't show himself often. She remembered the glow that emitted from Emrys's chest. One would have to wear a decent amount of clothing in order to hide it. From what she understood, Ipta was a very warm land.

"I'd like to meet him," Herlot said.

"I'll happily take you to Ipta one day."

"The way you describe it, Ipta sounds like such a wonderful place. Why would you and your father ever want to leave?"

Seum yawned. "I promise you, Eraskan, that is something you do not need to worry about. You know, they remind me of you and your people."

Herlot pointed at the golden-hearted people on the ceiling. "Them?"

"Yes. Them," Seum said. "There is a goodness in their eyes that feels light."

Seum's breath fell into a steady rhythm as he fell asleep, and the candlelight extinguished.

Before Herlot could worry about the dark, Devotio entered the room, lying down next to her, his coat shining like the birches in the night. It wasn't like the light from his alicorn, but it was enough.

"There might be golden-hearted people in Ipta, Devotio. If we go there, we might find one to blend the leaf," she whispered.

"Maybe. But not before your people are safe. My family was mistaken about them. They don't have golden hearts, but Seum is right. They're like the people in the paintings. And it will be to Eraskans that my family will return to one day. We hid not to hide forever. We hid in order to return again someday. Your people are hope that that someday may come sooner than later. Even if we do blend the leaf, without them, it does not matter," Devotio said.

"What exactly are you saying?"

"I really need you to do something for me, and it may not be easy," Devotio said.

Herlot stood up. "I will. Anything."

"Herlot, I want you to hide the leaf inside a space in the cave wall in this chamber."

"Well, that is simple and a good idea. We don't want it crushed. But what if I happen to start blending if I'm next to a tree?" she said as she slid the leaf into a crack in the wall.

"There's more to my wish. Herlot, I want you to completely forget about the leaf until Felix is no longer a threat to your land."

"What?" Her heart seemed to freeze. She couldn't believe what Devotio had said. "No, absolutely not. I promised you I would wait to try until we brought the Eraskans to safety. They now have a safe place to hide and train."

"If we don't protect your land, there will never be a safe place for my family to return to, even if you did blend the leaf. Your people are the beginning, I am certain, and it's more important that we protect them now."

"How can you be sure of this?"

"It feels right."

Herlot did not know what to say. "What is it exactly you want me to do then, Devotio?"

"Ask Seum to train you as an Iptan warrior and then we will fight, together, and give King Felix a fight like he has never seen before."

She had promised to keep Devotio safe, yet he wanted to fight alongside her? What would Emrys think of this idea?

"It is all I ask of you," Devotio said. "Please."

Herlot nodded, slowly. "Alright, alright." She exhaled. "Are you certain?"

"Yes."

Herlot sat deep in thought until the first light penetrated through the tiny holes in the ceiling.

She walked over to Seum and shook him awake. "Get up. We have a lot of work to do."

He stretched, groaning and rubbing his eyes. "Asm can run the patrol without me, and the others know what exercises to work on."

"Iptan tradition says we start at sunrise."

At this, Seum's eyes flew open.

"You said I was capable of an Iptan warrior training. Teach me."

● ● ●

Enri giggled with a toddler as she bounced Benyamin's seashell doll on the girl's stomach. She spun the string, causing the doll to twirl. "Where is her home?" the girl asked.

"Benyamin! Where is seashell doll from?" Enri asked.

"Why, everywhere, of course!" he called, standing up and making his way toward them. "The bottom of the sea and the Alonian beach, but one of the shells on her right arm was carried over by a sea lion from an area near Ussela! She traveled quite the journey to come together, had hundreds of different homes in people's palms and pockets. But how she came to be the way you see her today was first in my wife's imagination, so she is from the world of dreams. You see? Everywhere!"

Enri exchanged a confused look with the toddler. Most people thought Benyamin foolish, but there was a hint of an otherworldly wisdom in the things he said that made her feel like a child who still had much to learn.

Two Ruelderian men and two children entered the caves, followed by Movo. Enri's heartbeat sped up. That could only mean one thing—they were the only survivors. Her cave family rose to their feet at once and soon, they surrounded the Ruelderians, hugging, comforting, and welcoming them before she could utter a word.

As she waited in line, only a few were eager to see Movo, avoiding him after their greetings with the Ruelderians. From conversations she had overheard, it was evident that most were still wary of him because he had been one of the soldiers who'd help spread crowpox.

Enri noticed the exhaustion apparent on his features. He had given everything he could for the people of Ruelder, and he had done it mostly alone. She stepped out of her place in line and headed to the rations before approaching Movo.

"Thank you, Movo," she said. She handed him a cup of ale. "The others are grateful, too. It's just that—"

"Where is Herlot?" he asked.

"I don't know. The last few days she has been with Seum. They come back late at night after everyone is asleep and are gone before anyone wakes up. She seems to be doing well, though."

And she was, from what Enri had glimpsed of her. The dark circles under her eyes had disappeared and her cheeks were rosy.

Movo nodded. He sipped the ale, thanked Enri, and handed the cup back to her before leaving once more.

• • •

Herlot kicked at the sun-warmed gravel as her staff sailed into a tree next to the rapids.

The wooden staff Seum had constructed was more of a challenge than she'd expected. She could swing and sway it at her sides and above her head, but whenever she increased speed, she either let it go or was too late braking, causing it to ram into her side. She was covered in bruises.

They had made tremendous progress, but training was not as easy as Seum had said it would be, and took much longer than he had expected. The warriors he'd trained in the past hadn't been traumatized like her. She winced and pressed her chin into her shoulder whenever she lunged forward. She could kick, but she shook when hitting and elbowing, as if he would take her other arm right then and there. She had mastered the flip, but only backward to help an escape. Going forward was suicide. She kept seeing the horseman charging at her over and over again.

She was disenchanted at how hard it was to use a weapon that wasn't her sword, which Seum had prohibited her from using. He told her he didn't know if her sword was magical like the Eraskans believed, but she had to learn to use her own "magic." *I will never be the hero my people need me to be,* she thought. *There was never a hero in any Alonian story who was traumatized and disfigured at that.* But then she remembered the one-antlered elk she had seen fighting while she was hidden inside the hollowed-out oak as a child. She had never found out if he had won—but she knew for sure that he had tried.

Gathering herself, Herlot retrieved the staff and spoke softly but sternly to Seum. "I can do everything you have taught me, but I know I am missing something. It doesn't flow like it does when you do it."

Seum crossed his swords in front of him, the clear blue sky glinting off them. A spark shone through his eyes before he spoke. "Freedom—you have to fight with freedom."

Herlot angled her staff toward Seum. She closed her eyes, smelling the water and wind around her. What was freedom? She remembered the day by the stream—what felt like a lifetime ago now—when she had struggled to write a story for her never-completed Alonian rite of passage. The flock of birds that had taken off into the sky had felt free to her. They'd spread their wings and flown without anything stopping them.

"Attack," Seum said.

She swung the staff in looping patterns around her body, and this time, she did feel the speed increase. She attacked Seum's side, but Seum blocked it. Then she whipped the staff at his opposite side. Her heart leapt as she realized her staff had made contact with Seum's vest.

"Good!" he exclaimed.

They continued to duel, the speed of the strikes and blocks increasing in magnitude. It was exhilarating.

Herlot scooped the staff behind Seum's knees, knocking him off his feet. "Yes!" she shouted and jumped into the air, raising the staff. She had done it. She couldn't believe she had done it.

It took her a moment to notice that Seum wasn't cheering. He was untying his boots. He kicked them off and then unbuttoned his vest before throwing it onto his boots. He walked right past her, grabbing his scabbard harness and pulling it over his head. He sheathed both of his swords so they stuck out from behind his head.

Had she upset him?

"What are you doing? Am I ready for the sword now?" she called.

Seum didn't respond. He closed in on the edge of the path, after which the rapids raced. He stepped onto a protruding rock and leaped onto one farther in.

"You're insane!" Herlot called.

He continued to hop the rocks in the rapids until he had made it to the middle. She could see the rapids fall from the horizon behind him.

"Come on!" he called.

"Never."

"Come here and be free!"

"I can be free here just fine, thank you." Herlot turned to walk away.

"You're sure about that?"

"Yes."

"You're wrong!"

Herlot stopped in her tracks.

"What did you do back there? Think about birds?" Seum shouted.

She turned her entire body to face him, glaring.

Seum lifted his leg and balanced on one foot. "Thought so. See, that's a royal version of freedom. That's the freedom you pack and live with in a place like Felix's court. It's good for decoration, but it's not real."

Herlot approached the edge of the path as Seum jumped up and switched his footing on the rock.

"What do you say, Herlot? Are you going to stand there on the edge and watch my story of freedom, or are you going to come here and write your own?"

The water rushed faster, creating a mist around the area, making it hard to see. Seum jumped and, this time, landed on his hands with his legs in the air.

"Real freedom you can have when a slip could cost you your life. Or when a horseman strikes your arm off your body." He pushed off his hands and landed on his feet on another rock. He smiled and spoke as if he had taken a bite of a crisp apple. "With real freedom, you'll go over the waterfall and still soar. And, next time a soldier strikes, you'll flap your wings and tangle him in the strings of royal freedom he wraps himself in."

The mist thickened like a dense fog around him.

"In real freedom, you don't need to think of birds. In real freedom, you are the bird."

Herlot jumped into the fog, landing on a rock in front of Seum.

"What do you say, Herlot? Be a bird with me?"

Herlot struck her staff at his knees. Seum pulled his two swords as he leapt into the air.

That day, the rapids charged furiously over the rocks while two birds danced a fight of freedom toward the crest of the waterfall. They both landed, one leg each, on a rock protruding at the crest. Not even when the jagged rocks at the bottom of the waterfall sang a seductive song of danger, threat, and fear did their freedom cease to thrive as they relished the bird's-eye view of Eraska.

● ● ●

As Herlot made her way up the path to the waterfall, every muscle in her body aching, she could hear the voices of the villagers.

"I wonder what all the commotion is?" she said to Seum.

"Maybe Hans finally learned to hold a sword," Seum said.

"Listen, I think someone is playing the drums. And there's a flute!"

"Emperors help me."

"Why do you hate music so much?" Herlot asked. "Maybe we should try testing your skills by having you fight while Hans is playing one of his lullabies." She nudged him in the side.

"If that were to ever happen in battle, it'd be the end of me."

Once they made it to the top, Herlot's heartbeat quickened when she saw the scene in front of her. "Norway and Bundene are here!" she exclaimed and ran into the crowd. People were introducing and greeting one another left and right. Others were rolling barrels and carts of food and every person had a cup of ale. Even the chickens ran around clucking from all the excitement.

To her right, two men lifted Lucinda up onto their shoulders and began turning her in circles as the others clapped their hands.

"Enri! Mahtreeh!" Herlot exclaimed as she spotted her friends.

Mahtreeh stumbled toward her, pushing a mug into her hand. "Herlot, you have to try this. And there's more than enough barley and oats for everyone." Mahtreeh smiled at her with a lopsided grin. He poked her cheek. Then, he poked it again. "Your cheeks are rosy. Enri! Herlot is alive again!"

"How much ale have you drunk?" Herlot asked.

Enri snickered. "Too much."

"Is that a fire in your eyes?" Mahtreeh asked. "You find Seum and tell him I want one of these trainings. Maybe the women will like me more after."

They watched as a family from Bundene nearly crushed Benyamin with hugs before each one of them gave him a scolding. A girl who must have been Benyamin's granddaughter came up to Enri and kissed her hand. "Thank you for helping my grandfather." Herlot's throat tightened as she imagined what it would be like to reunite with Ambro. How she wished it weren't such a risk to return to the fortress and search for him. But even if she could, there was no way of knowing that he had not been sailed away on a ship already.

"Where's Movo?" Herlot asked, looking around. She thought he would have been easier to spot.

"He stopped in this morning and then left right away," Enri said. "He hasn't slept here in days. He asked about you the night when he returned with the Ruelderians. I thought he would have found and spoken to you by now."

Herlot frowned. What could he be up to? She had not seen him since she woke from her injury.

Then, as if on command, he entered the cave. Herlot wove her way through the crowd toward him. Movo didn't notice her even when she was only several feet away. She tried to follow after him. He stopped when he reached Asm and whispered something into his ear.

Asm stepped up on a wooden crate that broke right away under his weight. Several men helped him up, including Benyamin, although Asm was the last person to need help and Benyamin the last capable to give it.

Asm cupped his hands over his mouth. "Eraskans!" he called.

Ever so slowly, the crowd hushed.

"I hate to break up the celebration. I know we all want to celebrate the friends from Noray and Bundene who have safely joined us, but Movo spotted a group of scouts along the river. A group of forty men have set up camp in Ruelder, as well."

So that was it. They had finally returned from the fortress with reinforcements. Seum appeared at her side. "Are you ready?"

She nodded. "Yes," she said. It may have been the most confident yes of her life.

No one spoke as they listened to Asm's strategy. Their first attack would be on the scouts. They would cross the river and stay hidden behind the trees, scanning the other side for the scouts, and then attack when the soldiers were most vulnerable.

Once Asm finished speaking, Herlot was surprised that the atmosphere had not been completely crushed. The conversations started up again. Herlot pushed her way forward as she spotted Movo heading toward the waterfall. "Movo!" she shouted.

She thought she noticed him slow his pace, but then he rushed outside.

She picked up her pace once she reached the path. She turned in a circle looking in every direction, but he was nowhere in sight.

It was a beautiful evening—no clouds in the sky, and each star seemed to be glimmering to its fullest potential.

She heard hoof steps on the path behind her and turned to see Devotio.

She smiled wide at the sight of him. It may have been something about the beautiful evening, but all she wanted to do was to spend time doing something enjoyful with Devotio. She wanted to forget about everything, just for a little bit. It couldn't all just be hiding and fighting. She wanted to know that she could still feel pleasure, at least a little bit.

"Would you like to go for a swim?" she asked.

Devotio rose on his hind legs before he presented his side for her to climb on.

They trotted up a path that rose around the cliff and broke into a gallop along the rapids. They turned to follow a stream until they found a spot where the water was still, lined by sand on the brink.

Herlot stacked her leggings and what was left of her dress on the grass. She ran into the cold water, shouting for no reason but the fun of it, the freshness luring her in until it reached her neck. Devotio waded in, swimming and then dunking under before coming up with a splash.

Herlot cheered as the water sprinkled on her. She leaned back, floating and swishing her feet back and forth. "Ahh," she sighed. She hadn't felt this good in a long time.

A movement to her right caught her attention. She noticed a figure roaming in the shadows beyond the shore. What if it was a soldier? She frowned, realizing she felt no panic at the idea. As her eyes adjusted, she recognized the silhouette.

It was Movo.

This time, she was surprised to feel her heartbeat quicken. His head hung low, as if he hadn't even noticed them in the water. She waved her hand in the air.

"Movo!" she called.

He didn't startle, just lifted his head.

"Come here!" she called.

"You shouldn't be out here alone," he said. "You heard Seum, there's scouts in the area."

"I'm not. Devotio is with me. Besides, I'm not afraid of them anymore. Let them come."

He kneeled at the brink, and she swam toward him.

He cringed as she approached, looking in the direction of her shoulder. She didn't blame him. She knew it was not pretty.

"Come in. The water's great," she said as she reached his shore.

He raised his eyebrows. "No."

"Very well, then." She dove under and swam toward the muddy bottom. If she stayed under long enough, he'd probably get concerned enough to dive in after. Sure enough, he dove in and she kicked off toward the surface.

She waited for him to come up for a breath, hoping he wouldn't be angry at her trick. The moment he appeared, she met him with a splash aimed right at his face.

"Ha haaa!" Herlot laughed.

It could have been the fresh water, the splash, or a coincidence, but something in Movo's expression lightened. He answered her laughter with a splash twice the size of the one she had thrown in his direction. She squealed in delight, water dripping from her lashes.

They played for hours, all three of them splashing, chasing one another, and diving under. They didn't even notice the dark clouds approaching and intermittently covering the moonlight until they were floating on their backs while Devotio treaded water.

"A storm is coming," Herlot said at last, loathe to interrupt the joyful mood. "When I left the cave, the sky was so clear...I could see all the stars. Now, there're so many clouds I can't see a single star. It's strange how quickly things can change."

They floated in silence and listened to the thunder grow closer while the wind picked up.

"I'm sorry," Movo said.

"What for?"

"For everything that has happened to you..." He trailed off, then spoke again. "Why did you come out onto that field when I told you to stay back? None of this would have happened had you listened."

Devotio's voice wrapped around her. "You can tell him the truth. I trust him."

Herlot brought herself back into an upright position in the water and glared at Devotio with wide eyes. True, Devotio had been fond of Movo since the beginning, and had urged her to help Movo when he was injured, but did he really trust him enough for Herlot to tell him the truth? Devotio had said that he believed the people of Eraska played an important role in helping create a world for the unicorns to return to. Movo was not an Eraskan, though. And as much as he had helped them, it was also true that he had stood by and done nothing while the Alonians were locked in their homes with the crowpox. Yet out of all the people aside from Enri and Mahtreeh, it was Movo who Devotio trusted with the truth of him really being a unicorn and Herlot needing to use golden-heart magic to save his world? Unbelievable. She was unbelievably grateful for everything Movo had done, and she did believe he had changed; however, she also thought it would be smart to see if that change would continue to last before letting him know that there was a family of unicorns with golden alicorns hiding in a leaf. He was from a gold-hungry land, after all.

"You tell him," she mumbled.

"It wouldn't do him well if he heard me speak. I tested it before on the path to Temes. He will only question his wellness if he were to hear me again. You need to let him get accustomed to the idea of magic and unicorns first. Please. Try."

He had tested it without letting her know? She should have been angry but Devotio had said the word please. She couldn't say no to him. Not after her breakdown that he had had to witness. Not after she nearly broke her promise by coming close to death on the field of Ruelder. And especially not after he had made the decision to forego her learning to blend the leaf until her people were safe. She sighed. She would do it, even though she had no idea how to explain her true story of magic to someone like Movo. This was not going to go well. "I—"

"Do you know what it was like to see you stand there, weaponless, while that soldier charged at you? And to be too far away to do anything?"

Herlot paused. "I couldn't help it."

"You couldn't help it? Nobody forced you out onto that field from what I saw."

"From what *you* saw."

They were both in an upright position now, treading water and facing each other.

"Ah," he said. "It's another one of your stories."

"It is." She treaded in a circle around him. Tipping her body back, she lifted her foot out of the water. "This one is about my magical feet."

He scoffed.

Herlot smiled. "And how they made me chase after a unicorn," she whispered in his ear from behind, "who lived a long, long time ago, when humans with golden hearts roamed the earth."

"I don't believe it."

"I know. Maybe that's why I'm allowed to tell you."

"Maybe a long time ago I may have," he said.

"What changed?"

Herlot focused on the sound of the water swooshing as she parted it repeatedly with her hand, waiting for Movo to answer.

"There're places in this world that magic like you speak of could never exist, much less help someone out of a situation," he said after a while.

This time, she treaded to face him, fighting the urge to wipe away the wet strands of hair matted against his cheek and his neck.

"Does this have anything to do with why your father really sent you to Eraska? Enri told me that he's really not seeking a way to make the crowpox elixir on his own."

"My father invaded Eraska, along with several other lands, because he believes a sorcerer will grant him a magical power to conquer Ipta. And this is all because my uncle once discovered more gold than my father did. This is how magic possesses people, to a point where they would kill for it. You think magic will help you through all of this when, in fact, it's the reason you're suffering in the first place."

Herlot floated in the words Movo had shared. Herlot and Devotio's story was confusing, painful, disorienting, but not once, even for the amount of time it took a butterfly to flap its wings, had their story been dark. Yes, the unicorns had had to hide because of dark times, but Devotio was good. His unicorn family was good. Emrys was good. Their magic felt like kindness, freedom—it felt like flying toward the horizon. However, based on what Movo had said, Herlot doubted he would give the good kind of magic a chance. His father had destroyed magic for him. She cleared her throat. "And you're afraid that, if you believe, you will be mad like your father is?"

"I don't have many wants in my life, Herlot, but one of them is to be nothing like my father."

She digested that and felt for him. There was one thing that made Movo different from anyone in Eraska—he had been raised by a monster and somehow found a way to not be like him.

"I understand. But there is something you should know about me. I would never do anything like your father. In the real story about my sword, I was told that it was made of that which is good and pure and that's why I should never attack with it. And, from what I have heard about your father, I don't think it's the magic at fault. It's his greed and vengeance."

The world around them lightened as the first lightning of the storm made its grand entrance. The rain began to pour to the point where they couldn't see the shore. But Herlot wasn't afraid. She remembered the last time she had been stuck outside in such a storm, and it had resulted in the greatest gift in her life—Devotio.

"Race you to the fork and back!" Herlot shouted. She dove under, not waiting to see if Movo would play along. She kicked her feet and undulated her body forward, catching glimpses of Devotio's legs ahead of them.

Devotio won the race, but the pouring rain made it impossible to tell who came in second. When they finally made their way out of the water, Herlot laughed as the rain poured down on her, just for the sake of it. She did not stop when they climbed on to Devotio and then galloped back to the cave. She soaked in every raindrop on her face, every smooth glide of Devotio's step, the sound of his hoofs against the mud, and surprisingly also the feel of Movo's chest against her back. The first time she had been in this position with him, she had despised him.

Only Benyamin, who was mumbling to himself while turning the gears on his gadget, was awake when they came back to the cave. They changed out of their clothes and wrapped themselves in blankets. Movo took another one to pat Devotio dry. There was something Herlot really liked about him caring for Devotio. Once they were dry, together, they rested against his side, trying to contain their laughter while listening to Asm's snores.

She was falling into a dream when Movo spoke.

"I do believe there is something different about your horse. Maybe someday I'll ask you to tell me your real story about magic. Goodnight, Herlot."

• • •

During breakfast the next morning, Herlot and Devotio snuck away into the tunnels to the chamber with the paintings.

Herlot knelt down beneath the painting and unfolded the blanket she had carried in with her. Devotio took her sword out of her scabbard and set it down on the blanket. They had decided to store it in the cave room for the time being. It would be the safest place for it while Herlot was using Seum's sword and the staff he had made. They did not want it to get into the hands of someone who did not understand its magic.

She then took the leaf out of its hiding spot. "Emrys and all of Devotio's family, I made a promise to you and I will keep it. But I have to protect my family first, and I hope you understand that it's

Devotio's family too now..." She looked at the picture of the man in the clouds on his unicorn.

"If it's not safe for them, it will never be safe for you. It will be the Eraskans who create a safe world for us again. We need to protect them, too," Devotio added.

"Eleven moons now. I promise." She kissed the tips of her fingers and touched them to the leaf. For a moment, a gold color pulsed through the veins of the leaf.

"Thank you for understanding," Devotio said. Herlot hid the leaf back in the crack in the wall.

As they were about to leave, Herlot paused and looked at the carved-out space in the wall, the one that was about the size of a handprint. She couldn't remember any details from the last time she had blended in that spot, but her gut told her that something serious had happened at that spot. Something that felt dark.

"Is something wrong?" Devotio asked.

"No. Yes. I don't know."

"Are you worried you won't be able to fight?"

"No." She smiled. "Surprisingly, not a bit. I know I have to fight, and I want to...it's just a strange feeling that I'm not fighting the right enemy."

She shook her head and tore her eyes away from the crevice. "Come on, the others are waiting."

● ● ●

The villagers took turns holding and admiring Herlot's oak staff. One end of it was bound in leather, for sturdiness, the other carved to perfection to allow for flexibility. Seum was busy sewing another scabbard onto her baldric so she could carry the sword and the staff.

It was a murky, cloudy morning outside. It felt strangely peaceful to Herlot, the same way she felt about their mission to find the scouts.

"The woods are clear—" Asm began when his eyes focused in on the staff.

"Seum made it for Herlot!" Hans said.

"I did not know my son was a craftsman. And he taught you to use it?"

Herlot nodded.

He pointed to her new sword. "I see you have a different sword."

She was not ignorant of the fact that everyone had noticed she had a new sword and what that meant. This one carried none of the burdens of a magical story or legend. This one came with no limits as to how she was allowed to use it.

"After she learned the staff, she didn't need me to teach her the sword. By then, she was already an Iptan warrior. It took a little longer than a day, but then she sparked like a golden pyramid in the sun's noon rays. She would fit right in if we were back home." Seum ruffled Herlot's hair, causing the side to stick out at an angle.

Before long, Herlot was in her element, taking in every stir of the forest, following behind Devotio. Asm, Seum, Movo, and Mahtreeh were at her side, walking the edge of the forest as they scanned the opposite side of the river. The other Eraskans followed alongside them, but deeper in the forest.

By noon, the humidity made it hard to breathe and Herlot was aware that the morale of their troop had plummeted. At first, everyone's hearts had seemed to pump faster at the slightest sound. However, at this point all they could speak about was going back to the cool cave and standing next to the waterfall.

"I'd give anything to take a dip in the river," Mahtreeh said, wiping the sweat off his forehead.

"Don't even think about it unless you want to be bait," Seum grumbled.

"Everyone cheer up," Hans said. "Yesterday we were complaining about being stuck in the caves. Now we're complaining about being outside. Let's not forget the old saying that you can make music everywhere," Hans said.

"That's the dumbest thing I've ever heard. Thank the emperors it's not true or else even our wars would be infiltrated with these rosy child's ear-washing melodies," Seum said. He stood on his tiptoes and squeezed his knees together as he mimicked Hans playing the psaltery.

Hans lifted his chin. "King Cloudian told me that saying."

"King Cloudian can—"

"Enough!" Herlot swatted Seum on the head. She was about to do it again as he opened his mouth, but then she noticed Devotio stop in his tracks and pull his ears back. She nudged Mahtreeh and swung her chin toward Devotio so he would notice. Mahtreeh whistled the song of a mistle thrush, a signal they had all agreed upon beforehand. Everyone crouched low to the ground.

Herlot crawled forward to peek through a bush. On the other side of the river, five soldiers emerged out of the woods.

"Scouts," Seum said, crawling next to her. "Movo, do you think there will be more?"

"Doubt it."

"Now what?" Mahtreeh whispered.

"Herlot, you take them," Seum suggested.

"Wait—" Movo said.

She ignored Movo and had already submerged into the water before hearing the rest of his plea. She didn't bother to hide once she reached the other side. She was hungry for her enemy. She was yearning to dance. She was thirsty to show these men that the Eraskans were now a different people from the ones they had invaded in the beginning. From here on out, each step of her dance would be for every Alonian who had died before being given the chance to know what it was like to be truly free.

"There's one! Attack!" a soldier shouted.

Herlot swung her staff at the incoming soldier.

"She has a weapon!"

She spun the staff around her body, creating an impenetrable sphere around herself. They staggered back. Then she tucked one end behind her, and spun toward them, knocking their swords out of their hands. On the second spin, the staff clashed into their midsections.

"Watch out! She's left-handed!" one of them shouted. Seum had said this would work to her advantage since most soldiers were used to mainly fighting opponents who were right-handed.

A soldier lunged at her, but she pivoted away and dug the leather-bound end of the staff into the ground, freedom rushing through her veins, using its support to kick off and meet his forehead with her foot. Dropping the staff and jumping forward, she extended her hand toward a branch above her. Without making a sound, she landed behind them, sword ready. Their heads were turned up, still searching for her in the trees. Was it wrong that she smiled with satisfaction knowing she had outsmarted them? She made eye contact with Seum across the river. He nodded. Without a second thought, he sliced at the backs of their legs. They toppled over and she was given the view of Devotio. He must have crossed the river during the fight, rising up on his hind legs and then crashing his front legs down with full force on top of a soldier's back.

"Good work," she said.

She ignored the Eraskans' cheers as she made to clean the blood off her sword in the river but stopped. She didn't want to clean it off. She wasn't ashamed of it. She grabbed Devotio's mane and kicked up to mount him as her troop crossed the river. Asm stopped his horse next to her.

"Looks like you have yourself an army of Iptan warriors," he said, pointing at the troop.

Pride beamed through Herlot's body. These weren't the vulnerable peasants Felix's men had planned to invade anymore. They held their chests high, and there was a fierce light in their eyes as they cheered, holding their weapons in the air, the current of the river unable to budge them. One could almost hear their hearts beating in harmony. In that moment she knew with every fiber of her being that this was an army that could defend Eraska. It was time for them to take their mission a step further.

"No, Asm. They're Eraskan warriors." Herlot said. "Eraskans!" Herlot shouted over their cheers. "Today, we take Ruelder back!"

● ● ●

Percival of Damalathum sat inside one of Ruelder's homes, sharpening his sword. He heard rain begin to hammer down to the ground, but when he glanced out the doorway, he could only see fog. He stepped outside, wondering why he couldn't feel the rain. What else could the sound be? He marched ahead, his hand shielding his forehead, hoping to see better through the fog.

"Ey!" he called to the others, when he realized what the sound was.

He heard and felt the hooves, accompanied by the fierce battle cries. Percival took his guard.

Then he saw them, blurred by the fog as they rode and ran down the hill alongside Ruelder's cliff.

As they closed in, a woman on a white horse leading the group came into focus. Her gray eyes pierced Percival as she stood on the horse while holding on to its mane. Before he could throw himself out of her way, she kicked off, extracting her sword in midair and emitting a cry that resembled the shriek of an elk. The impact knocked the air out of his lungs as she toppled and rolled him to the ground. And, as her sword pierced his chest, he could hear the strong beat of her heart, more alive than anything he had ever experienced. His body shook as he choked on his own blood. Out the corners of his eyes he saw more and more of his men fall to the ground. All he could hear were the wild calls of this woman's people. The blood in his mouth gurgled as his lungs fought for air. Then, his body eased and became still. He knew he was about to take his last breath. Right at the top of the intake of his last taste of air, the world seemed to pause and all he could hear were the heartbeats of his attackers, all drumming in unison. It was this woman and her people who were responsible for his death, yet he felt no need for even a drop of revenge, for their heartbeats were the most beautiful thing he had witnessed in his life of adventures and travels to all parts of the world. He couldn't help attempting one last wish even though his life was at its end. *If perhaps I am given another chance, I take back my wish of the golden coins I was promised. Instead, may my heart beat strong and alive like theirs, and may I learn more of this beauty I never had a chance to know existed until now.*

● ● ●

The next evening, two hawks, carrying a message, set out from the Eraskan fortress to Damalathum and to any allied ship in the northern seas.

We seek immediate assistance in Eraska, having suffered heavy losses due to a rebellion led by two Iptan warriors, a one-armed peasant woman, and Prince Movo, son of King Felix.

-Dartharus

CHAPTER 20
The Sacrifice

"**T**HAT WAS A LOVELY story," Benyamin said. "Even though the fairy couldn't have children of her own, she visited all of those orphans in their dreams."

"She gave them all the guidance a parent would. Thanks to her, they escaped from the thief," Hans said.

"What is it called?" Benyamin asked.

"'The Goodnight Fairy,'" Herlot replied. "I wish you could have heard my father tell it."

A sly smile spread across Benyamin's face.

"You look like you're hiding something, Benyamin," Hans said.

"Who? Me? Ah, never." Benyamin winked.

The Eraskans were stretched out in the main chamber of the cave after the day's training, watching serenely as Seum tattooed the bottom of Herlot's big toe. A pyramid with a gracious S in black ink with a smooth undertone of gold. Although the pricking of the needle stung, she smiled. Seum said she was probably the only non-Iptan in the world who would have one, an Iptan trainer's signature. Now, wherever she took a step, the land would know that a warrior walked upon it. For her, it was an engraving of what her people and she had accomplished together. Now she would never forget that she could lead.

A week ago, they had chased the soldiers out of Ruelder, watching from atop a hill as they had tripped and stumbled over their feet.

"Next time, we'll have the sheep trained to smother your arses!" they had shouted, as sweat mixed with rain dripped from their hair and faces.

Their voices were still hoarse, and many bruises hadn't faded, but cups of ale were clanked together without end. Herlot had never been more proud of the Eraskans and of who she was.

A young girl with two loose teeth crawled over to Benyamin and ran her finger over his face. "Benyamin, you have many folds on your face," she said. She poked at the ones around his eyes.

"Those were some of my first. My wife gave them to me. She made me laugh so much that my lips and cheeks were always sore," Benyamin said.

Everyone laughed.

The girl then crawled over to Movo. "Do you miss your home, Movo? I miss mine."

Herlot thought she saw a moment of hesitation. But then, in a clear, sturdy voice, he said, "No. I don't."

"If you're a prince, have you ever danced with a princess and twirled her until both your feet raised off the ground and you grew wings and could fly?" she asked.

Movo chuckled. "Yes. I have danced with a princess, on many occasions. But most of the dances at the castle are very rigid. You have to memorize all the steps, and there is less twirling than I would like." He winked at the little girl.

"Oh, show us, please!" Enri cried.

Movo ran his fingers along his jaw. "Maybe another time."

"Oh, come on, Movo. Please?" Herlot asked.

"Yes! Don't be shy," Mahtreeh said. "I know! We'll show you how we dance, and then you show us how you do!"

He grabbed Enri and Hans's hands and they skipped in a circle like children. Herlot slapped her hand against her thigh as they spun faster and faster, while more and more people asked Movo to teach them. Herlot had never seen Movo lack confidence, but now she wondered if he was on the verge of blushing. He could teach them to fight, so what was stopping him from teaching them to dance?

Movo finally agreed and had them form two rows—one with women and the other with men. Movo stood in front of Herlot and demonstrated the first part of the dance. They took two strides toward each other, pressing their palms together and walking in a circle. Herlot's heart skipped a beat and she quickly looked away to avoid making eye contact with him.

She had only known Movo as a soldier and nearly forgotten that he was a prince. What was he like in Damalathum? He said he had danced with princesses. Had they also felt somewhat...dizzy, with him?

When it was time to circle the other way, Movo made his own change to the choreography and pressed his shoulder against Herlot's for the turn. Instead of feeling insecure about her shoulder, she enjoyed it. Holding their palms together had felt delicate. Shoulder to shoulder felt natural, as if they were preparing to duel, and this time she looked straight into his ice-blue eyes with ease.

Herlot noticed Hans pick up his psaltery as he studied the steps of the dancers. He then began to play a melody that matched them in rhythm—smooth and connected notes during turns, and shorter, staccato notes during the stepping sequences where the women held their dresses out to one side. Right away, she noticed a subtle grace in the clumsy dancers. "How do you do that, Hans!?" cried Asm. "This is the first time I have not stepped on someone's feet while dancing!" Asm's partner, Hans's mother, didn't look too assured, though.

"I didn't think I'd enjoy this," Movo said.

"Why is that?" Herlot asked as he held her hand up and guided her into a slow twirl.

"I can't show your people my city with its buildings, markets, and performers. But maybe teaching them this dance might show them that my people aren't only vicious."

She thought about that, trying to put herself in Movo's footsteps. He was helping a people who thought no good things of his. *Yes, Movo's people are probably much smarter and have better things, a lifestyle we have difficulty imagining, but that doesn't change the fact that he is an outsider among the Eraskans, even though he is helping us. He doesn't have a home here, and maybe sharing the dance is his way of bringing part of his home with him.* Then, she had a realization.

"You know, none of us have a home anymore—each one of us, here in the cave, except for Asm and Seum who can return to Ipta whenever they would like. But here we can have a new home where we don't have to be either my people, or your people. We can just be us."

"Maybe," was all he said.

For the rest of the evening, Herlot thought about her parents and all the Alonians who had died, and what they would think if they saw her dancing with her new family of Lorfiners, Temesians, Ruelderians, Noraynians, Bundeners, Iptans, and one from Damalathum. She wished she could share this moment with them, even as tragic as the events were that had led up to it. It was beautiful and they should have been there. Simon could have played his recorder and Agatha would have tapped her hips.

They were far from an end, and Movo said more soldiers would arrive. But they were happy in their own traumatized way. They didn't know what the future would bring, but, for now, they were dancing as if none of it and all of it had happened at the same time.

● ● ●

The next morning, Herlot awoke to the screeching sound of metal against metal. She must have slept in because Devotio wasn't behind her and Movo was helping a group sharpen their swords with a stone.

"Good morning," Movo called.

She liked how he knew she was awake even though his back was turned toward her. But what she didn't like was the thought of another day of training. She'd prefer a full day of dancing like they had the night before.

She wasn't the only one. Many families still lay under their blankets. Children cuddled against their mothers—men yawning, stretching their arms above their heads.

"Can you take that yammer outside?" a woman cried, pulling a blanket over her head.

Thankfully, Movo and his students abided and left.

Herlot tried to fall back asleep, but she was wondering what the weather was like. One could never tell from inside the cave. She missed that about her Alonian home. On sunny days, light peeked through the thatching in the morning, and on cloudy ones, gray haze so relaxing that she could sleep all day filled the home. It was on those days that everyone looked forward to taking a nap after working the fields. The only thing that made it more perfect was if the rain fell and tapped on the roof. In the cave, it was dark all the time and all she could hear was the waterfall. She wondered if there was a way Mahtreeh could whistle his bird calls so they would come in the cave one morning and everyone could awake to bird songs once again.

One thing she did enjoy was how the sky outside was always a surprise when living in the cave. Just behind the waterfall, a new day had risen. Herlot stretched, leaning from side to side, and bent forward to touch her toes. She scrunched her face at the dirt around her toenails. She doubted princesses danced with dirty feet.

She also noticed that her hair stayed clamped against her head. It was time to bathe. Immediately. The idea of feeling fresh and clean was so tempting to her that she couldn't wait to get in the water.

Her instincts took over. She ran at full speed, jumping over a sleeping family, and down the path along the ledge. As soon as she knew she was above an area where there were no rocks on the bottom, she jumped. She caught a glimpse of the sky before she dove in, racing the waterfall to the bottom. A family of fish scattered away from her as she pierced the water's surface. Once she reached the bottom, she let out a cheer, swallowing a bunch of water and regretting it right away.

"Are you insane!?" Movo shouted after she came up.

He and his group had dropped their work and gaped.

"Sunny!" Herlot called between coughs. "It's sunny!"

It seemed that her sudden run outside had stirred everyone inside awake, for they were rushing out of the cave looking alarmed.

Herlot found a spot where the water only came up to her knees and hopped from foot to foot in a circle. "Come in, everyone! The water is great!" she yelled.

Asm and the children raced down the ledge and along the shore. He stripped down and kicked off from the edge, keeping his legs squeezed together and his toes pointed as he dove in.

He didn't come to the surface alone. "I caught it with my bare hand!" He raised a fish up for everyone to see. But the fish wiggled back and forth, sending him into a fit of giggles as it tickled him under his chin with its tail until he let go.

"It's probably telling its family to stay clear of the big, hairy feet now," Enri said from the shore, resting her hands on her knees, trying to sneak a breath between her fits of laughter.

The sun shone high in the sky when Herlot and Enri finally climbed out of the water. They wrapped long pieces of cloth around their bodies and laid their dresses and leggings out to dry on the grass.

Asm and the children still had not had enough. The children blindfolded Asm, in preparation for a game of tag, ordering him to spin in circles and count to ten while they swam away from him.

"Six...seven...eight—"

"HELP! HELP! HELP!" Mahtreeh screamed.

Mahtreeh ran out of the woods, his entire face red and swollen, his knees wobbling each time one of his feet hit the ground. All the splashing ceased, as did Herlot's heart for a moment. She looked around, realizing she hadn't seen Devotio all morning. Mahtreeh gripped Movo's baldric. He swayed back and forth until Movo grasped his shoulders and held him still.

"What happened?" Movo asked.

"Th-they took them. Hans. Seum. Devotio," he stuttered.

Herlot dropped to her knees. "No," she cried.

Mahtreeh spoke quickly, only the centers of his stretched lips touching as he tripped over his words. "Hans and I wanted to do the patrol alone, and Devotio came with. Hans fell into a trap, and I went to find Seum. But, when we came back, Hans and Devotio were gone and they threw a net over Seum. I'm sorry, I'm so sorry."

Lucinda and Asm were already dressed. Asm was fastening his ax and other weapons into the saddle of one of the horses.

Movo slouched so he could be eye to eye with Mahtreeh. "How many soldiers were there?"

"I think six."

"Did they have a wagon?"

"No. Just horses." Mahtreeh wiped his nose on his forearm.

"How long ago?"

"Around sunrise," Mahtreeh choked. "I tried to get here sooner. I tried so hard, but everything went black. I must have fainted."

Movo looked up at the sun. His lips moved, speaking a jumble of numbers.

"Get up, Herlot. We have to go get Devotio," Enri said. She tucked her head under Herlot's arm and helped her to her feet.

"Yes. Yes. Now. My weapons are in the cave," Herlot muttered.

Movo stuck his hand out and blocked her from leaving. "Nobody is going anywhere."

Herlot tried to duck under his arm, but he grabbed her by her shoulders.

"Let me go!"

"Calm down!" he shouted.

She continued to fight against him, but he shook her three times and shouted in her face.

"What do you plan on doing? You're going to ride out so you can fall into a trap, too? Devotio needs you alive to help him!" He glared at Asm and Lucinda. "And so do Seum and Hans."

Herlot sobered.

"How will we find them?" Lucinda asked. "Hans isn't strong like Seum. He's fragile. We have to help him as soon as possible."

"I understand, Lucinda. We won't have to search for them. They're without wagons and on horses—they'll be at the fortress before we catch up to them." He continued speaking in a steady rhythm, raising his voice whenever someone tried to interrupt him. "Once at the fortress, they will be tortured unless they answer Dartharus's questions—I can guarantee you that. If they break, they will tell him where the rest of you are hiding. In order to rescue them, we will need to go to the fortress. This is probably what Dartharus would most want. He'll have lookouts who will spot a large group right away. Asm, we will sit down and make a plan first. Our only chance is if we get in and out of the fortress unseen. I need everyone else to gather their supplies, fill the handcarts, and have weapons ready in case the soldiers find out about the cave."

"My son would never tell Dartharus where we are!" Hans's mother exclaimed.

Movo closed his eyes. "Ipta may have the best armies in the world, but my father is the emperor of torture techniques and I promise you that Dartharus is just as sadistic. He'll break anyone, even a warrior like Seum."

• • •

Hans whimpered from pain as he awoke. He was in a plain, dark room made of gray bricks. His wrists were tied together behind him. He had no feeling in his arms. The air knocked out of his lungs as a boot wedged into his stomach with excruciating force. Before he could register the pain, he was forced into an upright position.

"That's enough, Nicholas. Now, Hans, that's your name, right? Tell me, Hans, where are your people hiding?" another man asked him. This one was older and more polite than the one who had kicked him.

Hans gritted his teeth.

The older man shook his head and then walked over to a table against a darker area of the cold room. "My name is Dartharus. Your people have made me look very bad in the eyes of my king, and now, you are going to help me set things right, Hans."

Shivers ran through Hans' spine as Dartharus sharpened a mystery object laying on the table. Dartharus approached him, displaying the object in the thin beam of light that shone into the room through a small window.

The door swung open and three men carried in a thrashing Seum. His feet were tied together, as were his hands behind his back. A cloth was tied around his mouth. All of his clothing was soaked in his own blood. "Careful, this one bites," one of the men said to Nicholas.

"Shall we begin?" Dartharus said. "Listen, Iptan, each moment you refuse to tell me the hiding place of the Eraskans, I will inflict some sort of damage to Hans. Deal? Deal. Now, since you've proven rather difficult already, I think we have some time to make up for first."

Dartharus studied the sharp hook in his hands. "Actually, let's begin with bones. Nicholas, both knees, please."

"Wood?" Nicholas asked.

Dartharus shook his head. "Let him bite his tongue off."

Hans started to pant and convulse with fear as Nicholas approached him with an enormous-sized hammer. Seum's muffled shouts emanated through the room.

"No, sir, please, please, sir, don't," Hans begged.

He could hear the crack of his knees reverberate through his head. His mouth filled with a warm liquid. Another crack.

Tears streamed down his face as pain pounded through his body. Out of the corner of his eyes, he saw someone undo the cloth that was wrapped around Seum's mouth.

"Don't. No matter what, don't tell them," Hans wheezed.

"Elbows," Dartharus said.

Someone untied Hans's hands. He reached for Dartharus, gripping his hand. "Please don't do this. I beg you," he choked. Dartharus slapped his hand away, as if he were disgusted by it.

More cracks. His body went limp from pain. Blood poured from his mouth, he could feel it pooling beneath his neck.

Dartharus raised the sharp object.

Somehow Hans managed to turn his head to look at Seum. "Don't tell," he mouthed.

● ● ●

Herlot paced back and forth, biting her nails while Movo, Mahtreeh, Enri, Lucinda, and Asm strategized on the cave floor.

This was her fault. She shouldn't have let Devotio get involved in their matters. She shouldn't have let him wander by himself. She should have taken him far, far away and worked on blending the leaf. And, even worse, he had helped her in her endeavors and made them his own. He had put her people first when she hadn't even tried for his.

As the plans unfolded, she felt Lucinda's pain. Movo was giving her the most difficult job, asking her to stay behind instead of Enri. He explained that they would need Enri because Seum and Hans would require medical attention, and someone with strong, decision-making capabilities had to stay back in case there was an attack on the cave.

Herlot couldn't imagine staying behind, but Lucinda, with a straight face, agreed and didn't offer an argument.

Movo used a rock to scratch an outline of the old fortress of Eraska. "Our odds of being undetected will be better at night if we stay low to the ground between the tall grasses. Luckily, we will be going into the least busy places, the cellar and the stables, where our chances of being seen will be the smallest."

"We'll have to disguise ourselves once we're in," he continued, pacing back and forth. "There's a shed near the entrance. We can find a way to lure in some soldiers so we can take their clothing. On the south end of the fortress, straight across from the shed, a staircase leads underground, which is where they'll most likely be kept. There are several hallways. The hardest part will be getting into the hallway with the rooms where the prisoners are kept. The door is locked from both sides, and there will be a guard inside."

"I'll ax it down," Asm said.

"Too much noise. We'll need a distraction."

They continued to strategize until a plan was set.

"What about the ring Hans told us about? If we are already at the fortress, we should make an attempt. If Vincent returns with news of having spotted our allies, we'd be ready to act right away. It's our chance to gain people, which we will need if Dartharus's reinforcements come," Enri said. "And, if Seum and Hans broke, the mountains might be the only other place left for us to hide."

Movo ran his thumb and pointer finger along the stubble around his jaw. He drew a specific outline of the eastern side of the fortress. "On the ground floor is a dining hall where the soldiers eat. To the left is a staircase that leads to the upper levels, where only a few soldiers are allowed. Dartharus sleeps in this chamber here."

"And my brother, Ambro. Where would we find him?" Herlot asked.

"I'm sorry but he could be anywhere, including the ship. He is safe, having survived the crowpox, of that I am certain," Movo explained. "Searching the entire place will be too risky, especially because Seum and Hans will need Enri's attention as soon as possible."

How could Herlot get so close to Ambro and not try to find him?

"Movo, I have to try and find my brother."

"No. You either agree to the plan or you stay. Herlot, all of you, I need you all to understand that we are risking our own lives to save two people who may be beyond saving. If we do manage to find Hans and Seum, they will need to be carried, and that alone might hurt them."

"Exactly what does Dartharus do to them?" Herlot asked. Then she caught a glimpse of Asm's expression. "No, don't answer that," she said. The last thing Asm and Lucinda needed was to imagine how Hans and Seum were suffering.

It was midnight the next night when the group arrived at the fortress. They observed the fortress from high up in a tree. Strangely, the portcullis was raised and there were no lookouts, not on the walls, or higher up in the bell tower. But there could have been someone looking out one of the windows from inside. Either they didn't expect anyone to be brave enough to come, or they really wanted them to have no trouble entering. Movo argued back and forth if it was a better idea to wait and observe longer, but every second they waited meant another second of torture for Hans and Seum.

Herlot led the way, crawling through the grass beneath the clouded night sky. Devotio was only a meadow and a wall away, and that was all she focused on. She didn't even feel the stones cutting at her knees and her elbow, or the bugs that were taking bites out of every bare part of her body.

She didn't hear the slithering alongside her until the snake cut in front of her and she almost stepped on it with her hand. Her instinct told her to run, but her desire to rescue Devotio overcame it. She would not, for the life of her, make a ruckus and bring attention to them—even if it meant a snakebite.

She sat back on her heels and supported her weight with her arm, attempting to scamper away from it. She kicked her leg at it as it moved toward her, but that only made it easier for it to slither its way up her leg. She felt its cool, dry skin and muscles contracting as it invaded up her torso, claiming her body and stopping at her neck.

"Don't move," Movo whispered.

Herlot's heart drummed in her ears. The snake's tongue flicked against her neck and under her ear. She frantically gasped for air, aggravating it and causing it to tighten around her neck.

"Slow your breathing," Movo hissed. He positioned himself on his knees behind her. "Lie your head back very slowly." He supported the back of Herlot's head with one hand.

With perfect grace, he began to uncoil the snake starting at the tail. "One more moment. He is just as scared as you are," he murmured. He massaged the bottom of her neck, helping her relax until she was free of the snake.

"Thank you," Herlot gasped.

Movo took the lead this time, and everyone was on high alert for snakes. When they made it to the fort's wall, they took a moment to gather themselves.

"That was mighty close there," Asm said.

"On the bright side, we won't have to crawl out of here," Enri added. "We'll be either dead or on horseback."

They tip-toed with their backs against the outer wall. Movo and Herlot peeked through the entrance. There were several men staggering around. Some of them could barely keep their balance. Music and clapping echoed from the dining hall, and she also recognized some feminine voices.

Then she saw them and her stomach sank. Behind the fortress, the tip of a third set of sails protruded. Three ships. Dartharus had already received reinforcements. "Movo, look."

They huddled back to the others.

"Bad news, the reinforcements arrived. Good news, the ship came with dancers for entertainment and they're currently celebrating their arrival," Movo said.

He signaled the others to be ready to run and chucked a rock at the shed, just as a group of soldiers walked by.

"Hey! I think there's something in there!" one of the men slurred.

"Good. They're drunk," Movo whispered.

As soon as the group of soldiers neared the door to the shed, Movo sprinted as fast as he could across the dirt. Herlot followed, as did Asm, Mahtreeh, and Enri. They crept up on the men from behind, strangling them until they lost consciousness.

Movo cursed when he realized the door was locked, but Asm nudged it loose with his ax. They hauled the unconscious soldiers inside.

"If someone notices the lock is loose, we're roasted frogs," Enri said as she adjusted a hat with a feather on her head.

"They're too drunk to notice," Movo said.

"Let's hope they're drunk enough to not notice we're girls," Herlot said, tucking her dress into the pants.

They lined up behind the door once they were finished. Movo took a look at Mahtreeh and let him know that his hat was on backwards.

He looked Herlot up and down in the soldier's pants and sweater. "We need something to hide your face," he said. He lifted his hooded cloak over his head.

"Raise your arm," he said and pulled it down over her head. He then tugged the hood forward so that her face was hidden in its shadows.

Movo looked through the hole created when the lock had been ripped off the door.

"Enri, Herlot, go, now."

Herlot leaned against Enri and pretended to be drunk and off-balance as they headed toward the stables located across from the dining hall. She was just footsteps away from Devotio. They held close to the shadows of the fortress. Once they saw there were no soldiers at the stables, Herlot forgot all about keeping up her disguise and barged through the doors.

"Devotio!" she cried as she climbed into the stall where her sweet friend was curled up in a corner. She pressed her forehead against his. "I'm here, Devotio. I'm so sorry. I'm here. I won't let them near you again," she whispered. He felt rigid, and his breathing was hard.

"He seems very shaken," Enri said.

"Did they hurt you?" Herlot asked as she examined his body. Physically, he seemed to be unharmed except for a few raw spots on his coat, but the longer she waited for a response that didn't come, the more scared she felt. She had to get him out of there as soon as possible.

• • •

I wish I had my summer sweater, Mahtreeh thought, sensing the cold of the fortress. Or was the cold from his fear?

Movo signaled Asm and Mahtreeh to halt as he reached the bottom of the stairs. Footsteps approached. He leaned forward to sneak a peek, a few seconds short of colliding with the soldier heading toward them. Before the soldier could react, Movo had him pressed against the wall, forearm against his throat until he fell unconscious. Asm slung the soldier over his shoulder, and they proceeded down the hallway.

"This is it," Movo said when they arrived at the locked door to the hallway with the rooms for the prisoners.

Now it was all up to Mahtreeh. He lowered onto his belly so his lips were right by the barely visible space between the door and the floor. He jutted his lower lip out, pulled the edges of it toward his chin, and tucked his upper lip against his front two teeth. A high-pitched squeal, somewhere between a mouse and a hawk, escaped him. He paused, and then began a procession of squeals, leaving no interludes between.

● ● ●

The soldier on the other side of the door stuck his pointer finger in his ear, rapidly wiggling it. When the noise wouldn't stop, he tried the other ear. When that didn't help, he thought either he was going crazy or there was something incredibly annoying in his vicinity that needed to be silenced. He scavenged the space, looking for the source.

"Great," he mumbled when he realized it was coming from outside. His orders were to not open the door unless Dartharus's voice was on the other side.

He went back to the other end of the hallway, hoping that creating a distance between himself and the door would make the sound less annoying. It didn't work. It only became more irritating. Each time the squeal sounded, he was certain it would be the last. These things always silenced eventually. But this one didn't. Each time he hoped it would, it squealed ten more times.

He finally decided that the noise did resemble Dartharus, which meant he had to open the door. He stuck his key in the lock, turned the handle, and pulled the door open. He saw stars the moment a fist made contact with his nose. Strangely, he felt relief when he heard the crunch of his nose bone because at least the squealing had stopped. He faltered to retrieve his balance and was knocked again, after which all he saw was the color black.

● ● ●

Mahtreeh pressed his ear to a cell door. "Hurry, Movo. There's someone in here, I can hear them."

Movo fumbled the keys, trying each one on the first door to the sound of Asm's huffs and puffs as he resisted smashing his ax into it.

Finally, the correct key entered the lock and Movo swung the door open. A man who had been leaning against the door spilled out into the hallway. He was wearing Eraskan clothes, but he wasn't Hans. There were several curls on his head, but the rest of his hair had been matted down by dirt and grease. He was thin, his legs thinner than Mahtreeh's, so fragile they looked as if a child could snap them in half. His face was heavily bearded. Mahtreeh winced as the man scrambled to his knees, afraid to hear his bones crack.

He bowed at Movo's feet. "Thank you, thank you," he cried.

Asm helped the man stand up. "What is your name, son?" Asm asked.

"Ambro," he replied, "of Alonia."

"Ambro?" Mahtreeh leaned forward to move the hair out of the man's face. "It really is you. Herlot will be so happy."

Ambro frowned but then his eyes softened. "Holy Basil! How strange it is to recognize the older features of a childhood friend." Ambro's speech was slurred and his eyes somewhat dazed, as if he were still in a dream. Mahtreeh wondered if he could be on the verge of delirium after what he had suffered through in the cell. "Mahtreeh of Lorfin! I never thought we'd meet in such conditions, but I am so happy to see you. You're with my sister? Where is she? How is she?"

"She is waiting for us in the stables, hopefully."

"Ambro, have you heard other prisoners in here?" Movo asked.

"The room next to mine," Ambro said. Mahtreeh noticed that Ambro's hands never stopped trembling.

Movo opened the door right away. In the corner of the room lay a man on his back. His leg was limp and twisted out to the side. His clothes were shredded and soaked with blood from his wounds. Had it not been for the black braid, they may not have recognized him.

Movo and Asm knelt down next to him while Mahtreeh held on to Ambro. A fragile, wheezing escaped Seum's swollen lips.

"He's alive," Movo said.

• • •

Asm checked his son's body. Several of his ribs were surely broken. Deep cuts from a dagger covered his body. Seum's face was unrecognizable—swollen, bruised, and encrusted with dried blood— but Asm knew something much worse had happened between these walls because he could feel that Seum's spirit was just as broken as his body was. In Ipta, they had both been trained on how to escape being held hostage. The moment Asm had seen the shards of brick in some areas along the wall of the fortress, he had been certain Seum would be fine. Even if his arms and legs had been tied together, Seum could have bit down on a sharp piece and used it to either free himself or attack his capturer. But he hadn't. Somehow these people had managed to break him to a point where he wasn't even willing to try.

Asm lifted his son, causing him to arch as if preparing to shout from the pain, but he only managed to gag. Most of his vest was torn in back, and there seemed to be hundreds of cuts from a whip across his back. The blood had dried to the ground beneath him and tore from his skin.

"We have to get him out of here as soon as possible if he's to live," Movo said.

"We still have to find Hans," Mahtreeh said.

At the mention of Hans's name, Seum did something he hadn't done since he was born. He cried. His beaten body shook as tears streamed from his black eyes, filling the valley between his lashes and swollen cheeks.

"Hans is dead, Father. They killed him."

"Herlot," a voice said before Herlot could turn around.

She didn't even stop to make sure she had heard right. She would have recognized her brother's voice anywhere, no matter how weak it was. She rushed into his arms, not stopping to take in his appearance. He felt fragile, but still like home.

Ambro jolted when his hands ran into the sheaths holding her weapons on her back. Then he patted his hand up her side. He pushed her away from him, his eyes wide as he stared between her face and her shoulder. "Sister, what happened to you?"

"A rather painful accident that we don't have time to explain now," she said.

She watched in horror at Seum as Asm lowered him down on the hay. "Where is Hans?" she asked, terrified of the answer.

"Hans is dead," Mahtreeh said.

Rage pulsed through Herlot's body, burning and disintegrating the feelings of helplessness in her belly, grief in her heart, and agony in her head. "Damned beasts," she blurted. Whether she meant to or not, she looked to Movo when she said it.

He was the closest thing to her that connected to the people who had harmed her friends. He came from the same place and wore the same clothes. And he had known that this would happen, and by the look of shame in his eyes, she understood that it was because he had done such things himself in the past.

Herlot marched to a window where she could observe the dining hall.

Her father had been wrong. It was an insult to think anyone could ever be happy before the end—at least, not in the real world. In real stories, the happiest a person could ever be was when everything that had been lost and broken was restored to what it once was. For her, it was about having her father and mother back the way they were before the soldiers invaded. It was about Oliver and the way he was before a sword pierced his heart. Seum, Ambro, and Devotio without the traces of vicious beasts on their bodies and spirits. And Hans, alive and playing his psaltery. Quite the paradox. The more one lived, the more one lost, hence the more one knew what happiness truly was, while at the same time knowing it was something impossible to actually experience. *I will never experience that happiness. Neither will any of my family and friends. But I will get the blood of those who caused our losses.*

Herlot marched back into the stable, her head high. "We are going to get the ring."

"Do you not see all the soldiers inside the fortress?" Mahtreeh said.

Herlot curled her hand into a fist by her side. "How long do we intend to hide? They'll scavenge us one by one like this. With our allies—if they exist—we will ravage these monsters so they never harm another soul again."

"I agree." Enri stood. "We can't hide forever, and they'll keep coming. We will fight them to our deaths if that's what we have to do, and we have to take our chance with the allies if we want to scare them from our land for good." She raised her voice as Movo opened his mouth to interrupt. "This might be the only chance we will get to be this close to the ring. This time, we follow my plan."

They watched out the window of the stall as a group of soldiers stepped outside for a breath of fresh air, spilling the contents of their tin cups each time they moved. Enri stood near the entrance, waiting for her cue.

A woman stepped out, holding a gold cup of her own. Ambro slammed his palm against his chest.

"Thank the skies. Manni, my love, you're alive," Ambro nearly sang. "She will help us. We must go to her."

Hope flourished in Herlot at the thought of at least Ambro and Manni having a happy ending after what they had been through at the fortress. But then she noticed Movo's expression.

Movo's lip curled as he followed Ambro's gaze toward Manni. "You will not go to her," he ordered.

"Nonsense," Herlot protested. "She's my brother's fiancée from Alonia. She'll help us."

Movo closed his eyes and pinched the bridge of his nose. "I-I remember her. Ah." He rubbed his temples.

Herlot frowned. Never before had she seen Movo disoriented.

"How could I have forgotten this? She was there." He swayed a bit as if his head hurt so much that he could not keep his balance.

Herlot stood in front of him. "Movo, what are you talking about?"

He dropped his hands and opened his eyes. "Your brother's fiancée met us in the woods and told us to wait to attack until her wedding, so all the Alonians would be gathered in one place. She said a group of hunters was late in returning. She gave this information in exchange for having the honor to serve Dartharus. But how did she know what we were there for?" Movo's voice drifted off.

"Tha-that's not true!" Ambro sputtered.

"Movo, why are you only telling us this now?" Herlot asked. Something was very not right.

"Listen, I don't know why, but I didn't remember until I saw her. It's like the memory was invisible until now. We all listened to her, did not question who she was and why she had come to us. It was like we were hypnotized."

Movo's eyes were wide. He actually looked scared. What he said made no sense, but based on his disorientation, she was certain that he was not lying.

At that moment, Herlot felt the familiar wind of Devotio's voice at her ears. From their reactions, she knew he was speaking to Enri and Mahtreeh, too.

"Stay away from Manni." As furious as she was about Manni, Herlot's heart sang at having heard Devotio speak. Next to her, Mahtreeh and Enri sighed in relief. They must have heard Devotio, too.

Herlot met Mahtreeh and Enri's gazes. "Movo, hold Ambro back if you have to. No one is going near Manni," she said.

"Who are you? Just listen to yourself," Ambro said, his eyes searching Herlot, pleading with her. "How would she even know who Dartharus was back then? This is my fiancée we're talki—"

Herlot cut him off. "Why did she disappear for so long before the wedding? You spent all day waiting for her to show her the home. And the hunters *were* late. If there is the slightest possibility that Manni did what Movo said, I swear, I'll slit her throat myself." She didn't bother checking for Ambro's reaction as he took a step toward the exit, but before he could get anywhere, Movo grasped Ambro's hands together behind his head.

"The soldiers are headed back inside," Mahtreeh said.

Enri took a deep breath. "Here I go."

• • •

Enri inched along the fortress wall. She had visited the fortress once with her father on his trip throughout the land. It wasn't her home, but a sense of entitlement grew in her belly for each stone that her fingertips grazed. *How dare Felix believe he can send his people here to do with our land as they please? This should be the last place I don't feel safe. This should be a place of kindness like it was when King Cloudian was alive.*

She passed one window where she could hear shouting, cheering, and the clinking of glasses. Standing on her tiptoes to get a better look, she saw long, wooden tables filled with fruits, pies, nuts, meats, and drinks that the soldiers were splurging on. Her mouth salivated at the sight of the food. There were beautifully dressed women walking along the aisles, too, refilling cups and food platters, while other women danced on a wooden stage. She didn't see a man matching Dartharus's description. A good sign. She needed him to be in Cloudian's chamber.

Enri continued along until she'd reached another window, which was glowing from candlelight. She listened as women gossiped inside and assisted one another in fixing their hair. She peeked through and saw some of their reflections in mirrors. They had colors on their faces, and their hair was woven into beautiful formations.

"This might be much harder than I thought," she muttered. She gazed down at the dirt covering her hands. She waited until the women left the room and hauled herself through the window, congratulating herself on her arm strength.

Getting the dirt off her body was her first priority. She found a sponge in a bucket of water and scrubbed her face, her arms, and her feet. Next she needed something to wear. She found a red, two-piece set that matched the ones the women leaving the room had worn.

After she'd dressed, she looked in the mirror and realized her exposed belly needed to be scrubbed, too. As she reached again for the sponge, she noticed the door handle swivel in the mirror. She dropped the sponge and pressed her back against the wall.

A woman with long, chestnut-colored hair entered. Enri pounced and knocked the woman to the ground, snatching a piece of fabric off the floor and wrapping it around her mouth. The woman squealed as Enri tugged out several pieces of her hair while tying the knot. The fabric was long enough to use the ends to tie her hands behind her back, as well.

Not giving the woman another thought, Enri sat in front of the mirror and looked at the painting tools the women had used while nervously tapping her fingertips against the table. The woman's muffled protests did not help her concentration.

Enri gave up on the task before touching any of the tools. She spun around on the chair. "I'm going to make a deal with you. I'll untie you and you're going to help me paint my face like yours. If you scream, I'll do much worse than tie you up, deal?"

The woman, looking up at Enri with one cheek squished against the stone floor, nodded in agreement. Enri untied her, and to her satisfaction, the woman did not make any startling movements.

"Sit down," the woman said. With a straight face, she took a brush and dipped it into one of the palettes. Then she used her pointer finger to tilt Enri's chin up.

Enri pulled away when she felt the coldness of the paint on her lips.

"If you stay still, this will go quicker," the woman said and got to work moving all different types of brushes and colors on Enri's lips, her face, and her eyes. "You're with them—Movo and the one-armed girl, are you not?"

Enri gave her a warning look.

"It's not every day one hears about a group of peasants defending their territory from King Felix. It's unheard of, actually. No one understands how you were able to do it. Whatever your plan may be tonight, you are very brave. I admire your people," she said. "

"Then why are you here?" Enri asked. "Why don't you just leave? These people are monsters."

The woman smiled sadly. "My parents sold me to King Felix when I was very young. I was trained to serve, to dance, and to entertain. This is all I know how to do. My sister was sick and they needed the money for medicine. It is not a bad exchange for the life of my sister," she replied calmly.

"My father knew medicine and taught it to me. We never asked for anything in exchange for saving a person's life if they didn't have anything," Enri said.

"That is why I hope your people will defeat our soldiers," the woman said as she finished her art. Then, she picked up a red veil embroidered in gold, which she placed right over Enri's nose and tied behind her hair.

Enri didn't bother to look at herself in the mirror. She didn't really know what to do at this point. She thought of tying the woman up again, but if anyone walked in they would know there was a threat. But she couldn't just let her go, either, because of the risk of her telling someone.

The woman sat back to admire her work. "What is it that you need to do?"

Enri paused, wondering whether to trust her. "I need to get to Dartharus's chamber," she said at last.

The woman nodded and told her to follow her. "After we pass the dining hall, I will tell the guard at the stairs that Dartharus sent for us," she explained.

As they walked down the corridor, the yammer, flutes, and drums from the dining room grew louder and louder. The music sounded nice, but nothing compared to Hans's psaltery. Enri couldn't bear the reality that she would never hear his melodies again.

Enri was so deep in thought about Hans that she almost didn't notice the figure walking toward them. Manni. Enri followed her gut reaction, pulling the woman along as she slid into the opening on her left.

"What have you done?" the woman muttered through her teeth.

Enri could feel eyes on her, and she cursed herself for the move she had made. They were in the dining hall.

"Do as I do," the woman said.

Enri followed her toward the stage, attempting to mimic the sway of her hips as she walked. On the stage were several women dancing to the sound of the flutes and drums.

"Go in back," the woman ordered. "Right behind me."

Enri did as she had been told. She bit her lip, focusing on undulating her body in the snakelike motion of the other women. This was a nightmare. If anyone paid any attention to her, they would notice she was a fake. *Movo said his people's dancing was rigid. Liar*, she thought. Circling around slowly, the woman signaled with her eyes toward the opening to their right, letting Enri know that they would go in that direction after the dance.

Enri continued to mimic the dance moves, moving her fingers in a wavelike motion in front of her face. Then she realized she had not given her nails much attention when she had been washing. *Skies, please don't let anyone notice.*

Another dancer joined them on stage. *This is the part where the situation gets worse, and it's Manni right next to me,* she thought, looking out of the corner of her eye. *Once again, my instincts were right.*

She tried to assure herself that Manni would not recognize her, since the last time they had seen each other, they had been children.

The music finally stopped, and the women dispersed off the stage. Several men whistled and made a comment about the color of Enri's hair, and she quickened her pace out of the room.

She was so close to getting to Dartharus now. She kept her eyes on the ground while the woman explained to a guard that they were ordered to see Dartharus. Without hesitation, the guard stepped aside, making room for them to head up the stairs.

Another guard stopped them at the top of the stairs, this one much more speculative. "What are you doing here, Lila?" he questioned.

"Dartharus sent for us," the woman, Lila, answered obediently.

"Who is she? I didn't see her among the others when you arrived."

Enri could feel his eyes on her, moving up and down her body. He bent over to get a glimpse of her face. There it was. The moment she had trained for. She had thought she would hesitate, but she didn't think twice, knowing her family and friends' lives were at stake outside. She pulled the dagger from his scabbard, pushed him against the wall, covered his mouth with her hand, and dragged the blade across his throat. Then she stepped aside to avoid contact with his blood.

"We need to hide him—right now. Help me with the body, please," Enri said.

Enri pulled the man by his feet into a storage area. A trail of blood led from the place of impact to the room.

"Clean this up and get out of here," Enri said, marching down the corridor. But she rushed back to grab Lila's hand. "Thank you, Lila."

"You're welcome, and give my blessings to Movo if you get a chance," Lila replied and grasped Enri in a quick hug.

Enri straightened herself before Dartharus's door and knocked. A man much older than she, wearing a colorful robe, opened the door.

"Oh my. What do we have here?" he slurred drunkenly. "I don't think we have had the pleasure of meeting."

Enri pushed past him. "Lila hasn't permitted me to make performances or serve yet. She doesn't think I am ready, but I think otherwise. I just couldn't wait to meet the great Dartharus," she sang as she circled the room. "May I serve you a drink?"

Dartharus spilled the contents of his cup onto the floor and handed his cup to her. "Please do. Something sweet," he said as he sat back on a wooden sofa.

A splurge of rage rushed through her veins as she noticed the intricate detail of the sofa. Only Rudi of Alonia could have made something that perfect. *How dare he sit on that. It was made with heart for a good king. A friend.*

Dartharus's chin rested against his chest, and Enri wondered if she even had to mix the herbs into his drink. She pulled out a tiny sack that had been fastened to her leg using a leather strap and shook the contents into Dartharus's cup before pouring the wine.

"This is for you, Father," she whispered. She had been waiting for her moment to grieve, after having kept strong for Mahtreeh for weeks. This would be it. Her grieving would not consist of crying, though. Revenge. It would be about revenge. Usually she was the healer who quietly, and patiently, waited on the sidelines. She was happy to play that role, but just this once, with no one else aside from her reflection in the mirror watching, especially Mahtreeh, she would get to be free in the darkest place within her being.

She sat next to Dartharus and held the cup up to his lips. The smell of the mixture woke him slightly.

"Oh, thank you," he said, grabbing the cup.

He tilted the cup for the first sip, but she grasped it and tilted it more, forcing him to drink every single drop.

"Well, I can see why Lila has kept you hidden," he said. He put his arm around her waist and she cringed at the sense of his arm hair against her exposed back and his dry fingers grasping on to her waist.

Hold yourself together and don't do anything he might understand as suspicious. It will be over any minute. Try counting something. She focused on the nails in the floorboards and prayed that the mixture would work sooner rather than later. She had given him twice the dose. All of a sudden, he attempted to put his other hand on her leg, but she stood abruptly. Anger flashed across his features and she knew she had made a mistake, even though her move had been so instinctual she doubted she would have done otherwise if given a second chance. *Think quick, Enri!*

She knelt in front of him and took both of his hands into hers. Then she widened her eyes and looked up into his, fluttering her lashes as she spoke. "Dartharus, I would like to tell you a story. I made it up just for you."

"A story? Oh, how nice—a story," he mumbled. He moved the tip of his tongue back and forth along his lips. Enri tightened her abdomen to prevent herself from gagging.

"Once upon a time, a girl had to put many people to sleep," she started.

"Sleep? Why sleep?" Dartharus slurred. His eyes started to close and his back began to slide down the back of the sofa.

"Well, you see, the people were in tremendous pain because they were sick. And they didn't have a chance at healing. So the girl gave them a mixture to drink so they could sleep forever and not have to suffer. And when they all fell asleep," Enri continued as she leaned close to Dartharus's ear, "she made a mixture for the man who had brought the illness and made him drink it. But this mixture would not help him sleep. Oh, no, she made sure that this mixture would give him a painful death."

Dartharus's eyes opened wide as he began to choke. She sat next to him, crossed her legs, and, for a moment, enjoyed the sight of him choking as his body seized. Then she stood to search the room, humming.

She rummaged through the deep drawers of an oak desk in the corner, but there was no ruby ring. There were several chests against a wall. Enri pulled the contents out frantically. She found a few rings, but they were not rubies. Next, she tried a coffer. It had many treasures, but not the one she sought.

She sat back on her heels, sighing and looking up. This couldn't have been all for nothing. Then she noticed pink shimmers dancing across the ceiling. They were coming from Dartharus's convulsing chest. His robe had opened slightly at the top, and a ruby ring was hanging from a necklace around his neck.

"Yes!" she cried. She ripped the necklace from around his neck and clenched it tightly in her fist.

At the same time, the door flew open and Manni barged in, trailed by a group of soldiers.

"That's her! I told you so!" Manni yelled as the soldiers made their way toward Enri. "You thought I wouldn't recognize you with that stupid flower in your hair and your dirty fingernails," she laughed.

You're going to have to do a lot more than recognize me in order to stop me, Enri thought as she sprinted toward the window, shouting to alarm the others.

● ● ●

Herlot and the others waited by the entrance of the stables for any sign of Enri while Mahtreeh filled Ambro in on the story of everything that had happened since Herlot had appeared in Lorfin. The entire time, Ambro could not stop staring at Devotio.

Herlot rocked back and forth on her heels, running her hand over Devotio's back while Asm held Seum in the corner of a stable.

374

He recited what sounded like an Iptan prayer to those who might die. He repeatedly asked the emperor to guide his son's soul to the land of forever.

The sound of yelling erupted from Dartharus's room, followed by Enri's shout. Movo didn't waste a moment and took off toward the building, leaving a cloud of stable dust behind him.

"We're going to have to make a run for it," Herlot said, blood rushing through her veins. "Asm, get Seum on a horse and out of here now!"

"I'm sorry, son, but this is going to hurt for a bit," Asm said as he slung Seum over the horse's back before climbing on himself.

Herlot gave the horse a strong pat on its side to make it go faster. They charged out of the barn and toward the open gate.

"Ambro, get on Devotio," she yelled.

"I'm not leaving without Manni!" Ambro yelled back.

Herlot pointed the tip of her sword at Ambro. "Get on right now or I promise you will not live to see Manni!" she ordered viciously. "Did you not recognize your precious fiancée's voice up there? The one who has been dressing in foreign clothing and entertaining the monsters who killed our family and people?"

Ambro winced.

She brought the sword closer to his chest, and he obediently got on Devotio.

She was getting ready to climb on behind him when Mahtreeh made her stop. "Herlot, soldiers."

She whipped around to see two soldiers running toward the window.

"Enri, jump!" Movo yelled. She could see Enri's outline in the window.

Enri scrambled out the window, falling right into Movo's arms, and at the same moment the doors to the dining room opened, boots stomping against the gravel as more soldiers ran at Movo and Enri. Movo took his guard in front of Enri and then charged at the first two soldiers while Enri faltered back.

Herlot knew that Movo would not stand a chance against all the soldiers alone. "Change of plans. Mahtreeh, get off your horse and onto Devotio now," she said. She ignored the detachment in her voice.

"But what—"

"He's faster, hurry, now. I'll be right behind you," she said.

She gave Mahtreeh a boost.

"Devotio, go get Enri and run. I love you. And I'm sorry," she whispered.

Devotio hesitated.

"Please," she asked softly. "If anything happens, you know where the sword and leaf are. Enri and Mahtreeh will help you. Go to Ipta and search for someone with a golden heart."

"No matter what happens, the stars can see you, always, even when you cannot see them during the day. You're never alone." Devotio's voice wrapped around her as he charged out of the stables and she ran after, grabbing hold of the handle of her sword in its sheath, no intention to mount the other horse and follow behind Devotio.

Devotio managed to make it close enough to Enri so that Mahtreeh could grab her hand and pull her up at the same moment that Movo was engulfed by the group of soldiers who had spilled out from inside the fortress.

"Run!" he shouted, as the sound of metal on metal filled the space.

Devotio galloped toward the gate. Mahtreeh and Ambro shouted for him to stop, but Herlot knew he wouldn't listen. Good.

Herlot threw herself into the fight, and sword tips cut into her body. She and Movo managed to create a gap between them and the soldiers, then started to make a run for it. Herlot pumped her legs but stopped and looked behind her when she noticed that Movo was not beside her.

Movo limped behind her, holding his wounded side. "Go! What are you waiting for? Run!" he yelled furiously.

Herlot began to run but slowed when she felt the heaviness in her legs—or was it her heart? Asm's ax was laying on the ground a few steps away—he had dropped it on the way out. She heard the soldiers tackle Movo to the ground. One shouted orders to get on the horses and chase after the ones who had escaped.

Herlot barely felt her hand as she picked up the ax. But then energy and life joined her blood when she saw Devotio and his beautiful, white coat sailing through the tall grasses with Mahtreeh, Enri, and her brother on top of him.

She raised the ax above her head and aimed it at the rope holding up the gate at the entrance to the fortress. She felt Asm's strength as she swung it with all of her might. The ax met the rope right where she'd wanted it, and the gate came crashing down with a thud she felt in her feet.

Herlot let out a cry of joy as she was pushed to her knees and a foot came crashing down on her back. Her face smushed into the ground and her nose sounded a crack. But the joy didn't leave her even as they tied her arm against her waist, the rough rope burning her skin as they tightened it.

Her family and friends were safe, and the broken gate would prevent anyone from chasing right after them. It would take Felix's men until dawn to fix. Herlot's friends would get a good enough head start. They were safe.

CHAPTER 21
Histories and Legends

E NRI'S FINGERS SHOOK AS she stitched a deep cut on Seum's back. The water in her bucket was severely tinted red from his blood.

"More water," she requested.

Devotio knocked the bucket over with his hoof and took the handle between his teeth. He dunked it into the stream and set it back near Enri's lap.

Asm watched on his hands and knees. His worries for his son's life had him completely distracted from Devotio following Enri's verbal orders.

"Don't worry, Asm. He's not in a good state right now, but he will live—I promise you," Enri said.

Leaves rustled. Enri and Asm took their guard, standing back to back, and then relaxed when Mahtreeh appeared.

"Were you spotted?" Enri asked nervously.

"Don't worry. No one saw or followed me. I didn't even go inside. I hid in a haystack outside the fortress. They were preparing the ship to sail, and...and..."

"And what, Mahtreeh? Tell us," Asm said.

Mahtreeh sat against a tree and put his face in his palms. "They spoke of execution."

"We have to go back there," Ambro announced as he paced the area.

"No, we do not," Enri said.

"It's Herlot and Movo. We can't leave them there," Mahtreeh said, lifting his head up and then putting it back in his hands.

Enri gave her head a firm shake. "No. If they don't make it, their death will be for nothing if we get ourselves captured, too, and killed alongside them. They wanted us to get away. We can't go back there and risk everything, especially now that we have this." She put her hand in her pocket and then extended it to show the ruby ring.

"What is that?" Ambro asked.

"The ruby ring given to King Cloudian from Eraska's allies," Enri said. She waddled on her knees over to Devotio and put a cooling salve on the raw places of his coat.

There was another reason they had to stay alive in case Herlot didn't make it. Someone had to help Devotio save his family. After the mess in Eraska was over, they had to travel to Ipta and pray that they would find someone who could blend the leaf.

"I have to go back for Manni. She must have been forced into helping the soldiers. She would never do such a thing from her own will," Ambro said.

Mahtreeh turned his gaze to Ambro. "I have news of that witch, too. Supposedly, she kissed the feet of the man who took charge after Dartharus was proclaimed dead. She begged him for a chance to meet King Felix. I am pretty sure I saw her on the deck of the ship."

Ambro glared at Mahtreeh, who put his hands up in front of his chest. "Believe what you want. I'm just sharing what I heard and saw."

"Ambro, she informed them after recognizing me in there. Had it not been for Manni, I could have escaped without anyone noticing me and we would all be here together now. Movo and Herlot's death will be her fault," Enri said.

Ambro sank to the ground and ran his hands through his hair. "Why would Manni do something like this?"

Enri shrugged. "I don't know. That's a question I'd expect her fiancé to know the answer to."

Herlot groaned from queasiness when she woke. She kept her eyes shut, taking in the sensation of swaying back and forth. "Why is the ground moving?" she asked.

The way she had imagined it, the afterlife had either a normal ground or no ground, but she had never imagined a wobbly ground. She groaned again as her stomach churned.

"Because we're on a ship," Movo answered.

"Didn't expect it to be a ship, either," she said.

"What?" Movo asked.

Herlot opened her eyes and found herself in a small room with a wooden floor, ceiling, and walls. "Holy Basil. We're still alive," she mumbled.

There was a circular window in one wall from which the smell of sea water entered. Large sacks were stacked against one of the walls, and grains spilled out of a hole in one of them. In the middle of the room was a bucket of water, spilling out as the ship rocked from side to side. The ground swayed, and her vision went blurry. She leaned toward the open window, hoping the fresh air would make her feel better, but she was mistaken. The ship tilted so far that she could see the sea water below, and then tilted in the other direction until the horizon disappeared and all she could see was the sky.

The softest hands Herlot had ever felt stroked her arm, startling her.

"Here. Try drinking some water," said a woman Herlot didn't recognize. Her voice was just as soft as her hands. Herlot guessed that her wavy, chestnut hair completed the trio.

She was wearing an outfit much like Enri's, the last time Herlot had seen her.

"This is Lila," Movo said. He was leaning against the wall of the ship with a wet piece of fabric covering his side. Herlot furrowed her eyebrows in concern. He waved his hand away from his body. "Just a scratch," he said. "Lila helped Enri get to Dartharus."

"I'm Herlot. Thank you for helping my friend. It means the world to me," Herlot said, shaking Lila's hand.

Herlot watched Lila's hair waves float up and down in response to the hand shaking, and she begged her body to be polite, but it chose not to listen. She turned away, covering her mouth with her hand and breathing through gritted teeth until her stomach stopped churning.

"Seasickness happens to the best of us," Lila said. She ripped off a piece of her costume and dipped it into the water. Herlot let out a sigh of relief when she felt the cool moisture as Lila pressed the fabric to her forehead. "Thank you," she said.

Movo chuckled.

"What could possibly be funny right now?" Herlot asked.

"My apologies, but you're green," Movo said.

Herlot imagined herself with green skin and thought it actually might suit her. If she hadn't felt so sick, she probably would have tried to find a way to see her own reflection. But then, if she hadn't been sick, she probably wouldn't be green.

"Why didn't they kill us?" Herlot asked.

"Dartharus received orders from my father that I, and any of the Eraskan troop leaders, were to be brought to Damalathum."

"And what will happen in Damalathum?" Herlot asked.

"They will try to execute us," Movo said. "For the public to see. My father will be a greater source of fear than ever before if they see him kill his own son because of treason."

"Try to?" Herlot asked.

"I'll try to get you out of this, Herlot. I promise."

"Movo, you said that Manni told your people to wait. Did you tell her what you were planning? Why did you listen to her?" Herlot asked.

She examined Movo as she waited for his answer. His frowned and rubbed his fingers against his beard, as he often did when he thought hard.

"I never thought of it. In fact, it wasn't until last night when I saw her that I remembered. The memory itself feels like shattered stained glass put together again, but parts are in the wrong places." He shook his head. "You probably don't even know what stained glass is. The whole encounter was strange when I think about it. I do remember her saying that she would give us vital information if we allowed her to serve Dartharus. I don't think anybody, including myself, ever wondered how she knew Dartharus's name. Then she told us to wait because not all of her village members were present, that the Alonians were waiting for the hunters to return. It's extremely odd," Movo said.

"Manni? The beautiful woman with long, black hair, right? She didn't speak to any of us when we first arrived at the fortress, but one of the girls caught her talking to herself while in the dressing room. My friend couldn't make out what she was saying. But whatever it was, it frightened her. She said that just being around Manni made her feel dazed."

Herlot shivered, remembering Manni stumbling in the woods as a young girl. She had been speaking to something then, too. Was she still speaking to it? For so long Herlot had explained the incident as Manni rehearsing a story, yet perhaps there was something more to it. Was she still speaking to it? Then she shuddered as another memory of Manni's pitch black eyes the night of the recitation rose to the surface of her mind.

Herlot's stomach adjusted to the ship's swaying, and she sat next to the window, looking out at the sea and sky. A pod of dolphins raced along the side of the ship. She watched, mesmerized, as they exhaled. She would have loved to know what it was like to breathe so powerfully as she flowed forward in pleasureful undulations. Her own breath was so weak in comparison with theirs—shallow, her worries encapsulating her lungs and making it impossible to expand them fully as the reality of her situation sank in. Before, each uncertain step forward since Movo rescued her from the fire was also accompanied with hope. Now her future was a series of uncertain events leading to her execution. If only she had the breath of the dolphins, one that allowed her to glide forward with confidence and certainty.

"Movo, you won't be able to get us out of this, really, will you?" she asked.

It was a child asking the question. She didn't want to hear the truth, she wanted to hear comfort.

A sad smile spread across his face. "I'm going to try," he said.

"How will they do it—the execution?" she asked.

"Hanging. Rather quickly, I don't think it will hurt too much," he said.

Never before had Herlot heard Movo speak with such softness. He had managed to tell her the truth and comfort her at the same time. She looked back out the window and traced her fingers along her neck.

The boards creaked, announcing that there was a presence outside the door. Several soldiers entered and pointed their swords at Movo and Lila, while one of them fastened a rope around Herlot's neck. Herlot fought to swallow the tight knot that had formed in her throat. She was not ready yet. They were supposed to wait until they got to Damalathum.

Movo attempted to stand up, but the soldier with the advantage of a weapon pressed the sword closer to him.

"You were ordered to take us to Felix. This is going against orders," Movo snarled.

"*King* Felix. You would know about going against orders, wouldn't you? Calm down. We just want to play," the man said as he dragged Herlot out the door.

Herlot fought to keep her balance going up the wooden staircase with the ship rocking. The soaring, white sails came into view the farther up they went. Once on deck, she was overwhelmed by the size of the sails and all the ropes and nets that surrounded her. She had never seen such a big ship.

A large, bald man made his way through the crowd, carrying a staff. He held it out to her. "Heard you are quite the talented fighter. We would like to see this for ourselves," he said.

Herlot refused to look him in the eyes and did not take the staff.

"You don't want to show us? That's right—I almost forgot. You're the kind who only fights to save lives," he said mockingly. "In that case, you probably just need a little motivation."

Herlot snapped her head up to look at him, attempting to fluster him with her glare.

The bald man ordered two of the soldiers back down the stairs. They returned, each holding one arm of a struggling Lila.

"We're going to play a game. You're going to fight one of my men. You win, this woman lives. You lose"—he shrugged—"she doesn't."

Herlot knew there was no sense in pleading with him, so she snapped the staff out of his grasp and ignored the laughter of the others.

A short man with large muscles faced her. Herlot waited for someone to take the rope off her neck, but it remained there. She was a game to them—alive, but not enough to treat like a real human. Just a goldless peasant at their disposal.

Herlot took her guard, holding the staff out in front of her. She tuned in to the man's every move. She evaluated the power his muscles could yield with each strike and decided that she had to use her quick reflexes to her advantage. She spun the staff as he retreated and gained momentum as she closed in on him. Then her staff emerged from its blurred cyclone and lashed at his feet.

He hissed and lifted his leg, then regained his form and charged at Herlot with frustration this time, not humor.

Herlot waited patiently until he was close enough, glided to the side, and then got him with a horizontal strike of the staff on his back. He fell onto his stomach, and she thrust one end of the staff between his shoulder blades.

The men's roaring laughter transcended the flapping of the sails in the wind while Herlot and Lila sighed in relief. Just then, a man jerked the rope around Herlot's neck, hurling her onto her back. He dragged her along the ship's floor. Her skin burned as slivers of wood cut into it. Her neck cracked in several places and she wheezed as the rope cut off her ability to breathe. She tugged on it with her hand, desperately trying to create space between the rope and her throat.

"Enough," the bald man ordered and stood above Herlot, winking. "Woman overboard!" he called.

"No!" Herlot shouted. "He went down first!"

Herlot scrambled to stand, but during each of her attempts, the bald man pulled on the rope and she would come crashing down onto her back. The air knocked out of her lungs a little more each time. It was a futile attempt. There was nothing she could do to free herself and help Lila. She rolled on her side and tilted her head up to look at Lila, only to find herself staggered by what she observed.

Lila showed no resistance as a man led her to an open space in the barricade around the ship; only his fingertips touched her back and nudged her along ever so slightly. She walked right up, the tips of her shoes in line with the edge.

Lila turned to look at Herlot, with a hint of a smile on her face. She winked, and before the man could push her, gracefully stepped off the ship into the waves below.

• • •

Later, when Herlot was back in the room with Movo, she looked haunted by Lila's last moment. "What kind of life did Lila have to make her so eager to die?" she asked.

Movo told her how she had been sold to serve, in order to save her sister. However, now, she was considered a traitor for having helped Enri. Traitors were treated worse than prisoners in their land. In a way, Herlot had almost done Lila a favor and saved her the torture of the execution crowd.

"Why in the world do your people do such things?" Herlot asked, exasperated.

"Not my people, my father. Just the idea of torture prevents people from turning against him because they're afraid of what will await them if they do. A king has to maintain order in his kingdom," Movo explained.

"Yet, you and Lila still did things that made you traitors, didn't you?" Herlot pointed out.

The moment Movo had stood against his own at Lorfin, he had known he could never return to Damalathum. If someone had asked him to explain his choice at that point, he would not have been able to give a clear answer except for that he had found his father's mission delusional since the beginning.

Maybe he had volunteered for it for that reason. Deep inside, he wanted to see if he had the strength in himself to stop it, to show his father he could not control him, no matter how many nights he'd shut him in darkness. But it had turned into much more than that after he'd gotten to know the Eraskans.

I admire them. Each and every one of them. I don't want to live in a world without Eraskans. He had traveled to many places and met many different types of people, but the first time he'd felt alive had been with them. He couldn't speak for Lila—but he imagined her reason for helping Enri had been similar. *She could have easily informed the guards like Manni had, but she had chosen not to.* He thought back to the few times he had seen her at the palace. *She'd seldom spoken, just smiled, and she'd taken extra care to make sure all of my needs were met. I wish I could go back and actually engage her in conversation and learn about the woman who risked her own life for someone she hadn't known. How many more people are there in Damalathum whom I could have admired if I'd gotten to know who they really were beyond the fear my father had instilled in them?*

The ship jerked heavily and came to a halt, resisting the winds that blew against its sails.

"What was that?" Herlot asked.

Movo looked out the window. "We've dropped anchor, but I don't know why."

One of his father's smaller ships had anchored right next to their ship. He tilted his head up to see what was happening.

"Can you ease our load?" called a soldier from the smaller ship "We've got about fifty here and enough back in Ussela for three more trips!"

"Bring them over! We only have four!" someone on theirs responded.

"Aye, will be a big help. Now, we can just make our way back for the others!"

"Three," Herlot whispered. "One: You. Two: Me. Three: Manni. Four: It has to be an Alonian."

She grasped Movo's thigh, looking him in his eyes. "There was another survivor besides Ambro in Alonia. Who was it? Do you remember what they looked like?"

"I-I don't remember." He was ashamed that he had not cared about what their faces looked like back then.

"Try harder. Another Alonian is alive and on this ship with us. I need to know who he is."

"I'm sorry, Herlot. I don't remember. I chased after you before I could get a closer look at him or her."

A plank was fastened between the ships, and a group of peasants was pushed one by one to walk across it. *Fifty crowpox survivors just on this one ship*, Movo thought. His heart sank. He had hoped to make a desperate attempt to change his father's mind about Herlot because she had not succumbed to the illness. However, now among all the other survivors, she was only a threat, a peasant woman who had rebelled against him. He would execute her in front of the entire city so anyone who had heard her story would learn she was no match for Felix.

"What fate awaits them in Damalathum?" Herlot asked.

"They will be taken outside of Damalathum to a village. After that, I don't know."

They watched the Usselanians cross the plank. "My people could have been them. I wish there was something we could do for them—"

A woman screamed as the plank reverberated. A soldier was jumping on the plank as the woman clung for dear life to the arms of a little girl dangling over the sea. Thankfully, a peasant man came to her rescue, then braced over them until the shaking stopped.

"That woman and her child did absolutely nothing. You've said your men fear torture, hence why they follow your father's orders. But that...*that*? That woman and her child did *nothing* to provoke that. Your father did not order to taunt the survivors, did he?" Herlot cried.

Movo cringed. "All they know is how to fight. They never were given a chance to craft, plant, or tell stories. Their minds wander when there is not much to do. So they look for entertainment doing what they know how to do best."

Herlot frowned at him. "Are you making excuses for them?"

"No. I'm just saying they weren't born like this and it is not completely their fault. They didn't choose this life—my father turned them into what they are now."

She shook her head. "Vincent changed." *Others can, too,* Herlot wanted to say.

"Neither I, nor Vincent, have a family whose lives depend on us," he admitted.

"Oh, so, if you had a wife and children waiting for you, you would not have helped our people? I mean, my people." Herlot crossed her arms. "You would have let me burn in the forest?"

Movo dropped his head into his palms. He had asked himself this question many times. "I don't know."

Herlot pursed her lips and nodded. "It's nice to learn that you're a person who believes having a family makes it acceptable to attack and kill another."

"At least I have the courage to tell you the truth," he snapped. "What did you expect me to say? Alright, Herlot. Let me do it your way. I would find a magical dragon and save the people of Eraska and fly it home to my family and rescue them before they were hurt for my actions. Does my made-up story help you feel better like yours does?"

"My story is not made up!" she shouted so loud her voice cracked.

"Oh, really? Then why does it bother you so much that I don't believe your magical nonsense?"

Her jaw dropped.

"It's because, deep down inside, you know it's not real. But, if someone like me were to believe, you could justify lying to yourself a little longer."

He regretted the words as soon as they left his lips, but by then it was too late. Her eyes had already filled with tears.

• • •

It would have been better if Movo had punched her in the stomach—that was how much his words hurt. He was wrong. She didn't need him to believe in anything. Or did she?

Her mind was spinning again, and she wanted to be as far away from Movo as possible. She crawled away, then rested the side of her head against a sack, closing her eyes.

She felt sick, but it was not her stomach's contents that fought to push up into her throat. It was a memory—or, rather, a fact—a fact that she had hidden from and avoided since the day Devotio had rescued her from the fire. Devotio could very much just be a beautiful, smart white horse that she had imagined was a unicorn who could speak. So much evidence that he was who she wanted him to be, yet it all collapsed around one specific fact—yes, his coat was unusually bright and there was a golden patch where an alicorn could have once been, and yes, Enri and Mahtreeh could hear him, too. But all of these coincidences could not stand against the fact that every element to Devotio's character and history was not based on a legend of something that had once happened and could possibly be true. She finally allowed the memory she had been fighting to repress since Devotio saved her from the fire to rise to the surface in its full glory. She could see herself running to the shore, shouting her father's name, then swimming and meeting him at his boat. And then she remembered his response when she asked him about where he had received the legend of the unicorns.

She vomited all over the rice sack as she realized she might need the healthy spirits tincture more than her mother ever did. The warmth of her golden heart and blending was too much like the flustered, heated states and moments of disappearance that someone with nerve illness suffered from. As for Devotio, the legend of the unicorns was not a history. Everything about Devotio had to have been based in imagination, for the legend of the unicorns was just a story made up by her father, Ernest of Alonia.

CHAPTER 22
The Realm
of Dreams

"TAKE CARE OF EACH other. Don't forget to keep a lookout for Vincent," Enri said, embracing Lucinda and Mahtreeh and sniffling against their shoulders. Then she slid the ruby ring off her finger and onto Lucinda's.

Giffard, Lucinda's father, lifted a pack and helped her secure it on her back. Enri took a tea pouch from her dress pocket to add to the pack. For a week, she had made teas for Lucinda and her parents to help them calm their emotions, but their entire family in the caves had helped them through the hard time. That's what they had become. They were not just Lorfiners, Temesians, Noraynians, and Bundeners. They were one Eraskan family who missed their brother and son, Hans, and felt a hole in their chests when the psaltery did not play at night.

Enri was reaching to help Mahtreeh with his pack when she noticed Seum, standing up for the first time since the fortress. He winced as he straightened, and it looked like he was carrying the weight of a tree as he shuffled his feet forward. But he was walking, that's what was important. It was normal for him to be stiff and in pain after barely having moved for a week, let alone the broken ribs and cuts to his skin he was recovering from.

Benyamin offered him a crutch.

"Thank you," Seum said. This was also the first time he had spoken the entire week.

"Always happy to share," Benyamin said.

Seum was out of breath when he stopped in front of Hans's family. "I need to tell you something before Lucinda and Mahtreeh leave for the mountains."

Mahtreeh rolled a barrel over and helped Seum sit. Seum cleared his throat and, with sad eyes, began to speak.

"Your son is the bravest soul I have ever met, and I was an idiot for seeing him as weak. I would like to tell you what happened to him. It will be painful to hear, but his last moments deserve to be told. They weren't allowed to kill me—I was recognized as one of the leaders to be taken back to Damalathum if caught. They tried every other method possible to get us to speak. At one point, Hans held onto Dartharus, asking him to stop. Hans's heart was made of something else, something special, to believe that man had the good in him to stop, as if he were protecting that man's soul rather than protecting himself from pain. No matter what they did to him, he would not tell them our hiding place. Their last move was to kill him unless I spoke. The truth is that they gave him a painful death that I wish you to never imagine. But what I do want you to know is that, the entire time—at least until he lost his voice—he begged me to not say anything." Tears streamed down Seum's face as he finished, but he didn't wipe them away. "I am proud of my tears. It is an honor to miss your son."

Lucinda and her parents reached out to hold Seum's hands.

"Thank you, Seum," Giffard said. "It means the world to know what happened to my son. I can go back and comfort his spirit during his last moments now."

Lucinda presented Seum with a folded blanket, unfolding it to reveal Hans's psaltery. Her tears fell and split in two over the strings. "Hans would have wanted you to have this."

Seum stared at the psaltery. "I couldn't. I was so awful to him."

Lucinda set the instrument in his lap. "He admired you. Whenever we complained about you after training, he'd tell us to stop. He said that only a person with a passionate heart could fight the way you do, and a powerful one, too, to be able to be so cranky all the time."

"Huh... Cranky," he said.

The family managed a laugh through their tears, as did Enri.

Seum pressed the psaltery against his chest. "I will treasure this the way I should have treasured Hans when I had the chance."

All of a sudden, Benyamin stood, waving his gadget above his head, almost toppling over from the motion. "It works! It works! Thank the skies and the stars—it works!"

Benyamin's granddaughter rushed over to help him sit down. "You must look!" he cried.

"Grandfather, I'll take a look after you calm down. Last time you got yourself so riled up, you left Bundene and were lucky that Enri found you." She took the gadget from his hands.

"Why does everyone insist on treating me like a child when I am the oldest one here?" He reached for the gadget, but she hid it behind her back.

She let out a sigh and crouched next to him. "I don't mean to make you upset, but Grandfather, you already snuck outside once tonight. Wasn't that enough excitement for you? We're all just worried and want what's best for you. What would we do if something happened to our dear grandfather Benyamin?"

He crossed his fingers on top of his belly. "Well, when you put it that way, I guess I'll just have to calm down for now. But don't ever let it be told that I was one to believe that excitement is not good for the spirits!"

His granddaughter smiled and then looked at Enri. "Enri...could you—"

"Of course," Enri said.

Benyamin's family often asked Enri to give Benyamin one of her sleep mixtures, even during the day. She would give him a mixture, but it was only made of some crushed, dried berries. She knew Benyamin was an odd old man, but he was harmless, and when he had asked her to not give him the mixture, she'd agreed as long as he promised to pretend that it worked.

Seum sat in a corner, running his finger down each string of the psaltery. The texture felt unfamiliar to him, as did the delicate wood frame. It was strange holding an object that could break so easily when he was used to handling swords and knives. He slid a fingertip down one of the strings, and a distant hum hinted at how it would sound if he plucked it.

Seum strummed the string with his knuckle, imagining that it was upset about the amateur trying to play it and wondering when Hans would come back. He strummed another, this time with more pressure, and the note vibrated in the air around him. Before he knew it, he was strumming all the strings. Sometimes he felt proud of the sound, and other times his eardrums cringed.

"Please, don't stop," a child said. He looked up, surprised to see so many asleep.

He took a breath and continued to play, completely losing track of time.

He detected a warmth radiating from the strings as if they were alive, his palm tingling from the sensation. Then one string made his fingers tingle more than the others. He plucked it, and then another sent the same signal. He continued following the tingles until he was playing a real tune. It was simple, and sometimes he did not aim right, accidentally strumming another string at the same time and ruining the melody.

Seum startled at a bare pair of feet in front of him. How long had this person been standing there? He looked up and almost threw the psaltery, out of shock. He thought he had seen Hans, but now, no one was in front of him.

Then he saw Benyamin, wide awake, waving his arm in the air. Benyamin wiggled his fingers in front of his chest, mimicking the play of the psaltery.

Seum hesitantly strummed another note, and translucent colors appeared before him, then faded along with the dissipating note. Seum strummed a few more times, and the colors swirled until a replica of Hans appeared smiling down at him.

"You're doing a lovely job," Hans said. "Keep playing and follow me! We have work to do tonight!" He skipped into the tunnel, waving his hand in an inviting manner.

Seum strummed the note without end, his eyes wide, afraid to blink. *Have I gone mad?*

He was highly aware of any movements around him, trying to comprehend what he had just seen and feeling on edge about anything else out of the ordinary appearing. To his left, Devotio rose from his place among the other horses while Benyamin held his crutch for balance as he bent over to untuck his gadget from behind a sack. Devotio took one of the torches, which Seum's father had recently constructed, from where it was wedged into the wall, between his teeth, and then he and Benyamin headed into the tunnel.

Seum stopped strumming and shook his head. *Enri must have put something into my tea*, he thought. Then he remembered that he hadn't drunk any.

Benyamin poked his head out of the shadows of the tunnel. "Play, play. It won't work if you stop. Now, come. We have to hurry. Follow me."

At least I can occupy my time figuring out what Benyamin is up to. It's probably a good idea anyway, so I can stop him from falling into something. As silly as he thought it was, though, he continued to strum. Seum held the psaltery against his chest with his hand bent at an uncomfortable angle, playing it with one finger while he supported his weight on the crutch. Every step sent pain through his bruised bones. Once inside the tunnel, he followed the torchlight as a guide in order to catch up to Benyamin and Devotio. He wasn't as free as he had been before his injuries to move around in the dark. He wasn't used to not having access to his quick reflexes, and walking into a dark tunnel was definitely a place he'd want to use them, especially if there were bats. *Or ghosts.* He turned a corner and finally caught up to Benyamin and Devotio.

And there he stood. As if it were any normal day. Same height, same features, but somewhat blurry in places. Hans.

"What is happening?" Seum asked. "Benyamin, can you see him?"

"Why, of course. It's Hans! Let's hurry along, we will have more time for explanations later. And don't stop playing!"

Seum was mesmerized by how real Hans's ribbon looked as it brushed against his hair while he walked.

"Are you a ghost?" Seum asked.

"As ghostly as a ghost can be," Hans said.

At that, Benyamin giggled. "You lack musical talent, but you played that psaltery with so much love that you woke Hans from the dead!"

"Benyamin, do you know when?" Hans asked.

"Yes, of course."

"When what? Yes, of course, you know when what?" Seum asked.

"Why, when the sun will take a nap," Hans answered as he twirled in a circle. "What else?"

Seum decided he was either dreaming or was suffering the consequences of a head injury. Either way, it was useless trying to make sense of the absurdity of the situation. He wished it was real, though. He wished this was really Hans' spirit. If there was anyone who deserved to be a happy, twirling ghost, it was this boy.

When they entered the chamber with the unicorn paintings, he was even more certain it was a dream because he was the only one who knew about this room besides Herlot.

Hans and Benyamin took a seat against the wall, patting the space between them for Seum.

If this is a dream, it'd be nice if the pain in my ribs disappeared. Would be nice to be able to take in a full breath again, Seum thought as he took his seat.

Hans leaned over, pointing his finger to certain strings. "I need you to play a song that will help us do what we need to do. First, you will play this one. Then these two together twice. Then one below the first."

"And what is it we need to do?" Seum asked.

"Enter the world of dreams without actually dreaming," said Hans.

"Why would we want to do that?"

Hans rolled his eyes. "Because if you're asleep, you can't control what happens when you go into the world of dreams. But! If you can go there when you're only *half* asleep, well, then, you can do whatever you want!"

"Everyone knows that," Benyamin said, heavy at work on his gadget.

Seum sneered. Then he stared at Hans and decided there was no harm in trying to play the notes, especially because the music seemed to be easing his pains ever so slightly. He failed at first, but Hans remained patient. "Close. But, this time, try to think of a boat out on calm waves."

When Seum played again, Hans swished his hands to guide the rhythm of the song. Once Seum could play without his assistance, he turned his attention to Benyamin, who was humming along while turning the wheels on his gadget.

"Right...there," Benyamin said, pointing at a spot on the contraption.

"Perfect," Hans said.

"How much longer do I have to do this?" Seum asked. "My fingers are getting tired."

"As long as it takes," Hans and Benyamin answered simultaneously.

Seum was about to complain, but something about the melody had made him too tired to speak. *Great. I am falling asleep in a dream.* His cheeks sagged, heavy like Eraskan morning porridge, and he couldn't feel his face. Any pain in his body disappeared, and his eyelids closed halfway. He wondered how it was possible for his fingers to keep playing when he couldn't feel them anymore.

Through his eyelashes, he saw the painting of the man riding the winged unicorn in the clouds. The colors shifted and the unicorn seemed to be breathing to the rhythm of the song. Its head trailed from side to side, and shivers ran down its body, each time making it protrude more out of the stone wall, until eventually it stood in the chamber. It was translucent yet vivid in color, like Hans. The room was illuminated in light as the unicorn stretched its magnificent, white wings.

• • •

For a week, Herlot had spent her time sleeping or looking out the window, never answering Movo when he apologized, even though every time the soldiers brought food he wouldn't touch it until she did first. All she wanted was to sleep so she could spend as little time with her mind as possible. Every waking moment was one of questioning her sanity by weighing the evidence of Devotio being real against the fact that her father had imagined the story about the unicorns and how they were hunted and forced to hide in a tree. Neither version made sense. If he was just a horse, how come Enri and Mahtreeh heard him to? If it were just her who was able to hear him, she'd be more certain that it was just her imagination. She remembered how she and Ambro would pretend to speak for the toy figures they played with as children. Perhaps one of them would speak for Devotio, and for the sake of holding onto magic for survival, all three of them had convinced themselves that it was real? But then, where had this white horse come from in the first place? And where had she gotten the sword and leaf? Could a wanderer have lost him in the woods along with his sword? Perhaps. And how had she been able to fight with the sword? That was easy. Iptans were turned into warriors in a matter of a day. The fear and magnitude of the situation had forced her to unleash skills waiting to be mastered.

She simply didn't know what to believe, what to trust. She mulled over every detail, finding endless explanations of how Devotio could be real or just her imagination. Worst of all, she didn't know if she could trust her own mind. What good was she for anything if her mind was not well? The only relief she found was that somehow her imagination helped her survive Alonia's fire and get Eraska's people to safety. She also wondered if she'd see things more clearly if she could get a daily dose of the healthy spirits tincture. She couldn't hide from the fact that she could disappear just like her mother. Perhaps her mother had been imagining speaking to faeries the night Herlot climbed out of the tree and got caught in the thunderstorm. And perhaps that was why her mother had always worried so much about Herlot, because she could see that Herlot might be just as ill as she was.

There was only one truth that she was certain of, a truth that made it possible for her to sleep and put all her thinking to rest: none of it mattered anymore because soon she'd be at the mercy of King Felix, and since he certainly had no mercy in him, she was going to hang.

Soon she'd be in a place where it didn't matter whether her mind was well or not. Soon she'd be dead.

It was close to sunset when Herlot gasped as the city of Damalathum came into view. The scene stirred her from the grey fog consisting only of racing thoughts or sleep she had been living in. Movo had been right. His city was bigger than anything she had ever seen. Buildings, some taller than the tallest trees she knew, crowded the landscape up to the horizon. It was a geometric masterpiece.

There were so many people outside the walls, probably more than in all of Eraska, and so many other ships. Everywhere were horses and wagons and even animals she had never seen before. She wanted to ask Movo what they were, but refrained from doing so.

Thumps and creaks vibrated across the ship as it docked at the boardwalk, and the clicking of boots against wood sounded above. The door to their room flew open.

"Movo or the Usselanians first?" a soldier called to someone at the top of the stairs.

"Movo and the peasant!"

The soldier waved his arm as if inviting them out.

"You're not going to tie us up?" Herlot asked.

Instead of answering, he headed up the stairs and left them alone. Herlot rushed out, but she halted when she saw a man at the top of the stairs pointing a bow and arrow at her chest. Movo rushed in front of her, his broad back shielding her.

"Do as they say," he warned.

Instinctively, she grabbed his hand and avoided eye contact with the archer. Once on deck, she observed the men busy at work carrying barrels and sacks, adjusting ropes, seemingly not worried that she and Movo were not restrained.

Movo was tense, and it looked like he was trying to orient his body to a threat even though there wasn't one there.

"Do not make any rapid movements," he said.

Herlot followed his line of sight. On top of the city's walls she made out several archers, each one holding a bow and arrow aimed at them.

As they were marched down the boardwalk toward a carriage, a large crowd gathered, watching them the entire time. It was so *loud.* So many different voices and sounds. Talking. Singing. Yelling. Hammering. Sizzling. Barking. Wagons and hoof steps. So many aromas that she couldn't tell one apart from another.

A man dressed in intricate robes opened the door of the carriage. "Prince Movo, King Felix wishes you to have one last royal ride through the city."

Herlot needed Movo's help climbing in. Her legs shook so badly she could barely hold her weight. She sat on the cushioned seat, scanning their ship for the Usselanians, hoping to find her missing Alonian among them, but there was no sign of anyone she recognized.

The horses were ordered into a slow trot, and the carriage stumbled over the cobblestone path. The streets were lined with people, some pressed up against the doors of the shops, shouting harsh words.

"Look—that's the girl who turned Prince Movo into a traitor!"

"She's not even beautiful! Look at her shoulder!"

"When is the execution?"

Some even jumped up right at the carriage to get the best view of her. Each time she found herself sliding more and more away from the window and toward Movo. "Deep breaths, we're almost there," Movo said. Herlot tried focusing on other things—the plants that grew along the walls and the woven designs on the doors, the vases scattered in random places. Just when she managed to ignore the people, a tomato flew through the window and slammed into her cheek. The pulp and the seeds ran down her neck and onto her dress.

Movo held her cheek in his palm. "Are you hurt?"

Herlot squeezed her eyes shut, thinking of Devotio and her friends. There she found a warmth that protected her from the coldness of the strangers outside. "It was just a tomato," she said through gritted teeth.

As the shouts dissipated, she opened her eyes. Ahead was a gilded gate and a path with gardens on each side. At the end of the path were stone steps that glistened under the sunlight, leading to the palace.

Their greeter, in garb, opened the door to the carriage. "You know where you're going," he said to Movo.

Movo gripped her hand and led her up the stairs to the arched entrance. On both sides of the arches were fountains bubbling fresh water.

Once inside, they turned right down a hall. Herlot stared at the canvases drenched in portraits of King Felix. Some were just of him, and others were of him mounted stoically on a horse in a battle scene. He looked different from what she had imagined. She had envisioned him like all villains in stories—as unattractive as the vicious things he did. She could never like the looks of this man, but he didn't have warts on his nose like an evil witch or two heads like a sea monster.

On the left, Herlot viewed the courtyard through open windows between the paintings and statues. She could smell the fresh, colorful plants. Beautiful women in pastel-colored clothing strolled while fanning themselves. One woman nudged her friend and then pointed and laughed when she noticed Herlot.

A long rug covered the stone floor. She had never walked on anything so soft, and the new texture of the fibers tickled her worn feet. She was also aware of the dirty footprints her bare feet were leaving.

At the end of the corridor, two guards opened a heavy door. Herlot couldn't see what was behind it—it was all dark.

But Movo continued forward without hesitation the way she would have entered her home in Alonia at night, not needing a candle to prevent her from stumbling into a chest or pot. She knew he had grown up in the castle, but still was taken aback by his confidence in entering a place where no trace of warmth could be felt.

One of the guards nudged her into the cell next to Movo's. The moment the cell door closed, Herlot grabbed a bar and shook it. She had known they'd be locked in, but it felt against her nature not to try to get out.

Her breathing became frantic as she thought about how far below ground she was, imagining the ceiling collapsing on her at any moment. The water trickling from above seemed to grow louder with every drop.

"Stop," she mumbled, covering her ears.

"Calm down, Herlot. Sit down and close your eyes," Movo said, standing at the bars that separated their cells.

She sat against the cold wall, hugging her knees to her chest, rocking back and forth.

She began to recite Devotio's firefly poem intended for her rite of passage recitation. "I'm so sorry, Devotio," she whispered halfway through. She thought of the leaf she would never blend, and a sob escaped her because she didn't even know if it was real or a fantasy anymore.

She continued reciting the poem until she exhausted herself into sleep.

• • •

Movo grabbed two bars and collapsed forward between his arms. Listening to Herlot recite the poem while fighting for breaths had almost crushed him. The dungeons would break her before the noose could do her any harm.

Footsteps sounded on the stairs. A figure approached Movo's cell, and he recognized the sharp, cold eyes that stared in at him.

In two long strides, he met the figure at the door.

"Father," he said.

"*Your Majesty.* I am your father no more," Felix spat.

Movo's body jolted, as if to bow down as he had done so many times, but he was stronger than his past ways and held his head up high.

Felix smirked. "You pride yourself now, having stood up for the weak and innocent, am I right?" He leaned his face right to the bars, his voice lowering a pitch as he spoke. "I wonder if your friends know how you treated the weak and innocent in this very dungeon. Ah, I was so proud of you back then..."

The memories had been stirring in Movo since he stepped off the last stair. For three years Felix had not allowed him to leave the dungeon as a boy. For three years Movo had fought Felix's only condition to be set free, to see the light. He had begged every dark day and every black night for some magic to come to his rescue and give him another option. In the beginning, he had even imagined one of his toy figures coming to life and rescuing him. But the magic never came and finally, he had succumbed, torturing a young boy to death. He was set free, having finally learned his lesson, but only free enough to train to be his Father's best pawn in his army.

Felix presented a dagger, holding it by the blade, with the hilt to Movo. "You have one chance, so choose wisely. Take the peasant girl's life and you will save yours."

"Never," Movo spat.

"Look at you," Felix said, his lip curling, "about to be executed for treason with only a filthy peasant for company. You could have had everything you ever wished for. Riches, women, exotic dishes of the finest quality. Lands of people devoted to you. An army. The title of king—emperor. I was ready to give you Ipta after I conquered it. But you chose to spit on it all. And, now you are left with nothing. You and this heathen will be executed. You are not my son. My blood could have not produced an ignoramus like you. Your execution will be three days from now. All of Damalathum will be there to watch." At that, Felix turned on his heel, his robe swishing to the side, and walked away.

"You're wrong," Movo said.

Felix's shadow halted.

"I wouldn't have had everything. I wanted much more than you could ever give me," Movo said, not caring if Felix heard him. He left the cell door and sat as close to Herlot as he could.

• • •

The torch light grew smaller and smaller until the dungeon was so dark Herlot could barely see her own hand when she held it up in front of her face. She sought out Movo's warmth on the other side of the bars and whispered, "I'm sorry."

"What could you possibly be sorry about?"

"That you didn't get everything you wanted. Your life was taken away the moment you helped us, and it was all a waste," she answered.

She heard him inhale deeply. "I got it. Not what I expected, but I got it."

"I don't understand."

"Well, it all began one day when I saved a girl and her horse from a fire. She cried like a little child. It was quite painful at first. So painful I covered her mouth so I wouldn't have to hear it. But, thankfully, the damage was done. I had finally felt something for the first time in many, many years. I felt alive...awake. I was awake enough to howl at the moon with her when we rode across rolling hills under the moonlight. I was awake enough to really hear her laugh one night, swimming as a storm approached. The girl gave me more than I could have ever imagined or asked for, because something I'd thought I had lost a long time ago was returned to me."

Herlot held his hand between the bars. She couldn't see, but she could feel his smile, in his touch.

"And at the execution, no matter how awful, I'm grateful. I have a reason to wish I didn't have to die. I'll think of this girl and how death is robbing me of more memories I could make with her. I faced death numerous times in battles and sieges. It didn't scare me. I neither thought about it nor cared. But today everything is different. Thanks to you, Herlot, I will die alive."

Herlot lifted their interlaced hands and grazed her cheeks against them. "That was a beautiful story—told like a true Alonian," she whispered, and squeezed his fingers tighter.

• • •

Seum laughed as he ran his hands over the unicorn, humbled that such a creature was allowing him to touch it.

"What a beauty!" Benyamin said.

Seum's hand was as translucent as the unicorn, Benyamin, and Hans were. He looked behind him and saw himself and Benyamin sitting against the wall, chins resting on their chests, his own fingers still playing the psaltery. He understood nothing about this dream.

Hans bowed in front of the unicorn. "Will you take us to the realm of dreams?"

The unicorn turned his side to Hans, who lifted his toes and practically floated to mount the unicorn. Benyamin followed suit, floating just as gracefully as Hans had.

"Come on, Seum!" Hans called.

Seum took a step, but before his other foot could touch the floor, he was rising toward the unicorn's back as if he were climbing an invisible staircase. He sat behind Benyamin. The unicorn's wings lifted, and a gust of wind nearly knocked him off as they flapped down.

"Stop! We can't fly in here. We'll hurt ourselves!" Seum called over the sound of the flapping wings. But when he looked up, the cave ceiling had disappeared and only a star-filled sky hovered above. He wrapped his arms around Benyamin's waist and held tight.

The unicorn rose toward the sky, each swish of its wings taking them higher than the one before.

"Ah-haa!" Benyamin laughed, his outburst fading into a silent gust of air as he bounced his calves against the unicorn's sides. He turned to look at Seum, holding his mouth open in a silent laugh before looking forward again.

Seum looked down at the world beneath. He could see all of Eraska and the sea. He thought he spotted Lucinda and Mahtreeh riding toward the mountains on their search for the allies.

The unicorn broke through the clouds and they settled onto the cushioning. Hans and Benyamin leaped off, landing with a bounce on the cloud.

Seum looked at the cloud that was magically supporting their weight. "I'll fall through," he said.

"Impossible," Benyamin countered.

"You don't understand. I don't have what you have." He swiveled his hand at them and hoped the motion emphasized that whatever knowledge they had that made it possible for them to know the rules of this dream with such grace, he certainly did not have it.

"Yes, Seum, you do," Hans said. "Your music brought us here—so, of course, you do. Here. Take my hand. I won't let you fall."

Seum grabbed Hans's translucent hand and carefully dismounted. His feet landed on the cloud. He couldn't sense anything below his feet, yet he didn't fall through. It was strange to stand on something so sparse and unstable, yet still feel the same kind of grounding as he would standing on soil.

"Where are we?" he asked as rainbow-tinted fog floated toward them.

"The realm of dreams, where all souls can meet in spirit form. Come on, she's waiting!" Hans exclaimed.

"Who is waiting?" Seum asked.

"The Queen. She will be easy to find. There is only one dream that sings louder than one of a child, and that is one of a mother whose love dreams for her child. Listen. I can hear it already," Hans said, holding a hand up to his ear.

Seum strained to hear a song.

Hans skipped through a patch of violet fog, "This way!"

The fog began to disperse, revealing a woman kneeling with her palms pressed together at her heart. Her long hair flowed freely in the gentle breeze and moonlight illuminated her face.

"Go to her," Hans said to Benyamin, "and use as few words as possible so she can remember when she wakes. She is more likely to remember an image than words."

Benyamin knelt in front of her and put his palms over hers. Together they rose to a standing position.

"My son," she started.

"I know, I know. I have something to show you," Benyamin said. He lowered his hands and then his gadget magically appeared in them. He began to move the metal objects around. "This is today. This is tomorrow. This is the sun. And this is the moon."

The unicorn stepped forward and nuzzled his nose against the woman's cheek. Then he lowered his alicorn so that it touched the center of her forehead as the fog encircled them. The woman gasped. When the fog passed, she was no longer there.

• • •

"Did you sleep well, my Queen?" King Felix chewed a grape while buttering his bread.

"No, I did not," Queen Magdalene said stiffly.

The king chuckled. "And why might that be?"

She set her teacup down. The sound of bells filled the room. An image of all the mechanical gadgets in the clock tower and how they worked to spin the time crossed her mind. She counted the rings. One, two, three...five...eight. She looked toward the window. A beam of sunlight shone right on her forehead. It was so bright. Her eyes fluttered. All of a sudden, her body gasped of its own accord. Breath filled her being and she started speaking. "My King has given me reason to be embarrassed to call myself his Queen."

King Felix's chair flew back as he stood "How dare you!" he roared.

Magdalene rose, causing her chair to fly back, as well. Some distant part of her screamed in horror at what she was doing and begged her to stop. But something about the breath she had taken was stronger, and urged her on. She couldn't stop it; it was as if some hypnotic power had overtaken her. "You have a kingdom to rule! What will people think of us as you wait to let our treacherous son rest for days before an execution? No traitor has ever been granted such a luxury. They will think we are weak if they have not thought so already. Have we forgotten that people from meager villages have recently sent our troops running and killed Dartharus? They should have been hanged the moment they set foot in Damalathum." *What had she done?*

Felix crossed his arms. "My advisor suggested for the execution to be postponed so news of it has time to spread. It is of utmost importance for the entire city to witness my wrath as I take the life of my own son for treason."

Magdalene's mind screamed at her to run and hide, but her breath held her upright as Felix walked alongside the table toward her, one hand stroking his chin. "But...I may have to rid myself of my advisor. It seems to me that my Queen is better equipped to perform his duty. Tell me, when do you suggest we execute our son and the peasant?" His eyes shone with lust.

Magdalene's hand wrapped around the wooden toy figure she had taken off her dresser and put in her dress pocket that morning. She thought of the crowd, the awful execution crowd with its ruthless taunts at whoever was destined to hang. She imagined how much more awful it would be if the entire city were there. She couldn't save Movo, but perhaps she could spare him the taunts of an entire city before he took his last breath. She could not believe the words that were being spoken from her very own lips. "When the sun reaches its highest point today." She pursed her lips and met him with her eyes shining as bright as his. She was either cursed or had gone mad. She was now the sole reason why her son had only a few hours left to live.

Herlot had not let go of Movo's hand the entire night and then into the morning while the other prisoners were served bowls of something that smelled like porridge. They weren't given anything to eat or drink.

After a while, several guards paraded down the dungeon's corridor and opened the doors to her and Movo's cells. First, they tied Movo's hands together in front of him. Then they stared at her with disgust and then tied a rope around her wrist.

"Movo, what is happening?" she asked.

Before he could answer, two men tied cloths around their mouths. "Now is not a time for conversation. Now is a time for contemplation of your crimes," one of them said. Herlot's eyes widened in terror. They were going to execute them...now.

Movo thrust his shoulder against one of them, but it was a futile attempt. Two others were right there to restrain him.

Her heart pounded as they were tugged along like a pair of goats up the dungeon's stairs and into the empty streets of the city. Herlot wondered where all the people were who had lined the streets yesterday.

She got her answer when they approached a large, roofless, rectangular building made of bricks, with towering, open wooden doors. All around and within the building a crowd of hungry people was waiting to see her execution. They cheered louder and louder the closer she and Movo were brought.

The calls only grew in intensity as they entered. This time, rocks accompanied the various foods that were thrown at her. Instinct told her to run away and she halted, tugging the other way. The soldier gave a strong jerk, causing her to fall on her face. The crowd erupted in laughter as they clapped and cheered. Then they turned their attention on Movo and started chanting, "Traitor!"

A hand extended from the crowd and slipped something between Movo's tied hands. From what Herlot could see, she thought it looked like a wooden toy figure.

"From the Queen. Fly with the swans, Prince Movo," a short man with a strange-pitched voice called before they were pushed forward.

When they reached the back of the building, they were herded up a flight of creaking wooden steps and then positioned in front of two ropes hanging from a strong beam. Herlot noticed the unstable plank that would give way right underneath her. On the second floor of the building, straight across from her, sat the king with his queen. The Queen's eyes expressed a serene sadness as more food and rocks were thrown Herlot's way. Then her attention drifted to Felix. His upper lip curled up and eyes were wide with hunger. Never before had she looked pure hatred straight in the eye.

● ● ●

Movo examined the small figure in between his palms. It had once been his favorite toy out of the entire wooden toy collection his mother had always added to. He smiled up at his mother, letting her know how much it meant to him. Then he looked at the crowd with pride beaming in his chest as tears streamed down his face.

He had helped the Eraskans rebel against his father's men, but his tears were for his own rebellion against the awful man whose blood he shared. There was a time when his father had nearly succeeded in turning him into a monster forever. But he hadn't and each of Movo's tears that fell between the cracks of the plank beneath him and onto the dirt of Felix's land was proof of that.

● ● ●

The noon sky burned upon Herlot as Felix's hate continued to bore into her being. Ropes heated by the sun were adjusted around her and Movo's necks as a man unrolled a roll of parchment. When the crowd silenced, he began to read Herlot's and Movo's crimes.

Herlot took a deep breath and closed her eyes. She was back at the river that flowed toward the waterfall. Movo, Enri, Mahtreeh, Ambro, and Devotio were there, too. They were treading water as the storm approached. She leaned back in the water and looked up at the stars like her father and she had done out on the boat the night of Ambro's engagement. She sighed with relief. How good it felt to be here. Although she knew she really wasn't there, the glimmer of the stars and the pleasure of knowing Movo and Devotio's hearts were beating next to hers in the water felt more real than the ugliness and hatred she'd see unfolding around her if she were to open her eyes again. And those cold, lifeless, hateful eyes of Felix. She almost smiled at how more real the warmth in the scene in her mind felt than Felix's cold glare.

She gasped in realization. Real. They felt real. Even now she could feel them. Movo was next to her on the plank, but Enri, Mahtreeh, and Ambro were not. Yet she could still *feel* them. Even though they were far away, it was as if their hearts played a song that drifted anywhere and everywhere across the world, available for anyone to listen to. And amongst the melodies of Movo, Ambro, Mahtreeh, and Enri, there was another one, and there was only one being this melody could belong to—Devotio. Just as strong, just as clear, just as vivid, and just as beautiful and warm as the others', Devotio's heart sang a song. All her previous thoughts of whether or not he was real or a figment of her imagination dissipated. All the evidence and proof in the world couldn't come close to what she was feeling now, to what she knew with every fiber of her being—Devotio was real. Everything that could emit such warmth in its heart song was. How she wished it hadn't taken the contrast of Felix's cold hatred to realize that warmth—love— was the only proof ever needed to know if something was real.

She couldn't even hear the man read her crimes anymore. All she felt was warmth in her heart. So real, so powerful. This was a good end. *My story ends today. It doesn't end in happiness, but it does end in love. Love for my parents, Ambro, Enri and Mahtreeh, Asm, Seum, and Hans. Love for all the Eraskans. A new love I wish I had more time to discover for Movo. And love for my magical friend, Devotio.*

Then she noticed it, something she had never felt before. A subtle place hidden deep within. Like the layers of an onion, there was her body—her skin, muscles, and bones—then layers of thoughts, emotions, memories, and dreams...and then there was something else, something deeper, smaller yet larger, subtle yet ever-reaching, a place at the most perfect center of her chest. She breathed into it, and just as if she had blown onto a fire, warmth ignited in her chest for a moment quicker than a sparkle on the sea.

Her eyes flew open at the realization that she had finally found the place of her golden magic and that she had touched the surface of controlling it. *No, oh dear skies, no. I can't die now.*

"Pull!" a man shouted.

Herlot squeezed her eyes shut and remembered Devotio's last words. *No matter what happens, the stars can see you, always, even when you cannot see them during the day. You're never alone.*

All of a sudden, murmurs broke out through the crowd. The orange Herlot had seen from the sun's light behind her closed eyelids turned to black. She opened her eyes to catch a glimpse of the cloud that had floated in front of the sun, only to realize that there wasn't one there. There also was no sun. There was no light... Night had come in the middle of the day and the entire city was covered in darkness.

Movo crashed into her back, knocking them both off the stand and into the frightened crowd. She felt him grab the back of her dress as he helped her to her feet, still holding on as he pushed her toward the exit.

The darkness shielded them from recognition, even though numerous bodies pressed against them.

"Search any pouch you can find. We'll need the coins," Movo whispered.

Herlot nodded, her hand flustering in front of her until she felt a dangling pouch. She spread her fingers wide against the rope that tightened it shut. Luckily, the woman was too distracted to notice. Herlot grabbed the coins and leaned against Movo's chest to shove her conquest into his pant pocket.

As they pushed forward, she continued to raid. One pouch was extra heavy, but it had a complex knot she could not open with one hand. Urgency pumped through her veins. She bit into the leather strap and yanked until it detached. Her teeth felt loose in some of their sockets, but she held the pouch with pride.

Outside the execution building, the crowd dispersed into the streets. Herlot and Movo hustled among them through several alleys, Movo leading the way.

Herlot looked up at the sky as light began to return, the sun reappearing as if it were a moon flowing through its phases.

"In here," Movo said, squeezing into a tight alley and then through a large crack in a wall.

They collapsed against the wall, catching their breath. Herlot, her chest rising and falling, looked over at Movo at the same time he turned to look at her. Laughter rippled through their bodies.

Movo knelt in front of her, exposing his bound hands.

Herlot's one arm was a blessing and a curse. She was free to move it whichever way she wished even though the rope was still tied around it. However, she struggled with not being able to maneuver the rope around Movo's wrists out of its complicated knot, without a second set of fingers. Movo directed her to hold a specific part while he pulled in the opposite direction. He continued guiding her until there was enough space to pull the rope apart with the strength of his arms.

More and more light illuminated the room through the crack in the wall. Movo pressed his palm under Herlot's jaw and caressed her dimple with his thumb.

"Did that really happen?" He examined every part of her face as if he were searching for her even though she was right in front of him.

"A miracle," she whispered.

A deep chuckle sounded in Movo's throat. "No. Not a miracle. Magic." Then, he uncurled the fingers of his other palm, revealing a wooded figure of a unicorn.

Herlot's breath caught in her chest.

"Herlot of Alonia. Will you tell me your real story about magic?"

● ● ●

She couldn't wait to return to her master, she thought, as a man in the execution crowd coughed on her. She shoved her way forward toward the two nooses. She needed to get a closer look at the girl who had returned with the prince. Could this be the one she and her master had been looking for?

She nearly gagged with disgust as she got her glimpse of the girl. Herlot of Alonia. *Pathetic.* This could not be the person who had managed to trick her way out of the master's grasp. She didn't need to be here any longer. Her work was done. Herlot was not the one. Wedged between several strangers who had certainly not bathed in ages, she twisted around and then began to push her way back toward the entrance.

"May I know your name, my beautiful lady?" a man asked as she shoved him aside.

She ignored him.

She didn't have a name anymore. Couldn't remember it, even. It was a fair exchange for the ecstasy that only her master could deliver. He was the only one who could fill her with the sensations of pleasure and power even Iptan emperors could only dream of. She was already yearning for him to breathe into her mouth so she could taste the pure gold of thousands and thousands of souls.

She picked up her pace the moment she was out of the building. However, once she reached the gatehouse, a woman who stood among a group of guards caught her attention. The woman flicked her black hair over her shoulder and fluttered her eyes at a guard who was showing her his bow and arrows. It was like looking into a reflection. Could it be? It wouldn't hurt to ask her for her name. She rushed toward the woman.

As she got closer, the woman seemed to sense her. They made eye contact. The woman brushed the guard aside and stepped forward to meet her. She tilted her head. "Do I know you?"

"Perhaps you may soon enough. Tell me, what is your name?"

The woman straightened, clearly ready to speak with pride and confidence. "Manni."

It was the name her master had been able to call forth just before she had left for Damalathum. Oh, how satisfied he would be when she returned with the one who had willingly interwoven her thread with his reach.

All of a sudden, darkness encapsulated the streets around her. She looked up and dropped her jaw. The sun had disappeared. What kind of magic was this? She turned and glared in the direction from which she had come. Shouting and yelling emitted from the execution building. Was this some form of golden heart magic? Had she made a mistake about the peasant girl? She raced back toward the building, panting. Once she reached her destination, she hissed in frustration in how the darkness made it impossible to tell one person from another. If the girl had managed to escape from the noose, she wouldn't be able to find her.

A sly smile spread across her face. If it had been planned and magically contoured, and if the girl was the one who had performed the magic, she was impressed at how smart she was to hide her abilities by wearing such a filthy disguise.

She shook her head and laughed. *Herlot of Alonia, have you fooled me?* Her expression turned serious. *Let's find out, shall we?*

ACKNOWLEDGEMENTS

A big thank you to the extraordinary team of family, friends, and teachers who have played such a significant role in making Herlot's story possible. To my husband, parents, family, and friends, I am forever grateful for your enthusiasm and support throughout the entire story-creating process. Throughout the challenging times, you were my inspiration to keep going. To my teachers, I am grateful for all your wisdom and sharing, thanks to you I found and had the support to stay on my personal path of imagination. And a giant thank-you to every magnificent soul who helped in the story writing and image design process, Alexa, Elaine, Sara Kocek, Elizabeth, Mike, and Staci. Herlot and all the characters in the story are grateful to you for helping bring the story into words and images.

ABOUT THE AUTHOR

Maria Rosestone is a historian and instructional designer who can always be found with a book. She particularly likes ancient and medieval history. If she is not juicing, studying, writing, or yoga-ing, she loves to lie in the grass watching bugs and go for nature walks with her family and dog.

Contact: mariastone4@gmail.com